BACK OF BEYOND

BRIAN LEDSOM

ACKNOWLEDGMENTS

Kat Harvey (Editor), Lisa & Phil (Readers), Chulainn, Freja and Mark = model, IT, inspirers. Jonathan Capecchi (the Graphic King).

Dedicated to my childhood friend Richard, who introduced me to Sabbath, then left the party too early.

ONE
UNE PETITE MERDE

High up, a gull battles the rain sweeping in off the Clyde. His eyes, yellow orbs around pin-prick black pupils, gaze over Argyll's lochs, gnarled trees and bog-buried Iron Age forts as the hills roll away into the gloom for miles and miles, becoming more barren as the eye follows the brown mass north. Something sparkles, catches his attention. Gull blinks, turns his head and drifts down towards a shiny speck below him, driven by a mixture of curiosity and ever-present hunger. As he lands, a vicious hairy creature chases him off, then pushes the prize, a syringe, over the edge of the stone pier, where it tumbles end over end towards the water.

The road sweeper hates both seagulls and junkies; even remembers a time when there weren't any of the latter in this town. The seagulls are flying rats really, something you just put up with he'd say.

'As for those dirty junkie bastards – they should bring the army in and wipe them out once and for all,' the guy tells the empty pier.

Gull isn't sure who 'they' and 'them' are, but he senses

menace and hovers out of reach of the red-faced sweeper who stands, brush in hand, peering over the concrete edge at the lapping tide. Below, the syringe bobs against the sea wall, its sparkling silver–crimson tip caught on the emerald moss of the waterline – beauty from despair – dancing in the cool morning light. Gull glides away from the dangerous pink ape and over the swimming pool, then the bookie shop that has no food-spilling drunks outside yet, before cutting right onto the High Street. The grey spirit drifts unseen over the head of the wee fat baker from over the water whose sectarianism forces him to sing nasty wee songs when he thinks no one is around. A few flaps on and Gull passes the window of the dying moneylender from Glasgow. Cancer, he had overheard. She's always alone now, in the dark – no parties – no laughter – no crusts – just calls from people who make her frown. Gull sails on until the stone-bound gargoyle on the Burgh Hall curses him for his freedom. A mocking screech touches stone as the bird climbs higher, over the church spire that dominates the centre of town, higher still into the swollen low clouds. Against the wind, he sails up the steep slope of the town and over the slated roofs that help the rain find its way down to the shore during the long, wet winters. Beyond the rooftops, marching armies of sharp, foreign spruce darken the ridge that hems the Town in against the river.

Around the tree roots, thin topsoil barely hides the land's grey schist bones that run deep into the earth – cold and resolute as time. Even hardy bastards like Gull struggle to make a living from this moss-veiled rock, especially since the sheep farming died off. He's forced to track the messy apes for a living now, watching for when the gluttonous things spill their wealth from burst bin bags or outside chip shops. Yellow orbs wide again, Gull spots one of his new feeders in a metal box on the ground. The windows are steamed up, and the ape inside isn't moving. Gull drifts away, still starving.

'No!' Hughie shouts.

With a trembling hand, he rolls the window down and pushes his flushed face out into the Argyll weather. Cooling droplets of rain hit his cheek and wide forehead then bounce onto the ground to be washed away in the torrent that runs down the road. In the distance, a dog is barking within the hushing rain.

'We're fine,' he tells himself. 'Breathe deep, they're just thoughts.'

With his suit soaked as far as his shoulders, he's forced to pull his head back inside and roll up the window. His other scarred hand is gripping the steering wheel too tight while the rain outside gets heavier, dancing on the road like nine-inch nails spilling from on high. As he sits there alone, a shroud of dark cloud smothers the late April day, entombing the entire town and all its repressed Presbyterian emotions.

Bloodshot, teary eyes stare back from the mirror like a stranger is watching him.

'We're home,' he says and slaps away the mirror. He nods and tries to reassure himself. We'll start over, here in safe, windswept Argyll; where people die normally as the grease from the mutton pies stops their middle-aged hearts in their tracks during a morning walk with the dog. Still got pals here from back then, when I was a prince amongst barmen, horny, and just inside that zone of attractiveness and naivety that lets you think the world's yours for the taking. 'Safe?'

Parked near the top of Bute Street, he stares out the drizzly car window and on up the narrow lane that leads to

St Andrews Terrace, where he'll be heading. The tall, slate-roofed B&B leans over towards the dark stone of the church hall, the lane sitting between them like a small child, as the taller, long-coated elders conspire against it. He takes a chest-swelling breath and lets it out slowly; there is still a quiver in his breath that tells him he has to use some psychology. Don't get in so deep here, stick to small-town stuff, that's the answer. It's about arguing with those disgruntled parents over the contact arrangements for the kids they'd battered black and blue a few months before, or else anguishing over those tricky adoption details when the feral poor from the City get offered up to the seedless wealthy commuters who hide from reality on this side of the Firth. Let's just take the fucking money, Hughie, and resist the urge to don the armour. Go home at five, do the *Herald* crossword and then doze off on the couch watching *Sportscene*. Oh, and find a woman, preferably a good looker with nice legs and no major psychos in her life. He looks in the empty back seat and tries a smile as he says, 'Agreed?' **Nae chance.** The smile falters. He sits silent now, staring and breathing slowly as he's been taught.

A red Jag pulls up behind, its horn pamping. He puts the rear wiper on and adjusts the mirror to get a better look but doesn't make a move. After a short while, the horn pamps again in three short, impatient bursts. It is wee Chas, now waving like an agitated toddler for him to come over. Hughie swallows. I ought to give the man a chance, wind my neck in. He's showing who's the boss by parking behind and ensuring it's me who goes to him and gets the soaking. Fair enough, I guess. Pretty sure that the separate cars thing means he's not going to introduce me to the punter up the lane either. Hughie stares wide-eyed at the heavy rain. God, look at the stuff; it's relentless here. The horn beeps once again, angrier and more sustained than before, forcing Hughie to take a calming breath and step out of his comfortable car into the deluge. Strolling as slow as he can between the cars, to retain some dignity, backfires as rain darkens the rest of his suit to match his shoulders. He opens Chas's car door and bends his head inside. 'We goin straight up?'

'Just get in, Aqua Man,' Chas orders in his course Glaswegian accent.

Crushing his dripping frame into the passenger seat, briefcase upright on his lap, Hughie catches his boss smirking to himself. It is one of those smug-bastard smirks that you know is for your benefit. Hughie gives a nod and smiles back best he can. Don't get paranoid again – he knows nothing.

'You okay, son?' Chas asks, looking into Hughie's red eyes.

'Eh, fine, fine ... bit of a cold, that's all.'

The boss slowly looks over Hughie's wet suit. 'You sure?'

'Fine.'

'Just ... I've been thinkin; one minute you're a high-heid-yin down south, next you appear up here in the hills as a wet front-liner ... that cannae be easy on the old ego.'

'Developin a bit of an interest in me?'

Chas shrugs, his face dour. 'Not many people drop down the ranks outta choice – that's what I'm sayin.'

'I did!' Hughie says more sharply than intended.

Chas isn't put off by the nip back, keeps poking at the nest. 'Ah mean, who'd buy a one-way ticket tae here?' When Chas says this, he is wearing a perplexed look, gazing out at the rain-soaked streets, then back to Hughie, expectant.

'Had enough of paper shuffling,' Hughie says, 'wanted to get back to what matters—'

'I had a mate in the Glasgow Authority like you,' Chas interrupts. 'He was a real high-flyer. He left his job suddenly. He said it was his choice; they said it was stress, who knows?' Chas is pursing his lips tight together now, perhaps holding back a snort of laughter.

Uncomfortable, Hughie shifts in his seat, fighting the tightness around his throat.

'What really brought you back, Hugh?' Chas asks.

Hughie now feels like a small, cornered chanterelle mushroom beneath the grunting snout of an insatiable pig. He breathes deeper to hold the panic back but struggles not to let it show as he starts to doubt again. Why am I back here?

Tell Piggy, fuck all, a second voice in his head whispers.

Finished toying with him, Chas gives a shrug and turns his gaze to the clock on the dash, bored with the game and wanting to get on. 'Office door is always open if you need tae talk.'

'Yeah, thanks for that ... boss.' Hughie relaxes a bit.

Lifting a thin paper file from his side, Chas throws it onto Hughie's briefcased lap. 'Here you go,' he says as he sits back against the door, folding his arms. His eyes, which sit among the folds of a puffy, overindulged face, begin drilling into Hughie's skull again with that domineering overuse of eye contact, obviously one of the boss's favourite management skills.

'Shouldn't this go to Children and Families?' Hughie asks after clocking the date of birth on the front of the file.

'I make those decisions,' Chas says, then quickly pulls his claws back a bit. 'Susan Hendry's team are overrun, we sometimes ease the pressure on them, pick off the wee stuff to help them out.'

Hughie nods in understanding.

'Now!' Chas says, making Hughie look up. 'There's nae need for heroics round here.' At this point, he stares at Hughie's scarred hands for a second before going on, 'A lot of stuff round here gets sorted with a quick responsibility speech, a verbal clip round the ear. In and out, onto the next job.' He takes a breath, perhaps irritated at having to explain the obvious. 'Resources are tight; we're on the edge of Europe remember.'

Nodding submissively, Hughie pushes both hands down under his briefcase and out of sight. This twat knows nothing, he's just another rung climber, foraging for the competition's weaknesses in case I get out of hand. Aye, he's a pain sniffer, alright.

The car feels like it keeps shrinking, like it's in some sort of crusher – Chas's bullish lecture spraying over Hughie's face – domination complete.

'The Authority's broke,' Chas says, 'besides, I reckon families have the right tae fix their own fences.'

Hughie is nodding, hoping it's in the right places, as Chas goes off again, 'Costs a couple of hundred grand when we take a kid into care – what's that about?'

'We still have a statutory obligation,' Hughie cuts in, instantly regretting opening his mouth.

'Not easy to keep to,' Chas tells him, 'when those amateurs in that Edinburgh Parliament are squeezin our financial balls off.' He looks down at Hughie's shiny pointed shoes, looks troubled by them. 'You're no a socialist, are you?'

'Social–worker,' Hughie says.

'Ah, very funny, son.' Chas gives another fake smile. 'Right, where was ah?'

'You were sayin that the country's run by amateurs.'

'Aye, you're right there. So, if you walk into a situation that will *do*, that's fine – money pot's empty.'

'You mentioned that.'

Chas gives him a stern glance after that one. 'Those idiots in mental health are goin tae bankrupt us; I'm sure the Humpty Dumpties got by just fine before we came along.'

Coughing, Hughie rubs his throat as if massaging a rising response back down inside. Christ, if he mentions eugenics, I'm out the car. I guess that Humpty Dumpties are people who get broken and can't be fixed. Bet he thinks I'm a Humpty Dumpty. 'Don't we get stick from the public now we're pullin back services?' Hughie asks.

'Nah,' Chas says, waving that away, 'any of them start firing letters up the food chain, you dig them hard. Go for the cracks, and they fall to bits. We have a responsibility tae the taxpayer tae use our resources wisely.'

Hughie listens, knowing he isn't the first to be trapped by a man who doesn't know or care that he is a bullying bureaucratic bore. Without thinking, he folds his arms around himself and sinks further into his thoughts. Perhaps this prick is me two or three years ago when I stopped giving a fuck about *Homo sapiens* and started losing sleep over spreadsheets from Finance.

'Right!' Chas says, jolting Hughie from his trance. 'D'you know what you're about here?'

'Eh ... you phoned ... about a young lad—'

'Thomas Anderson,' Chas interrupts. 'We've been gettin letters from some malicious sod, sayin that wee Tommy is in danger.' Chas puffs through narrowed lips at this point and looks past Hughie out the wet window and up the lane. 'It's no the worst part of town.'

Hughie agrees with a nod and sits silent.

'The mum was a bit of a goer in her day, stranded when the old Russkies packed it in and the Yanks sailed off at short notice. She's a fly one Hughie, so don't fall for it.'

'Don't know her,' Hughie says after racking his memory banks.

'Aye, you've probably seen her in the pubs. No bad lookin back then, ah bet, but hellish rough now.' He leans in towards Hughie until his small sharp teeth show. He winks, whispers, 'She's missin the old Yankee dick, nae doubt.'

Hughie tries to feign a laugh, but it comes out all painful and stiff-faced without any spark in his eyes to convince. I'm weak. Hughie escapes his shame by hiding his head in the file he's been given. It is orange, a threadbare newbie containing two handwritten letters, both of which are anonymous, though the handwriting is neat and well ordered, probably that of an older or educated person.

'Course, it's typical o the letters we get round here,' Chas tells him.

Chas was right, these letters are often sent in by punters worried about their psycho pal who's been using their child as a punching bag, but the punter's too scared to say anything directly in case the psycho turns on him. Or sometimes, they're from twisted bastards wanting to cause a bit of good old-fashioned pain and humiliation to a neighbour they've taken a petty dislike to. The thing is, you can't dismiss a single one in case it comes back to bite you.

'Well versed in the art of skulduggery round here,' Chas says as he looks around outside the car as if he is in an urban jungle rather than a quiet west Highland town. 'Don't get sucked in.'

Hughie gets the 'austere times, step around the shit if you can' message that the boss is feeding him. The trick of this trade is to keep new orphan files, like this one, thin and nameless, that way you can soon make them disappear under the carpet if things are *satisfactory* – no need to build costly files that take up filing cabinet space and hang about for years. Besides, old files in this age have become forensic markers, proof of culpability, left in those cabinets until they are used against some poor overworked social worker ten years after the fact. The press doesn't give a damn about the others involved in these cases, the cops or nurses or even the drug dependent parent who killed the baby. It goes like this – the cops are in with the press and far too fly. The medical blunderers, they're forgiven, seen as angels who you might need some day when your heart starts acting up. As for the junkie parents, well they're expected to mess up, no fun in scapegoating those who are already neck-deep in life's cesspit. Nah, it's those bleeding-heart, lefty social workers that the tabloids love to burn at the stake for squandering our hard-earned taxes. It's the latest legal blood sport; dragging some bewildered social worker out of their dark office and through the glaring, flashing lights – the most hated sod in Britain – a sacrifice to our fracturing world. Rule number one, be careful of things handed to you by slippery, budget-conscious bosses, things that intitaily appear to be benign but might mutate into something rancid that swallows your lonesome arse whole. Hughie blinks, closes the file, puts it in his briefcase and looks up, eyes doubtful.

'Problem?' Chas asks.

'Has ... anyone looked at this before?'

'It's all yours, Hugh.'

'Guess that's a no then.'

'Anythin else?' Chas asks with a sigh.

'Is it allocated to me on the system?'

Challenged again, Chas takes his turn at moving uncomfortably in his chair. 'Let's see what happens,' he says, going pink around the gills. 'Not below you, this sort of work, is it, Hugh?'

Hughie looks down as he fastens his brown leather briefcase. 'No,' he says, giving a small shake of the head.

Good to see you've learned to swallow.

The big Jag's walnut dash and leather seats are shiny and professionally polished. Hughie can smell money; his thoughts speed up again. There's a fair chance that my new boss here is a political beast, a good one by the look of it. Talk for hours about nothing but himself and blessed with a Teflon skin for when the shite starts flying. **_Ask him_**.

'Are you not comin to introduce me?' Hughie asks, nodding towards the lane.

'No, no, no, a man o your experience doesn't need me watchin over his shoulder. Anyway, I've a meetin with the Finance Committee in twenty minutes.'

'Important, is it?'

Chas rubs at an irritation in his neck. 'They're gonnae start chargin folk fifteen quid an hour for support services.'

'You're kiddin!' Hughie says with genuine surprise.

'The welfare state is on the way out, Hugh, catch up.'

'Says who?'

Chas comes back after a moment as if he's worked out how to explain his point to a complete idiot. 'It's about spendin less, smarter, these days. _Comprende?_'

'Clever stuff,' Hughie says.

It isn't clear from Chas's facial expressions, whether he is picking up on Hughie's sarcasm; he either has a slow, arrogant brain or a reptilian skin so thick he can't feel the insects any more.

'Right, enough o this,' Chas tells him as he shoos him away with one hand and starts the car with the other.

As Hughie gets out of the car and closes the door, a scruffy guy in a combat jacket and mirror sunglasses dunts his arm. The guy swaggers away up the lane. No apology, shoulders poking up and down in a rocking movement that oozes casual defiance with every stride.

A bit wet for sunshades, ya dozy prick.

As if hearing this, the man's mirrored shades rotate right back around in a robotic twist, his grin dark and menacing; but it is hard to be sure without seeing his eyes. After holding Hughie's gaze for a moment, he turns and struts up the hill. Hughie taps on Chas's car window. The window burrs down and Chas whistles to drag Hughie's attention away from the creature in sunglasses.

'You know that guy?' Hughie asks, still looking up the hill.

Chas gives a shrug of the face, says, 'Some nobody.'

'Shifty lookin nobody.'

Chas clocks the concern in Hughie's voice. 'Don't you start overthinkin this one.'

'Do the boy and his mum stay in a private let?'

Hughie turns and looks in at Chas, but Chas doesn't bother to answer the question. Instead, he holds the pissed-off expression of someone wanting to be somewhere more important, talking to more important people about reasonably important things. 'In and out. We clear?' Chas orders.

'Yeah ... no probs.'

'Listen,' Chas says as he makes out to be sawing at an instrument by his shoulder. 'Can ye hear violins?'

'No?' Hughie looks puzzled.

'I'm deaf tae them myself,' Chas tells him.

'Should get your GP to check that out,' Hughie says, making Chas's jaw tighten.

There is a brief stare-off before the electric window shoots up, an angry, 'Don't suffer fools,' slipping out from inside as the rain comes down like a biblical punishment. The car sits there for a time while Hughie stands like a truant holding his briefcase in his left hand, trying to lift and hold his jacket collar around his neck with the other in a futile attempt to keep the cold rain from running down the back of his neck. He catches himself getting angry, takes a breath. Try to be fair, I walked in those management shoes not so long ago. The man's got a tough gig.

Mmmmm, let's think about that. Okay, there's the, 'Don't suffer fools' plus poor listener. Bullying eye contact plus a deep interest in both finances and his colleagues' weaknesses plus lack of patience with those less fortunate. He could just be stressed out of his box. *Or a complete and utter fuckin arsehole.* No, stop it, don't be bitter; bitter equals becoming what you hate. *And being naïve equals fuckin blindness.*

The Jag's hissing tyres roll off through the puddles, sending black water in small waves onto the tarred pavement and over Hughie's shiny brogues. The car speeds up, then takes the corner, gone.

Abandoned in the trenches like a newbie grunt; about to hand over some bad news to a total fuckin stranger. Hughie looks up the lane that leads to the Terrace and steps forward.

TWO

TERRACE OF SAINT ANDREW

Hughie is alone, apart from anyone who might be spying from behind a curtain in the tall B&B as he goes through a tear in the towns respectable veneer and trudges on up the neglected lane.

Within a few steps, the church hall on the right gives up the Christian charm of its façade, sporting distrustful steel grills and rusting padlocks all along its length that make pinging noises as the rain plays on the bars. Further up the hill, he slows to a standstill and leans back into the rain in meditation. A gull sweeps around in a low circle above his head. Hughie blinks. Wonder if the arsehole knows about Manchester? Maybe they all do. Stop it – get back in the flow. Soothing raindrops pit-patter on his forehead, calming his thoughts as he opens his mouth wide and draws in deep, deliberate breaths of mist. Above, the gull is gone and grey skies press down again. Focus on the here and now and don't let them in. Stepping, on purpose, into the stream that runs down the lane, the water seeps through his already damp leather soles and weaves slowly through the cotton of his socks until, at last, he feels cold rainwater between his toes. His head-storm calms, he is in the zone and part of that Universal Oneness again, only a slightly different, rearranged cluster of atoms than that swaying tree that's creaking in the breeze behind the hall, or the crumbling tarmac of the lane beneath his feet, or even that lone white-bellied gull that cut below the cloud. He puffs his chest out. 'Things are going to be okay here – they are.' The water from his eyelashes leads his gaze down to the lumpy stone wall he's been following up the track, his mind seizes hold of its bright lime mosses and the spiky crimson throats of raiding brambles that cling and slither through the crumbling mortar. Just a hundred steps from the main road and time itself has combined with nature to set about destroying the things that the good folks of the town have long since forgotten. 'Collapse the fucking system, man,' the voracious weeds demand as they ransack through sheds, walls and even an old rusting water tank that stands on stilts behind the church hall. Hughie nods, thinks an affirmation. Embrace change.

Yeah, that's it Sire – Fuck em all!

He suddenly becomes conscious of the fact that he is standing gormless, in the rain, a catatonic social worker spaced out on cosmic realities – a chilled Humpty Dumpty, perhaps. After a quick scan around, he walks off in squelching brogues.

He soon comes to the three slate-roofed houses that make up Saint Andrews Terrace. It is immediately clear that Saint Andrew is a bit of an absentee patron saint who has long since dissociated himself from these sandstone rain sponges. **_Beirut, in the pishin rain._** A shaft of light escapes the grey sky above to illuminate the wind playing in the long grasses on a bit of waste ground opposite. The light evokes a deep déjà vu as he remembers walking along this way as a kid, running to the chip shop late on a summer's night for a fish supper to save Mum from having to cook. Back in the late seventies, you could encounter anything around here, from a pair of cackling good-time girls, to drunken brown-skinned Yankee sailors, with eyelids as heavy as their owners' stumbling, stoned feet. Smiling, he feels the kiss of memories soothe him within, imagining warm, midsummer nights, kids laughing, ice-cream-van jingles and the sun refusing to go down, the day unwilling to leave him. The gap in the clouds gets noticed and is quickly shored up so that the gloom is restored.

Drips from the broken gutters glisten before splashing into puddles full of decaying fag packets by the front door of No 1. Something catches his peripheral vision as he passes by.

What is it?

Stopping dead, he sees a shape through the window of the first house. Half in shadow, it stands motionless, watching him. The clouds move, and the light shifts. Hughie moves off again as he realises it's the prick in the shades. As he walks, the weight of being observed falls on him like a familiar cloak of awkwardness that fills the legs with lead. The owner of the shades never turns his head but that evolutionary radar within Hughie says that gun-sight eyes are still tracking him from behind the dead reflective surfaces. Don't show the creepy bastard that he's got to me. Focus the mind, keep the shoulders loose and breathe, Hughie, breathe.

When he knocks on No 2, a small flake of door paint comes loose and sails down like a blue leaf, landing on the step by his wet shoes. Standing back to look for signs of life, it feels like the building is leaning over him, malicious, its deep eaves above a frowning brow. He smiles to himself, suddenly aware of music blaring from No 1; Oasis, 'Some Might Say', coming out at full power. Our pal with the mirror shades is trying to get my attention. Despite Hughie's efforts, there is a knot in his stomach again. The place has a whiff of hopelessness coming through the brickwork. After another knock, the curtain of the bay window of No 3 to his right moves, and a man peers through yellowing, lace nets, his lips making shapes behind the silencing glass. Hughie hesitates, then walks towards him, leaning closer to try to hear what the old guy is saying. This only succeeds in antagonising the man who rips the nets aside, his stubbled face pushing hard up against the dirty pane, shiny erratic eyes racing in the slits of a lined face – his mouth spitting words that are now audible through the rotting frame. 'Creepin back, eh?'

Hughie steps backwards. Who are all these half-breeds for God's sake? Holding out a calming hand, he says, 'I am looking for Thomas Anderson's mum, the lady at No 2.'

'Back again, a different one ... creepin round. She's in, she's in ... Christ sakes,' the crazy old guy shouts, little of the venom taken out by the glass.

The nets swing back and forth as the old guy moves away. Hughie shakes his head in disbelief, looking around for what might come next. **PEEDO** is spray-painted on the old man's wall, by his door. Hughie clenches his teeth. Jesus, this place is bizarre. ***Off the fucking gauge.***

Steadying himself with three calming breaths, he knocks again on No 2 with more purpose than before, then stands, arms folded, looking up at the leaking gutter that is dripping on him like yet another deterrent. Moments later, he hears steps inside and assumes his entry face that is made up of an amiable, empathic look with a slight smile which says, 'Just a few quick questions, Mrs, and I'll be on my way, honest.' After a time, a small, sandy haired boy's head squeezes into the gap in the opening door. The boy's blue, disc-shaped eyes blink up at Hughie.

'Mum's not in,' the boy tells him then glances backwards, as if fighting the urge to turn and ask someone else what to do next. Remembering the script, he bats innocent eyes and adds, 'She's definitely not in, Mister.'

'I think your mum *is* in, son. Ask her to come to the door, right now,' Hughie says in a firm, practised voice while maintaining the easy smile.

Closing one eye and screwing up the other, the boy thinks it through, then dips inside, seeking advice from someone more familiar with the interrogation techniques of strange men in wet suits. A few moments pass. Whispering can be heard, then a frizzy-haired, bottle-blonde woman of around fifty-nine-ish wrenches the door wide open and eyes him hard. She lets go of the door and holds her pink satin dressing gown together with one hand while lifting a fag to and from her red lips with the other.

'What the hell do you want?' she half shouts.

'I'm Hugh—'

'I'm no payin anything until that roof's fixed,' she interrupts. 'Bugger off!'

While he tries to find a reply, she looks him over again, more intensely than the first inspection, trying to suss out what type of door banger he is. Despite the bluster, her eyes are uneasy and distrustful in that experienced kind of way, her head tilts back, unconscious that she is showing her fear.

'Are you? Nah, you're not here for the landlord,' she says and blows smoke towards him through her nostrils.

'No, Ms Anderson, I'm—'

'Too soft lookin to be after money. Don't suppose you're here to tell me I've got a new house, are you?'

'Eh ... no, unfortunately not.'

He is struggling to get his bit in, while keeping it softly, softly.

'Pity,' she says, still calculating. With her worst fears and best hopes dismissed, her demeanour changes, and she starts to smile like a girl a quarter of her age. She is no stranger to the manipulation of men. Hughie squares his shoulders, but before he can get started, she's off again.

'You've got soft hands, almost effeminate,' she tells him.

'Well ... thanks ...'

'Social worker?' she says while narrowing an eye, almost sure of her bet.

Nodding, he feels lost for words, embarrassed that he obviously looks like a social-work grunt and impressed by her highly evolved cold-reading skills. His smile widens slightly. Hopefully, she'll let me in, thinking I'm a soft cunt; easy to manipulate. Let's keep the smile going until we're inside. Looks like she's handled the whole gamut of door bangers in her time – the educated type one debt collectors that should always be let in the first time, because if you don't negotiate the catalogue debt with them, they'll only go back to the farm and let loose a couple of type twos; the socially retarded ones that have blanker stares and bigger heads. No doubt, she's met plenty of them over the years, chasing her for poll tax or broken payments on pay-day loans. Her momentary aggression, followed by tired resignation, tells of them stomping around in the boy's room, sniggering at the mess of the place and her panties on the radiator. They'd have taken her last few quid, headed down to the club where they could have a pint and a good old laugh at the poor hoor up the lane.

Touching his tie knot, he blows out to take the tension

off his tight chest. 'Ms Anderson,' he says, 'I've come about your son, Thomas.'

'My Tommy?'

'Could I come in—'

'In!' she shrieks.

'Yes, to talk, in private.' When he says that he looks left and right at the neighbours' windows to emphasise his point.

It doesn't take long before she drops the shocked look, shrugs and walks away from the storm door, leaving it wide open. For a moment, he feels unsure whether he is to follow. No middle-classer would allow just any fucker in their door this easy, not without asking for my ID at least; seems the poor have become programmed for abuse, perhaps they always were. Looking over his shoulder, he runs an eye along the cloud covered hills that go from south to north, hemming the town in against the river. The clouds part, giving a glimpse of lines of jagged pine-tops, which reminds him of the broken green glass that ran along orchard walls when he was a youngster. The county begins folding in on him as if suddenly noticing one of its prodigal strays who's snuck back on the ferry, hidden amongst the commuters. The rain comes down again, dissolving his uncertainty and chasing him in through Ms Anderson's open front door.

Once through the door, it is dark, and he finds it hard to adjust his eyes. 'Ms Anderson,' he says, trying to slow her evaporating form.

Pausing at the sound of his nagging voice, she turns around, her baggy eyes clocking him surveying the place, her fag smoke following his gaze upward from a tin wastepaper bin that is noisily catching drips, to a hole in the peeling, papered ceiling where the rainwater has broken in. Her fag glows silently in the gloom as she watches him.

'Some place, eh son?' she says, face deadpan.

An unconvincing grin is the best thing he can find. Jesus, even the punters, are calling me 'son' now. In the hall, footprints on the wet carpet lead in three directions: to the living room, to the kitchen where he can see a stack of unwashed pots and pans, and up a flight of stairs, past peeling wallpaper to what he presumes are the bedrooms. The place stinks of damp in all three directions.

Kicking the living-room door open with her slipper lets light flood into the hall, exposing mouldy patches all over the carpet and yellow skirting boards. He takes a last disbelieving glance around, then follows her into the welcoming orange light of the front room.

'Take a pew, there,' she says, pointing her fag at a brown settee, before shuffling in her slippers over to her chair which she falls into like she's exhausted from all her efforts. As he sits, he scopes the place for signs of her ability to cope or the lack of it. The place is a dump, but it is well ordered. On the table, next to her chair, are an open pack of cigarettes, a full glass ashtray and a stained teacup. Next to that is what looks like a romantic novel. He squints, trying to read the author's name. She's a reader, good, good. Reaching for another fag, she keeps an eye on him as if waiting for something. After a few seconds, his professional smile begins to lapse in response to dampness oozing through the seat of his trousers; the only semi-dry part of his suit is now soaking up something liquid, of unknown source. ***Jeziz, that was student basics: always test the seat before plonking yer arse down.***

He moves along the sofa, hoping she hasn't clocked his reaction, but she has. She grins over at him – tables turning.

'Like the nineteen seventies décor?' she asks.

'Yeah ... very nice.'

'You're thinkin this is a hole, I can see it.'

Trying not to react, he notes the yellowing light switches and ornate skirting whose edges are all but buried under layer upon layer of torn and faded floral wallpaper. In the corner alcove, a white phone sits beside a dark green bottle of supermarket gin, its contents drained to within an inch of the bottom. Senses now on high alert, his nostrils tingle. Christ, what is that stench? ***Dead cat under the fuckin floor I'd bet.*** Oh, that's a thought; hope that wasn't cat piss I just sat on. ***Ok, let's just calm it down.*** He lets out a breath then assumes an open posture, knees apart, palms open in an attempt to offer less threat to his interrogee; she grins through smoke as she twists her fag into the ashtray.

'Right, let's have it,' she says, shuffling back into her seat.

'We received anonymous letters, concerning your son,' he tells her, his voice even toned.

'Letters!'

'As I'm sure you know; the authority is duty bound to follow this sort of thing up.'

'What kind of letters?' she demands. Their eyes meet, hers narrowing, irritated, his still calm.

'The first letter suggests that ... Thomas isn't safe,' Hughie says.

Her body takes a mini convulsion which she tries hard to control. 'My Thomas?' she asks. After he nods, her eyes start searching the floor for a reason.

'There was another letter,' he says, bringing her head straight back up, 'expressing further concerns about your son ... and your own situation.'

As he expected, her face jumps from disbelief to revulsion, then to outright anger in an instant after this information percolates down into her mind.

'They're feckin malicious, these letters,' she shouts across the room.

With her nerves now getting the better of her, she fights to get another calming fag from the packet. Fag lit, she inhales deeply and draws her head back in defiance, then blows a plume of blue smoke towards him. He notes her hands shaking a wee bit, perhaps the booze, perhaps just understandable anxiety. Early days, don't jump to conclusions.

'These things can be malicious, but we have an obligation to check them out. I'm sure you understand, Ms—'

'Bet it was one of those teachers,' she interrupts. 'That Miss Hendry's a stuck up lookin bitch – face like a cat with a sore arse. She's barren, y'know; can't have weans, jealous ah guess.'

'How *is* your son doing at school?' Hughie asks, bringing her back.

'Tommy's no keen on it but, he goes ... most of the time.'

'Most?'

'You a truant officer too, son?' She scolds him with her eyes.

'Just a social worker, Ms Anderson, just a social worker.'

'Nosey bastard mair like,' she tells herself.

Avoiding being drawn into a fight that will get him kicked out, he shrugs his shoulders at her. 'Okay, so he misses school now and then, but does he enjoy it when he goes?'

Wising up to his persistence, she stops answering for a while and bends over, feverishly rooting through letters in her bag for something. 'I'll show you somethin,' she says, 'when ah can find the bloody thing.'

'There's no need, Ms Anderson.'

'There's always a bloody need with you lot.'

The room becomes tense and quiet, save for the sound of her rummaging through a box that got pulled from under her chair. As Hughie waits on her, he remembers passing these houses when he was about twelve; it was a shortcut on late night forays with bored pals. Unlike everyone else, young Hughie had envied the inhabitants of this place back then, as it was always full to the brim with music, laughter, loud-mouthed Yankee sailors and cackling, delirious, good-time girls who wore glossy make-up on full lips. One night, a six-foot-six black American came out of this place, almost catching Hughie and his pals peeking in. The guy was like Clarence Clemons on crack, staggering coolly on the front step; taking a break from the life force that surged and pulsed behind the cracked window panes. He spotted them right away. The gang of Argyll pixies sniggered from the bushes as the Yank blew reefer smoke into the electric evening air.

'Yoah! White-boys, I see you, I see you little mowfuckers. Y'all come on out here. You want a beer? Alright, alright, you be shy,' he'd slurred.

The pixies stayed hidden, giggling and pushing each other into his sight. The Yank shrugged, flicked his joint roach away, and ambled back inside. A moment later, he came back out and threw two cans of Schlitz beer into the bushes where the boys were still sitting, pissing themselves with nervy laughter.

'Don't you boys take no shit from no man. You hear?' he shouted before going back inside towards the demands of a delirious, drunk woman. Perhaps it was the demanding woman or maybe he was about to fail a drug-piss-test the next day and get kept on board the USS *Canopus* (*Can–o–fuckin–Piss* as the pixies called it) for a few months. Hughie's Highland mother had called this lane, 'Hoors' Alley'. But the young girls who swarmed over the river away from poverty weren't whores. Nah, they didn't exchange sex for money, they were far more sophisticated negotiators who bought right into the glossy American dreams they had seen on Dallas and Dynasty. So, with years of sparkly American propaganda in the tank, they decided to fuck their way towards Hollywood, sell their souls to lust in exchange for the chance of becoming a Texan wife. Mind you, the Yankee sailors were horny enough to agree to just about anything to get their end away, so it was never a fair contest, really. For a time, even the ugliest female on the West Coast could bag a Yankee husband with the help of some cleavage, perfume and duty-free vodka.

Hughie looks at the losing lines on Maggie's face then up at the peeling ceiling, still hearing the echoes of deep sexual breaths from the past winners and the vision of an engagement ring sliding down over a red-painted fingernail. Unlike his Catholic mum and Presbyterian dad, he gets those crazy folks who once came here. He knew, even then, that true, blood-boiling life spirit doesn't have time for housework, trimming the hedge or wasting your whole weekend on DIY. ***Lust is life.***

'Got it!' Maggie shouts, startling him as she rises from her search, waving some sheets of paper. Her chin is stuck out in triumph and her lizard lips grin as she throws the papers across the room. 'Read that. On you go, son,' she orders.

'Okaaay ...' He looks at the two pages at his feet.

Remind the daft cow why we're here. 'Like I said, Ms Anderson—'

'Read it,' she says, banging her hand on the table and knocking over her teacup, spilling the dregs of cold tea onto her nightie.

Hughie picks up the report card, giving her a calming nod.

'Your lot know ma situation.' Making a sorrowful face, she mimics someone else, 'Oh, you'll be alright, Margaret, I know a guy in housing, don't feckin worry, Margaret, we'll get you and the boy a new place sorted.'

Saying nothing, he lets her vent and then simmer as he reads over the detail of the report card. After a bit, he nods again and looks at her.

'Can we talk about the present?' he asks.

'That's it, deny it, keep the daft cow quiet.'

'I have never met you before, Ms Anderson—'

'But you have eyes, can see the state of this place,' she says, throwing her hands up to the flaking ceiling. 'Aye, very carin, your lot – very bloody carin.'

'Have you had support before?' Hughie asks.

Without looking up, she says, 'Doesn't matter ... I'm exhausted with all this.'

I can see the fingerprints of one of Chas's amateur lackey's all over this mess. You're the daft brush, sweepin shite under the carpet.

Hughie shakes off the voice in his head, knowing he'll have to take control before she leads him towards a demand for a crisis grant for paint. Dropping his smile while raising his left eyebrow, he turns the volume of his voice up a notch or two and gives her his no messing about face.

'Ms Anderson, I am here as an officer of the Authority,

to find things out. No threats or promises. What I need is information that will let me assess any risk to your son, Thomas.'

She catches on quick – notes the friendliness veil had been dumped – the real power balance in the room exposed.

'I suppose you're right, son, sorry about that wee rant. I've been a bit down, not sleepin so well of late. Call me Margaret, son,' she says, changing tack in an instant.

'The report says that Thomas is good in non-academic areas - art, singing - and that he's pretty nippy on his feet.'

She coughs out smoke and holds her chest for a moment. When she recovers, she says, 'Sorry. I'll need to get back to the doctor.'

Chas was right; fly as fuck this yin.

She's certainly resourceful; a very adaptable woman, which is good for her and wee Tommy. By releasing a brief smile, he rewards her, evening up the balance in the relationship, for now.

'I'm here to assess that Thomas is safe. That's all.' His voice is calm, luring her in for the tougher questions. 'Is it okay if I have a word with your son, Ms ... Margaret.'

'Tommy! In here!' she bawls at the top of her voice. She shakes her head when she doesn't get an instant reply. Noticing Hughie studying her, she gives him a toothy false grin.

Racing footfall overhead, turns into a series of jumping thumps on the stairs. Wee Tommy then piles into the room and stands by his mum's knee, blinking. She tidies his hair, patting a persistent tuft flat.

'I can't understand it,' she says, 'the way he is. His father wiz a handsome big fella. A swine right enough – but all there.'

The boy says nothing, just stands there, blinking rapidly at their guest.

Hughie changes the subject to save the wee fella from any further revelations on his genetic shortcomings.

'When was the last time Tommy had his eyes tested, Margaret?' he asks her.

'He gets enough slaggin at the school; you honestly think I'll make him wear specs too?' She shakes her head at that, smiling into her boy's face, nipping his cheek with her thumb and finger. 'You're fine, aren't you, son?'

Tommy nods in reply like a ventriloquist doll.

Hughie gives up on the mother and tries to engage with the disc-eyed lad. 'Hi, Tommy. I'm a social worker. I help families like ... Anyway, your mum says you don't like school, why's that?'

'It's shite.'

Tommy's answer results in a skelp around the head from his mum.

'Margaret, you don't hit a child on the head.'

'Why?'

'It's illegal for a start.' After putting her right, he goes back to Tommy. 'How do you find reading the letters in the books, Tommy?'

The boy looks at his mum to get the nod, then says, 'They move about ... kinda fuzzy.'

'What the hell are you on about, Tommy ...' As if just remembering her part in the game, she bites her lip.

'Does anything help?' Hughie asks the boy.

'If I do this,' Tommy says narrowing his eyes into tight slits, his teeth showing as he grimaces.

Maggie shakes her head at this. 'See, he's away with it ...' Her words trail off again after catching one of Hughie's disapproving raised eyebrows. When the boy starts rubbing his teeth with a finger and staring at Hughie she's had enough, pushing him off towards the door. 'Go fill the kettle, this man expects refreshments.'

'There's no need,' Hughie says.

'Nonsense, it's part of the test; on you go, son.'

When Tommy is out the door, she leans towards Hughie and lowers her voice while looking from him to the door and back. 'See, *he* stopped me gettin away from this here.'

'In what way?'

'I used to write to his father in the States, when the Yanks left.'

'What's Tommy's dad's name?' Hughie asks.

'Larry,' she says after a small huff of the chest. 'He came back here for a wee while, and I got pregnant.'

'A late mum?'

Scowling for an instant at his blunder, she continues, 'Larry tried to stick it out here, till the wee man wiz about four. Larry couldn't get work. He asked me to put Tommy away somewhere, ah don't know, in a children's home ah think. Said we could both go to Texas, start over again.'

'Nice guy,' Hughie says.

'Guess I held out, hopin he'd change his mind, a sort of daft bluff that didn't work.'

'He left you?'

'Aye, he did that, son,' she says in a lilting, almost tender, voice.

'Do you regret your decision?' Hughie asks her.

After a thoughtful pause, she grows serious, shaking her head.

'You don't mention this to Tommy, do you, Margaret?' Hughie asks.

'God, no. He's got enough problems already, the wee soul.'

Her defensive facades have started to slip, showing the roots of real tenderness. She catches him looking and puts the fake smile on again.

'Does Tommy remember his dad?' he asks.

Maggie shakes her head again, pushing away from her thoughts and into her chair. In doing so, her legs uncross to show the flushing Hughie far too much.

Jesus, the old tart's got nae knickers on.

Hughie coughs. C'mon, C'mon, where's the humanity for Christ's sake?

Perhaps noticing his discomfort, she pulls her robe around, stands up, and goes to the alcove where she pours a small gin from the bottle; then hesitates, on the point of pouring what is left in the bottle into her glass. After a stalled moment, she thinks better of it, screws the lid back on and stands the bottle upright. Fingers trembling, she knocks the shot back in a oner.

'You've shattered my nerves turning up like this, son.'

When she sits back down in her tea-stained chair, waiting for the mercurial Tommy to come back, her gaze drifts out the window. He swears her eyes become moist, perhaps a small tear caught by the light. Maybe the conversation has set her off – reaching out through the clouds and rain to the Lone Star State where she can see her old, still handsome, lover sitting on his flaky-painted porch in a white shirt, faded jeans and those pointy shit-kicker boots she used to take the mick out of. He's staring out into the bright azure skies, looking back at her.

Hughie gulps. She's given up lots for the wee fella. ***Aye, she knows our old friend, regret, alright.*** Who gives a damn for virtue or sacrifice these days, who sees that in you when you're old, ugly and alone? Guess she's got to hold on to knowing that she once did the right thing. Good on you, Margaret of St Andrews Terrace; I see your glow. He smiles at her, and she looks confused as to why.

'Who's your landlord?' he asks, looking at a large crack above his head.

'Some company that never answers the phone.'

'I could contact them if it would help.'

'No,' she says, 'they know.'

Although she is back in the conversation, she looks sad, quite vulnerable for once and probably angry that he is getting under her scales.

'Tommy,' she bawls with bone-gnawing effect, 'where the hell's that tea?'

Rattling cups announce his return. Tommy appears through the door with a tray of three spilling tea cups, which he attempts to put beside Hughie.

'No, no,' she tells the boy, as she draws him on with a finger.

After a short-circuit moment, Tommy moves off and puts the tray on the exact spot on the floor, between the sofa and his mum's chair, where she pointed.

'He's already spilt tea on that sofa today, but ah guess you already felt that,' she says, a small twinkle coming back into her eyes.

Bitch, sat you right on it.

Pulling her robe between her legs this time, she sits forward in her seat, looks down at the flooded tray. 'Biscuits?' she says.

'Ehhh, I forgot,' Tommy replies.

She gets up and moves towards the kitchen. At the door, she pauses and tells Tommy, 'Don't let that man nick anythin.' She cackles at her own joke as she goes into the hall.

With his mum away, Tommy creeps closer, step by slow step until he hands Hughie a cup of milky tea. The lad has the roundest eyes Hughie has ever seen, shiny blue planets that cut to slits when he tries to focus on anything close, which now includes his guest's face.

'You doin okay, Tommy?' Hughie asks, putting his cup of tea down on the floor. He reassures the boy with a follow-up smile. With a bit of luck and a set of specs, the wee bugger will be able to keep a toe in the flow at school. *Just a bit o luck?* Hughie looks again at the report card Maggie has given him, one word catches his eye. *Potential.* Seems like there's hope.

'Got any crisps, mister?' the boy asks.

Hughie leans forward, unnerving the boy with a grin; the kind of intense grin people without kids give to wee ones when they get stuck and don't know what to say. Tommy backs off as Hughie lifts his cup up again.

'I won't bite,' he tells the boy.

Tommy isn't sure yet. 'You got weans, mister?'

'Eh ... no, not yet,' Hughie says after a sip of bitter tea. *Good job he doesn't know yer ex-wife ran off with a teacher from Aston, popped out two weans right off the bat.* Hughie blinks at the voice. Perhaps my wife's female intuition shouted, 'This one's a duffer, seedless, time to bail out'. That's the past, focus on the now, focus.

'D'you not like weans?' Tommy asks, after noting his guest is distracted.

'No, I mean yes; just not been as lucky as your mum.'

'Have you got a wife, mister?'

'No Tommy ... not got one of them either.

'You don't have a wife and don't have weans?' Tommy looks puzzled and Hughie put his cup to his mouth.

You're sussed, Jaffa.

The rain stops hitting the windows with the same suddenness as when a tap is turned off, both of them turn to look through the dirty panes and across the waste ground. Hughie's eyes spot and follow a narrow path that cuts through the long grass at the front of the house and goes through a gap in the fence to the rear of a grocery shop which sits between a garage and the undertaker. Hughie clinks his cup on the saucer in the quiet room.

'Does Mum send you to the shops that way?' Hughie asks with a nod of the head.

'Yeah, I go for sweets n crisps.'

'Red-hot keen on the sweets, I bet.' Hughie gives a more relaxed smile, the boy grins back and moves closer.

'Ah like sweets and Coke and crisps, specially cheese and onion ... and Thai sweet chilli.' After saying this, Tommy starts to do a wee swivel-hipped dance beside Hughie, hands to his sides, head gyrating up and down in a joyous salute to the sweet-gods.

'What do you think of carrots?'

'They're shite,' Tommy replies – dance over.

Hughie's relaxed approach brings Tommy even closer and they both watch the grasses outside bend in the breeze. Without warning the boy's affectionate arm slithers around Hughie's neck like an unwelcome snake.

Lifting the boy's arm from around his neck, he puts it gently back by Tommy's side without any word of reprimand. **Uh-Oh.** That's not good, too needy, vulnerable and inappropriate.

'D'you like sweets, mister?'

33

'Who else gives you sweets, apart from Mum?'

Tommy shrugs at that one.

Outside, the tap switches back on, and the rain causes the swaying grass to judder and stagger about as if being machine-gunned, a thousand pulsing rings riddling the puddles up the length of the empty lane.

'There's kittens out in the grass in the summer,' Tommy tells him, eyes glazing for a moment.

Unhooking the tentacle arm for the second time, Hughie pats the lad's shoulder in weak reassurance and places the arm back by the boy's side, hoping it will stay there. 'Do you get doggies out there too?' Hughie asks him.

Looking from the window to his guest, Tommy seems indignant at that question. 'Noooo,' he says, 'just fuckin kittens.'

That burst of cold straightness makes Hughie laugh out loud and Tommy frown. ***You just blew it there.***

'You're laughin at me, aren't you?' Tommy says, avoiding eye contact, a petted lip sticking out as the lad turns away to up the ante. There is an awkward quiet moment before Tommy says, 'You got any money for sweets, mister?'

'Fraid not, Tommy.'

Hughie nips the bridge of his nose, blinking to regain focus. All those years away from the front line, managing other disgruntled social-work troops and tight departmental budgets have made me rusty. ***You're about as useful as a fuckin hard-on in a women's refuge.*** C'mon, c'mon, assess this situation ... Maslow, Bowlby. 'So, Tommy, I hear you're an active lad, bet you go fishin; I used to love it.'

'Went once with Don from next door. Mum said that all we caught was colds, but we didn't, we caught a fish.'

'Mackerel?'

'Aye,' Tommy agrees then tries to put an arm around him again, saying, 'Are we pals?'

'I'm someone you can trust, Tommy,' Hughie says, lifting the boy's arm off his shoulder. He nods to reassure as he calculates. I'm speculating that this lad's been passed from pillar to post, attachment issues through a pattern of inconsistent parenting – far too familiar with strangers.

Tommy gives up on the sweet challenge and goes over to his cup, gulping down the cooled tea, drips coming off his chin onto his white T-shirt.

Let's be honest, Hughie, this wee grinnin octopus is paedo fodder. It's a case of severe fuckin neglect, obvious man. Hughie's eyes open wide as the croaky voice in his head grows louder, almost angry. Okay, she's lost hope, perhaps depressed; who can blame her. A drinker, she seems lonely. ***Aye, comes home now and then with another drunk – say hello to yer new daddy, Tommy ma boy.*** Mustn't jump the gun again. ***The mother's fuckin useless.*** He shakes the voice away. No, no, judgemental beliefs often hide the truth. You can see a broken family in her though; at least one alcoholic in her past, perhaps Dad or Mum. Her accent's from poverty, possibly the Port over the water. Guess she ran away from it with a pretty face and a tight wee arse on her side. Plan A – bag a Yankee officer in life's Love Casino. ***The wee shite, Chas, wiz right, yer over thinkin this one man.*** With all the excitement of the game, she forgets why she's playing, too drunk on attention and promises, ends up left with a busted flush of fading

looks and a big arse. ***What's yer thoughts on the boy
then smart-arse?*** Dyslexia? Autism is a possibility, the
lack of eye contact, the staring at patterns ... possible. But I
need evidence, facts. ***Fuck only knows. Einstein
would struggle to thrive in this fuckin shithole.***
Right, get out! The voice in his head falls silent.

'You okay, mister?' Tommy asks.

'Great, son.' Hughie comes back to the room and smiles
to reassure.

A loud crash, that sounds like plates smashing, comes
from the kitchen and the boy looks towards the door.
Hughie checks out the boy's scruffy clothes, the trousers –
too short, the polo shirt collar – filthy with a grubby brown
stain holding to its inner curve. ***Wait!*** Hughie sits forward.
There, on the back of his neck – what's that?

'Come here, son,' Hughie says as he catches the boy by
the arm and reels him in. Holding the sweaty collar aside,
he peers at a dull-red circular mark on Tommy's neck.

'Leave me, mister.' Tommy isn't having it, starts wriggling like an eel to get free.

Hughie stares, eyes narrowing. It looks like a ... ***a
cigarette burn?*** It's faded, but not a pox scar. ***It's a
burn!*** Oh, fuck, oh fuck! Please, not here. Hughie imagines Tommy fighting as someone holds him by the scruff,
perhaps, three, four months back. An image of a glowing
comet cigarette coming close to a soft white neck –
Tommy's face all contorted like a squealing piglet that is
too weak to escape. The ash hitting the soft skin first, a
prelude to the real pain. Then it lands, the skin shrinking
away from it as agony spreads – more pain – a child
screaming hysterically, arms flailing in useless terror.
'Mummy, Mummy.' No one is helping. Skin cells melt in

their millions, stinking, seething, as they form a circular crater. Tommy scurries across the waste ground, hiding in the long grass with tears streaming down his cheeks and his hand covering the pain. Keep watching; is the torturer following?

Hughie's brow crumples, his face drained, and his grip on the lad relaxes, letting go.

The wolves are inside the gates.

Tommy moves away, pulling his collar up tight. He looks quizzically at the strange expression on Hughie's zombified face as the social worker fights to gain control and shore up a smile for the sake of the lad.

Face up to it, they are HERE!

The boy isn't upset by Hughie's corpse act. No, subtle detachment is the best defence against reality – it gives less sport to the bullies, the irritating classmates or the crazies that would burn a child with a cigarette. Hughie sits forward, pats Tommy on the shoulder while resisting the inappropriate urge to hug the poor wee bugger. Don't let your own trauma colour your judgement, the shrink kept saying.

'Where's that mum of yours got to, eh?' Hughie says.

'Don't think we've got any biscuits left.'

Hughie nods at the stoic wee boy, still fighting his own inner panic.

It's spreadin, probably followed us up the road. I told you this would happen, ya naïve prick. Shut up! I can't listen ... must stay calm.

The guards on the walkways are just standin by, watching it all goin on. Hughie is looking at the boy, unable to speak, he feels his smile fading, his stomach churning, and his leg begins to shake. Hughie blinks slowly.

Don't listen. Don't freak out. ***I'm not freakin,
I'm ragin***.

'Do you like the football ...' Hughie asks the boy in a
shrill voice that tapers off.

'Cage fighting; a guy at school showed me on his phone.'

'You like to draw?'

***That's it. Yer a social worker; a knight in the
field.*** Me, a social worker – what a fucking joke that is.
***When the old cow comes back, we'll tear her
guilty guts out till she gives us a straight answer,
some names.*** Please go ... I need to focus. The voice
fades as if falling down a deep drain, then stops.

'You got asthma, mister?' Tommy asks as a bead of sweat
runs down Hughie's forehead.

After taking a chest-swelling breath, he ignores the
boy's question and asks one himself, 'What happened to
your neck, Tommy? Who ... done that to you?' His voice
sounds breathless, intense.

'I was a bad wee bastard,' Tommy says, rubbing
his neck.

'I don't believe that, Tommy.'

'I'm a dafty.'

'No, you're a smart lad, it says it on this report card.' As
they both look at the report card, Hughie adds, 'Smart
enough to tell me who hurt you.'

Tommy shakes his head with determination, cutting off
that line of enquiry. 'Wot's your name, mister?' he asks.

Still fazed, Hughie is slow to respond. 'Hughie, you can
call me Hughie, son.' Admiration for this young trench-rat
begins washing over him, quelling his own demons for
a while.

D'you think it could have been her... the mother... that done it?

Maggie sweeps into the room with another tray. On this tray are three small saucers; each holds two slices of fruitcake spread with cheap, bright yellow margarine.

'Here we go, one for the social worker, one for Tommy and one for the daft old cow.' She gives Tommy a look as he attempts to lift a slice of fruitcake, he drops his hand.

As she leans over Hughie, offering him one of the small saucers of cake, her sack-like tits hang in his face. The pink lipstick she's put on in the kitchen makes her dry, alcohol-blasted mouth look even more grotesque as it grins, a fag still held between those lips. The glowing fag end catches his attention as it dances in her mouth, small pieces of ash appearing on his white saucer like toxic pepper. In that instant, her eyes meet his.

'Thought you were a cake man, wis ah right?' she asks.

He takes the saucer from her and averts his eyes. Maggie backs away, tits still on show.

Draw your sword. Sitting the cake on the floor, Hughie moves right to the front of his chair balancing on the balls of his feet, both hands clasped together. She appears to sense the change in his mood like a shot and clocks a redness to his neck, his combative body language – she knows men, knows something is coming.

'Was the wee bugger being cheeky,' she asks.

He doesn't reply, still gathering himself, throat tight, eyebrows arching across his sticky forehead. His gaze becomes hard, an axe edge that wants to split into her brain. The soft, easily manipulated man is now sitting in her living room all serial-killer intense. She instinctively backs off to her drinking chair with her cake, wondering how the ground rules could have changed while she was out the room for such a short time.

'Tommy, can you give your mum and me a minute?' Hughie asks.

Maggie stops the boy from moving off towards the door, pulls him to her side.

'Wonder if you could help get ma benefits checked?' she says, testing the water.

He doesn't respond again, and she is left with little choice but to sip at her tea, before giving up a weak smile. Hughie holds the silence, glances at Tommy, then looks straight at Maggie. 'Tommy's neck, what happened to it, Ms Anderson?' he asks her.

'Needs a good wash, that's all.'

'There's a burn mark on it – the wee fella thinks he deserved it.'

Crossing her legs, she pulls her dressing gown tight around herself. 'Cruel features you've got when you start gettin all serious.' She puts her shaking cup on the side to stop it spilling.

Hughie is watching closely, analysing her response. She looks frightened, but I'm not sure it's me she's scared of. **Put the word on her, hard.** 'Ms Anderson, I am asking you: What. Happened. To. Your son's. Neck?'

'Hold on ... that ... that was ages ago ... I ... I ... was over in ... away in Glasgow, attending ma incapacity medical—'

Hughie interrupts her with a hand, pushing hard now that he has her wrong-footed. 'What caused the mark?' he says, holding her with strong eye contact.

Digging her way back into her armchair, she resembles an embattled pink crab within her silk-lined carapace. 'Ah know your angle,' she says, 'I'm telling you, I wasn't bloody here.'

'So, you left Thomas alone,' he states.

'No, I never said that ...'

'You said you weren't here.'

'Listen, I'm not—'

'Who was looking after Thomas that day then, Ms Anderson?'

With colour coming to her cheeks, she puts a hand on her son's arm, squeezing it. 'See, Thomas, you get bullied by those wee bastards at school, and suddenly, it's Ms Anderson; that's the way this lot twist it. Course, if I don't get ma money sorted and don't feed you, his lot will get me that way too.' She looks into the boy's face. 'You cannae win with his sort, Tommy; never.'

Tommy listens to her, eyes like plates, then looks over at Hughie. It was a great comeback, and clever using the boy as cover, but Hughie doesn't drop his accusing eyebrows or give an inch.

'Stop!' Hughie says, holding a firm hand out towards her again. 'I'm an officer of the local authority, and I have to establish if this child is safe in your care, Ms Anderson. Your son has, what looks like, a cigarette burn on his neck.' Pausing, he takes a breath, drops his hand and gives the shocked Tommy a brief smile. He turns back to Maggie. 'Who was looking after Tommy when he received the burn on the neck, Ms Anderson?'

She let go of the boy's arm, gives the question some thought as if trying to construct a plausible comeback. She then gives out a capitulating sigh and says, 'Don.'

When Hughie narrows his eyes, she goes on, 'He lives next door, that way.' Her thumb points towards No 3 where Hughie had seen that wild-looking old man at a window when he first arrived.

'I like Don; he gives me cornflakes ... and crisps,' Tommy says.

Once he acknowledges the boy with a nod, he looks back at Maggie, saying nothing, this makes her blab - anything to break from that cruel, axe-face stare of his.

'Don has always been in there,' she says, voice getting high in pitch. 'He takes care o the wee fella when I'm out, couldn't get by without the guy ... all that stuff they say about him is ... it's pish.'

'Does he live with his wife?' Hughie asks.

Coughing up her tea, she says. 'Don, well ... he talks to himself.' She's in the process of spinning a finger beside her head, making the crazy person gesture when she obviously twigs that she is building Hughie's case for him. Her finger spirals off towards the cigarette packet, keen to stuff another one in her mouth and keep from spouting any more incriminating verbal diarrhoea.

'This Don,' Hughie says, 'is he mentally ill? Is that what people say?'

'Well, we're all a wee bit odd; I'm a depressive myself.'

'But this man, Don, was watchin Tommy the day he got his neck burned. Is that what you're sayin?'

'Don was as upset as me; he's mad, no bad.'

After a thoughtful long minute, Hughie nods, says, 'I'll talk to this, Don, myself.'

'He cannae remember what happened yesterday,' she says, 'you're wastin your ...'

Feeling more in control, Hughie gives the boy a reassuring wink. Maggie's visible relief is brief as he comes back to her and asks, 'Do you find it hard being a depressive, as you said, and having a child on your own?'

'No.'

'Do you ever lose your temper with your son, Ms Anderson?'

Back against the wall now, she becomes defiant. 'Course I lose ma nut at times; but I'd never hurt him, he's my child, my son.'

'I have to ask these—'

'No! You're upsettin Tommy,' she interrupts, 'bringin this school bullies stuff back up.' Pulling her son close, she adds, 'It's not right.'

He rubs his stubble chin back and forth with a thumb and forefinger, making it hiss as he thinks. Perhaps it was the school bullies; perhaps it's me caught in my flashbacks, over amping it. Perhaps she's right.

Finish off the sleekit bitch.

Opening his briefcase to get his diary out gives him time to calculate. One answer would be to march Cuddle–for– Crisps Tommy out of the door and sort it all out later. That would keep the conscience happy, and the arse covered at the same time, but it would amount to Goon Squad behaviour. Chas's frowning face appears in his head, hands on his shaking brow, asking where the boy should go. 'You takin him home with you, are ye, Hughie?' Always important to remember the times we rushed into battle and got fucked by a lack of evidence. **_Fuck the rules!_** No, the idea is to hide out here, far beyond the southern front. Let the big guns of the city battlegrounds boom away in the distance while I scam the rations amongst the heather covered hills – home guard stuff really. Cowards are some of the wisest men. He pictures wee Chas's violin and a tabloid headline:

Dodgy Social Worker Screws Up Yet Again – Steals Tot – Never Told his Boss About his Mental Illness.

The voice bubbles up again from inside. **_Ya spineless_**

weasel, don't give up – Fight. You know nothing of people, nothing. Go! Now! ***Don't you dare*** …

Blinking, Hughie sits back in a pragmatic truce with Maggie, then points to the lad, his voice soft and easy for the young ear. 'Now wee man, can you shed any light on all this with the bullies?'

Shaking his head with a blurring determination and an oversized frown, the boy says, 'I'll go to school … promise.'

'Okay, okay, Tommy, we'll leave it there, for now. Clever lad.' Hughie looks at them with gentle admiration; the symbiotic allegiance between the embattled mother and apprentice/sweetie addict. That tells him there *is* some kind of attachment.

Both the interrogees visibly relax, perhaps sensing the end of the game.

'I'll go, mister,' Tommy says again.

'He'll go, I'll make sure,' she adds, nailing it.

'Course you will, Tommy,' Hughie says. 'Oh, and I'll make you an appointment at the optician; hopefully make school easier.'

'What are you on about …' Her voice tapers off, as realisation dawns on her face – she is about to get the social worker out the door.

'Call me Hughie from now on, Margaret.' This tells her he is planning to come back.

The first skirmish over, the lines on her face seem to have deepened during his short visit; that weight you carry when hiding things. Not used to front-line combat, his armpits complain as the adrenaline slows in his nervous system and the sweaty patches chill the skin beneath his suit.

The boy's neck? I won't let it drop.

Maggie stands up and looks at him expectantly until he

44

gcts up too. After a flashing fake smile, she shoos him towards the door. Tommy is already distracted by the untouched piece of cake Hughie has left behind, the boy sets upon it. His mouth chomps at the slice – ravenous – eating quickly before she turns around and catches him. ***Ahhhh, the wee grinnin octopus has been fed at last, so cute before they grow into burglars.***

'You can see yourself out, son,' Maggie says sweetly, holding the living-room door as he passes.

In the hall, he turns to say a proper goodbye to the boy. 'See you, Tommy—'

Hughie's eyes and mouth close and his eardrums explode as the living-room door slams in his face. He turns and walks the damp hall to the front door, his thoughts starting to spin in slow rotation. Man, what a dump and what is that fucking smell? ***Dead cat?*** And that burn on his neck? ***It's here; I told you***.

OUTSIDE, the limitless damp air cools his sweaty forehead and armpits.

But the entombing hills above still encircle him, and his thoughts are still rattling around too fast. A shadow moves away from old Don's window. Breathe, breathe. Three steps down the lane, he hears the music from the first house. Oasis, yeah, Oasis. Angry, moody music – suits this place. ***Hoatchin with nutjobs – we're in a fuckin crater again.***

At the end of the Terrace, the guy with mirror sunglasses, who is working on a motorbike in his muddy garden, spots him and stands up. About Hughie's age, he is thin, probably from dope smoking, or something more demanding on the body, and his clothes look like drug-culture high fashion or Oxfam surplus. Motorbike parts, feral dog shit and black bin bags lie around the grassless yard in a random feckless way that somehow manages to be artful and desperate at the same time.

As Hughie draws level with the guy, he sees a pale, pretty girl, with long dyed-blonde hair, watching from the far end of the backyard. She's caked on the make-up, like some of the Eastern bloc girls do, desperate to catch a man, as if she's nothing more than a polished gift. Her distant gaze adjusts, taking in the social worker for an instant, then goes back to where it was before as if she's seen nothing of consequence. Hughie nods and smiles at her anyway. As Hughie's feet crunch past, the mirror lenses seize him again. It is so hard to tell, without eyes, what the expressions on faces mean, but the guy's grin is cruel and perhaps made more unnerving by the visit to wee Tommy's house.

'What'd you come back to this dump for?' the guy shouts.

The girl picks up on a certain tone in her man's voice, unfolds her arms and walks away, around the back of the house. Mr Shades comes across the mud to meet Hughie. Not wanting to stop, but not wanting to seem afraid, Hughie adjusts the pace of his steps, slowing and smiling sideways without stopping. He can't make out the face, but the voice does ring some youthful memory bells. I'm exhausted, this is no time for meeting potential old dole-boy school pals. He lifts the pace again and moves off as the guy gets closer.

'Howz it goin?' Hughie says in a way that isn't wanting an answer.

The guy starts tapping his nose as you would to someone who is asking too many questions.

Don't let some hillbilly prick intimidate you, man. Hughie begins to tense, his step becoming unnatural, stilted. **_C'mon, swagger Hugh, swagger._** Rallying, Hughie swings his arms with manic energy, his crisp black suit and pendulum briefcase somehow irritating the slow stagnancy of the place as he makes his way along the side of the littered waste ground.

'Shite-bag!' drifts after him.

The sunglasses-wearing stoner, the damp brickwork, the bursting rubbish bags, the old man at the window and Tommy's neck, all amalgamate with a breeze that sweeps down from the hills and across the wet swaying grass – pushing hard at Hughie's back like an army of angry anti-bodies, rejecting him and his misplaced foreign concerns, driving him hard round the curve of the lane towards normal society.

———

BACK AT THE VOLVO, he fumbles for the key. His temper spikes as the key catches in the lining of his pocket and something rips, rage letting loose his deeper thoughts. White, almost translucent, skin, the burn mark, flashes, animal cries and dark glimpses of contorted faces – like liquid tar, pulling him under into blackness. He tries to shake it off as he puts his briefcase in the boot and slams the lid shut. Looking around the street, he's sure someone is watching even though the street is empty. With his eyes closed, the sounds come to the fore; frightened sobs filtered through clenched teeth. **_Don't let them in, Hughie,_** *they're evil!* I can't stop it. The Eyes surfaces in the centre of his thoughts and paralyse, rooting him to the spot with that stare he knows so well. *Look away, man – come towards me.*

All around him, the good folk of the town are going about their business, dodging the showers to trim their privet hedges, dead-head the early daffodils and hoover out the dog hair from the four-wheel drives, anything that'll help gloss over the murky goings-on of their own seedy wee parish; hide anything odd or chase it back across the water where it belongs. The indifference joins with the Eyes, the snarling sounds, burning fag ends and mirror shades – world spinning faster and faster. He falls against the car, his hand slapping the roof hard.

Get in the car man, fore you fall.

The door won't open when he pulls at the handle. Fuck, fuck! At last, the car key in his hand makes the car beep again, and the doors unlock. Scrambling into his car, he slumps in the driver's seat and presses his head hard onto the wheel, eyes closed tight.

Hughie, the rasping voice whispers.

Please no, not now, please.

You need to listen to me, son, before those fuckin Eyes come back again.

Hughie gulps.

I'm on your side.

He gulps again. It's the Knight; he's back. Ignore him; ignore it.

A moving weight comes into the passenger seat next to him.

Arms fold around his head, he pushes his forehead into

the wheel, refusing to look, to see its shape. Outside the car, the street is empty.

As always, he is alone.

Hugh, please, it whispers.

He sneaks a peek, then winces as he sees an armoured knee on the passenger seat. He hides his eyes again. Jesus, please go away; it's over.

Over, over? Is that a joke? Those fuckin Eyes are terrorisin you again, man. But even the Eyes is just a symptom o what's needin fixed.

Glancing again reveals what he dreaded. 'Fuck!'

Beside him in the passenger seat sits a small, shrivelled, old man, covered in rusted bronze armour; his thin, grinning face poking out of an ill-fitting helmet with the visor up. The armour rattles with the little Knight's heavy breaths, rattles like death. Bile seeps from scales by his pulsing heart, dripping down onto the seat where it pools. Hughie feels the Knight's staring eyes on him, knows they hold malice, rage and wisdom within them. He hides his head from him. 'I'm losin it all over again; the PTSD … it's back.'

You are losin it again, Hugh, but no because of o me, it's them out there, the wolves and the cunts, remindin you o what can and has happened to the weak.

You're part of it.

Okay, play that game, but you saw what I saw on that boy's neck. You know what kinda stuff means. It's here – face it.

Sitting up and rubbing his face, Hughie tries to reorder his mind or ignore the creature but ends up angry, slapping his own face. He stops, clenches his fists to control them. 'Okay, okay, don't freak; just don't freak.' It's not psychosis, it's an internal defence mechanism, the PTSD exaggerating and catastrophizing it all, triggered by … that poor wee boy. Ignore the Knight. Don't embrace delusion or hide in fantasy, that's what the shrink told me, don't connect everything to yourself or that mess in the city.

He closes his eyes tight, his head gently shaking. 'Jesus.'

So, yer shrink bitch called all this 'Post-Traumatic Stress Disorder', said your thinkin's all wrong because of o the nightmare down south. Psycho fuckin babble! Waking to reality, that's what's really goin down here, Hugh. What you just witnessed was worse than wolves do; wolves might eat other creatures alive to survive, but only people do it to one another on full bellies, for fun.

'No …'

Aye, Hughie, it's here and you need to reconnect your spine.

'Don't know if I can.' Hughie falls forward against the steering wheel, head buried again. The plastic becomes sticky and hot on his lips as he breathes hard, the heat running up his cheeks to make them glow; his knees begin trembling.

The Knight holds a bile encrusted, chain-mailed glove out in front of his own face, making a fist and then laughing manically until the car shudders. The hand opens and comes towards Hughie's shoulder, making him flinch when it touches him. Its breath touches his neck as it whispers close in.

You've never been one of those tossers who hides their head, Hugh. One o those smiley benighted bastards, kiddin themselves on that everythin's alright with the world. The chain-mailed hand shakes him. ***Yer a revolutionary, man, a fixer and a fighter, a Knight o the Light who knows that we get the world we forge.*** A bristly chin touches Hughie's ear, the croaky voice singing along in unison with something else within him.

You used to laugh in the face o wee pricks like that guy wi the shades – mighta given him a hard skelp in yer day. Yet you just ran off like a wee lassie there.

'I can't get into the physical stuff again.'

I'll only go when the wolves are muzzled, and you've found the torch, yer spine – not till then.

You can't say that.

You can't fuckin stop me! The Knight laughs as you would at a naïve child, then says softly, ***I'll let you lead, Sire, promise. All you need to do is let me help.***

They sat silent for a time. 'We can try.' Despite finding solid ground within his mind, Hughie doesn't lift his head from the wheel.

Hey, remember ole Uncle Malky's stories about the Bruce, the cunning Wallace, MacAlpin and old Charlemagne? Tell in ye, this modern lot have nae vision or bottle; they're consumers who'd rather flick the channel and phone another kebab than face the blackness creepin in on us.

'I don't know what I've got left in me ... not much.' Hughie's head shakes from side to side, still not looking.

Little things matter, Sire, wee gestures, first moves. That boy, Tommy, he matters.

Hughie's head stops shaking, a stillness coming over him. 'What if we ... can agree?'

Refuse to look on like a goat-eyed punter at a dogfight, Hugh. Accept that actions will redeem – wade in there and get about the bastards. Reconnect your spine ... spine ... spine ...

Hughie doesn't move for a time, then sits bolt upright, eyes staring straight ahead. 'Okay, okay ... I'll try,' he says. When he doesn't get a response, he slyly glances to the side, then spins right round, searching the empty car – the Knight is gone. The stains of black bile on the leather are gone too, that rasping breath and those cruel eyes are also gone. But despite the vanishing, something has changed, something feels different inside him. Deep down, by his amygdala, a bubbling gated forge has been left open intentionally, his past oozing out of it in slow glugs of molten resentment to form something shiny and black, something of use. His fist begins to beat on the window in rhythm with the clanging forge hammers in his head; his shoulders straightening as he feels it cooling and setting within – a keen hard point forms in his soul.

'I will,' he tells the empty car.

Red eyes fixed ahead, he sinks his boot to the floor and belts down Bute Street, spraying a big puddle up in the air. Inside, he is razor sharp, pig-iron, while outside, he assumes his usual, likeable, gentle mask for the good people of the Town – knowing that deception is critical in warfare.

THREE

GREEN EYES ON THE CROOKED PATH

Gull stares at the tuna sandwich from a post, twenty feet away, and Hughie stares back, golf club in his other hand, holding it like a walking stick to one side.

'You'll have to wait,' he tells the bird and takes another bite.

Gull's impatient shriek resonates across the still of the Town's reservoir, just as the sun starts to seep through the hill mist and paint orange cracks on the still water. The occasional tall, pointed tree begins to poke out of the soup, like guardians of the far shore. Beneath the feet of these watchmen, Hughie imagines the scattered campfires of last summer, forgotten shell holes full of burned beer cans, and rusting oil drums the forestry workers forgot to go back for.

The sign below Gull's feet warns you not to light fires, camp, fish without a permit, swim in the reservoir or let your dog foul. Spray-painted underneath this are the words, **'FUCK OFF'**. Hughie grins, recognising something he'd have done himself twenty-five years ago. In fact, one of the reasons he's come here is just that; this place and his youth haunt him with memories of stone-head parties under night skies, girls' shrieking laughter skimming across star-drenched water and heavy metal bellowing through the dark woods like electric gas. Those distant memories of carefree pleasure come on a lot at the moment and make him smile despite the throes of social-work chaos. The edited past gives him hope, and he wants to carry that again. But it doesn't take long for dark realities, like yesterday, to sink that boat. He's come here today to plan, not to dream. Walking along the earth and stone dam that holds the deep waters back, he begins fretting on his conundrum. *Eyes, knights, neck burns, wolves, Amygdalanians; all these things need so much energy to deal with – energy I just don't fucking have. Anyway, isn't it like that sixties' saying: fighting for peace is like fucking for virginity.*

You agreed. We fight … Sire.

He looks at the remains of his tuna sandwich, his face tired, white and drawn due to last night's poor sleep. *Not sure if I'm overreacting, personalising it all.* He throws the bread in the grass at his feet as Kilbride Hill appears from the mist. He imagines it forming under some giant, mythical, Druidic arse from the dark days of the Iron Age when the Eppidii tribe ran the show around these parts; slashing lost Romans in the days they ran for the south. By seventeen, he'd told those stories to scare his tripping pals, or to bring some giggling lassie closer so you might sneak a sly kiss or grab a feel by the campfire. He'd always absorbed that side of things, the lie, the truth within; like how Christian hearts see a nod to St. Bride of Kildare in the names round here, but even that was a typical Argyll conceal-ment, hiding the pagan fire goddess, Bridgit, among the etymologies of a thousand years of ecclesiastical misdirec-tion. As he stands in the scattering mist, Bridgit wanders around him; part of an older brain wiring that makes you sure you are being watched through the marsh reeds whose roots sink below brown water until they grasp her cold stone heart.

Eeeeeeaaaghhh, Gull shrieks, pouncing on the bread.

Hughie takes something from his coat pocket and rubs it on the cloth of his jacket until it holds a white sheen. Dropping a golf ball onto the grass, he cranks back his club and takes several practice swings as the Knight wakes again.

There'll be no crappin out of today's mission. The Knight is sat on the dewy grass by Hughie's feet with his helmet off, looking up at his creator. Long sprouts of marsh grass spike up between the rusty armour plates of his skeletal legs. Hughie doesn't want to show the Knight that he is terrified by his reappearance, but also knows that, in the end, you can't hide anything from yourself. Yawning, the Knight shows his scaly pink throat and dodgy collection of black teeth, while Hughie shakes his head at what is either his own relentless self-defence mechanism, or a persistent visual hallucination that points towards a future stay in a padded room.

The golf club ratchets back, then fires the ball high up into the calm morning sky, the bright dot soaring free for a while before surrendering to gravity, falling back down to a distant plop. Hughie raises a rare smile as the small surface ripple grows and grows. Small things can have a large effect, but what to do?

C'mon, social work isnae a winnin game, Hugh, never has been.

Hughie's smile drops off.

If you take a kid away from some old tart, yer a child snatcher; if you don't, and the kid gets mangled, yer one o those limp-wristed-

fuckin-lefties. Nae prizes for indecision in war –
just do what has to be done and fuck em all.

He nods at the Knight in agreement. I know that wanting to be understood is student stuff. But there are better ways, theory-driven possibilities that this boss won't want to fund.

Forget that prick.

A heron wades out of the wispy reeds not far from him, sure that it has heard an over-active trout. It sees Hughie and hears something else it doesn't like, wading back into reed cover as Gull flaps off along the water's edge, breakfast in beak. Dropping another ball, Hughie thinks about how to handle his boss, imagining Chas's face as he lines the clubhead with the smirking ball. His meditations are spoiled as his hearing catches up with that of the birds'. Pausing mid-swing, he turns his head to the side slightly, catching the sound of mumbled singing floating up through the birch trees below. Within seconds, the singer, a small, bespectacled man with dark hair and a cheap zipper jacket, rounds the corner of the path below. Looking down, Hughie tries to put a name to the old face. The guy pushes a heavy wheel-barrow, full to the brim with plastic-covered electrical cable, pausing now and then to rest his skinny legs, before moving on up the track towards Hughie. The Knight disappears, and Hughie hopes the old guy will pass on up the track without bothering him, but as he prepares to strike another ball, he feels the old man's eyes on him. His hard, nervous swing is all wrong from the start and the ball shoots away to the left where it skites out a choppy trough in the water.

It's that creepy old fucker's fault.

The old boy laughs and moves off again, waddling with

his heavy load up past the Scots pines then on up into the hills. The eek, eek, of the wheelbarrow fading as he goes.

Hughie looks at his watch, his chest tightening.

No scared o wee Chas, are we?

'Right, okay, okay.' I know where I'm going with this; we'll throw money at it, resources, see if the mum can float.

After a quick suspicious squint around, he hides the driver behind a gorse bush. Marching off, he looks full of purpose, his swinging arms out of place within the slow-moving county of Argyll. Without stopping, he takes a last look over his shoulder at the Goddess Bridgit and sees small wisps of black smoke from melting plastic cable begin to seep up from the trees on the hillside.

Good to see cottage industries takin off in the Highlands at last.

Hughie stops dead. 'Jim.' That's his name, the old bugger with the wheelbarrow of scrap.

Industrious old fucker, got to give him that.

Racking his memory for his mum's and gran's stories, he finds some detail: old Jimbo was flown home from the Korean War; there was something about him shooting a wee Korean girl ... through the head, by accident. Ahhhh, Argyll myth-making; if you don't know, make it up. The poor old bastard probably never ventured past the pier.

The burn on the boy's neck – the mission?

'Shut it!'

Hughie leaves part of himself behind and marches down through the birch into town as a cloud blocks the sun and the goddess blows on the branches.

'IT'S all got a bit bloody chaotic since you turned up.'

Chas sits back in his chair, hands behind head, both feet on the desk, observing how his jocular hand-grenade affected his junior. Hughie feels nervous in the gut as he looks down at his boss but doesn't buckle or give up on the first go. The wee shite stinks of the arrogance that comes from toerags who do better than expected, promoted beyond their ability through cunning and a fair amount of social climbing, end up as the head key jangler. God, listen to yourself, Hughie, that was you not so long ago.

Don't be so slow for fuck's sake, he's laughin at you. The Knight's armour can be heard rattling as he shakes his head and tuts at his master's rubber spine.

'What did I tell you?' Chas demands.

'All I can do is report the unmet needs I see—'

'You can think first,' Chas interrupts. 'We don't have your big city budgets round here.'

'I'm not asking for that—'

'I specifically warned you about jumpin tae conclusions.'

Hughie's shoulders lift and fall with a quiet breath. 'What about the burn?'

'So, you're a doctor now, are you, Hugh? Could be a chicken pox scar or bullies like old Maggie said – why dramatise it.'

'I'm not new to this.' After saying this, Hughie looks to his boss for some acknowledgement.

'And that should stop you takin it personal.'

Chas looks irritated but sure he can close this down. His eyes flash to Hughie's scarred hand for the second time in two days. He shakes his head, and Hughie tries to hold the line. Both are staring, refusing to back down; stags caught up in the usual social-work rut. Hughie breaks first, dropping his eyes in defeat, feeling the gnaw of shame and humiliation deep inside.

You let the weasel-snake in easy there. I've lost that confidence that used to break the putrid smugness of idiots. Since Manchester, the psyche's got big holes in the hull, and the rudder, well ... it broke off. The Knight jumps around within the mind, trying to shore up the self-doubt that is spraying from everywhere.

He's a wee scheming weasel-snake, nothin more; find his fuckin weakness, push the cunt back. Well, he fears new blood, frightened he'll lose the throne to someone smarter. That will allow room for negotiation as he'll want someone on his side in a big office full of folk he's probably pissed all over. *Still be easier to just nut the wee shite.*

'Four hours' respite for the boy's mum?' Hughie says, like a last bet.

'More money.'

'But Ms Anderson is an older mum who's strugglin ... their place is falling apart. A bit of proper support will give them time to sort things out ... then we can step back, see how things go.'

'I said no; bat it back to the school.' Chas swings his legs off his desk.

There is nowhere to go after that and all the certificates on the walls are rallying to their owner's aid; black-framed, post-grad merits with gold stamps from this trainer and that university. They strangle the usurper's voice, any right to reply and insist on compliance with a superior being who you should not and could not question.

In Hughie's mind, the Knight has wee Chas tied naked to a rack and is sharpening the inner edge of a crested knife.

Tight little cunt, are we? Guts spilt out in a loud sloppy gush, a muffled scream cut short.

'The boy's vulnerable, the place is a pit,' Hughie says, catching his volume as it begins to rise.

'Hugh,' Chas says as a reprimand.

'Sorry, but I see ... difficulties if we don't act.'

'Tell you what, why don't you phone Housing or the boy's school, let them do their bloody jobs for a change?'

Time to bring out the big blade, son, get statutory.

'I think you are obviously missin the child-protection issues here, Charles.' Hughie gulps after saying it. This move is a direct insult – calling his boss out for a fight. When Chas doesn't react, Hughie starts again, 'I'll—'

'Shhhh,' Chas interrupts, holding a finger to his own lips.

Flushing with anger, Hughie goes quiet. ***Neutered, like a fuckin dog, man.*** Maybe he's negotiating.

Chas rummages in a low drawer of his desk, both of his hands disappearing into the drawer, leaving his vulnerable, grinning ball-face floating just above the desktop looking up at Hughie.

Please, smack that wee face, for fuck's sake.

Hughie holds it in.

'Right,' Chas says as he comes back up. 'This is how it works; pick a card and don't show me it.'

He is holding out a curve of playing cards towards Hughie.

After a bit of huffing and puffing, Hughie feels forced to play along by the clown's insistent stare, reluctantly picking a card. It is an eight of spades. He holds it against his chest. Please get it wrong.

'Eight of spades,' Chas says with a big cocky grin.

'Yep,' Hughie replies. ***What a fuckin dickhead***.

Putting the card down on the desk, Hughie is unsure what this naff card trick was supposed to prove.

'Now take another,' Chas insists.

Hughie moves slow, trying his best to show that his obedience is grudging, then picks another card; it is the same, another eight of spades. Chas then rolls over the pack onto the desktop. They are all eights of spades. Hughie shrugs, still confused.

'This pack o cards is like me,' Chas tells him. 'You'll keep gettin the same message again and again.' He nods towards the phone. 'My bosses say what I can afford to spend every year; I tell you what you can.' He becomes all patronising, 'If I teach you one thing up here, it'll be realism.'

Hughie tries to take the lecture, his fists balling behind his back.

I'm sure the cunt's aware o the realism Maggie and the boy have drippin on their heads every night. Looks like child protection doesn't exist this side of the water now – either that or he's just enjoyin rammin his cock down yer throat.

'Now! Your other cases; looks like you're behind with most of them,' Chas says all serious – trying to turn the blade back around.

Hughie's neck flushes.

1 – 2 – 3 – 4 – 5 – trebuchet away.

'This is nonsense!' Hughie shouts at the top of his voice, storming to the door where he stands with one hand trembling on the handle, his neck veins pulsing.

Chas's eyes are wide and the office outside the door is silent, nine or more pairs of ears listening intently now. But Chas can't find a reply. The transformation in this witty, if seemingly ineffective, social worker is frightening. This guy is all Mr Hyde compared to the usual underlings who might sulk when slapped down, or at worst, go off sick, before coming back full of apologies when the message gets through.

Opening the door, Hughie starts to leave, then looks back, his face half in shade, an incendiary anger growing in him. The space between the two men is filling with a thick expectant hush that is suffocating.

Behind his eyes, Chas is calculating fast with little beads clattering into one another and scenarios being rushed through in hyper mode to find the best outcome, but he can't think that quick, and this mental-case bastard hasn't behaved as he should have.

The door is fully open now, so the crowd might hear what comes next, but Hughie isn't moving for some reason, taking the kind of breaths you do before going completely Tonto.

'Right! I've got a plan,' Chas says and jumps up. Snatching his coat off the back of the chair, he swings his arms into it and meets Hughie on the threshold. He pats his underling's shoulder, whispering, 'I care more than you fuckin know, son,' in the other man's ear.

They exchange a brief hard stare. Chas smiling like it is all part of the test and to reassure the rabble who look on; Hughie looks quiet and wrong-footed again.

'Follow,' Chas demands and Hughie traipses behind him towards the exit without a clue as to what is going on. The work ants that had been gawking click back to work mode and looked away in unison.

Before they get to the door, Faye, who is next in line to the throne, waves a hand and sails over from her desk. 'Is there a problem?' she asks.

Chas doesn't answer and gives her a domineering stare which she instantly adapts to.

'I've made the changes you wanted to our response to the new permanency legislation, Charles,' she says. Her eyes are flicking between them both for tells of what is going on.

'Aye, you'll have to get up early to beat this filly in the races, Hughie,' Chas tells him. He winks at Faye and gives a scoffing laugh.

Faye is thin, elegant and as cold as her staff nickname, Snowball, suggests.

On a drive to the head office last week, Chas told Hughie about the competition. Faye is divorced with no kids, no life, but very ambitious. Despite wearing the tightest suits to work, she'd never waste a second flirting with anyone of a lower or equal rank, no point in diluting the gene pool. She runs the lives of five adult-care social workers, plus Hughie, and three slave-like social work assistants. Hughie's job is funded as a multidisciplinary worker to take the pressure off the other two teams; he answers to Faye if it is adult care and Chas if it is work for another team. Faye's attitude is intense, focused and simultaneously aloof. She is a born manager – control freak.

Aye, cold as fuckin ice; no chance o gettin near her panty line in this lifetime, Hughie ma boy.

'And where are the boys off to?' Faye asks, voice curious and sarcastic.

Chas ignores her and moves away, while Hughie raises

his shoulders and eyebrows like a lost tourist. As they pass the social work assistants' desks near the main door, Chas smiles down at Joyce, a girl of about twenty-eightish, who has a pretty, round face and sparkly eyes and happens to be Hughie's only ally in the team so far.

'Hiya Joyce, how's the Weight Watchers goin then?' Chas asks her.

'I don't go to Weight Watchers any more.' Her cheeks flush, and the spark leaves her eyes.

'Sorrrraaay, I thought you were still at it.'

'Eh, no ...' she says to his back as he walks away.

'Got to show an interest in yer staff, but you know all that,' Chas tells Hughie over his shoulder.

Hughie gives Joyce a reassuring smile as he follows on.

The doors flap, and they go down the stairs, leaving the office quiet bar the tapping keyboards. Joyce nestles her hurt and rage, while the Snowball stands arms folded in the middle of the office shaking her head; left to steer the ship while the Captain and his new first mate float out to fuck around in the world, as boys do.

DRIVING ALONG AT SPEED, Chas rolls down the window and blows his cigar smoke out into the slipstream, letting the silence between them breathe a bit. He throws the cigar into the day, after a few puffs, and accelerates along Queen Street, doing at least forty.

'Karen is the lassie's name,' Chas says out of the blue.

'Where are we goin?'

'She's a carer; you wanted a carer.' He looks at Hughie at this point and Hughie nods. 'Bit of a goer in her day, but she's one of the best carers we had.'

64

'Had?' Hughie says.

Turning into Kirk Lane far too fast sends Hughie sliding in his seat and scrabbling for the grab handle above his door.

'She's no fosterin kids now, but maybe you could charm her into it,' Chas says as he takes his eyes off the road for far too long while giving his sweaty hostage a peculiar grin. 'What d'ye think?'

'Me?'

'Why not give wee Tommy a couple of weeks of her popping in and out? Maggie gets a bit of parentin advice, then pull her out again – job done.'

'Yeah ... that might be ... okay.'

Wee shit's up to somthin, I'm tellin you.

The car thankfully slows as it groans its way up Argyll Road, built on one of the many steep hills that lie beneath the houses and tarmac of the Town, then speeds up as it turns into the brown roughcast estate of Ardenvale. A few sweat-inducing bends later, they swerve in close to the kerb at the end of a long, drab crescent of semi-detached council houses.

'She lives here,' Chas says, gesturing at a semi that has a red door. 'Number Eighty-Two, Stalag Thirteen.' He smiles to himself.

'Not a fan of social housing then?' Hughie says.

Chas gives a dismissive shrug of the shoulders. 'Shows a certain lack of ambition, does it not?' After seeing Hughie's face frown, he adds, 'Just a wee joke aimed at subvertin political correctness, Hugh, relax.'

Clenching his jaw inside his face, Hughie avoids shaking his head and looks at his feet to stop it all surfacing again. He's probably overloaded with stress. I know there's no budget left, and I'm sure he needs a few malts every night, just to get a sleep. ***Wee fuckin SS commandant; note the reference to a prison camp – prick.*** Hold on, this was what I wanted, was it not? The peace, the slow pace of life. ***The small-town bigots.***

Parked opposite 82 Ardenvale Crescent with the engine off, both men sit silent for what seems an age, waiting. Hughie feels confused. I don't want to come across as an idiot by asking daft questions, like: What is going on? ***What the fuck is goin on?*** He senses that his boss, who is constantly sending guarded texts like a bored teenager, likes it this way, keeping people always on the back foot, off balance. Chas fills the gaps between his texting with second-hand gossip from other members of staff. Hughie listens and takes deep, quiet breaths. Maybe he's trying to paint a picture of the town, clue me up. ***Aye, propaganda always works best in drip, drip form. Like wee stones dropped over the neighbour's wall, one at a time, durin the winter, till there's a big fuckin pile o rocks on yer lawn come summer with no obvious cunt to blame.***

In between jokes and patter, there is a short tale that hints at the Snowball's lack of sexual control in the past – some embarrassing moment at a wedding in the bowling club toilet that involved a visiting rugby player or perhaps two. Joyce's name is deftly sullied too to gauge from Hughie's facial tells just how close he's got to her. The stuff is fine sewn between work chit-chat, every line a smearing half quote from someone else, quickly refuted as outrageous by Chas after the seed has been planted. To reduce budgets without a revolution, you must first misdirect the flock, drive them into the dark, keep them powerless and at one another's throats.

Tipping his head back, Chas gives Hughie a curious look. 'You and Joyce?'

'Nothing to tell,' Hughie tells him.

Chas is watching Hughie's eyes again. 'It's just that you seem kinda ... close, the pair o you.'

Don't get caught in his wee detour.

'She works hard,' Hughie says abruptly, cutting Chas off.

For five more minutes, both look out the window in an uncomfortable silence.

'Here's my girl,' Chas says with relief.

Hughie clocks a woman coming around the corner, head down. Their attention leaves her for a moment as a stray mongrel crosses the road and begins to lift a leg to piss against Chas's shiny Jag. He hits the horn to send the dog scurrying off, but this breaks their cover and alerts the woman, who looks up at them. Hughie sees her pretty, sad face for the first time.

'Now, Karen here is no the brightest girl,' Chas says. 'I like my foster carers like ah like ma soup.'

Hughie furrows his brow, waiting for it.

'Warm and thick,' Chas says, then winks. 'Black humour, Hughie.'

'She looks ... tired.'

'But not bad lookin – what d'ye think?'

He is studying Hughie's facial responses, like that entomologist again, waiting for the bug to react to stimuli, flip itself over and give away its triggers

'She looks okay,' Hughie admits, giving in.

'Aye, looks after herself alright. Goes to the gym down the front – lycra, the whole lot.'

The woman dawdles towards them, her hair bottle blonde, with dark roots showing; her auxiliary nurse's uniform is perhaps one size too small, hinting at a very good figure under the worn grey cloth. The two heavy shopping bags she carries pull on her arms, her shoulders and face until she is a walking scowl. Hughie can't picture her fostering vulnerable young kids who have their own deep-rooted problems.

'Great with wee ones, but Andy Mac, in Finance, says Karen was a very friendly girl when the Americans were here, especially with the black boys.' Chas is staring out the window at her as he says this.

'Nice guy, this Andy?' Hughie asks.

Chas doesn't answer.

She comes further up the road, Hughie squinting to see her face better.

'She looks ... disappointed,' he says.

'Cannae have kids.'

Hughie turns to him. 'She can't have kids?'

'Always guessed, that's why she used to foster.' Still watching her, Chas's lips pout, and his head tilts to the side. 'Maybe you can stir up her maternal instinct again, bring her back to the fold.'

Despite trying to hold it back, Hughie's head gives a micro shake. The wee bastard calculates endlessly, doesn't he? ***Weighs everyone's worth in the basest system o value, their cost to the Authority in pounds and pence.*** He's given us this opportunity to get Tommy's mum help; focus on that. ***He's playin us here somehow, don't be soft, Hughie.***

Chas starts the car, then gives another of those looks that tells Hughie he's had enough of his company, and it is time for him to get out the car and get dirty.

'Give her a try, Hughie. She's still registered,' he says as hc pushes the release button on Hughie's seat belt, sending the belt slinking across his passenger's chest.

As Hughie opens his door, Chas catches his shoulder. 'You of all people will know the pressure I'm under?' he says.

'Yeah, yeah, I remember it,' Hughie says picking his briefcase out of the footwell and pushing his way out the door. Glancing back as he stands outside, his boss looks suddenly vulnerable. *I smell a trap.*

The Jag roars off just as Karen gets to her gate, opposite where Hughie stands. She looks after the car then goes in her gate without a word or glance towards the gleekit social worker who's been left by the kerb. Following her, Hughie waves a raised hand to catch her attention, then pulls it back when she doesn't see it. He has no choice now but to stalk after her uninvited.

Got that unmistakable look of a pissed-off female about her – careful.

'Karen,' he shouts from just inside the gate, his voice sounding too familiar and loud in the quiet street. ***Miss …? Oh, that's right, your wee boss mate didn't bother to tell you her proper name.***

She turns on her doorstep, gives him a withering look that makes him feel both guilty and, for reasons he does not yet know, strangely excited at the same time. He gives a wary smile as he gets closer. God, she's pretty, if a bit hard looking. Her eyes flash him again, softer this time, and he glimpses a tangible ember of empathy hidden well below the weariness of a long day cleaning bedpans and geriatric arses at the hospital. Perhaps she is someone who could influence wee Tommy in a positive way, after all.

'Karen,' he says, lifting a finger then dropping it.

'Who're you?'

'Sorry, I don't know your second name. I'm not well prepared.'

'Who. Are. You?' she repeats.

'I'm ... eh ...'

'You for real?' she says with a look of tired annoyance on her face.

He fights with his breast pocket. 'Got my ID here, somewhere.'

'It doesn't matter,' she says, 'I saw the wee creep drive off; you're from social work.'

Trying to hold her big green-eyed gaze makes him blink. 'Yeah, that's right.'

'Got a child needin looked after, by any chance?'

'Eh ... yes.'

Her eyes begin probing the self-conscious social worker until he begins to feel that he is outside his own body looking down at an utter imbecile.

'It's okay, it's the way the wee shit leaves everyone feeling – like a fool,' she says. Her gaze holds him, it's expectant.

'Hughie's my name ... MacDonald.'

'Not Ronald then.'

The joke goes over his head as he holds out a hand for her to shake. She folds her arms, and he drops the embarrassing wriggling hand to his side, wanting to chop it off. Peeping out from behind his frontal lobe, the Knight licks his lips and gives a lecherous growl, ***Frisky lookin wench; stick to the mission, nae nooky detours***. Hughie banishes him to the dungeon in an instant, the sound of laughter fading as if he's fallen down a well.

'Could we have a talk; about fostering?' Hughie asks.

'No point.'

'A bit of advice then?'

Her green eyes search his soul for intent as he shrinks inside. Turning her back to him, she glances up and down the neighbours' bay windows, lifts her shopping and goes inside, leaving the door wide open. 'Five minutes,' she says over her shoulder.

By the time he has paused, gone in and turned to close the front door, she has gone. He edges up the hall, noting a cork pinboard above the phone table that holds four take-away menus and numerous taxi firm cards. Along a bit further, in the small alcove under the stairs, a computer screen shows a Facebook screensaver. Next to the keyboard, an empty glass and wine bottle tell of another lonely night on the web. The living-room door on the left is ajar, and he can see half a dozen CDs sat by a cheap hi-fi. David Gray's *White Ladder* sits next to Snow Patrol's *Final Straw*. He smiles. Good to know she's into music rather than a greatest hits type of girl, shows depth, even curiosity. Both artists are kind of safe, mind you, prefer more avant-garde stuff myself, the pretentious prick music, as the ex-wife used to say. 'What do you have in your coffee?' her faint voice asks from somewhere further up the hall.

'What?' he asks, even though he has heard, needing a better fix on where she is.

Can we try not to look any more rapey than necessary, Sire.

He hears cups clinking.

'Are you a bit deaf? Milk and sugar?' she shouts.

He leans around the kitchen doorframe. 'Milk and two,' he says as he steps onto the shiny lino floor. She puts two hot cups on a small table by the back door and sits down, crossing her legs. Lifting a cigarette and lighter while watching him, she places the cigarette between her thin lips, lights the end and inhales slowly, eyes still on him. A welcome sign of nerves within her coolness comes when she nods to the seat opposite, her head jerking slightly. He is sure that his brogues are covered in super glue as he walks the five steps to the seat while avoiding the optical draw of her slender legs.

This wench is freakin me too, no sure why.

He stands awkward, opposite her, as she puts two heaped teaspoons of sugar and then a drop of milk into both cups, pointing with the dripping spoon at an empty chair. The fag bouncing between her lips as she says, 'Sit. Shouldn't stand over people; your mum never tell you that?'

'She did, in fact,' he says.

'Well, sit.'

'Nice place,' he says as he takes his seat.

The room is bare-looking with matching cream chrome kettle, toaster and a pedal bin. No sign of any mess or family life getting in the way; perhaps some control issues under the surface. On the wall, by the fridge, hangs a black and white framed photo of a naked black model with his tight muscular backside thrust towards the camera.

Maybe yer pal was right about her bein man daft.

'Listen, before you ask, I'm not fosterin,' she says, her sharp eyes pinning him, 'haven't for over a year – the Creep knows that.'

'The Creep?'

'Yeah, your tight-fisted pal, Chas.'

They give one another knowing smiles, holding eye contact for a long, uncomfortable moment; he looks away first. Lifting the cup and having a sip gives him time to settle. She's tired and disappointed, a real last gasp beauty

alright. Check out those big, womanly, forest-green eyes –
wow! *Fuckin desperate, more like.*

'He spoke highly of you,' Hughie lies.

She snorts out smoke and shakes her head. 'Yeah, right.'

Behind her defensive tone, he senses a life of regrets
and dormant plans that got swept away by bad timing; all
those small events that give folk that buried-alive look. He
listens to her complain about the Jaguar-driving Chas's
money orientated approach to foster care; how people who
do the dirty work at the front line have to beg for crumbs
while others, further up the food chain, diddle their
expenses for thousands as well as taking home a good wage.

'D'you know that your lot pay the lowest rate in the
whole country?' she says.

He stops sipping his tea, gives a guilty nod.

'That little shit told me that it wasn't ethical to pay folk
to look after kids,' she says. 'It's a vocation, seemingly; we
should eat dirt.'

'He's ... budget conscious.'

She narrows her eyes a bit. 'Priests and doctors do
alright for cash and look at their track record with the
vulnerable.'

'What have doctors done wrong?' he asks, giving a wee
jokey surprised face.

'Shipman. Crippen. I don't have to tell you about the
priests, do I?'

'Fair point.' *Sharper than she looks – watch her.*

In between moaning about the complexities of trench
life, she betrays her love for the kids she's cared for
through small changes to her tone, that warm lilt in her
voice when saying their names or talking about that visit
to the swimming pool. There was hyperactive Jaden, who
spat at the guy next door, oh and smiley wee Alex who

used to nick money from her purse when she went to the toilet. Catching her beautiful sad eyes flashing, it suddenly dawns on him. In that very instant, he knows the game.

Bollocks! It's a set-up.

He continues listening with a twisted smile, his mind now speeding up. Wee Chas is good, fucking good. It's that lilt in her voice that gives it away, that sigh like ending to some of her words. Most wouldn't spot it, and others might think she is a cold, hard-faced bitch, burned out, scary even. But if you pay attention, listen, you know she has a soul, maybe it's a bit lost, but it's there, throbbing beneath life's waves.

As she gets up to wash out her cup, Hughie sees her thigh push against the inside of her auxiliary uniform. Damn, Chas has baited the hook well. Some sad beauty, with a jaded warm heart, who's got trapped in a run-down housing scheme, and me, a once optimistic, fucked-up, gawky looking, crestfallen social worker – both looking for another shot at the happiness title, a cause to follow, or the beacon in the misty distance.

It's the perfect desperado stitch-up. The Knight gets mad when he catches Hughie imagining driving through Las Vegas – her drunk on tequila, with the wind blowing through her tangled hair, him at the wheel, sunshades and white teeth, The Doors pounding out 'LA Woman' on the radio. ***Stop it!*** I've always been plagued by the same romantic notions for the gone-astray ones, the maiden-lost-in-the-woods ones; all that futile chivalrous optimism which Chas could smell a mile away. Is starry-eyed romantic so clearly marked on my forehead? ***I think it's more a gullible fanny tattoo, myself.***

'You *are* weird Hughie MacDonald,' she says from the sink as she catches him daydreaming.

He tries his best smile, but she's turned away, washing her cup out and placing it on the drainer. Taking another Marlboro from a packet on the side, she takes her time to light it, then stands over him, resting her backside against the unit, her legs crossed at the ankles, the look on her face suggesting she is waiting for something.

'Sorry, never slept last night,' he says with genuine tiredness.

'Me neither; must be our bad consciences.'

'Bet Chas sleeps like a bloody baby, eh?'

They both snigger at this, him into his tea, her as she blows out smoke. Through the blue haze, he sees a soft zest begin to seep out in the easy creases of her eyes. It is difficult to know what will get her back on track with the fostering or if she is too burned out and angry to find her way back to that particular road. ***Ten more years and this lassie will be headin into mingin Maggie territory, so focus on why we're here.*** Hughie looks at her smooth calves and her fine ankles, noticing she has no shoes on, making him worry that he's broken a house rule.

'Who's needin to be looked after?' she asks.

'Eh ...' He looks flustered; caught perving.

'You're here lookin for a carer – no?'

The boy – the reason we're fuckin here, ankle licker.

'Oh, yeah, yeah ... a young boy, about ten,' he says.

'And?'

'And ... the mum's a bit exhausted ... can't keep him safe. He's on his own a lot of the time ... poor school attendance. Possible abuse from unknown other, but I'm not a hundred percent sure of that one any more, if I'm honest.' Hughie's speech has become pressured, so he pauses to breathe, focusing on her face. 'He's a crackin wee lad, honest – glows like a star.'

He watches her react to this, softening, then stiffening as if catching herself straying towards a familiar trap.

'Wish I could help,' she says and gives a sad smile.

When he keeps looking, she takes another draw on her fag, smoke escaping her lips in a thin cool plume. *She's not budgin*.

'It won't be a long placement,' he says.

Moving in herself, she looks conflicted for a second, a small crack in the armour perhaps.

'No,' she says, 'I'm not in the right place.'

'Just for a month?' He lifts his hands up and smiles at her.

'I can't ...'

'If things are a bit difficult for you right now, a week will do,' he says, knowing he is pushing it now. She doesn't answer, so he jumps in again, 'I know it can be difficult to commit at short notice; I understand how it goes, but—'

'I said, no!'

He flushes as she knocks him onto the back foot. 'I didn't mean to make out that I know you,' he says.

'You don't know the first thing.'

We need to get some respite for old Maggie – it's urgent!

'Listen, we all go through things,' he says. 'I got cynical too, moved back here to recharge.' *Ah, got you now, sob story time.*

'So, I'm a cynic now?' she says, folding her arms.

'No, no, it's me I'm talkin about.'

'You're the cynic?'

Nodding slow, he sees some welcome concern on her face. 'Yeah.'

'What happened?' she asks.

'It's a tough game social work—'

'No. I meant to your hands?'

'Oh ... I dropped the car bonnet on them ... a while back.' *The old lies are the best; sound authentic.*

She grimaces at the thought, her face becoming soft and pitying to the point he feels the need to put his hands up and wriggle the fingers about to show they work okay.

'You get through it okay?' she asks, taking a seat and leaning on the table, chin in her hand.

'No choice.'

We've got her; now reel her in for fuck's sake.

Clearing his throat, he sits up straight, saying. 'This boy I was telling you about ... he might be at some risk if we don't find help.'

She takes her elbows off the table and leans back in her creaky chair. 'That's why social-work types like you get paid so much.' The softness is gone again – he's pulled too hard on the line.

'Pity,' Hughie says, 'he'd be happy gettin spoiled for a while.'

She snorts, says, 'Happy? Here?'

Ach, you're losin her.

'I went away, lookin for happy,' he says to prick her ears.

She seems vaguely curious as she relights her cigarette, lighter waving side to side as she asks, 'Why come back?'

He thinks for a minute. 'Don't know, to be honest. Maybe I want to pay something back.'

'Feel good does it, helpin the lost?'

Their eyes link as smoke seeps out of her glossy lips and up past high cheekbones. Hughie feels her on his skin, inside it, that resonance that he hasn't felt for so long.

Hold on, there's somethin happenin here; who's hookin who? Shut up. Keep out of this.

'It gives me a purpose, I guess,' Hughie says, their eyes still linked.

'Least you're honest.'

'The lad, he just needs a couple of weeks.'

Her face holds a pondering stillness for a moment. 'This lad, is he high tariff?'

'Don't think so. You give the mum a wee help out, a bit of respite and see how it goes.'

'Learning difficulties?'

'Possible Dyslexia.'

'Health?'

'Good, as far as I know.'

This catches her attention. 'As far as you know?'

'It's a new case, just gettin a handle on it,' he admits.

'What about behaviour, attachment issues?'

Are we on fuckin trial here?

Hughie feels exhausted inside, the lack of sleep catching up, his head dipping into her last question. He takes a breath. 'That ... might be an area where he needs some attention,' he admits with a slow nod. 'But you can leave the technical side of it to me.'

Fuck me gently, how long's this gonnae take – c'mon, c'mon, c'mon.

'Did he attend nursery?' She is insistent now.

Put this cheeky wench back in her box.

He is blinking now. 'Wouldn't worry about all that,' he tells her, 'it's just that the situation, well ... it needs to be addressed right now … we're kinda desperate.' As that last tired word leaves his mouth, he wishes he could catch it, suck it back out the air and swallow its nasty shape whole.

Her shift's-end face goes rigid as his clanger flies right through her façade, catching her just as she has let down the guard. Those beautiful green eyes show a cavernous hurt, then sharpen until he feels she is looking straight through him.

'Just another bloody chancer, like your boss,' she tells him.

He sees her chest redden as he sits like a smacked mullet, not daring to show any emotion in case it is the wrong one. ***Crazy fuckin bunny boiler!***

'I'm sorry,' he says, squirming. 'I didn't mean to offend—'

Holding out a hand is enough to stop his excuses and give her a moment. 'Listen. I'm tired, it's time you went,' she says. There is real fragility in her voice, yet something more savage in reserve; when he doesn't look like he is about to move anytime soon, it rises to the surface. 'Out!' she shouts.

Like a string operated puppet, he flies up out of the chair, scrambling to gather up his briefcase and follow her silently into the hall.

Obviously some sorta mental, hormonal, fuckin nutjob? Poison in the tea sort? I must have trodden on her low self-esteem there, I'm so tired, not on my game. ***Don't be surprised if some clown with a gimp mask and a cosh jumps out of one of these doors any minute; pops yer skull open.*** Leave it.

'Didn't mean to upset you there, Karen,' he says in a dry-throated voice. 'I'm really sorry.'

It works, and he can see the tension in her shoulders drop, her pace slowing.

'I'll let you off, this time,' she says over her shoulder.

He tiptoes close behind, trying not to get too close. 'No, I'm genuinely sorry.'

Don't overdo it, succubus, she's schitzo, change in a fuckin instant – shout rape.

'It's these shifts; make you all ...' Her words drift off, absorbed by the narrow hall and he misses the last bit.

'I've done shifts – knackering.'

She pauses by the computer table, half turns, and holds her hands out; her fingertips showing him a slight tremor. 'See,' she says.

'How long you been doin them, the shifts?' he asks, all concerned.

'Six, no, seven years.'

'Whoa, bit of a killer that.'

'Most of the others don't mind,' she says, 'it still gets to me.'

'Don't suppose I helped.'

She looks at him as if trying to figure him out, then moves on; he hates himself but can't help staring at her slim waist and feline shape from behind.

Awww, you're havin me on here, Hughie – she's a fuckin psycho. Piss off, she's stunning, a fragile beauty. The house is sterile like mine, so I know she's alone. The Knight screws up his face in utter revulsion. ***She's a fuckin bunny boiler, man.*** The Knight's shouting sprays venom over the frontal lobe, but Hughie is now picturing her face when she spoke about the kids she'd looked after. She's quite something, this one. ***You haven't learned from Manchester, have you.***

'Thanks,' he says as she pulls back the front door to let him by.

'Sorry ...' She makes a crazy-woman face for an instant that is quite convincing and funny.

'Listen, I'm tired too ... the desperate thing ...'

'It's fine; you're fine,' she says.

Why would a good lookin lassie like that still be sittin on the shelf at her age? Must be a nutjob.

Her eyes flash, soft, and then back to harsh in an instant as he smiles at her. She's got depth – haunting. ***Bi-fuckin-polar more like, the promiscuous type.***

Stop. Stop. Stop!

'You going?' she asks after catching him drifting again.

He spins on the top step and offers a shake of the hand; she takes his hand and he feels hers, soft, warm. He thinks something goes between them, but he doesn't really have a clue about this sort of stuff anymore.

'See you later ...' she starts to say.

'Hughie,' he says, finishing her sentence.

'Good luck with the boy.' Her soft eyes catch him one last time, green, green, green.

'If you change—'

'Bye, Hughieeee,' she says, the door shutting, suddenly breaking their shared gaze.

The Knight looks at the closed door then at Hughie with disbelief. ***That sexy wee lassie voice, what's that about?*** She's something else. ***Yeah, a nutjob. Still, you must be gettin kinda used to women slammin doors in yer face. Ha ha ha ha ha ha.*** *She* didn't slam it. I could have asked her out. I mean, she doesn't work for us now. ***Ha ha ha ha ha ha—***

Hughie cuts the Knight's throat within his imagination and the Knight disappears as bile squirts from the gauntlet that still holds his throat together.

At the gate, he gets his car key out and scans along the crescent. Only when he's walked down the pavement a bit does he remember that he'd been dropped off by Chazzy boy and will have to walk across town to pick up his car. He feels for his phone. Left it on my desk.

'Fuck!'

BACK HOME, he climbs the echoing stone stairs with weary steps until he is in the blackness of the first-floor landing. He stands, looking up at the missing light bulb, his keys tinkling in his pocket as he searches for the right one.

'What is it with this place?'

His neighbour's door is sealed shut like a tomb, and the hall stinks of damp stone and earth with a sprinkling of fungus that catches the lungs. It is a relief when the key goes in first time, and the flat door swings open. He steps over the junk mail and slams the door behind, entombing himself.

He goes straight into the kitchen, where he lifts a glass from the mess in the sink, the dishes clattering as he leaves. He frowns. What the fuck? The living-room window is open, the curtains billowing about. Before closing it, he looks around for the photo of his mum and uncle that usually sits on the sill. Weird, where are you two? After a look at the floor, he pulls back the curtain and scans the street below for it – nothing. **Did you look at it in the night; you do that sort o sad shit when you're steamin**. He grimaces and shakes his head. No idea. If it fell down there, wee Lenny the Sweep will have tidied it away by now. He forces the stiff window shut, its squeaking reluctant frame making a man look up from below.

Sat on the wooden inner sill, Hughie pours a large Highland Park and watches the street traffic die away to a trickle, the shops close one at a time, and the people drift and dawdle home from work with their bags of stuff. From where he sits, he can see both ways, up and down the main street, as far as Reno's Chippy, which is warming up for the tea-time heart-blocking clinic; a whiff of hot fat seeps through the rotting sash windows of his rented flat.

Across the way, in the opposite flat, a young woman comes home from college, peels off her coat, and stands in the kitchen drinking fresh orange juice straight from the carton. After her drink, she'll shower, dress up, then go out with her dark-haired pal who comes up around nine. He knows her routine well and suspects she knows his just as well, as do all the neighbours who live on the High Street, above the shops. He sighs.

We all pretend we are blind, not taking an interest in our own kind, not really social creatures; apes with Timex watches, that's all we can ever be.

About half Hughie's age, the student across the way is right into trance music, has the wasteful busy life of a moderately good-looking twenty-two-year-old, and has no idea that this is her time, or that she will never be so hopeful or blissfully ignorant again. One day last month, when she was sat watching the street while wearing a bored petulant look on her face, he'd wanted to phone her up and scream down the phone, 'Live every moment before it runs out.' He'd written off that idea as he was sure it would be more creepy than inspiring. Besides, he knew how easily the police could trace a call when they really wanted to – like for pretty girls.

Pouring another big whisky, he puts the glass against his cheek, feels the coolness as he looks inward. Poor wee Tommy. 'No, no, no,' he tells himself out loud, his voice bouncing around his big flat. No more caring today, it's far too difficult to cope with. Let's think about something else, look after your own needs, recharge the batteries. The gorgeous Karen floats in and out of his mind as he drinks and spins the golden glass in front of his face. *Jeez, ah knew this would happen*. What? *This, the morbid sad-sack routine.* I'm not well, remember ... and Karen's like me – lonely. *She's certainly your type – Loop the Loop.*

'Okay, I am a fucking loser; least I'm not imaginary,' Hughie shouts, making the Knight vanish.

The whisky shines gold as he knocks it back in a oner, bringing a grimace to his face. The girl in the flat across the street turns on her lights as the sun to the west sinks low, a deep aching blue dominates the sky now; triggering thoughts of his youth around here when summer skies meant drinking games and rounds of pool with the lads. He can still feel the tickle from a young girlfriend's breath on his neck, touching a lace bra strap with sweating fingers, and those wet lips that crackled with life – alive. *Alive? That's a joke.*

Another whisky. Drinking slowly is better, numbing his throat while avoiding the contorted face. Half an hour later, the girl comes out of the shower, drops her robe and stands looking at herself in the mirror. He watches from a chair, his cock hardening despite the self-disgust he feels.

The Knight appears at his shoulder, smirking now. *I*

have to say it, Lord MacDonald – yer one sad, creepy bastard these days.

Looking away into the evening sky, he remembers that tiny-waisted Goth he went with when he was a nineteen-year-old barman at the Tavern, how she trembled in his youthful embrace as if made of some form of liquid ecstasy, how she'd woken him from his damaged childhood, even before he knew it was holding him ransom; endlessly teasing him about his scheme-boy nihilistic attitude to get him riled, and then telling him in the same breath he could do anything he wanted in this life. He shakes his head. 'I believed her too.'

While spilling whisky on his shirt breast, he looks out at the same skies that watched his first love take hold; those same skies now sniggering at his empty existence. He falls forward in the chair, hand holding his glass to the floor.

All this halcyon days shit is a bit of a fuckin embarrassment if I'm bein honest, Sire. And that wee lassie across the street there, she hasn't even got proper tits yet. Jezis. Do somethin man; let's scope the dodgy old paedo or the druggie at the Terrace, find some intel. I'm so tired. *Okay, nae balls, you wallow there like a fuckin eunuch. Whine, whine, whimper, whine.*

Around the dull flat, things feed into the Knight's song, the unopened crates of vinyl records and the boxes of history books, that his ex called his obsession, all sit like witnesses to his middle-aged fall from grace. The landlord's threadbare, fourth-hand, furniture and the empty walls whisper too. Finally, in the bedroom, the closed curtains and unmade covers tell of the terrors that control him, even in his sleep. His shoulders and chest tense as he takes a big breath. The glass makes a loud shriek as it hits the wall, the whisky dribbles down the plaster, soaking into the powder-dry surface while the shards settle on the dirty carpet. His door slams and feet pound down the stone stairwell to the street.

'YOU ON A PROMISE?' the taxi driver asks, all chirpy.

'You a detective?' Hughie replies.

'Alright, alright, pal, just makin conversation.'

As they pull up opposite, Hughie feels a bit of guilt for snapping. He gets out onto the street and hands the man a fiver through the window, telling him to keep the ninety pence change. The driver takes it with a shake of the head then speeds off up the road and around the corner. Hughie's gaze drifts to the gate and the house. He swallows.

At first ah was thinkin that you had changed, were more focused. Go. Away! I need a distraction, see if I can actually feel. *Listen to you, just listen to you. I offer you the cure, a crusade and all you want is a hole to batter into.* Crude, misogynistic, and typically blind. *Grunt, grunt, ape boy.* Fuck off! The Knight falls through the pavement without warning.

The lights shine through the blinds, making the place look so warm and welcome as the cold comes in from the river. Cupping his hand, he breathes and sniffs for signs of whisky breath, but you can never smell it, not after the first few. The early summer sky is a dark blue now and calling on him to try to live. Marching up the path, he prepares what he will say, but as soon as he knocks on the door, his instinct is to run for it. Inside the house, there is movement, and he hears someone coming towards the door. It'll be worth a bit of embarrassment – this is a good move.

The chain on the inside of the door is undone. Right, don't freeze up, be casual, just passing by sort of thing. *Just passing by, stinking of whisky – aye right.* Fucking weirdo, that's what she's going to think. C'mon Hughie, cool as fuck, cool as fuck. Door opening, cool as you like, cool, cool.

When the door opens, a big hairy guy in his underpants stands there, staring at Hughie with a furrowing brow.

Big muscle bound type, in Karen's house, in his underpants; too late son.

The man's frame is wide, the glow of the hall light glistens on sweat beads along his hefty shoulders and face. Hughie stands in dull shadow, aware that his skin looks anaemic, like some desperate door-to-door salesman who is working late in an attempt to make up the bad numbers.

'What the fuck do you want?' the big guy asks as he scratches his hairy chest.

'Is Karen in?'

'*Is Karen in,*' the guy mimics in a five-year-old's voice. 'You sound like a wean wantin someone to come out and play on the swings.'

The guy's broad jaw holds a smirk as he shakes his head at Hughie.

'Is ... she in?' Hughie asks. *Weak.*

The guy's head goes back, half laughing now. 'Who the fuck are you, pal?'

Before the ground can finish swallowing Hughie, Karen appears by the big lump, still sorting her nightie. She looks sweaty and flushed too.

Nae monkey business for you the night, Hughie – he's already had her, son.

'Hughie,' she says, out of breath, embarrassed.

'Forgot to give you my card,' he says.

She steps in front of the Caveman, trying to push him inside with her backside. 'I know where to get you, Hughie. You're a social worker, from the social work department, remember.'

Despite the drink in him, Hughie stands stuck to the spot, head dipping as he recognises pity in her voice.

'Where's your card?' the Caveman asks.

Good point, big cunt. No as daft as he fuckin looks, this guy.

'I ... I forgot it,' Hughie stutters.

'Forgot it?' the Caveman says, shaking his gorilla-sized skull from side to side. 'Are you for real, pal?'

Karen turns in towards her boyfriend's chest and pushes him right back inside the door. As she turns back to Hughie, her eyes dismantle his childlike ego in an instant. 'Just go home, Hughie,' she tells him with a deep sigh, then closes the door on his red face.

He stands for a bit, his left knee shaking, unable to move.

Good old humiliation, you cannae whack it.

As he walks off down the path, something makes him pause, and he remembers where he put his cards. Taking one from the back of his wallet, he writes Sorry on it.

What is it with you and this woman? She made a cunt of you, man; and it looks like the tart's had some nooky already, despite the fact that it's barely half-nine.

Creeping back, he pokes his card in the letterbox as

carefully as he can. About to begin this week's third undignified retreat, he hears a sound, looks sideways straight through one of the half-open blinds. Karen is naked in the warm glow of her living-room lamp. He tries not to gawk, cursing himself as he cranes his head until he can see her better. The Caveman can be seen, sitting back on a chair, also bollock-naked, eyes closed tight shut, Karen kneeling between his legs.

This is the time for Hughie to do the honest thing and bail – he can't. The moaning starts, her head bobbing up and down, hair flicking back and forth. Something basic, ancient, and primaeval holds him there, salivating as he becomes the perennial rogue-male outcast, watching the tribal fire from the dark woods of bitter envy. She mounts the Caveman, and Hughie watches the curve of her back move up and down, her narrow shoulders rolling forward as her pony-tailed head begins to bob and flick. Like that outcast, he takes the scraps offered by opportunity, lets the guilt grow in the background like bile to be consumed later.

He is now hard, standing in Karen's garden, looking at someone fucking the woman he had only hours before asked to help with caring for a vulnerable child. He begins to turn away, but the Knight is in on it now, tongue slithering from his mouth like a snake. ***Nah, no way man, she's goin fuckin wild in there.*** Shame edges forward for a second, but the Knight runs it through with unsheathed desperate lust.

'Oh no,' Hughie whispers. Manchester is happening again; I am out of control.

'Hoi! You!' a voice shouts from behind, making Hughie spin and the Knight disappear.

A blinding flash. Then again. Hughie's eyes narrow. The shouting gets louder as he holds his hand up to block the light that comes from a bright, waving torch. It flashes across him and up the wall then hits Karen's window, cutting through the blinds and onto the living-room wall within.

'Peeping Tom!' the voice screams again and again.

The commotion and the waving torch alerts Karen's boyfriend. He throws her on her back on the chair and runs to the window. The window is banging now, the Caveman in a rage, the torch blinding and the voice on the pavement shouting, 'Pervert. Peeping fuckin Tom!'

Run. Run Hughie.

No, I can explain this; it doesn't look that bad.

Hughie, you've got nae chance. Run, man. RUN!

Hughie is off, around the gable end of Karen's house, his heart pounding, the adrenaline turning fear into outright terror. Behind him, he hears the nosey wee neighbourhood watchman tell Karen's caveman lover, 'Peeping Tom, looking in your windows, son.'

Dogs begin barking in the next-door garden. Shadows, dark, hard to see where he is going. Hughie runs at the back gate as footfall, and torch beams come around the corner after him. Shit, the gate's locked. Shite, shite. I can't get caught, humiliated – unemployed.

MOVE IT FER GOD'S SAKE!

He throws himself up and over the high gate.

'There's the bastard!' the Caveman shouts as Hughie's dark silhouette disappears.

Tumbling down the other side, Hughie's trouser pocket catches on the bolt and tears. Karen's boyfriend is now banging on the other side of the gate, only inches away, screaming with rage. 'You're fuckin dead, pal – deeeeeeaaaad!'

Pushing a wheelie bin against the gate, Hughie tries to slow the lump, then runs off blindly into the dark. There is a loud crash as the gate bursts open and the wheelie bin is kicked off the path into something glass that shatters.

This clown's way out of our league, run for yer fuckin life, Hughie.

Throwing himself into what turns out to be a holly bush and legging it through next door's garden, he is forced to kick a wee yappy dog off his leg as he goes. After crashing through another half-dozen hedges, he comes out on the other side of the crescent, running up the middle of the road. The shouting and the barking dogs fade as he runs into the once-promising night, trouser leg flailing behind. The Knight closes his heavy eyes and stops communicating; a bronze shield sliding over him like a cockroach's carapace. **Go home, Hughie, just go home**, the Knight whispers as he sinks into the fissures in the amygdala.

Hughie speeds past warm, lamp-lit windows, those welcoming squares of orange, where normal folk live, and kids' drawings are attached to fridges by magnets bought on family holidays to Crete. In there, the normal people cuddle one another on the sofas, watching scary films, eating midnight snacks of cheese, toast and contentment, while wondering what sort of idiot is running about the world at this time of night. He keeps running, the night air heavy with a smog-like paranoia that follows him home; the odd lonesome car headlight searching him out and exposing the so-called social worker in all his torn-trousered patheticness.

3 A.M.

His neck quivers as he pushes the bottle upward until it is pointing straight down his throat, the whisky flowing in slow punishing gulps, the rain tapping at the window as the streetlight seeks him out. After another hard slug of the bottle, his gaze follows the lumpy shadows across the dark room, through the flapping curtains and out into the night. Raindrops look like sparks as they shoot past the orange light of the lamp post. Somewhere out there, a dog barks.

'Wonder if wee Tommy's feeling terrified too?'

FOUR

SKULDUGGERY

No sign of the police yet.

Rubbing his hot neck, he looks around at the whispering lips. Was it Sartre who said that words are loaded pistols? Some shots get fired inward – that familiar voice that doubts and weakens our resolve when we hit real resistance. In this office, word-bullets are often fired by colleagues, to tease, to undermine and to dent the self-esteem of a rival without the escalation you'd see on a building site; all reprisal must be with similar weapons, regardless of the level of provocation. Hughie, like most of those brought up in poverty, struggles with these restrictive imaginary rules of combat. Since his return to the Town, he can see the well-established cliques and age-old hierarchies that need to be preserved at all cost; it is so claustrophobic for returning escapees like him, but to the inmates, it is just the way it is, it works somehow, so keep your nose out. Hughie's defence is to trace the trajectory of any nip or jaggy joke, as you would a real bullet, follow it back across the staff tea room, through the barrel-like gap in those painted lips, up to the trigger larynx and into the explosive powder of a bitter mind. Now inside, you find the usual accelerants lying around – the domineering father, the divorcing parents or, worst of all, a blood relative who visited the bedroom too often when you turned eleven. Bitter minds build weapons to share out the pain. Luckily, these verbal gunslingers shoot themselves more often than they shoot you; most slugs not making it out of their minds, ricocheting around till the day they die.

A flush runs right through him; the sweats have started. If the peeping Tom thing gets out, I'm finished around here – for good.

Failin means yer playin. Anyway, fuck em all.

As he bends forward to take his diary from the lower desk drawer, acid shoots up his windpipe like escaping lava and the room begins to spin. Sure he is going to be sick, he cups a hand around his mouth. Jesus, I'm dying here, melting; never, ever going to drink again.

We'll give the peepin in windows a body swerve too, eh?

In an effort at not fixating on the door through which the police will come for him, he looks around the office. It is an open-plan affair, designed to aid supervision of the maximum number of unruly inmates at one time and reduce private phone calls to a manageable level. Dust dances in the shafts of sunshine from tall Victorian windows, while the low burr of chatter and clacking keyboards continues. Hughie is dressed in one of his good black suits, ironed shirt and combed back hair, awaiting that summons to the boss's office at any moment. He looks up as the main door opens. It is only the duty worker from downstairs who puts a file in the filing cabinet and wanders back out; Hughie watches her face for signs of insight or glances towards him – nothing. Despite the attempt at a confident façade, he knows he looks haunted, sweaty, even ill, watching every face for anything that will betray a familiarity with last night's manic events. No sign of the boys in blue looking for a peeping Tom. **For now, at least**. I'm fucked, I'm finished.

Calm it, Bo Peep.

As the clock ticks away, the hangover goes from bad to tense, paranoid and horrendous, with anxiety scouring the lining of his veins like hot brick-dust that makes his neck pulse red, sweat running under his greasy hair. He jabs at the keyboard, struggling to focus.

'C'mon, c'mon,' he says, stirring some of the drones.

Calm it, Bo. In fact, why don't we get outta here; doesn't look like the cops are comin for you. Can't. Too much to do. He tries to focus on his screen while gulping from a water bottle. Around him, the work drones rattle away at overdue reports; most of the dour-faced social workers are burned out wash-ups from the City, looking for an easy life in the sticks - few figured that the chaotic, feral poor might have had the same idea and followed them over on the ferry. He shuts his eyes tight. Must stop negative thoughts; they build negative beliefs.

Jesus Christ. Let's get the fuck out before you need a nappy. No!

Lifting the phone, he dials Tom-a-Mhoid Street surgery and asks the receptionist to put him through to Dr David-son. Only because it is Sadie Thompson, who went to school with him, is his wish granted.

'Yes,' a stuffy voice says.

'This is Hughie MacDonald, social work—'

'Can't reception deal with this?' Davidson asks.

'No, I need some information.'

'We don't need to share private medical data, you know.'

'I'll record that on the child protection report I'm about to complete, will I?'

There is a pause, then Davidson sighs. 'What do you want?'

Thank you, Baby P.

'I'm enquiring about Thomas Anderson, No 2 St Andrews Terrace. We have some concerns about him—'

'What do you want?' Davidson interrupts again.

'Well, he hasn't been seen by your surgery for some time.'

'He's probably not been sick for some time.' Davidson's tone, as usual, exudes contempt for an inferior profession.

'Has he been tested for dyslexia?' Hughie asks.

'Why would we test for that?'

Hughie saw old Davidson driving his boat to the sailing club the other day, the season is about to start, so his head will be full of nautical maps and early retirement plans, not poor working-class runts.

'Was there ever a suspicion of autism with Tommy,' Hughie asks.

'No.'

'Any concerns that I should be aware of?'

'No. None at all.' Davidson says this in a way that is far too quick to be based on any form of clinical recollection.

Hughie pretends to start another line of investigation, 'I'll talk to—' as he pushes the receiver cradle to cut the prick off.

A shiver of reality comes over him as he remembers that he has seventeen open cases that need his urgent attention.

Tommy's name keeps floatin to the top o the

guilt pile, I hope. Time to look outward. ***But not in
windows.*** Enough!

A door opens then slams shut, making him flinch.

It is Faye, the queen of the work drones, coming out of
Chas's office, all stern faced. She looks directly at him, but
he can't read her poker face, no one can, and she doesn't
give much away, certainly not when important stuff is going
on. Maybe she knows the police are on the way. She looks
suspicious. Nah, she always looks at me that way.

***She's next in line to the throne, what do ye
expect. On the scan for possible usurpers –
that's you now, Hughie.*** What if it is the police? ***We
run for it.***

Faye bends over at her filing cabinet, her navy pencil
skirt riding up her thigh. ***Fuck, you are on heat.*** He
shakes his head at a million of years of evolutionary
programming that are trying to kick in – from an amoeba to
an amphibian to a mammal to an ape, to get him to his fully-
fledged *Homo sapiens* brain, that can invent retractable dog
leads, Dengue fever vaccinations and spaceships that crash
into Mars and don't work – and yet a woman bending over a
filing cabinet at work, still makes him feel both excited and
sort of pathetic in the same bestial moment.

He looks away from her as the Knight starts on him.
***Listen, I'm not excusin all your voyeuristic
malarkey last night, but the modern woman
does seem to forget how primitive the male
brain is at times – or maybe she doesn't.*** Think,
Think. Wee Tommy's neighbours?

Faye is still stood across from him, frowning. He feels
she can hear the Knight, read his thoughts, or perhaps, she is
expecting the police at any moment, so he stares at his

screen, pretending to be deep in thought. To make a show of it, he types wee Tommy's name into the system for the umpteenth time. Faye stands there as if deciding whether to come over. He feels her attention on him, like the eye of Sauron, but refuses to look up again. His computer flashes up an answer to his search.

Thomas Anderson NO MATCH FOUND
= Redefine input.

Give me a break! Hughie rubs his sweaty forehead, then tries to enhance his search by typing in wee Tommy's address: 2 St Andrews Terrace, PA22 777. Still nothing, but he is drawn to other close matches to that postcode. Both No 1 and No 3 St Andrews Terrace are highlighted in yellow bands that indicate service input. After a bit of rooting around, he finds that Mr David Stantz, obviously the son of a Yank, and the weirdo with sunglasses at No 1, has a file with criminal justice for three minor drug charges and one for assault/domestic dispute. Hughie's nodding. Looks like our Davy here is teetering on the third rung of the criminal career ladder, just about staying out of prison.

That's our man; fuckin dealers! That's all I need.

Hughie double-clicked on the other name, Mr Donald Cameron of No 3. Old Don, he guesses, who also makes the grade with a compulsory Community Treatment Order for his crime of having paranoid schizophrenia and allegedly having the ability to see through people's souls. Seems the poor bugger went to a local politician's office in 2002 in just his underpants, told the man he possessed mind-reading abilities he'd got from his mother who had just died a month before. After a phone call to mental health, who aren't retiring arsehole doctors, Hughie is pleased to discover that old Don is just schizophrenic and odd, with no trace of paedophilia – on record at least. There's a slight shake of Hughie's head as he stares at the screen again. 'That one's a paedo,' has long-since replaced, 'Get the witch', when you want to ostracise any poor individual who doesn't fit in, looks at you the wrong way, or owes you a few quid from a hash deal.

There's at least one good thing here, that wee Tommy has some very positive male role models around to guide him through aw life's travails. Stop. ***It'll be the dealer, you know it already.*** Just stop, now.

The Knight responds with disgruntled mumbles that echo as he drops the visor of his helmet, hiding those edgy eyes, and fading into the depths of the subconscious. Hughie pauses while he copies the names into his notebook. Wonder who wrote the letter to social work and got us involved?

Faye's phone rings, and he steals a glimpse when she picks it up and stands opposite, feet together. She is about thirty-nine, wears close-fitting, elegant outfits in dull blues and dark greys which give the idea that she is meant for the top – that this is just a stepping stone en route to cleaner, more sophisticated waters where her class will shine through and her salary will reflect her combined gifts of intelligence and attractiveness. The drones call her 'Faye dear' to her face and 'the Snowball' behind her back. She looks at Hughie while nodding to someone on the other end of the phone. 'Alright,' she says and hangs up.

His mind races. Oh, shite, the police are on their way! ***Calm it, Bo***.

Lifting the file she'd dug out of the cabinet earlier, she comes towards him in cool, confident, feline strides. He tries to hide a gulp in his throat as she puts the file down on top of the work that is already there and pats it.

'Chas asked me to give you this,' she says, as she stands over him, reading what he has on the screen.

'Another job? Chas is trying to sink me,' he jokes, voice stilted.

Ignoring this completely, she points to the file she's put down. 'This is a record of the work that Karen MacLean, the ex-foster carer has done for us.'

'Thanks,' he says, struggling to look her in her face. Shit, they know about last night. Nightmare!

'Karen's not fostering again, is she?' Faye asks.

'Eh, no, no.'

'Why do you need her file then?'

He looks to see if she really wants an answer, or if this is a cruel wind-up. 'I'm hoping to persuade her to give it another go.' He smiles, but Faye doesn't.

'You met her?' she asks, eyes on him.

Fuck, fuck, fuck. 'Briefly ... yesterday.'

After a tense moment, where he feels he is being read like a book and anything he says will be taken down as evidence in the peeping Tom case, her eyes relax.

'I've already tried to tempt her back,' she says. 'Don't waste your time.'

'I'll give it a go, all the same.'

'Who's the child?'

This bitch is diggin deep.

'Tommy Anderson ... Margaret Anderson's boy,' he says. 'What's with all the questions?'

She ignores his question about questions, asking another. 'Is that the woman Chas calls Minging Maggie?'

'Aye, it is. Good job he's not judgemental.'

'Good with names, our Chas is,' she says.

He is sure something troubles her thoughts just there but doesn't ask what she means.

'This lad, Tommy, is not on the system for some reason,' he says, 'only got a thin paper file. Is that right?'

Her brow falls into a slight frown; everything she does is in small, considered increments. It isn't smart to rock the boat or slag off the boss in these days of austerity, one-year contracts and short straws.

She looks around, he swears it is towards the main door, then leans in.

'Weren't you in senior management down south, Hugh?'

'What?' He is confused, sure something is about to happen. ***The cops are at the door.***

'CYA, Hughie,' she says.

'What?' He fights a rise in his heart rate.

She seems to pick up on his confusion, leans even closer and whispers, 'Cover Your Arse.'

'Oh, yeah ... very good,' he says, trying hard to make a viable smile.

The main office door opens and Geraldine, one of the HR managers, comes in and looks towards them. Hughie freezes again, and the keyboards around him seem to slow.

'You ready for lunch, Faye,' the woman shouts.

Instantly detaching from him, she goes to her desk, picks up her phone and bag, then moves off towards the stairs for an early lunch.

His shoulders slump with relief as he watches her slim legs criss-cross to the door.

Spinning back to his work, he catches the chattering drones at it, confident enough to stare back now, he makes them look away. Faye's trying to help, and she's right, of course, about the untold rules of this game.

Why's she helpin you? God knows, but cover your arse is the signal you give to recently drafted recruits in troubled front-line battalions; warn you before you become fodder for the arrows of the tabloid press.

Joyce, his only ally, gets up and comes past him.

'You fer tea or fuck-offee?' she asks.

Everyone watches as Hughie follows her into the small kitchen that has no door to hide behind, where they stand by the boiling kettle and look out of the tall windows at the Town. Reaching down, he pulls on the brass handles of the sash window which opens about eight inches, the cool air of the day washing up around him as he leans into it.

'You on the drink last night?' Joyce asks, frowning. 'You look shit.'

Suspicious of more female questioning, he gives a wary nod and pushes his face further down towards the gap in the window, taking big gulping breaths. 'I'm dying.'

'Hasn't stopped you being a perv,' she tells Hughie, her eyes sparkling with mischief. 'Seen you, looking at the Snowball in her tight skirt, again.' There is a certain tormenting glee on her face now.

'Here's me thinking you're asleep, like the rest of that lot in there.'

'Pervert!'

'Okay, okay, you caught me out; I'm a heterosexual man for Christ's sake,' he says as he straightens up, feeling dizzy.

'You've got no chance anyway.'

He shakes his head at this and puts it back down into the window draft. 'Howz that?'

'Soon as Petite Merde slips up, she'll be the boss round

here.' Her thick drawn eyebrows arch. 'It doesn't pay to be shaggin plebs on the way up the ladder.'

'Don't fancy her anyway.'

Joyce puckers her face in scathing disbelief. 'You are such a liar; you'd hump the hair on the barber's floor.'

This makes him laugh. 'Is it that obvious?'

'Fraid so.'

'Takes a perv to know a perv,' he says.

She gives one of her filthy cackles in response which sails out into the sunlight.

'Bloody harlot's laugh you've got there.'

This makes them laugh even more. He starts to fill the cups from the kettle, stirring in two spoons of sugar to each as usual.

'Apart from Snowball, is there anyone else you fancy?' she asks as she takes the hot cup from him.

'No ... eh, not at the moment.' She knows nothing, don't be paranoid. 'On my lonesome, as usual.'

'You'll find someone, promise.'

He feels himself relaxing for the first time that day.

Do ye trust this bit? I like her because of her laughter – the dirty laugh, the really happy laugh, and her best, the mocking-Hughie-to-bring-him-back-to-Earth laugh.

These half-breeds are all in one another's pockets; trust none o them.

Opening her handbag, she takes out a packet of penguin biscuits, unwraps one and begins to chew on it before noticing him looking at her. Holding the biscuit in her mouth, she goes back in her bag and takes another one from the packet, handing it to him.

'Saves me thinking of fags,' she says apologetically.

'Anyway, why you gettin torpedoed with all the work? Been a naughty boy?'

'Faye says someone's off sick ... stress, I think. I've got appointeeships to chase up and three oldies on the delayed discharge list.' He shakes his head at the thought of it all.

'Face it, you're getting torpedoed, Hughie.'

After a sad nod, he says, 'You're right.'

'Ask one of the others for a hand,' she says, chewing her biscuit.

'That lot?' Hughie is looking back at the main room, face doubtful.

'God. They're nice people; you just don't make the effort.'

He looks all serious now.

'But you're still enjoyin it here, right.' Joyce's voice becomes warm and childlike in an attempt to reverse his perplexed expression.

'I'm not so sure any more.'

'Why?' she mumbles, still eating.

'I'm working with this wee boy,' he says and takes a big gulp of the tea to ease his dry throat. 'The boy, and his mum, they're up against it.' He's staring into his cup.

'Why've you got a child's case?' she asks.

'Children and Families are overrun; I'm it.' He looks right into her face after he says this, wondering what she knows. Joyce often knows a lot but seldom gives it away. 'This boy's vulnerable,' he adds, still watching her face, 'and it seems every arsehole is against me.'

'Anythin I can do?' Her voice is sincere.

'Not right now.'

'Anyway, only one lad,' she says, going back to her usual smirking face. 'It's about outcomes and numbers, not emotions,' Joyce says in a strange voice that is perhaps mimicking Chas.

'Quality before quantity I go for, unlike you and your men.'

They burst into laughter, the way only people who trust one another can.

Hughie's shoulders rise, the lines on his face relax as he stops laughing. It feels like the sun is shining brighter on the walls of the tiny kitchen, the drones' keyboards somehow magical, relaxing. ***You do trust her.*** She's authentic.

They continue munching their second biscuits and watching the street below. One of the well-known local heroin addicts scowls up at the window as he cuts through the car park towards the Jobcentre. The anaemic man walks across the flowerbeds, trampling flowers, then steps onto the road.

'Not often you see him up this early,' Joyce says, watching the guy's progress.

Remembering her encyclopaedic knowledge of the Town's inmates, Hughie asks, 'Do you know a guy, mid-to-late-thirties, thin, lives up St Andrews Terrace? His missus is a looker, sort of East European, maybe. David Stan—'

'Davy Drug you mean. Idiot. Dealer.'

'Does he sell smack?'

'Don't think so, mostly hash, but they move up at some point.'

'Violent?'

She shrugs at that one. 'He's part of a wee pack of losers, all on the dole and into the dope.'

'Would he hurt a kid?' Hughie asks.

Pausing him with a raised finger, she crumples her face, in the end process of swallowing a half-chewed piece of her biscuit. 'He hit his last girlfriend, a couple of years back, got community service.'

'The other losers?'

'One called Scatter-cash,' she says as she stifles a burp. 'He's been inside. Think Davy carries the viable brain cell, going by the look of both of them.'

'Scatter-cash?' he says.

'Aye, you'll know him when you see him; heavy set git, smelly looking, with mean sad eyes.'

'The Davy one looks like a devious wee bastard.'

His sudden change of tone catches her attention. 'Not keen on drug dealers?' she says.

'Hate them.' His jaw tenses as he speaks.

'You must've had big problems with them down south, eh?' she says.

He freezes inside for a second, stares, before shrugging his shoulders. 'Not really.' *What does she know? Just don't mention Manchester fer fuck's sake – not a word to the bitch.* Stop the paranoia for Christ's sake, she's a pal, a good pal.

Over the road, the gaunt addict dodges a couple of young hoodies who are blocking the way as he enters the Jobcentre. Hughie looks sideways at her, watching her sipping on her tea cup. She seems transfixed by the street life outside. Despite her jolly façade, she is full of a single woman's worries about her weight and lack of a husband to produce that baby she's always wanted, the baby that will allow her to give up caring for complete strangers every day of the week and let loose the ocean of nurturing instinct that she has dammed up behind her patter and sarcastic jokes. He feels guilty for seeing her as the enemy for an instant and lets out a long, silent breath. *Nah, she knows*

nothin about down south, how could she? Girls got a fair bit o character though – fragile inner glow, pretty in her own way and great pair o paps. You leave her alone – Fuck off!

'What about his neighbour, Don?' Hughie asks.

Coming back to the conversation she gives one of her smiles. 'Old Donald, he's, well ... a bit weird.'

'Bad weird?'

She shrugs.

Across the way, the addict storms out of the Jobcentre with a flea in his ear, throwing the door backwards as he pushes through the young hoodies, who dance away while jabbing the air to show they don't take that kind of shit from any old smackhead.

'Ever think that addicts are like vampires?' he says thoughtfully.

Turning her gaze from the street to him, she looks bemused.

'Think about it,' he says through a crunching biscuit, 'they live by different rules, a different dimension really. They're white as hell, gaunt faces ... they don't go out unless they must, creep about at night most of the time, hungering for somethin unpleasant and taboo. They live off others and no one has much sympathy for the poor traumatised bastards.' He lifts an eyebrow and adds, 'They're invariably found dead with sharp things sticking out of them.'

As she thinks on his black humour, she sips at the tea, eyes floating above the rim of the cup, looking at him, a mischievous grin spreading across her face, deepening her dimples.

'You're that caring sort who always find their way into social work, eh?' she suggests.

'And you're man daft.'

'I just want a decent one, with a job and no ex-wife.'

'And plenty of cash,' he adds.

He finds himself smiling as he watches sparkles dancing in her eyes, the furrowed brow he's carried for the last eleven hours vanquished.

'Bet you sniff Snowball's seat when you work late,' she tells him, poking his chest with a sharp finger.

He catches her finger. 'Yours too.'

'Sicko,' she says in a high voice, pretending to be offended. Their laughter echoes into the main office, making the others slow and listen.

A door bangs, making the keyboards speed up, and Chas ambles towards them, coffee cup in hand, his dour face strangling any illegitimate moment of elation before it grows. Both go quiet as he enters the kitchen. He clocks that they both subconsciously move towards one another and gives his head a slight shake.

'What are you *meant* to be doin this mornin?' Chas asks Hughie.

His two employees feel that practised negative weight he carries into every room.

'Taking Tommy Anderson to the opticians,' Hughie answers.

'Oh, ah see, so we pay you thirty-five grand a year, and you take kids to the shops, great.' He hammers home his point with yet another dismissive headshake. 'Here's me losin sleep over wee things like an eight percent budget cut, silly old bastard, eh?'

Chas crafts this tension expertly, even if you can't see him, you often know he's there just by the atmosphere in the room.

'What made you give up the Weight Watchers then, Joyce?' Chas asks. 'You were doin brilliant.'

Her hand, with the biscuit in it, falls away to her side as if to hide the evidence, her cheeks go pink.

After a pitying grin, Chas turns and saunters out of the kitchen and through the mosh of ear-wigging drones, towards the exit. The hurt on Joyce's face grows like an unfolding storm, until all areas are dark, and her happy-go-lucky façade has dissolved like cheap tissue in lashing rain.

Hughie scowls after his boss, making tight fists at his side without meaning to. ***That prick finds the cracks without even havin to think about it, wee shite.*** Wee rung-climbing shite. After a second, he remembers Joyce, who stands silently beside him, and his white fists loosen.

'Don't let him know that he winds you up,' Hughie tells her. 'He's a prick.'

'Hate him.' She looks at the biscuit in her hand.

'He's just keepin the hierarchy in order.'

Her biscuit thuds into the open bin. 'Were you a bastard, when you were a big-shot manager down south?' she asks.

He gives her a wee side on hug, his head shaking, then frowning when he thinks about what she said. 'Why is it that everyone knows about my past?' he asks her.

Joyce looks up, all sheepish. 'Small town – loose tongues?'

'How do they find things out?'

'They smell skulduggery a mile off. What they don't know—'

'They make up,' he says, finishing her sentence.

Her face is scowling down into the car park where Chas

109

is getting into his Jag. 'It's always been like this here; you just don't notice when you're young.'

This wisdom pushes seriousness onto Hughie's face. She's right. Just wait until the peeping Tom story gets out, it'll spread like Aids at a fucking orgy; nightmare, an absolute fucking nightmare. *In the name o King Robert, do you actually care about this wee lad Tommy, or are we just gonnae self-obsess. Let's get on with it – crack some fuckin skulls – let some of this bile out o the system.*

Joyce goes back towards her desk, body slumped at the shoulders, eyes devoid of the wicked sparkle they had carried only moments before, before Chas pissed all over it for no good reason. Walking behind her to her workstation, he massages her shoulders for a few moments in full view of the drones. 'Perhaps he's impotent,' he whispers in her ear.

A dim light glows again, somewhere within her, and she chuckles to herself.

'Wears his wife's panties too, I bet,' she says.

Making his way across the room, Hughie pauses to give her a wiggling fingered wave goodbye. The smile holds on her face until he is gone, and the double doors are closed. Smile gone, her head goes down and she submerges herself in the flow of the other tapping keyboards – work, work, work – prove I'm good, prove myself and that I'm worth something – go back on the diet next week and don't tell anyone, especially Hughie, coz he'll say I'm great the way I am; he lies too.

FIVE
SHADOW PLAY

St Andrews Terrace is bathed in mid-afternoon sun when he appears on the lane; its porous pink sandstone and flaky woodwork glowing with relief. After a long winter campaign in which the rain has made serious advances towards the houses' final destruction, their structure appears both decrepit and resolute, like an old watchman with nowhere to retire to. Despite the pause in the seasonal wars, the place seems hostile, like its irritated by him as he marches doggedly towards it on another of his unwelcome incursions. The Terrace's brow eaves and blank-eyed windows hold the shadow; set in its ways, and more than willing to fight to the death for the damp poverty it understands as normal. Like the Town itself, it has always struggled with the idea of change and the endless waves of smart-mouthed outsiders who break on these shores, full of odd ideas that they just have to share. It knows that dumb stubbornness will pay off in the end and the newcomers will succumb or leave.

Perhaps it is the sun that makes him remember a blonde girl he knew, who lived up here when he was nineteen and falling in love with everybody on a daily basis. She must have gone away with the Yanks or gone back to Glasgow when that particular ship sailed. The image of her dancing barefoot, drunk on Bacardi, in the Paul Jones, comes to him as beautiful, half-seen shards of his past. Her name won't come to him, but her blue eyes, glowing cheeks and blonde curls bring back his youth in alternating welcome and unwelcome bursts – welcome for remembering he has lived a passion-soaked life, unwelcome because they remind him that he has become a wanking loner in middle age. The Knight who is clanking beside him, armour leaking muddy bile, grins. *You had to watch your wenches back then, did ye no?* Aye, those Yanks were bold, flashing wads of dollars and parking their red, six-cylinder, Trans-Am next to your BSA sirocco bicycle, with its slow puncture. Woah, that memory-blonde might be old Maggie's niece. *Let's get on with the mission, pussy brain.* Yeah, why dwell on sunny memories of shiny lipped, blonde-haired women in pencil-skirts, when I've got a potential child abuse case to fascinate me? *Taken off the breast far too early, you were; obsessed.* It isn't the sex I miss. *Liar!* It's that feeling of being alive and wanted, the dopamine rush, holding girls tight, and the pools of boundless hope you find lying around in your head when you're nineteen and invincible.

The blast of Orange Goblin stoner riffs shake him out of his daydreaming. Apart from the music, there is no sign of life at Davy Drug's window – no sad, pretty girl or psychopath in mirror sunglasses grinning back as he passes by. Across the waste ground and over the iron fence, a shop-keeper comes out of the back of the grocer's and throws a cardboard box onto an already blazing bonfire then stands watching it catch alight as he combs his oily, chip-pan hair. It's Jim, the guy he'd seen pushing the wheelbarrow of scrap electrical cable up the Bishop's Glen the other day. Hughie thinks the blaze seems hellish close to the adjoining garage's tyre pile and oil drums, but the old fella leaves the flames leaping towards the phone lines and goes back into the rear of the shop, slamming the door behind him. Blue pungent smoke from the blaze drifts through the weeds towards Hughie, seeping silently between the tall rushes until it rises into the intense rays of the sun in front of him, where it turns white. It stalls for a moment, like a curious stinking spirit who has no better place to go until the early summer breeze convulses and coughs out a much-needed breath.

The spirit-smoke fades up towards the green hills, leaving only the sweet residue of piss-poor industry in his nose. Hughie is alone – even the Knight has disappeared, and he is standing at the door to No 2 St Andrews Terrace again.

He feels something through the sole of his shiny brogues as he knocks on Maggie's door. Lifting one foot back, he sees the step littered with small stones, pebbles really. Bending forward, he squints, looking for a pattern. Stop being paranoid. **_No, there are letters._** Without effort, he aligns the pebbles on the worn, red stone step. **_Oh, fuck._** His face goes a bit pale, and he looks around before turning back to the message.

URNOTWANTD

There is a small gap, then:

B WARND

Hughie feels another uninvited presence creep into his mind. With the crackle of the fire in his ear, he looks around once more, eyes darting from windows to the tall rushes and then along the length of the empty lane. Straightening up and taking two steps back, he looks at Davy Drug's window and tries to control his breathing. But the sun is out and all he can see are the leaping flames behind him, reflected in the dirty glass. Even old Don hasn't appeared at the window of No 3 this time.

It's a crater alright – back on the battlefield. Stop it!

That warm feeling he's enjoyed from thinking about the drunk blonde is gone, replaced by a subtle tightness which sits across his chest and a low current trickling through his nerves on repeat. Sweeping his hair back, he tries to look casual, breathing deeply without letting it show. Christ, I'm getting paranoid again. I mean, who makes pebble warnings? Wee Tommy, trying to avoid our appointment at the optician? Nah, bit advanced for him. This is some sort of mind game.

My money's on the druggie cunt at No1; the old nutjob, Don, has got good odds too. Right, time to man up.

With a firm left foot, he sweeps the step clear and looks along the Terrace in both directions again.

Don't act so obvious, these sociopaths like to see how ye react to this sort of shit.

The door echoes inside when he thumps it again; the hollow sound making him sure that No 2 is an empty house today. Pushing open the creaking storm door, he shouts. 'Maggie, it's me, Hughie! I made an appointment with the optician, remember?'

She's off out shoppin or boozin.

He imagines Tommy standing outside a pub with a packet of crisps in the afternoon sun. He shakes his head.

Stop the cynicism. ***Realism, ye mean.*** Twisting his head around the door a bit further, he snoops for the wee stuff that can tell the tale of a life. There are bills, some official looking letters and a tide of junk mail lying squashed up behind the door like a makeshift draft excluder. She's struggling to cope with the day-to-day stuff.

This is the job, to know something in your gut, then spend forever trying to find the evidence for what was so glaringly obvious in the first place, but without the evidence you won't stand a chance in court. Oh, and always, but always, cover your own arse. He tears a leaf out of his diary and writes a brief note to Maggie, wedging it in the inner door at eye level so she can't say she missed it. He then writes the time in his diary to cover his arse.

Don't get caught up in rules fer fuck's sake. Why don't you open a bill, see if she's in the shit with the gas board? No, we play by most of the rules. ***For now.***

Closing the storm door gently, he shuffles backwards down the step while pretending to check his mobile phone – still wondering who might be watching, who was warning him off coming here, and who wrote the anonymous letters to his department about wee Tommy in the first place. Lots of players, all keeping quiet. The Knight appears in his head, cooking what looks like a dead rat on a skewer, its dark flesh hanging loose in the flame. The Knight's eyes flash at Hughie, full of a black knowing. The Knight's black teeth bite into the dead rat – forcing grease and blood to pop out onto his wrinkled cheeks and roll down a matted beard. Knight looks defensive for a moment as Hughie watches, then shrugs. ***Looks like someone has a decent view o this dump, know whit I'm sayin?*** The Knight nods over his master's shoulder and Hughie raises his eyebrow in agreement at the logic of a well-observed lead.

The Knight sits in the dark, chewing on a thin rat leg while Hughie follows Tommy's well-worn trail through the hushing long grass and rushes of the waste ground. Skipping through two bent bars of a spiked fence, he avoids suffocation from toxic fumes by covering his mouth and nose with a hanky as he passes the fire. Beyond, the yard at the back of the shops is a chaotic zone where the adjoining corner shop, funeral home, and garage store, recycle or leave to rot the hidden debris of their various trades. Parked cars, in the process of cannibalisation, sit alongside splintered wooden pallets and piles of tyres. Jim who owns the middle shop is burning sweetie boxes from the supermarket that have **not for re-sale**, printed on them, while the Stevenson's funeral home has a hearse sitting there amongst the chaos, its battery charging via long leads that run across concrete from the garage window. On the passenger seat of the hearse, sits a box of tomatoes bound, in time, for a wake. The air behind the shops is scented with rotting fruit, burning boxes and diesel fumes, a chaotic mix that feeds the Terrace most days of the week. He smiles at the reciprocal small-town microculture that has evolved, stashed away from the grieving, pie-eating, MOT-needing public who haunt the shop fronts on Hannay Road. Hughie looks in the hearse before stepping over things towards the alley that leads to the street. Hope that coffin's empty.

JIM'S GROCERIES, it says on the sign above the door of the shop; it is hard to tell from the window what is inside as faded special-offer banners and handwritten 'for sale' slips block a clear view. Inside, he stands looking around a tired shop that seems to be stuck in time.

'If you're selling anything, turn round and fuck off!' a voice shouts from behind a stacked counter.

Accustomed to rejection, as a social worker who few want at their door, Hughie doesn't blink. Instead, he looks around some more as if searching for something in particular. The owner, Jim, gets up and puts his *Sporting Times* away under the counter for later, glaring over the rims of his cheap wire specs with suspicion after clocking Hughie's briefcase and black suit.

'I'm just in for a roll ... a can of Fanta,' Hughie lies as he comes forward, claiming more ground.

Jim's eyes leave the briefcase and stare at the visitor's face. 'What's with the case?'

'I'm not sellin ... I'm in social work.'

Unsure, Jim watches him closely, his grey, unkempt eyebrows creasing in the middle. 'I know that face?'

'I'm Hugh Mac—'

'MacDonald. Aye, ah see it now,' Jim says.

'You do?'

'Knew your uncle.'

'Did you?'

'Didn't you move away ... London?' Jim's brow now creases further.

Right nosey cunts round here still.

Hughie throws up both his hands in fake annoyance. 'Manchester.'

'Aye, you must've been a bad, bad bugger to end up back here.' A knife-cut grin crosses the old man's lips before he adds, 'You weren't involved in one of them dead baby cases the red-tops go on about, were you?' When Hughie shakes his head, Jim asks another question, 'You goin to stay around?'

'Christ, you do like to suss people out.'

The grocer doesn't react to this assertion at first, keeps watching from behind the brows and the wire rims. After a short time, something goes on in his head, and his face relaxes, perhaps he believes that Hughie is telling the truth and isn't one of the smart arses from the tax office. 'Fraid us natives are nosey by necessity,' Jim says.

'Not much to worry about round here, is there?'

'Most people comin in at this time are either hopin to sell me somethin or askin for somethin for free.' Jim's face is deadpan.

Coming further forward, Hughie looks along the counter. 'I'm just in for a roll and a drink.' He studies the handwritten list of cooked snacks on the wall behind the shopkeeper's back.

The writin's very fuckin neat.

The shop itself is a sparse, dank affair; shelves of white bread, tinned goods, ravioli, beans with sausages, that kind of stuff; a wall of booze, lager and cheap cider and a small freezer full of oven chips and chicken nuggets. Above all this, a top shelf of dirty mags looks down on their red-topped sister tabloids that give you the message in short sentences. Two trampled scratch cards are melted into the dirty green carpet tiles with the losing face up. Hughie leans on the counter, still pretending to take great interest in Jim's menu.

'Social work you said?' Jim asks.

'Yeah. I work with adults, and kids.'

The shopkeeper doesn't blink, but a hardness comes to his eyes again. 'Good for you, son, good for you,' he says with sarcasm.

'Do you happen to know Mag—'

'It was a roll you came in for, wasn't it, son?' Jim says,

interrupting as he wipes his hands on the front of his cardigan.

'Right, yeah, eh ... sausage with sauce, brown, no salt.'

Hughie gives a friendly nod. Slow it down, he's still on the defensive.

Nosey and defensive old git with good, neat handwriting = anonymous fuckin letter writer. Yeeharrr!

Still in his slippers, Jim takes his copy of *Sporting Life* from under the counter, turns and saunters through a beaded curtain into the back room where he watches stuff on TV, cooks stuff, stores stuff, and throws stuff out the back door onto fires. Even from where Hughie is standing, you can see its minging carpets, soaked in age-old margarine from years of roll preparation, and a sink with a window above that looks out the back towards numbers one to three Saint Andrews Terrace. A frozen sausage hisses as it slides into the frying pan. Below this, badly fitted units hold a big old gas cooker in place, its once-white enamel surface now light brown with splatters from the spitting grease. Jim sits down in an armchair and watches the horse racing on the telly while his customer stands abandoned on the other side of the beaded curtain. Hughie remains silent. I come in to bait a few hooks and ask a few questions, now I'm caught here waiting for a greasy roll I don't want ... **Like a spare prick at a hoor's weddin, while the Town's last Korean War veteran watches the early race at Kempton Park. Old prick's havin you on.**

Through the swaying bead curtain, Hughie clocks the raft of crunched up betting slips under the telly; every other space in the back room is stacked high with cheap tinned goods, twenty or so cases of lager and more piles of dirty magazines still to be put out for perusal by the shop's clientele.

'I seen you up Bishop's Glen, the other day,' Hughie shouts through the beads as his sausage begins to smoke. 'Were you pushin a wheelbarrow?'

'Fuck it!' Jim says as he throws another betting slip onto the pile and gets up to salvage the frying pan from the heat. He comes back through with a more severe face than he left with and puts the burned roll n sausage next to the till while he sorts out a bag for it. He looks suddenly irked as he remembers Hughie's question. 'What's my barrow got to do with social work?'

'Nosey ex-native.'

'Smart-arse,' Jim says while grinning and pointing a butter knife like an accusation. 'Far too fuckin smart.'

'I used to help my uncle melt scrap. Old git paid me fifty pence an hour.'

Jim stares, thinking back. 'Aye, old Malky was a grafter; liked the gee-gees alright.'

'Looks like you're as successful as he was at it.'

This breaks a slight smile on Jim's face as he thinks of Hughie's wayward family. 'Price o scrap's gone through the roof, it's the Chinks, you know – found capitalism, buildin everywhere they say. You have to diversify in this modern business environment, stop the country goin down the fuckin pan,' Jim tells him, and Hughie nods at the wisdom of a backstreet survivor.

'I was lookin for Maggie Anderson or her wee boy, Tommy,' Hughie says as he hands over a fiver. 'You know them?'

The old boy scoops change out of the till, says, 'Two-ten change,' as if he hasn't heard the question.

'Well, do you?'

'Do I what?' Jim says, smile gone, face sharp.

The shopkeeper is carrying a weight behind his eyes again; like a small bit of his scrap lead sits on his thoughts, growing heavier as their conversation gets more challenging. Hughie tries smiling more. **The bastard's hidin somethin.** I see it. Everyone says he killed a few folk in Korea, before getting sent home in a straightjacket. Some say he shot a wee lassie in the skull by mistake, while others say he shot his commanding officer after an argument about tobacco. Anyway, those are the two main versions on the subject of Jim's mental health and military service that have been bandied about this part of Argyll for decades. **Time to man up!** Squaring up, Hughie looks him in the eye. 'Do you know Maggie Anderson?' he says.

'Thought you just came in for a roll,' Jim says, stare intensifying.

'You can see her house from your back window,' Hughie says and glances over the man's shoulder. 'See all sorts out there, I bet.'

They give each other a good eyeballing at that point, Jim's stare so deep and cavernous. As they break from it, Hughie shrugs and turns to leave.

'I'm no a bloody snooper,' Jim says, bringing Hughie back around.

'Maybe you just care,' Hughie replies.

'Maybe I don't.'

'I don't believe that, Jim, not for a minute.'

This brings the game to a crucial point and a pink tinge flares on Jim's neck, his eyes drifting off before returning to Hughie quickly. 'You brave, son?'

'I do my best,' Hughie says.

There is another lengthy pause as Jim takes on the look

he normally has before placing any bet over a fiver at the bookies. 'There's drugs and all sorts gettin dealt up there,' he says.

BINGO!

'At St Andrews Terrace?' Hughie asks.

Jim catches himself again, as if rolling the odds around in his head, still unsure.

'I'm just trying to help the boy,' Hughie says. 'You need to give me what you know ... help him.'

Jim gets angry at the bag he is trying to fit the roll in, a darkness forming under the eyes. 'Help, huh? Kids bein used as drug runners while the police sit all day out on that High Road, watchin for speedin cars.' He pauses, throws one of the paper bags across the room and picks up another, his face now scarlet. 'What kind of country is this?'

'Did you write to the police, then us?'

The shopkeeper shakes his head hard at that and his jaw locks. He manages to open one of the paper bags and hurriedly stuffs Hughie's roll inside. 'Don't be a smart-arse, son.' He spins the bag around several times while holding the corners.

'Well, all I know is someone is tryin to help me do my job,' Hughie says, all casual and clever-cunt insistent.

Jim breathes, trying to get back in control of his anger, then hands over the hot brown paper bag and a warm can of juice. 'Help you,' he says, staring, the urge swelling up again. 'Jesus. I reckon the idiot who wrote your letters might o wanted to help a mother and her boy.'

'Same thing is it not?'

'No really. The police need to get tough round here, do their bloody job, kick in doors. It's like a bloody Brazilian slum up there.' He is violently shaking his head now. 'Society, it's fragmentin.'

You've got him.

'We all work together now, nurses, police, my lot.'

'Oh aye, I can just see it, the cops holdin off the screamin mother while *your lot* drag the lad off to some kids' home.'

'That's the last thing I want, but we need proof if there's drug dealers involved.'

Stroking his beard, Jim finally catches onto the game. 'Only an idiot would grass up a dealer these days – end up in the witness box, the clown you fingered starin you out till he's let off and you're on your own back home, listenin for bumps in the night. No thanks.'

'No one needs to know where we get our information.'

'Are you for fuckin real, Hughie MacDonald?' he asks.

Hughie acknowledges the weakness of his last point with an accepting tilt of the head and a shrug of the face. Both men go quiet and stare, then put away their blades.

'Thanks,' Hughie says, holding his bag up as he walks away. 'Thanks for the roll.'

Jim goes back through the rattling bead curtain, adjusts the aerial on the small portable TV and sits down to watch the end of a race. As he leans back in his seat, Hughie opens the shop door, pausing with its handle in his grip.

'Tell you what, Jim,' Hughie shouts through the shop, 'I'll give you a shout when we're startin a lynch mob.'

The volume goes up on the TV as an excited racing commentator's voice comes to a crescendo and The Dog's Bollocks wins the two o'clock at Kempton Park.

Outside, the sun makes Hughie squint and realise how dark and dingy the shop was. Holding a hand up to deflect its glare, he watches the sea plane from Islay droning along in the clear blue afternoon sky, its sound vibrating against the hills as it heads for Loch Lomond. He feels natural warmth for the first time this year and turns his face into it and smiles. Well, at least I've found my letter writer.

Aye, some other fucker who gives a shit.

Sauntering away from Jim's shop, he looks at the roll he's bought during his info hunt. The rat, which the Knight had scoffed, comes to mind as grease seeps through the brown paper bag in his hand. Whisky hunger swirls back into his brain, making him almost swoon, demanding some ammo to fight the hangover that is now making his mouth feel like desiccated snakeskin. Without hesitating, he opens the bag, lifts the dripping roll to his mouth and bites into its soft surface. He has to jump backwards and lean forward at the same time to stop the eruption of grease and brown sauce from hitting his clean suit. Shit! He laughs and bites into the roll again, the taste of salt and pig fat exploding onto his tongue, telling his brain he will survive. He ponders why it is that dead fatty animals are so tasty. The Knight then shows a flickering film of his ancestor waiting in the thorn bushes for the lions to finish, after that, the hyenas and vultures take what is left – then, and only then, does Hughie's skinny, half-starved descendant creep over to the herbivore skeleton, before quickly scuttling off with a bone filled with sweet fatty marrow.

Guess we're kinda lucky these days really … nae predators to worry about – only humans, who act like wolves, preying on wee defenceless weans.

Still standing in a ski-jumper's position, he glances up the side of the funeral director's towards the Terrace, his teeth freezing on the last of the dripping roll as he spots something move. It's wee Tommy running at speed down the lane away from something. Did he come out of Davy

Drug's? I'm sure he did. **Wolves, bastard wolves! They're after the young!**

What is left of the roll hits the floor, oozes onto the pavement as another evolutionary urge kicks in, and he runs behind the shops, towards the Terrace. Pushing the can of Fanta into his jacket pocket, he trips over the electric leads coming from the hearse, sending sparks dancing across the filthy yard. Tyres fall around him, and he clatters his head on the fence as he flies through its bent bars, trying to make ground on rabbit boy.

Coming out of the tall rushes, he pauses, wiping the grass from his best trousers and catching a breath.

Forget yer image ponce – he's gettin away.

As he draws level with No 1, someone moves behind Davy Drug's dark window; a force is observing, it feels malignant. They're watching me. **Fuck the dealers – Move!** He refocuses as Tommy's blue jumper evaporates around the bend in the lane. Off again. puffing hard now, he feels the greasy roll move inside him like an aquatic alien. I'll struggle to catch him now. The Knight bursts into his head, hitting sword on shield, **'C'mon, ya lazy shite, catch him. He's only a wean for fuck's sake!'**

Briefcase locked up against one oxter, his flashing trousered legs take him around the curve and down to the bottom where the lane meets with Bute Street, his feet splaying as he skids to a halt. The boy is nowhere to be seen. Eh?

Left, go left – go, go, go, GO!

Puffing uphill, he comes onto Hannay Road just in time to see wee Tommy in the middle of the road, three hundred yards on, looking back at Hughie over his shoulder.

'Tommy,' Hughie tries to shout, but he is out of breath

and his voice falls off into a wheezing gasp. 'Tommy!' he shouts again, louder this time.

The boy ignores him and runs over the crossing with John Street, almost getting hit by a Post Office van that swerves and screeches its brakes. The driver mouths unheard abuse through the closed window as the van mounts the opposite kerb – Tommy keeps running, passing a row of small cottages before disappearing up another branch of the Town's rabbit warren of shortcuts. Hughie stops a few steps from the crossroads, his grass-stained black suit and cream shirt feel uncomfortable, clinging to his skin as a beetroot flush hits his cheeks and transparent patches of sweat spread from his armpits to his chest, the booze gushing through pores. *I look like a stalking paedophile.* Most of my workmates would let the boy run off, tick the box and slope off back to the house for a brew or down the Lorne for a glass of Prosecco. ***The boy needs to be caught, searched for evidence; he wiz nearly killed there fer fuck sake. Got that adrenaline resolve ye see in bag-snatching circles.*** He certainly looks scared stiff for some reason. Even if we catch him, where will this all end up? ***Will ye sleep if Tommy runs under a bus or into the police on his own?*** If he gets nabbed delivering a couple of ounces of hash, he'll get the 'Go to Jail' card – end up in a children's unit in the City. ***Gettin groomed by the latest Jimmy Saville clone. Ah fer fuck's sake, get after him ya tart!***

Hughie runs on; the angry postie watching in disbelief as another frantic idiot pelts across the road in front of him.

'That wee bastard could've died there,' the postie screams out his window.

After following the boy up another lane that comes off the main road, he pauses, pinching a stitch in his side. Ahead, bramble bushes, sycamore trees and old cars block the way – no sign of Tommy. Eventually, a clattering sound gives away the wee man's position and Hughie goes on, negotiating his way through a herd of half-crushed scrap cars that had once been a nineties start-up business until the government grants dried up, and it returned to being a rusty pile of broken cars up a track in a small town. He avoids sharp metal edges, his ears reaching ahead while fighting off triffid brambles that catch and stab him through his sweaty suit. Just as he is about to give up, he spots something through the smashed window of a dead Ford Escort – Tommy, frantic, trying to free himself while snagged on a rusting gate that separates off the upper reaches of the junk-yard jungle.

'Tommy! Don't you move!'

Skipping round the Escort and over axles and tyres, he focuses on Tommy's panicked eyes as the youngster fights to get free. I've got you now. Just as he imagines his hand on the back of Tommy's neck, the thread holding the boy snaps, sending Tommy flying off to the end of the yard where he crashes into a thicket of rhododendron that fall back into place behind him.

'Tommy, for fuck's sake! Give us a break!'

Running at full pelt now, he attempts to jump the gate, catches his leg on barbed wire, screams and hits the deck hard on the other side, his briefcase bouncing away into more brambles.

Rolling over in the dirt, he examines another pair of ripped thirty-quid trousers. I let Tommy escape – probably dropping off an ounce of hash as I lie here like a knob. I'm losing it here, but there's nowhere else to run after this, no lower level to crawl into. His eyes moisten as he imagines Tommy in the back of a police car, crying, then that prick Watson on the Children's Panel asking, 'Where was the social worker when all this was going on?' Tommy was now being led to another car and driven to a children's unit over the water.

Stop this, Hugh. Get up!

Staggering to his feet, he fights with a bramble bush for his briefcase and goes through the gate which creaks with a mocking laugh.

Jesus, that little prick's fast.

'Fuckkkkk!'

He swings a kick, almost breaking his toe on the wheel of an innocent rusting Mini Metro. This brings him down onto his arse again with a sharp pain in his toe and his side. I'm having a heart attack! The pain stops when he shakes free the forgotten can of Fanta that was digging into a left rib. The metal cools his flushed face as he holds it against his cheek. But when he tugs back the ring pull, the foaming juice shoots up in an arced fountain, falling over him like sticky orange rain. He doesn't fight it or try to stem the gushing can, just lets it piss on him like every-thing else has for the last few years. Resistance was, and is, useless. The sun breaks through and shines hard as a breeze comes up the track, carrying powder-dry British Leyland rust. He groans. What in the name of fuck is wrong with the universe? Across from where he sits, a tyre begins to morph into an eye and a tremor starts in his leg.

Hugh, don't look at it. Get up, man.

Rising to his feet, for the second time, he pulls bramble thorns from his forearm and does his shirt collar right up to the last button, limping off. Should I tell Chas any of this dealer stuff? Nah, he'll laugh me out the room.

It's me and you, Sire, just me and you. Bit sad, when your only pal is your own ego, but beggars ...

A WHIFF of Jim's bonfire comes up off his suit as he struggles up the steps of his close towards the landing he shares with Mrs Murchison, tired footfall projecting his mood ahead of him.

The only window that might have offered light was broken in the January storms and is now boarded up with shuttering ply. Thankfully, some bad workmanship has left a thin crack to one side that allows a bit of weak illumination onto the worn grey stone steps. At the top of the next flight, the last of that light is gone, so he flicks the light switch on the wall up and down – nothing. That's strange, I only replaced the bulb yesterday. I'll phone and leave another message for the landlord; he's harder to meet than the Dalai fucking Lama. Flapping at his jacket pocket, he frees his door keys, his nose now catching the musty hint of damp or something else that oozes from holes in the crumbling plasterwork. After a day of mental fatigue, his eyes refuse to adjust, and he has to suffer that annoying scratching noise that follows a brass key refusing to mate with a keyhole. Something moves under his left foot. He feels small lumps under his shoe.

Cockroaches?

He feels around the floor with his foot as a fireman or a blind man would. Stones? Perhaps fallen plaster? It comes on slow and builds up before rolling over him – that sensation of being watched. He turns, looking up where the stairs to the roof should be but only sees darkness and little static dots dancing and sparking on his retina. Opening his door, he throws the briefcase inside and lets some light out into the hall. After a glance up the stairs to the roof fire exit, he kneels, resting his weight on his tired calves and cut toe. Small quarter-inch pebbles sit along the threshold of his front door, the soft light casting small shadows that define them into what looks like letters.

U AR... DEAD

This pushes him back up onto his feet as a tingle of standing hairs and goosebumps crawls over his neck. He makes fists and raises them up, an instinct he took on when forced to learn to box at twelve years old by his father.

Wolves, abroad in the world.

He analyses every splodge of drifting darkness around the hall for signs of a human shape or movement, his freaking mind making out a possible creature from nothing, then disregarding it as he moves back towards reason.

Behind.

His fists tighten further when he hears the unmistakable sound of a person's weight shifting behind Mrs Murchison's door across the landing. He shows the first sign of a tremble as the door opposite cracks open a quarter inch, and a warm orange light cuts its edges like molten iron running around the frame. A single, beady eye comes to the gap, peering out into the hall before coming to rest on Hughie – its intent hard to fathom, because it is detached from any discernible body. The eye holds him there.

'Hi there, did you see anyone ... at my door?' Hughie asks what he hopes is Ms Murchison's floating eye.

The door is pushed firmly shut and the locks go on, one by one, the weight moves off down the corridor behind the closed door. He blinks, looking back down at the stones by his feet.

'What's goin on?' he whispers.

In the silence that follows, his consciousness reaches out further until he can smell the mould growing within the walls, hear the mice licking their fur and feel the old building breathe in and out around him. His whole body pulses as he senses other things that he cannot be sure of – a stalker perhaps. No, no, don't overreact, you can cope with this.

This is voodoo … told ye we shoulda got a blade … I fuckin warned ye, get a blade! Gaslighting, that's what this is; getting inside someone's head, making them doubt their own sanity. Oh Christ, not again, not here. ***We're obviously pissin some maniac right off, again. You're a psycho-fuckin-magnet!*** Maybe the old guy, Don, is a sociopath ... and Jim, he asked a lot of questions. What if the Eyes ... what if it's found us again? What— ***Or, maybe it's the drug dealer whose distribution network yer fuckin with, genius. Think about it. It's obviously Davy Drug or one of his pals; must've seen you after the boy on deliveries. Cunts!***

As he goes to hurry inside, something makes him sniff his hand. He throws his head back in disgust. 'Fuck.'

It's shite. Dirty druggie bastards!

Hughie fights off a vision of the Knight repeatedly jabbing two steel-clad fingers through mirror shades. ***Eeeh, eeeh, eeeh!***

Skin crawling now, he reverses inside his front door, kicking it shut with his foot. With his clean hand, he slides the deadbolt across, the mortice and Yale locks following into their tight slots.

'What the fuck!' he says to himself, before lurching up the hall towards the bathroom.

The landing outside his front door is black again, empty bar some scattered pebbles. The lonely faint purr of passing cars washes up the stone stairs and over the tightly closed doors.

SIX
FEW PLANS SURVIVE FIRST
CONTACT ...

This one's face is so wrinkled that it is hard to find an inch of smooth skin, even on the cheeks. Lines run in gullies from her nostrils to her thin lips, making her look like a small beaked bird; the lines are also the sure sign of a long-term smoker. Strangely, the eyes are still sparkly, if slightly prominent, as she peers at him without questioning who she has let in her front door. She smiles with a row of yellow teeth that resemble corn kernels.

'Do you know why I'm here, Mrs Beattie?' Hughie asks, while sitting with his body language open and a soft reassuring smile.

Another day in the big muddy.

'Bobby's just gone out, to get bread,' she tells him with assurance.

'Bobby? Is that your husband?' Hughie asks.

She ponders on this for a moment, then says, 'Aye,' though doesn't look so sure this time.

'Love of your life, no doubt.'

'Oh yes,' she replies now he's guided her to an emotional anchor.

'Well, all I'm here to do is see if you need any help with anything.'

'Oh no, son,' the wee bird says as she shakes her head, 'I'm fine ... me and Bobby are fine.'

'Your sister—'

'My sister?' she interrupts, as if she doesn't have a sister.

'Agnes, your sister Agnes, she lives in Corby,' he explains.

Looking around the carpet she thinks on this, her expression telling him she is sending out nets that only return empty.

'Agnes is a bit concerned about you, Mrs Beattie. She asked us to come and see you,' he tells her.

'Oh, she did, did she?'

Get on with it, before she gets shirty. On fuckin Pluto, this yin.

'Mrs Beattie, have you ever been seen by Dr Chowla at the memory clinic?' Hughie holds eye contact, asking his questions in a soft, clear tone.

'Eh ... I don't know. Ask Bobby.'

Bobby's been dead for years love; you've got dementia, its rippin out o you doll.

'Are you drinkin, taking your pills?' he asks the small woman in her furry pink dressing gown, who grins back from oblivion.

Although dusty, the place is well ordered, except that the medicine blister pack in the kitchen hasn't been touched since the Tuesday morning pills were taken out, three days ago. Even these are unlikely to have got into her system as he spotted pills in most of the cracks in the kitchen floor on his way in.

'Are you drinking okay, Mrs Beattie?' he says in a louder voice, suspecting she is also deaf. It works.

'Are you wantin a cuppa tea, is that it?' Now agitated by Hughie's probing of her small world, she starts calling, 'Bobby, Bobby!' When Bobby doesn't answer, she gets up. 'Don't know where he is. I'll make it, son, I'll make it.'

He takes the opportunity to follow the little pink bird through to the kitchen and see how she coordinates making two teas.

The sink holds a single half-empty porridge bowl, a single cup and a used teabag. In the cupboard she opens to get the sugar, he can see cornflakes and a wall of soup tins that the sister in Corby has said a neighbour gets for the widow, Doreen Beattie, on Mondays. Hughie pretends to help and lifts a teabag out the sink. He stands on the pedal for the bin; there is little evidence in the almost empty bin of her using up her shopping. Although she is blunted by her condition, he can see she is nervous of his presence now, her small eyes flicking sideways at him as she flits about between the kitchen units. She picks up things – the spoon, a fresh teabag, and after a ponderous moment, a second cup – like a bird, surprised that it keeps finding fresh crumbs.

The isolation huz speeded it up, nae doubt; this is you in fifteen years. It's all of us in time.

She fills the kettle and then looks at it, on pause again, then switches it on.

'Doreen, do you mind me calling you by your first name?' he asks, trying to build a small bridge.

She doesn't answer, goes to the window and looks out for something or someone. In time, comes back to the bubbling kettle. She pours the water into the cups as it boils, without turning it off, then stirs two sugars into her cup, while looking up at him with a wee lost smile. She pauses, as if something has fallen over in her mind, then goes to the fridge and gets the milk. Bringing the milk back, she seems unsure of why she has put down two cups.

'You okay?' he asks.

She pours milk into her own cup, the carton hesitating mid-air for a moment before she puts it down. With shaky hands, she lifts her cup and moves away.

'We'll sit at the fire,' she says as she passes him and goes back towards the living room.

He picks up his cup without adding anything and follows her. I think she's kind of enjoying the company now, but her sequencing isn't great.

Aw, poor wee soul. Let's head, we know she's El Loco. Job done – back to the Fort, send out the foot soldiers to make her meals.

As she sips the tea, she watches him with curiosity on her face, as if trying to work out who he might be. Her mop of wiry white hair reminds Hughie of candyfloss, or the wee clouds that float alone in blue summer skies.

'I'm not happy with the dog being away,' she says.

'Right ...' When she doesn't add to this, he asks, 'Doreen, would you mind if I came back tomorrow with an occupational therapist?'

Pausing mid-sip, she says, 'No therapist, just you.'

'I'll have a word with Dr Chowla, get you an appointment if that's alright with you.'

'Robertson!' she says.

'Sorry?'

'Dr Robertson, have a word with him.'

He's been dead three years too, love.

'If I can get someone to help you out, would that be okay?'

She looks at him as hard as a pink bird can. 'Help out? Nah,' she says and waves the idea away with a frown.

He gives a reassuring nod of the head. ***Job done.***

'Okay, before I go, do you want me to get you something to eat?'

'Where you goin, Bobby?' she asks in a petted voice.

Oh, fer fuck's sake!

'It's Hughie, and I have to go back to work, to talk to your doctor. I'll come back, okay Doreen?'

Her eyes try to calculate something, but she has fallen into a maze, a maze where everything is complicated; even door handles, how they open and lock. Even the tins have become complicated, worse than doors. Worst of all these things, is the fact that Bobby and the dog keep disappearing – leaving her all alone.

She looks up at him with her wee bird eyes, mutters, 'Tomato soup's nice.'

'I'll make you soup,' Hughie says, taking off his jacket.

Fuck me gently, you're at it again.

As he stirs the soup, the silent pink bird goes about her flat from the bedroom to the bathroom to the living room as if looking for things that she can't quite visualise. She carries a towel from the bathroom into the hall, then thinks better of it and takes it back. She never seems distressed, but occasionally looks up to ensure he is still for real, not just another one of those fleeting ghosts. Back in the living room together, she spoons the soup between her too-dry lips.

When he starts to put his jacket on, she stops, spoon in the air, says, 'Where are you going now?' There is despair in her voice this time.

'I won't be too long, Doreen,' he lies.

She puts the bowl down. 'Well, I'm not happy,' she says

with sorrowful lips, her face now that of a small bird peeping out of the nest, looking for mum.

Hughie rubs his knees. I hate the extraction moment.

Jesus, Chas wiz right; Mother fuckin Teresa syndrome.

As he stands up, she looks at his briefcase on the couch, says, 'Don't you forget that baby this time,' as if telling him off for a common behavioural flaw.

'Oh yeah ... I won't forget.'

Lifting the briefcase, that Doreen would swear in court is a baby named wee Derek, he walks to the door – her beady eyes and pointed beak following him all the way. Something deep inside her says the pink chick will be alone again.

'I'll be back again with a lady called Linda, from our service. Will you be okay?'

'Just you come, no lady,' she tweets.

'Okay Doreen, you're the boss.'

The bird beak smiles.

IN THE GARDEN, he checks the bin. It's empty. He walks round to the street. The area is working-class and almost desolate with everyone being out at work. He phones the office, asking for Joyce.

Before he can speak a word, Joyce asks, 'Are you at that wee lady Beattie's house yet? Her sister's been on the phone again, and she's a right stroppy cow.'

'Joyce, Joyce, forget the bloody sister!'

'Alright, don't have a go at me.'

'Get hold of Linda from the care team. This one's like a wee pink bird; one that can't fly.' He pauses to get his spinning thoughts into order, then adds, 'Oh, and call Dr Chowla in the dementia team, ask for an urgent referral this week.'

'You'll have to call Chowla,' Joyce tells him. 'His secretary's a right stuck-up bitch, won't take anythin from a pleb like me.'

'I'm on my mobile, can you not do it, please?'

'What happened to you not needin help?'

As Joyce speaks, he clocks wee Tommy running up to a door two hundred yards down the block. 'Hold on,' he says, putting the phone by his side, watching as Tommy knocks on one of the Dunan Court two-bedroomers. *Caught.*

'Hughie, Hughie,' his phone screams.

Lifting it to his ear, he keeps watching while the door Tommy tapped on is opened. Tommy stands with his hand out for a bit as someone's head comes out the door and looks around. I think Tommy's handing something over? *He did, he did.* The boy runs off fast, up the street towards the top of McArthur Brae which runs down the steep incline towards the heart of the Town.

'Joyce, I'll have to phone you back.'

'Chowla won't take an *urgent* from me, you'll have to use your stripes—'

He hangs up on her and starts walking at speed up the road towards where Tommy has disappeared. *No point chasin the wee bugger, we tried that the other day, ended up on our arse in a car dump.* No, but what's he doing round here? *Drug dealin.* He handed something over, but I'm sure he never took payment. *Perhaps Davy doesn't trust the boy with cash returns.* Or perhaps it was a distribution of supplies, rather than a sale. *Mm-hh.*

Opposite the door Tommy had gone to, Hughie stops and looks towards the brae, instantly giving up on any idea of another second-prize chase that he knows will end in torn trousers. He rubs the back of his neck, thoughts starting to roll. Is this boy actually involved in dealing?

Neck deep in it.

The world is unreal again and the road beneath his feet a battlefield trench, his briefcase a broken shield. Drawn in without conscious agreement, he finds himself at the gate of the delivery house, unhooking the metal latch. Moving up the path, he no longer sees the lush green grass of the houses that reminds him of how they were built on hard rock that keeps the soil wet; he'd forgotten the fact that their walls were built cheaply with no cavity within, a cavity that might keep the dampness from seeping through and into your bedroom and lungs. Lost too, the fact that these tenants, who can ill afford to burn a hole in the ozone layer to avoid a lung-hugging mould, are vilified by the tabloids, slagged off for squandering their giros on cheap, fat-ladened food and sunbeds that stop you looking like an asthmatic corpse. Only wee Tommy's fate and overlooked childhood spark the fuel spill in his mind. The Knight is at the helm, riding him on.

Right, let's do some man's work – check this bastard out.

Hughie knocks on the door. There is a noise inside, then someone comes to the frosted glass and hesitates. The door opens, and an odd-looking man with long hair, bald on top, and loose joggers stands staring at him with big anxious eyes.

Don't tell the twat who ye are.

'Hello, sir. I have just seen Tommy Anderson at your door ... looked like he knew you,' Hughie says all accusatory.

'Who is it?' a woman screams from somewhere inside.

'It's the polis,' the guy says, still in shock – frozen to the spot, eyes flicking from side to side.

'Can I ask how you know him?' Hughie says.

'What?'

'Do you know the boy?' Hughie asks again.

'Sort of,' the sweaty guy says, his fat jowls forming a frown.

Cunt knows him alright.

'Sort of?' Hughie says and stays deadpan quiet.

'Aye, he, eh ... he runs to the shop for me, now and then.'

'What'd the boy deliver this time?'

'Delivered? Eh, a loaf.' The guy is scared, on the back foot with his mind racing.

'No, it was a small thing, not a loaf.' Hughie tells him straight.

Unable to answer, with one eye almost closing, the guy fights to get a grip on what is going on.

'Can you tell me what the boy handed you, please?' Hughie says as he squares up, arms folded. ***Mistake!***

'Hold on,' the guy says, waking up to something not quite right and stepping forward. 'Are you a cop?'

Ye said please, he'll know yer soft.

'No, but I am that child's—'

'Fuck off,' the guy interrupts as he moves fully out onto the steps and pulls the door closed behind him, so his girl-friend can't hear. The guy is two steps above Hughie and looks bigger now. He has the whiff of sweat and hash about him, his big sad eyes hardening just as Hughie recognises Scatter-cash from Joyce's description.

'You deaf? Ah said, fuck off!' he tells Hughie, pointing a finger at his face.

Hughie pushes back his shoulders in his clean suit and faces the guy up with the arrogance that comes from social capital. Brought up around here, he knows how to put on a front, and that quickly backing down from a threat is a weakness that's hard to come back from. Scatter-cash starts a staring match that the Knight is having none of.

Don't back down to this druggie prick.

Scatter-cash softens first and starts glancing up and down the street, while Hughie shakes his head in total disrespect. He gives the dealer his hardest stare, then turns his back, starts ambling down the path. This one's a bottom feeder, Davy's drone, no doubt. I'll pass it onto the police when I get back to the office, they can pop around after dark and kick the door in.

FUCCKKKK!

Hughie lets go of his briefcase as he is dragged backwards by the hair and thrown hard against the rough-cast wall of the dealer's house. His chin jars on concrete, pain shooting up his jawbone to the brain. As he turns, Scatter-cash gets a hold of his throat. 'Aaaghhh.' The dealer is using his weight now, pushing hard on Hughie's windpipe, the rough wall behind digging into his skull. The guy's fat sweaty wrist is impossible to get a proper grip on, sending panic through Hughie's mind.

Nut the bastard!

'Now there's no need—' Hughie starts to say.

The dealer looks different now, no sad eyes, those puffed folds of the face forming a demonic grimace as he leans on the social worker's throat again. 'You know who you're messin with, prick? Do you?' he shouts into Hughie's face, his breath stinking of fried food and hash.

Hughie, wake up man – fight man, fight!

Like a rag doll, Hughie is pulled by the hair into a tight sweaty headlock, his shiny shoes flailing, unable to find purchase on the damp, mossy slabs. The fat arm around his neck squeezes ever tighter, constricting like a snake as Scatter-cash pulls him up the step. Blood pulses in Hughie's forehead and water comes to his eyes. The man's too strong, can't get a grip. Scatter-cash flaps his other hand, trying to get hold of his door handle, only stops when Hughie spasms again.

'You're goin down,' Scatter-cash whispers in his ear. 'Down!'

The dealer can feel it now, the strength and fight slipping away from his victim. Numbness flows up the legs and arms, telling of a horrific end – being dragged inside the house, then burned with cigarettes while Scatter-cash and his bird hang over him, drunk, laughing at his contorted expressions of pain. Wolves' teeth flash in Hughie's mind, a deep gurgling sound growing as the Eyes comes and goes in terrifying bursts. No, not again. Please! A set of pointed teeth respond to his plea, biting at morphing shadows, the beast's slavering tongue running over sharp canines.

Hughie, wake up!

Hughie digs his nails into the fleshy snake that is intent on draining him of his last. As it loosens, he turns his head to the side and lets a precious shot of cold air into his lungs. He begins growling as his feet push him upright. Scatter-cash responds, trying to pull his prisoner's head back down to get the fat snake on the windpipe again. It is too late. Hughie is somehow coming back to life, snarling and bucking before sinking teeth into the man's finger that is flapping invitingly by his mouth. Headlock loosened, Hughie throws his head around until it thuds into something soft; nose blood floods his hair as skull meets cartilage. Scatter-cash lets out a cry that holds real fear when a hard elbow hits him in the guts. Tables turned, the dealer goes reeling backwards, his hands flapping in defence. It should have been over at that point, but Hughie is red-crazed and possessed, no longer Hughie.

Kill it, kill it, kill it!

Two hard jabs to Scatter-cash's sweaty face and the dealer is gone, his nose in tatters, strange bleating noises coming from his throat.

Again, again, again!

The right cross digs hard and Hughie feels bone at the end of his fist. The man's eyes, that were first terrified, roll back into white as he staggers, trips and falls with a sickening thud onto the concrete steps. He lies still, then momentarily jolts back to life when Hughie's boot meets his face; his belly quivers and he gasps for air, holding out a hand for mercy.

'Sheena!' he tries to shout through his closed door, but he can hardly speak.

Hughie stands over him now, fists tight, teeth showing, a watery madness in his eyes. The dealer tries to shuffle away. ***Cunt's movin!*** Hughie sinks a boot into the dealer without warning, feels his foot hit soft fat and then ribs. The man gives out a muffled grunt, now looking like the overweight, middle-aged, unemployed, failed bully that he is. His tone is desperate, like a child wondering what this creature in a suit is, where this thing that pretended to be a cop came from. Perhaps another drug gang – more ruthless, crazier – are on the patch.

'I'll kill you,' Hughie says.

A pretend lunge makes the dealer recoil with fear, his body now shaking, tears running down a fat, blotchy face.

Stove his dome in!

'Please ... don't hurt me,' the thing on the step begs.

As if released from an invisible grip, Hughie shakes his head and sees his opponent as he is. The snarling wolf disappears in echoes like it's lost in a long corridor.

Stamp on it!

This order brings a heavy jolt of electricity to the brain and the snarling comes back for an instant, Hughie fights the urge to smash the dealer's face to a pulp. He breathes deep, his balled fists relax, and the monster is gone. Holding out his hands, he watches hairy claws become his scarred fingers.

'I've become one of them.'

A high-pitched sound rises from his gut, the blood draining from his face as he stumbles back from the pitiful dealer. Oh God, oh, my God.

Baldy-fuckin-mutt, kick it again. Kick it!

'No,' Hughie tells the Knight.

Scatter-cash's frightened eyes peer around to see who Hughie is talking to.

Holding out an apologetic hand, Hughie bends to pick up his briefcase, then backs away down the short path and out the gate. On the pavement, he glances back, sees the dealer still lying there, folds of white belly fat escaping a T-shirt that is pulled up to chest-level; the guy's hands now daring to fumble for a grip on the door to pull himself up. Across the way, Hughie's wide glistening eyes see a gull turn its back and fly off the rooftops. Then his gaze finds the rows of windows, watching like stern judges; each pane knowing his sins and shouting out – guilty, guilty, GUILTY!

'All this will come back on Tommy.'

He breaks into a panicked run. ***Stop!*** Catching himself, he slows to a forced march along the pavement, towards the car, no looking back.

I created this.

You're kiddin me on, right? That baldy, retarded mutt attacked us first. Fuck witnesses, no fucker cares about his kind. You were attacked by a drug dealer for askin a few questions about a wee lad; you done him over and he deserved it, worse ah think. Hughie shakes his head, but the Knight is grinning. ***We're sendin the message out into the woods that we're no fuckin messin about; we're no some bottle-fucking-merchant amateurs.*** It's not right, I'm getting drawn in all over again, like before, running on adrenaline and rage. ***Jeezo, what are ye like, you complete spasm – we won – enjoy.***

At the car, he puts his case on the roof and throws up just as his phone rings. Heart thumping, he straightens up and fights to get the mobile out of his pocket. Oh shit, this will be bad – bad, bad, bad.

'What happened there?' Joyce asks down a crackly line.

'I ... I ... what?' he stammers.

'You hung up on me earlier.'

'Oh right, sorry ... I'm ... on my way back to the office.'

'You've been to the pub, haven't you?'

'No, no.' His voice sounds guilty.

'Well, are you not going to ask how I got on?' she says, her voice now upbeat.

'With what?' He looks up the empty road, lost.

'You asked me to call Linda, from home care, for the

wee pink bird woman, whose sister's never off the bloody phone.' She becomes sceptical. 'You must be in the pub.'

Swapping the phone to his other hand, he notes that both hands are now trembling in response to the slowing adrenaline spike. He closes his eyes, so he can focus, sure that he looks like a guilty, sweaty beast as a young girl with an old Silver Cross pram passes on the other side of the road.

'Eh ... did you get Chowla?' he asks her, blinking now.

'No, but Linda can visit the lady tomorrow. Chowla and his dragon secretary are down to you.'

'I can't deal with this right now,' he shouts, dropping the phone to his side.

'Don't get all angry with me, grumpy bollocks,' she says, but he doesn't answer. 'Hughie, Hughie ... you okay?'

He is stood by his car, staring back along the estate towards the dealer's place, jaw so tight, vomit-wet lips. Scatter-cash's bird might call the police; witnesses file out the houses opposite and then I'm done for. He remembers the phone, lifts it to his ear again just as she says, 'Hugh, are you in trouble?'

'I'm fine ... I'll talk to Chowla when I get back,' he tells her.'

After a silence while they both wait on the other to speak, she says, 'Oh, some guy phoned.'

'What guy?!' His minds racing again.

'Jim,' she answers. 'Told me he was in your lynch mob; said it was urgent, didn't say what.' She recounts this as if it is a normal Hughie type of message.

Tiredness comes over him, and he opens the car door. 'Okay, Joyce,' is all he says, then he hangs up on her for the second time that day and gets in his Volvo. Once inside, he rolls the window down and then thumps the steering wheel with both fists. 'Fuck!'

The scheme around him, where he and most of his friends grew up, closes in, accusing him of betrayal, for an assault on one of its own lost souls, someone who he should understand and know how to deal with. Somewhere, two dogs bark one after the other. He pokes a finger in his ear to make sure the dogs aren't imaginary. A small man with a shopping trolley waddles towards him along the street, looking nosey.

'What have I done?' he asks himself, winding the window back up as quick as he can, his damp hand slipping several times as he tries to close the window before the guy gets to him.

'This can't come back on Maggie or the boy.'

As soon as he closes his eyes they are open again. There is movement on the other seat – the Knight dripping bile all over the leather, grinning with those broken black teeth that come to small pointed ends.

'Get lost,' he says, his face contorting with disgust.

Without saying anything, the Knight starts to slowly clap in appreciation of Hughie's survival skills and Scattercash's complete and utter defeat – the sound of the metal gauntlets clacks and bounces around the car and off the windows in a steady nerve-shredding beat.

'That was totally and utterly mental,' Hughie tells the Knight as he closes his eyes again.

Stop being a fanny, Hughie – this is the grizzly reality of the endless war. Me, you, Maggie and wee Tommy – we're born to struggle for our very existence, day after day after day. There's never been rules on these streets and

**don't, for fuck's sake, expect an acknowledge-
ment from society for yer efforts. Darwin
opened our eyes to the interminable horror of it
all; it's endless, but at least we're winnin for a
change.**

'Are we?'

Hughie is ignored like a naïve conscript, the Knight's voice gets stronger, emboldened rather than terrified by getting into a fight in broad daylight – he sounds drunk on the violence – triumphant. *Just getting started on the bastards, eh Sire?*

Hughie's blank eyes look straight ahead. 'I hope not,' he says to the empty car.

SEVEN
POW-WOW

After driving around for an hour, he pulls over on Hannay Road. It is getting late and he'd go home if he could handle it. He moves his face to the side as he looks in the visor mirror, sees the red rash the snake has left and looks away out of the window. He is too tired to be angry and feels his body isn't quite his to command – sore all over, running stiff and sluggish like his Volvo that's seen better days, days when it could cope with the rough road.

He pats the steering wheel affectionately and gets out of the car in slow motion, rocking his head about to loosen his tight neck. Walking over the road to Jim's place, he follows a man into the grocer's shop, while an almost identical man to the one he followed, except he has a more sullen demeanour, longer hair and a bigger Roman nose, stands outside as if keeping watch.

The Knight appears behind the watcher, holding a knife to the man's throat. ***Brigand on the rob.*** Hughie shakes his head.

Inside, Jim looks perplexed as Hughie and the guy he followed in both stand silent in front of the counter.

'Hughie,' he says over the tinker's head.

'Serve this gentleman first,' Hughie tells him with a nod towards the guy.

'No, no, not at all,' the tinker says. 'If yous gentlemen have more important business, I'm a man who is used to waitin, no problem there, Jim sir.'

'What you after?' Jim asks the tinker, voice irked, impatient.

At that moment, the tinker senses a vulnerability in Jim's voice, an urge to get him out the shop fast, so he can talk to Hughie alone.

'Well, sir, I am needin a bottle of ... your whiskee.' When Jim does not immediately lose the rag and throw him out, he smells further weakness and adds, 'Oh, and four, eh no, six cans of your strong lager, Jim sir.'

'Will that be on tick?' Jim asks, voice thick with sarcasm.

'Oh yes, that would be fine, Jim, just fine.'

Jim put the six cans on top of the local newspaper and walks along behind the counter to the spirits, his hand hovering over the whisky bottles.

'A nice malt would be just fine,' the tinker says, his voice tapering off when he senses he's pushed too far.

Jim picks his cheapest blended whisky, takes it to the till and puts it in a bag with the cans without any negotiation. He opens a worn book and writes in pen:

£4.50 lager, £10 whisk/budgt = £14.50 the twins bill;
NO MORE.

As Jim hands the bag of booze over, the man grasps the handle, half turning away, but Jim still holds a firm grip on it, the tinker caught between Jim's stare and escape.

'Tell your brother, who I can see standin outside, that

it's up to forty-eight quid. The next time either one of you appear in here, I'll be expectin payment, in full.'

At that, Jim lets go and the man gives a wee stagger backwards. 'You know us travellin folk, Jim, know we're good for it. Wully out there is waitin on a payment from the man, any day now, any day—'

'See you later,' Jim interrupts, allowing the man to scurry out the door and away.

They watch the brothers walk off up the road through the open door for a moment then turn to one another. Hughie knows he looks burned out, shaking, and Jim is carrying something important that shows in the added lines on his forehead.

'Travellers, hah, what a joke. Tonight, those two chancers will be sittin on their arses drinkin my booze in a council house,' Jim says with dry regret.

'I see them everywhere,' Hughie says, struggling to contribute.

'Their mother made the most amazin intricate wicker baskets, you know; it's only poly-bags full of my booze with those two.'

Hughie doesn't even try to smile, just says, 'You called for a hanging?'

After locking the shop door, Jim gestures for him to follow and walks off into the back room without saying much. In the back, he turns off the TV and looks out the window above the sink that faces the Terrace, his eyes flicking left to right then up towards Maggie's place.

Watch him, he's old, but if the Korean shit's true, he could pull a knife, big fucker too ah bet, chib us.

After locking the back door, Jim puts his back against it.

Here we go.

'You hungry?' Jim asks.

Hughie looks at the dirty cooker and frowns. 'Not particularly.'

'Listen, I wiz a wee bit rude the other day,' Jim says with little apology in his voice. 'You're from good people.' There's an awkward moment before Jim adds, 'You must be starvin after your work.'

He points to a wooden chair with an open hand. 'Have a pew, sir.'

Tired resignation sits Hughie down on the seat by a table with a red checked tablecloth. From here, he watches the old guy fire up the frying pan. He senses a secret to be revealed, and a fair lump of loneliness at play too.

'You like beans with a fry-up?' Jim asks.

Hughie shrugs.

'Good for the guts, ah find,' Jim tells him, rubbing his belly.

'Fine.'

Pausing and narrowing his eyes, Jim says, 'You okay, you look ... worn out.'

'I'm guessin you didn't ask me here to give health and dietary advice. What's goin on?'

The shopkeeper doesn't answer at first, too busy peering at a scratch on his guest's cheek. 'Bacon, sausage, beans,' he insists as he stands in his slippers and tired blue cardigan, flipping lengths of bacon into the frying pan with his nicotine fingers. The cardigan has greasy marks by its side pockets where he's wiped his hands again and again over the week. He hums along with the radio as he empties beans into a small pot and loads toast under the grill which explodes into life with the help of a match, forcing him to pull his hand back quick.

Hughie leans back as the fat begins spluttering on a high flame, bringing a certain greasy aromatic life to the dull back room. He finds the pensioner hypnotic. Aye, you've got to be a duck-n-diver in the crumbling world of the back-street grocer's shop during this endless austerity. ***Old crook.*** Not this guy – bend the rules, maybe, wise to the game, defo; but old-school honest with his fellow inmates. ***Just because he's an old fucker doesn't mean he's lost the killer instinct. Anyway, why we here again?***

'You called me,' Hughie says but gets no answer.

As he sets plates by the cooker, Jim looks out the window, his eyes lingering on the waste ground. When he's sure it's safe, he takes a small packet from behind the teabags and throws it on the table where it hits the brown sauce bottle and settles on the tablecloth. He gives Hughie a blank look and then goes on cooking. On closer inspection, the small cellophane packet holds a dark, oily cube. Hughie stares at it, then up at Jim who hasn't bothered to turn back round to see his reaction.

'What's this?' Hughie asks.

'That's why you're here,' Jim answers sharply, turning the toast over then sucking a finger he's burned in the process.

Picking the packet up, Hughie peers at it. 'Looks like ... cannabis resin.'

'Looks like?'

'I'm tired,' Hughie tells him. 'Anyway, I'm not a fuckin expert.'

'It stinks,' Jim says as if sharing important information.

'Where'd you get it?'

Jim is watching now but doesn't answer.

Tearing the wrapping, Hughie gives the contents a sniff. 'Definitely cannabis resin; we called it dope in my day.'

'Is stinking good?' Jim asks, lifting his eyebrows.

'Guess so. But they didn't teach me about that at university, well not at lectures anyway.'

'My tax money's obviously been squandered over the years.'

'You goin to tell me where you got it now?'

'Well, it's no bloody mine, is it?' Jim says with a scoff.

Hughie shakes his weary head in his hands. 'Must be living on your own that does it.'

The frying pan is lifted off the purring gas for a moment as Jim thinks for an answer. 'Aye, the wife's long gone; it changes you,' Jim says with a wee sigh in his voice. This admission builds a bridge and makes the dinner suddenly a more serious affair.

'I think I saw wee Tommy delivering one of these today,' he tells Jim who is peering in at the toast in the grill.

'One thing at a time,' Jim says between a series of ouches.

After a few more minutes, the ounce of hash looks quite at home in the back of Jim's shop amongst the nicotine coloured ceiling, the damp, peeling 70s wallpaper, piles of newspapers, scud-mags and hundreds of litres of cheap cider and lager. This is what austerity is doing to the back-street grocers who are competing with multinationals that can fly fifty tons of grapes in from southern India at short notice while Jim here has to pay twenty quid just to get his ten-year-old fiat Punto over on the ferry, hoping it doesn't break down on the way back. Fighting globalisation isn't for those young and smart enough to know about choices or having an actual life. Hughie watches through heavy eyelids, knowing the man has more intel to give. The old bugger's lonely, so he's drawing it all out. *If he knew how mental I am, he'd put rat poison in the food.* ***Focus, nancy boy.***

'Hope that bacon is in date this time,' Hughie jokes.

'You find me a successful small businessman in this rocky part of the world, and I'll show you a crook by necessity,' Jim replies with a knowing glance over his specs, then a wee grin.

Two well-filled plates are put on the table, the one in front of his guest has an extra sausage. Jim scoops up two glasses out of the sink, shakes water out of them, then carries them with a new bottle of brown sauce and a can of lager to the table. After another shifty glance out the back window, he sits down opposite Hughie and opens the lager, sharing it into the two glasses. 'Eat up lad, you're at yer auntie's.'

'The dope?' Hughie says with irritation in his voice.

Jim points a knife at the food, grinning at having his date on the hook.

With a shake of the head, Hughie starts to cut up a sausage. *The old bastard's El Loco.* ***Nae doubts there, but there's more.***

Both drink their lager in no time and Jim opens another can, which goes down the same way. Hughie dips a piece of toast in his beans and eats it as Jim tucks in at the speed you'd expect of a widower who eats alone every night. After a minute of silent chewing, Jim spins in his chair and brings a bottle of dark rum from under the sink, showing it to Hughie, who nods. The rum is served straight, in small glasses, and tastes strong after salty bean juice.

'Where'd you get it,' Hughie demands as he continues to chew, still looking at Jim.

That's it, poker face Hughie, poker face.

'Out there on the waste ground,' Jim finally admits.

'Does it belong to who I think it does?'

Jim's face is smirking, eyes twinkling. 'Seen him stash it the other night.'

'Will Davy guess you took it?'

'He might,' Jim says, showing too much of the food rotating in his mouth, tipping his head back to keep it in.

'You not worried?'

Shaking his head, Jim changes tack. 'What's it like, smokin dope?'

'Is there more, or is that all of it?'

'I think the clown spreads it about – eggs in baskets sorta thing.'

After that, they both have another rum shot each, and Hughie feels the anxiety circuits being shut down, one at a time, his eyelids becoming heavier still; his gaze takes on a stillness, and he feels quite at home.

'What's it like?' Jim asks again, staring at the packet.

'This conversation's like the magic fucking mystery tour.'

'Yeah, but wha—'

Hughie holds up a hand, interrupts the question and leans towards his host. 'Listen, I haven't smoked since uni.'

'So, ma tax money did go up in smoke.'

'You actually pay tax?'

'Funny. Does it make you feel happy, the dope?'

Hughie starts massaging his aching neck and shoulders. 'Not if you're a miserable git to start out.'

'We should smoke away that wanker's profits.'

This catches Hughie out, stops the neck rubbing. 'Thought you hated drugs,' he says.

'I hate drug *dealers*.'

'You old fuckin hypocrite.'

'Listen,' Jim says, now drunk and grinning, 'I'm almost dead, so all that doesn't count, none of it. Anyway, I fought for ma country, why should these lazy clowns get aw the fun on the dole while I work myself into the grave?'

'Fair point,' Hughie says, 'for a bigot.'

Poor old bastard's right, kept the country goin through thick and thin, he'd give you his last piece o toast, yet nae cunt gives a toss about him. Ah, you've found our soul at last. ***This gives us an advantage.*** How so? ***He's a lonely old bastard, we can use that, get the best out o him, get at the druggies.*** You're vile. The Knight sniggers.

Jim tops up the lager with yet another can, and they have another shot each before the cutlery hits the plates. Jim takes the plates away to the sink. He keeps looking down at Hughie, then at the dope, without speaking.

'Okay, okay, go get some fag papers and tobacco,' he orders.

Jim grins and scurries through the bead curtain like a teenager on a promise, bumping into the door frame en route. In seconds, he is back with two lighters, two pouches of tobacco and three packs of fag papers.

'Fuck's sake,' Hughie says, 'you only need a few fag papers and a sprinkle of tobacco.'

'Well ah don't know what's needed, do ah.'

Excited now, Jim stands over him, slapping and rubbing his hands together.

'You're an oppor-fuckin-tunistic old git,' Hughie says.

The old boy's specs move up and his eyes widen as Hughie takes the dope out the bag. Sticking several fag papers together, he lies them on the checked tablecloth, then sprinkles in some loose tobacco. Taking a slice of card from the paper packet, he rolls a small filter and aligns it with the tobacco.

'It's been a long time since I've been near a joint, never mind rolling one, so don't rush me,' he tells Jim who is hung over his shoulder like a hungry crow.

After cutting a small piece off the chunk of dope and heating it with a lighter, he sprinkles the crumbly resin onto the tobacco, pausing to look over her shoulder at the old hoodie.

'You'll be revising your notion that the police should shoot drug dealers without trial then,' Hughie says.

'Nah, Davy's sellin worse stuff.'

Hughie stops what he's doing. 'Says who?'

'Says the gangster who pops in to see him. Drives a new Merc; you don't get one of them frae sellin a wee bit of cannabis, do you?'

'How long's this been goin on?' Hughie asks, staring at Jim until he answers.

'Ages ... maybe three, four months.'

'Might be an insurance salesman.'

'Listen, if you'd seen the big cunt, you'd know he's a gangster – big gut, grey hair and a shiny suit,' Jim says, then shakes his head in disappointment, nodding for Hughie to get on with the joint.

We're gettin in deep now, Sire.

Hughie tenses, pain shoots up his neck, somehow connecting his jaw to his spine and an anxious mind that flashes with his own choking face, crying fat drug dealers on concrete steps, and big gangsters in red Mercs. Totally distracted, he forgets about the joint prep, frozen.

'Geez it here, for fuck's sake,' Jim says as he snatches it out of his guest's hands.

As the shopkeeper skilfully spins the joint into shape, Hughie is drawn out of his trance. 'Thought you hadn't ...'

'Ah smoked roll-ups for thirty years till *she* died of lung cancer ... you never forget how,' Jim says, a wee smirk on his lips.

'You can light it then, Drug King.'

'Nah, nah, you go first,' Jim says trying to hand it back, like it's a bomb.

'Nope.'

'C'mon,' Jim pleads.

'All yours, Grandad.'

Putting the reefer to his lips, Jim lifts it away for a second, nervous.

Back between his lips, he takes the cigarette lighter from the table and quickly flicks the wheel to ignite it, the joint end glowing bright orange under the flame. His cheeks thin as he inhales too deep, eyes narrow with the effort. It ends in a loud eruption of smoke and spluttering lungs as Jim flails like an epileptic having a fit. Hughie laughs out loud into the room of pungent smoke and sweet, fat fumes. Now that Jim is disabled by the coughing fit, Hughie wrestles the joint from his grasp, inhaling slowly to avoid a similar embarrassing performance. This time, the smoke blows out in a long, casual, refined plume into Jim's face. It goes on to form a smog about head height, a smoke screen that helps Hughie avoid the grasp of the overzealous pensioner who is frantically attempting to secure the next shot of their new-found toy. Taking his time, Hughie steals a second puff, stopping to smile through at Jim.

'Hurry,' Jim demands, wiggling beckoning fingers.

'Christ, "Drug-Crazed Pensioner Kills Social Worker After First Toot".'

'Has it started workin yet?'

'It takes time. Chill maaaan,' Hughie says, laughing at him.

As the third puff comes out of his lungs, Hughie feels the buzz slowly float around him like a long-forgotten friend, his eyes close without much resistance. This makes him vulnerable to attack, and sure enough, he feels the joint being torn from his grasp. Two more short goes each and it is gone. The wee transistor radio by the window trickles out Otis Redding's 'Try a Little Tenderness', as the light dulls in the west and the waste ground grows too dark to see. 'Nothing's happenin,' Jim says in a dry, croaky voice.

'Listen.'

'To what?'

'The radio.'

Otis's voice has never sounded better, clawing at their souls, pleading, lonely, each note seems at home and made just for them, right there, in the squalid, smoky, bacon and hash scented back-shop. Neither says a word until the very last note of the song has ended.

'I'll roll another,' Jim says, agreeing with himself.

When that decision has been made, they both get up and move with their drinks and essentials to a pair of worn armchairs that sit against the back wall, next to the door for the toilet-cum-storeroom. They conspire in lazy coordination to open a few more cans then roll another larger joint, which the shopkeeper holds out in front of him in a tight, proud grip. They grin at each other, Jim looking like a druid, somehow younger, and Hughie feeling less sore and more relaxed, as if he's found safety at last. After some chit-chat that makes them both giggle at nothing, Hughie, exhausted, goes off into a trance. Scatter-cash's face is there, bloated, but distant, windows reflecting the violence with no sound.

'What?' Hughie says, startled.

'I said, does one child really matter to you lot?'

'To me, at least.'

Jim chews on this for a wee while. 'See my son, George?'

'Mm-hh.'

'When my wife was alive, he ignored her, seemed bored when she spoke, disinterested you might say.' Jim pauses, turning his thoughts over, licking his lips. 'When she died, he starts goin to her grave, always leavin flowers ... what's that about?'

'The dead don't answer you back, I guess.'

'He doesn't talk to me now, think I've lost him,' Jim says, looking over at Hughie and giving a wee shake of the head.

'Is that why you worry about wee Tommy so much?'

'Perhaps,' Jim says, his eyes losing focus and his thoughts turning inward.

'Listen, we've no choice but to care.'

Jim sinks back into his chair, pulls his feet up, his whiskers moving up and down like an old rabbit peeping out the burrow. 'Nah, society, it's broken.'

'We're social apes, wired by hundreds of thousands of years of evolution ... to care, to worry,' Hughie insists.

'Is this the dope talkin.'

'They've done experiments with morality; something about people on a train track. If you pull a lever, you divert the train from people on the track and no one gets run over.'

'They tied folk to a track?' Jim says, popping his head out the burrow and peering across.

'No, for fuck's sake, it was a hypothetical question-y

thing. Anyway, ninety-nine percent, regardless of race or religion or lack of it, made the same choice.'

'What'd they choose?' Jim asks, now lying back with a deep frown.

'To divert the train.'

It seems like an age before either of them speaks, both staring at the ceiling.

'What about the Nazis?' Jim asks from nowhere.

Hughie's face grows troubled. 'We have other evolutionary circuits ... earlier, darker ones, from when we were selfish amoeba ...' His words trail off for a while. '... Hitler tuned others into their fear, that other side.'

'That'll be the drug dealer side.'

'It's complicated ... to do with childhood, environment and genes.'

'Pity that wee cunt Davy Drug wasn't on that track, with me at the lever, eh? Cut his fuckin heid right off him,' Jim says, tittering to himself.

They go silent after that exchange and five minutes pass without a word, both in Pluto mode.

Remember you're still on the clock MacDonald, undercover, so get on with it.

'You seem to know the Terrace well,' Hughie says, breaking into their space-out.

'Maybe,' Jim says.

'The old guy, Don, is he interested in kids?'

With one eye screwed up, Jim considers this. 'Yeah, but not like that.'

'You sure?'

'Forget Don,' Jim insists, 'it's that drug dealin weasel and his pals you want to be goin after.'

Jim is too stoned to sound angry, but his voice has a

certain edge. Hughie nods again to show he is listening, before adding, 'I'm already on it.'

This makes Jim sit up on one shaky elbow for a few seconds. 'What've you done?'

Don't tell the old git anything about Scatter-cash, he might freak, clam up or reach for his bayonet. Jesus, we're off the rim today, fightin in broad daylight, risking the sack.

'What'd you do?' Jim asks again; stoned, curious, one eye half-shut.

Keep stoom.

'People crack me up,' Hughie says, his heavy eyelids blinking in slow beats. 'They expect social work to do the dirty work in the shadows, clean up the shite no one wants to touch, not bother anyone in the process; we're like a secret caste.'

Melting back into his seat again, Jim gives up, goes off on his own. 'I've decided I'm going to help you ... where I can.' There is a pause before he adds, 'It was me, by the way – I wrote the letters.'

'I know, you old fart.'

'Listen,' Jim says, trying to prove his point, 'I will, I'll help.'

Hughie shrugs his face. 'I'm sure you mean it – until you sober up.'

'I'm serious; Maggie and the boy ... they deserve it ...'

Hughie now listens with his eyes closed as Jim chatters, the radio drifting in and out. He feels his body going limp and the day's mad events begin slipping to the back of his mind, the room feeling like childhood nights at Gran's or Uncle Malky's. The talking falls away, and he hears Jim's breathing deepen. Blinking, he fights the inevitable pull towards another troubled sleep. 'It's getting late,' he whispers in a croaky voice, his throat feeling dry and shrunken.

Jim jerks upright at this, startling Hughie.

'No need to rush off,' Jim says, then smacks his lips and stretches his legs out from his armchair like some cosmonaut coming out of the capsule after years in deep space and suspended animation. Shuffling his bum forward to the very edge of his chair, he starts wrinkling his face about with his jaw to wake it up, before clapping and rubbing his hands together. 'Right,' he announces, 'another wee fry-up, eh Hugh?'

Grinning, Hughie struggles to his feet, feeling stiff all over, especially his neck. When up, he looks at his watch and goes towards the beaded curtains. 'Will you keep an eye on my car? It's over the road.'

'I'll open up a new packet of bacon if you want,' Jim says in a last attempt to keep him there.

Hughie doesn't dare look at the pensioner, avoiding the lonely, lined face and widower sadness that might pull him back. 'Enjoy the munchies.'

The curtain strands regroup behind Hughie with a protective clinking as the pan rattles on the cooker and the tranny gets turned up to ward off the ghosts. As Hughie crosses the dark shop, opens the shop door and peers out into the night, Jim shouts something. Hughie doesn't answer.

'Don't forget that boy!' Jim shouts again, his voice haunting, like the last cry from a wounded soldier in no man's land.

Hughie goes out and closes the door behind him.

As Hughie traipses off along the street, the cool air wraps around him, evaporating the warm feeling of the last few hours, bringing in bad memories to flatten the mood.

Above, bright pinholes, that poke through the cloth of the pitch-black night, peer down in judgement at a supposed Knight of the Light, a Knight who is half-beaten, a Knight who has given the poor a kicking this day. As his shoes tap out the beat of a hasty retreat on the pavement, his eyes are drawn between the buildings to glimpse the dark, brooding lump that is Saint Andrews Terrace. There is one light on at Davy Drug's window; it glows a lonely red through thin curtains while the rest of the Terrace hides in darkness. Something bad oozes from the faint glow that becomes the red eye of a great silhouetted beast.

Sensing growing anxiety in his host's stomach, the Knight comes back from his slumbers. ***Chin up, soldier. We've got a spy on enemy soil now, but it's down to us to do the dirty work – our duty.*** Hughie looks behind before answering. But there's still so little to go on, apart from hearsay. Chas won't buy any of this, the rabbit-like Tommy, the stones, the lump of dope evidence we've just smoked, the possible paedophile and the list of loosely connected idiots who might make up a drug network. Oh, and then there's the shit on the door handle and my psychotic assault on a member of the public in his own garden, explain that and look sane – they'll push me out like they done down south – the nutter.

That's why we sort it ourselves, under the radar stuff; we sink the druggie cunt, Davy, like we did his pal. Chas will only point me back to Karen and I'm not going there again in a hurry.

Hughie blinks as he fights off a tidal wave of pity, fear and guilt. ***Light is Right. Trust yer gut, Hughie. We take the fight to the wolf's lair, dig out more*** *intel, then snare the mutt.* No violence this time. Promise? **Grow up.**

The dragon's eye fades and all is black save the odd street light. He pictures Tommy under the covers, listening to the creaking house around him, waiting for the voice of the fag burner to return, fighting the memory of the screaming, the pleading that no one answered – the boy's praying to God now, anyone, or anything, that will help make it okay. Tommy's wee steepled hands shake as he prays.

Cold gets inside Hughie's collar, bringing him back as the stars roll over black hills into the west. At the crossing, he turns down Bute Street, the lamplight hardly able to hold his dark suit as he moves on like a ghost. The paper shop, the tall B&B, and the spire of St John that disappears into the sky, all sit around him like silent mechanisms within the comatose town. Faint music escapes one of the dim-lit rooms at the B&B where passers-through stay. But there is no one to be seen in the second-floor window. The music is dreamlike, infecting the cold air, perhaps Pink Floyd from an album he doesn't know or heard when he was young and stoned. He imagines another lost soul, who has fallen asleep with glass in hand, stereo playing the sounds of their youth, vodka bottle empty on the floor and a picture of the ex-wife in shreds next to the spillage. He looks away from the dull lit window above. Why can't all the lonely unite, all the wee sad souls at their one-man parties come out into the dark streets and meet up – not be alone? He suddenly pictures the staircase up to his flat – it is dark and damp, and someone is in the shadow by his door.

We need a blade, Hughie, a Stanley would do; that was fuckin close today, too close.

I'm losing it, not sure I can keep this up, not after today ... it's wrong.

Don't wallow in pity, man, get the job done, kill the beast. We are defined by the things we manage to defeat.

'Enough!'

Hughie turns the corner, pushes his hands into his pockets and hunches his shoulders as he makes his way down towards his flat on the empty high street.

EIGHT

THE GRAIL

Bulging, they draw him deeper into their depths, easily reading every phoney, long-practiced facial expression in the so-called social worker's repertoire. Once they get past that defensive façade, he is, like everyone else, so damn vulnerable, some wee bug that has lost its carapace, left wriggling in its weakness under the sun-like glare of close observation. Despite years of training in the art of objectivity, they soon latch on and suck at his very marrow. There isn't much sympathy in their draw either, just an intense, almost cruel, unrelenting curiosity for this new world they are forced to inhabit. The magnification has the effect of making the pupils so big and dark they are like gaping holes in reality, variant blue and grey splinters shining out as the irises catch the harsh window light. Hughie sits face-to-face, meeting them square on, feeling a presence in his soul, something searching through it like a clumsy inexperienced thief, ransacking and scattering any stuff it comes across that it doesn't understand or value. The eyes blink and Hughie lets go of the frames and sits back.

'Now is that not better?' Hughie asks.

'No,' the lad says.

'Told you so,' she adds.

Slap her.

'Try to be supportive, Maggie.'

'Ah, it's *Maggie* again, see that, son? We are in the good books now, do what you're telt and get in the good books. Prison screw, this one, nuthin more, son.'

'Maggie!' Hughie warns without looking at her.

She cracks a momentary fake smile for her son, says, 'The new specs look brilliant, son.'

Tommy isn't convinced but continues gawking around his mum's hovel like it is a new boundless universe full of exciting hues and textures that cut the mind like a scalpel. Despite everything he's lived through, the wee lad now shines like a pulsar, his glow flooding over the jubilant social worker. Not much can lift Hughie these days, but this has.

'It's brown,' Tommy says.

'What is?' Hughie asks.

'Where the water comes in,' the boy says pointing up at the ceiling as if the young explorer in hand-me-down clothes has just discovered a fork in the sacred river Alph, in long-lost Xanadu.

'With a bit of luck, you'll be out of here by Christmas,' Hughie tells him.

'Aye, we'll believe him when it happens, eh son?' Maggie's voice mocks at the social worker's optimism, threatens him with failure and hides her own bitter fear of hoping for good things that tend to never, ever happen.

Tommy's new laser vision locks onto Hughie's opening briefcase as a bag of sweets comes out. His grin falls into a frown as a tube of toothpaste and two toothbrushes, one lime-green, one fluorescent aqua-blue, follow.

'Now, Tommy,' Hughie begins, 'if you keep the old

Gregory Pecks on, I'll give you a pick-and-mix every week until you are happy wearing them. Deal?'

Tommy moves his tongue around inside his cheek, surveying first the sweets, then the toothbrushes, his eyes narrowing as he calculates. 'Do I have to use that?'

'Fraid so.'

Maggie watches the growing relationship with the suspicion of an old hand.

'Deal,' the boy says, his fingertips already dancing on the table next to the sweets.

Baby fuckin fox, this wee bastard.

'On you go,' Hughie tells him.

Tommy rips open the bag, throws a sweet in the hole and crunches it until it breaks, sucking on its sour inside. Maggie leans over and jolts the boy with a hand to stop him grimacing. It is then that Tommy locks onto an old eighties photo on top of the telly. A grin grows wide on his wee round face. The faded colour photograph is of Maggie and a bearded man in a pub, the couple hugging and smiling above a mountain of empty beer glasses. You can almost see rays from the old photo warming the boy up inside now that he can look deep into his dad's eyes. He is not a mistake or a bust condom as the bullies tell him, he has a mum and a dad who once sat together in a pub drinking and smiling. Tommy's face holds a holy glow.

Aye, okay so you've done somethin for a change, but the place is still hoachin with dealers.

'I need to ask you something serious, Tommy,' Hughie says.

The boy moves closer to his mum.

'Last Friday,' Hughie begins, 'I chased you through the

scrapyard off Hannay Road. The day before yesterday, I saw you at a door up the top of town.'

Tommy shakes his head in denial as his mum pushes back in her chair.

'What were you up to?' Hughie asks.

'Christ, can you no leave it,' Maggie says. 'He's happy.'

'I can't,' Hughie replies.

In that moment, distrust creeps onto both their faces.

'Are people making you deliver things, Tommy?'

'I was playin with pals.'

'Look at me, Tommy,' Hughie says. The boy reluctantly lifts his head, unable to make eye contact. 'Have any of your neighbours asked you to do things you don't want?' Hughie glances at Maggie to stop any prompting, and an uncomfortable silence fills the room.

Tommy shrugs. 'I wis just playin.'

Maggie pats his shoulder.

The boy knows how dedicated these fag burnin dealers are; code o silence. We need facts. ***They're scared; yer talkin to the carrion.***

Hughie nods in resignation. 'Right, how are we doin at school then?'

'Tell nosey parker about school,' she insists.

'Who's Nosey Parker?' Tommy asks.

Maggie gives a sly nod towards Hughie.

'Oh ... Miss Clark says I'm makin a bit of an effort at last.'

'Mum get you up in time for school?'

Maggie sucks on her fag, fighting that urge to intervene.

'Don gives me cornflakes in the mornin,' Tommy says.

Maggie splutters out smoke and interrupts, 'Don't start

slaggin Don off ... If it wisnae for him, we'd be struggling big time ...'

Hughie looks at her, and Maggie avoids his gaze altogether.

'The old man next door gets you up?' Hughie asks Tommy.

'Aye.'

'Every day?'

'Most.' A sucking sound comes from the boy's mouth as another sweet breaks inside the mixer.

'You okay with that?'

'Don't like the flashes; like his jokes,' Tommy says between slurps.

'What does he mean by the flashes?' Hughie asks Maggie. 'Are they from a camera?'

'Hold on a minute,' Maggie says, shaking her head at the boy. 'Don gets Tommy his breakfast, puts his uniform by the bed and goes, that's all.' Hughie gives her a stern look that drives her on again. 'Don's an artist, he cannae sleep, y'know the type, nervy, erratic – a bit like you.'

'What kind of artist?' Hughie asks her. ***Paedo type?***

'Listen, I'm depressed, cannae face the world at that time of the morning – Don's a great help.'

Hughie hits back, 'Tommy is your responsibility. Don't you cop out of this, letting people you hardly know get him up. Tommy's needs come first; before your own, before anything; that's what being a parent's about.'

Her cheeks flush, and they lock stares, her eyes mean now, his calm and provoking.

That's it, stir up the dozy old cow, see what's under the bonnet.

'Do you think these things out?' Hughie asks her.

'Don't judge me. Don's a great fella who I've known for years, twenty almost.' She screams this at him without any reserve, and he absorbs it without reply.

That's ma girl, show the boy ye give a shit.

'Tommy's ma son and ah love him,' she continues while looking at the boy. 'More than you'll ever know ... ah do my best.' She turns to Hughie now. 'What business is it o yours if a friend helps me out.'

'Alright, Maggie, you've made your point,' Hughie says, glancing at Tommy, who is smiling at his ferocious she-wolf of a mother.

Hughie unhooks himself from her angry stare and turns to the boy. 'Tommy, when Don comes in, what is it that flashes?'

'Pola ... roid, the wee picture comes out the bottom. I'll show you.' The boy runs out into the hall as if on an important mission.

Maggie sits silent in the armchair and fiddles with her lighter, unable to get it to work. A few silent moments are necessary at this time in order to let the responsibility speech he's given her ferment. Outside the window, dropping grey cloud seals the Town in again.

Tommy comes back into their silence and hands Hughie a photograph.

'That's me!' Tommy says proudly.

'Oh yeah, so it is.' Hughie makes sure he looks suitably impressed.

In the photograph, Tommy is sitting up in bed, bare-topped, smiling with a bowl of cereal on his lap. It is dark, but Tommy's smile cuts through the gloom and shines out like a little uncorrupted moonbeam. Hughie nods at the boy. The lad's smile's relaxed. **Everything**

can be faked or shaped for a small fee o
sweeties.

'Are there more photos, Tommy?' Hughie asks.

'Course.' The boy gives him a look filled with suspicion.
'Where are they?'

Tommy points at the wall with a dismissive hitchhiker's
thumb.

'Don's house?' Hughie says.

Tommy nods while sucking on another sweet.

'Are you in all those photos too?'

The boy pauses, stops chewing, looks at Hughie as if
he's said something stupid, 'Naaaahhh.'

'Right!' Maggie shouts. 'Sorry to break up the camera
club meeting, but Tommy and me are off to the shops.' She
picks up her coat then pulls Tommy away from Hughie.
Cursing, she wrestles an anorak over the boy's head, the
sweetie bag in his firm grip getting stuck inside the sleeve.

'I have a few more questions,' Hughie says.

'You'll soon moan if ah don't feed him.'

As he stands up, Maggie is holding the living-room door
open, nodding for him to leave.

'No cup of tea today then?' Hughie says.

'I'm trainin you up; if you annoy me, nae tea.'

As he passes her, they share a smile, his is brief,
knowing and perhaps patronising, while hers is even
shorter, forced and obviously holding back real anger.

Tough lookin ol witch, but it's aw show. She's
back in charge and I'll always bolster that for the sake of
Tommy. ***Aye, but she cannae protect him frae
dealers and photo snappin paedophiles.***

Maggie blows smoke at the back of his head as an
awkward silence follows them all up the hall towards the

175

front door, only the incessant crunching of little teeth on hard sweets cuts the atmosphere.

OUTSIDE, fine rain falls, the dwindling glimmers of early summer eaten up by heavy grey cloud. He hesitates, caught in thought, as Maggie locks the storm door and drops the key into her cavernous shopping bag. As she turns to head off, Tommy's hand in hers, a scruffy couple are making their way up the lane towards the Terrace, both with hunched shoulders, tracksuit bottoms and matching hoodies.

Junkie alert, junkie alert! Problematic drug users.

'What are you lot after?' Maggie asks them as they get within shouting distance.

They ignore her and keep advancing.

Look at the nick o these cunts.

The woman is squat with a certain manliness about her and wiry, salt and pepper hair. She looks like she wants to have a go at Maggie but says nothing after clocking Hughie's suit. Her tall, skinny, hooded pal, another methadone addict by the look of his black teeth, intervenes. 'Just visitin old Don, see if he's awright, if he needs anythin out of the shops.'

'No, you're not; beat it,' Maggie tells the tall one.

'We'll just check on him aw the same,' he replies.

'Beat it,' she tells him again.

'You the fuckin polis nowadays, are you?' the tall, skinny one spits out – any pretence at niceties gone – his mean piercing eyes now on the rampage.

Maggie points to Hughie. 'Naw, but he is.'

As the pair take time to warily study Hughie, a mini stand-off takes place. There is perhaps a whiff of potential violence or escalation. Hughie wonders if they work with Scatter-cash and Davy Drug.

Maggie reaffirms her advice. 'Now beat it, the both o you!'

The wee squat one doesn't blink, catches Hughie with a cold stare. She communicates her plan of action to the tall skinny one with a guiding nod towards the waste ground and a tug on his shrugging sleeve.

The wee, fat yin's obviously got the viable brain cell in the outfit, feign retreat in the short term, avoid comin to the notice of authority types and creep back like cockroaches later.

The boss addict pulls her hood up over her head, draws her chin down into her jacket and plods away across the wet grass towards the hole in the fence. After a brief attempt to stare Hughie out, the tall one retracts his viscous eyes and runs off after his boss, dancing alongside her, gesticulating and acting like a daft juvenile who's got distracted and wants to make it up to a wiser member of the goat-eyed tribe.

Junkie scum. Symptoms of the wider disease.

Maggie looks unperturbed after the encounter, the misty breeze taking any sting out of the threat as the pair continue their foraging trip in the direction of Jim's shop.

'Nice caring types, visiting the disabled,' Hughie jokes.

'Junkies, lookin for money or pills.'

Told you.

'Do they target Don?'

'They try.'

'Will they visit Jim next?' Hughie asks with concern in his voice.

She smirks. 'He'll chase the bastards before the door's half open.'

Tommy stands listening to his elders, taking in the coarse wit and wisdom needed to survive in modern times.

Grey cloud and rain ride down off the hills in spiralling shoals towards them, a damp chill running in front to cut through their thin clothes.

'Guess summer's given up,' Hughie says.

Only a loud hiss replies as the rain falls on the trees, grass and roofs – the droplets getting bigger, the hissing growing to a soft roar that seems to signal the weather's intent to wash the Town straight down into the Clyde, then off out into the Irish Sea.

Maggie takes the wee man's hand, dragging him at pace along the rutted lane which is becoming a river.

'See you,' Tommy shouts.

'Bye, wee man.'

From far down the lane, Maggie's plastic hood keeks back over her shoulder, not in the social worker's direction, but to where the addicts have gone through the iron fence. Hughie smiles to himself and stops following. She's a sly, defensive old she-wolf.

Right, it's time to tap the David Bailey of the paedophile world?

Davy Drug's girl watches him run back towards No 3.

Foreign spy witch!

Wonder if she's okay?

Would she really be stayin with that clown if she was?

There is movement behind old Don's net curtain when he chaps the door; something moves then wilts away. **Turn the screw.**

He knocks again, counting to four before knocking again.

The door springs open, catching Hughie napping. Don's scruffy face scowls out, confused at his social quarantine being interrupted by some clown in a black suit.

'Stop, stop, the fucking knocking,' Don shouts.

His face is thin and sharp, his long, white, yellowing hair runs back to a ponytail, held together with an elastic band. It looks like he used a broken bottle to shave and his eyes are insanely sharp and bright blue. 'What do they want,' he says to himself. 'They're not getting it ... no way.'

The old man seems to be talking to Hughie, himself, and perhaps, the prowling addicts, or worse. Stepping out of the rain and onto the top step, Hughie forces the old guy to draw back and narrow his eyes.

'Can I come in, have a word with you, Mr ...?'

'Donald Cameron,' the old boy answers, then begins to rant under his breath, eyes darting about the place. 'Asking questions at this time of the day ... nosey bastards, eh ... what you expect from them, what you expect.'

After a warm smile, Hughie asks again, 'Can I please come in and talk Mr Cameron? I'm a social worker from the Authority.' Hughie feels for his ID and lets the rain in under his jacket.

'Getting soaked?' Don says, grinning.

'Yeah, a bit.'

'Five minutes,' Don says, then shuffles inside – bottom of the pile, little resistance, little point.

Hughie goes inside and stamps his feet on a worn patch of carpet by the door. He draws back his collar and shakes his jacket, nose catching a certain stink.

Jesus, it reeks in here.

Mumbling to himself at a rapid rate, Don slopes off

down the hallway in purple slippers and goes through an open door.

'Thanks for invitin me in,' Hughie whispers.

Leaving his briefcase by the front door, he follows Don into the living room, nose still twitching. I tell you, if Maggie's place has a dead cat under the floor then this place has a corpse, a human one, maybe even two, both further down the road of decomposition.

'It's the sewer. Landlord won't fix it,' Don says, catching his guest trying not to inhale.

'You complain?' Hughie asks, glancing around the place.

'Aye, but I'm on benefits,' Don says. 'Powerless – they don't even write back.'

The right-hand wall of the room is covered in coloured pictures and collages, some drawn in what looks like kid's crayons, some in acrylics and some made of odd things. They run horizontally and vertically from stained skirting to the old worn cornice, with only small gaps between. One collage made from beer cans and carrier bags is nailed onto rough wooden planks with nine-inch nails; it says WASTED.

Most of the art material looks as if it has been dug up from the long grass on the waste ground on a wet spring day. The sparse room has two armchairs and a coffee table full of beer cans, copper and silver coins and ten-pound notes. The carpeted floor feels sticky underfoot and sucks at the soles of Hughie's brogues. ***Shit, what is that?*** Probably the grease, spilled beer, and mould you get from a cold, lonely, chaotic lifestyle. He spots Polaroid photos to the right of the front window. ***Bingo!*** Don't look towards them, not yet. He might guess, sling us out. Need to give some chat. ***That's it, smile for the nutter, wee reassurin nods as we move up the room towards the photies.***

'What you after?' Don asks straight out, his arms folded, his back against his wall.

'I'm Hugh MacDonald, a social worker ... I'd like to ask some questions.'

'I know who sent you.' Don shakes his head.

'Who'd that be?'

'Ahhh right, I've got you now, it's daft game time. They wear the same uniform and think we're all daft. Right, son.'

That's fuckin hilarious, even the nutters call you son now.

'You can call me Hughie.'

'You can call me Mr Cameron.'

The old man refuses to shake Hughie's outstretched hand and stays by the fireplace, sunk into himself. He looks at Hughie as you might a sticky-fingered nephew or heroin addict. Pointing to a stool, Hughie waits until Don nods in agreement before he sits down, hand patting the cushion first.

Fuck me, Hughie, you're back amongst your own kind at last. Yeah, the ones who listen to disembodied voices.

Hughie smiles, trying to avoid any further glances towards the Polaroids.

'You know Tommy, who lives next door?' Hughie asks.

'I'm mental, not simple.'

Hughie nods with understanding. 'Tommy told me you get him up for school.'

'Tommy isn't simple either, you can trust him if he tells you stuff – if he trusts you, that is.'

'Does he put his trust in you?'

This catches Don off guard, perhaps he thought the game would take longer to warm up. 'Least I don't have him running around town delivering—' Don clenches his jaw, stopping himself going on.

'Deliverin what?' Hughie asks.

Don stares back, his arms coiling tight around his cardiganed chest, his legs spreading out defensively, like Andy Murray on the baseline as he waits for another probing shot. Hughie decides to sit for a wee while in total silence – let the pressure build, try and look casual, as if here to stay for the rest of the day.

Fuck this shit, get to the photos. Patience.

'Spacemen don't talk,' Don says suddenly, bringing Hughie's gaze back to him.

'You consider yourself a ... spaceman?'

'No.' Don is grinning at him.

'You said, spaceman.' ***Oh, oh, psycho time!***

'Neil Armstrong didn't give interviews, ever.'

Hughie's mouth feels dry. 'And ... you are like Neil Armstrong, because ...?'

'We experienced things that go beyond.'

'Beyond?'

'We've seen the world from a different place.'

Hughie nods thoughtfully, the old man's words sinking in.

Man, he's out there. Shhh, he's thawing. 'I tried to do a bit of sculpture myself, at university,' Hughie tells him. 'Liked Henry Moore ... Kandinsky. I was hopeless.'

'Kandinsky's not a sculptor, but Moore was very good.' Don's hands relax their grip on his rib cage. 'You should try again,' Don says, his voice almost tender.

'Where'd you study?' Hughie asks.

'Glasgow ... got a second in Art and Photography.'

Aw, fer fuck's sake hurry up, pull the hook.

'It was social work for me, Manchester. But I suppose that's a bit of an art in its own way.'

Don tightens up again, perhaps sensing the lure. 'Art?' Don shakes his head.

'Well, in its own way.'

'What, checking up on folk, pokin at them through the bars. How's that art?'

Christ, listen to the manky old git, gettin smart with you, rein the cheeky old cunt in a bit. Keep out of this.

'The art is in fixin complicated social problems with no easy answer. To do that I'm always interpreting what people say they will do into what they will actually do.'

'So, you're a mind reader,' Don says, smirking.

'Well no, but if someone is nervous about discussin certain things, she might put a cigarette in her mouth to push back what she's scared will come out.' Hughie holds Don's eye and smiles, adding, 'But it all seeps out in the end.'

Don's inner voices are clashing, his face strained, and there is a gradual sedation flowing into his eyes as this morning's mask-inducing anti-psychotics kick in, perhaps remembering Hughie's cold-reading skills, he throws his hands back around his chest.

'Clever cunt, this one,' Don says to himself.

Hughie doesn't react, casually looks at the art on the wall again; the Knight ranting, demanding a tougher approach and **a good look at the Polaroids.**

'Do you have a nurse?' Hughie asks.

Don tries to focus on reality, blinking. 'Eh, yeah ... she gives me paints and moans on about the mess, goes on about the pills.'

'You get on alright?'

'Bit of a pain ... but she means well.' Don's jaw loosens off at last, and his tone suggests he likes and even pities those who stumble around him trying to help him with his thing. 'She's on a diet again ... don't see why. Keeps saying she likes art but doesn't do it ... life usually beats it out of them.'

The Polaroids fer fuck's sake, PO-LA-ROIDS. Calm it; motivational interviewing, remember that?

'You sell any of your stuff?' Hughie asks, sounding curious.

'My work? Nah, not for years.'

Getting up slowly, Hughie points to the wall. 'Can I look at ... your work?'

A tentative nod from Don, and he is free to peruse the objects on the walls of the dingy house like you would in a gallery, taking his time, angling his head as he looks at the strange things, one by one. While he works his way down the room, Don sits silent and uncomfortable, watching the latest in a long line of authority goons who wade into his life uninvited.

Can you feel the psycho's eyes boring into yer skull? He might be frightened of a possible negative reaction to his life's work. *Or, might be ready to pounce when he's been found out.* He's got schizophrenia, not psychopathy. *Paedophilia, perhaps?* Nah, doesn't fit the profile, I don't think. *Maybe we'll wait till we check out the photos before we decide that yin. Hold it! The cunt's movin behind you.*

Hughie holds his breath and listens then nods.

That's it, pretend yer interested, keep goin, away from him till you get tae the photos.

The room goes cold as a breeze rattles through the house and shakes the window, disturbing the smell beneath the floors, sending it up around Hughie like plague miasma. When it stops, the atmosphere is thick and tense. Perhaps it's Hughie's imagination or a result of the Knight's impatience, but within the still that falls on the room, he is almost sure Don holds his breath when his guest draws level with the Polaroid collection.

This cunt's creepin me out, the Knight whispers.

The photos spin out on the fading magnolia coloured wall in six, long, arcing spokes; some of the spokes stretch from the chipped skirting boards to the flaky cornice eight foot above.

Check out mad-skull.

Hughie sneaks another glance back, Don is frozen, eyes locked on him.

Guilty as fuckin sin that yin, but what's he got behind his back? Stop!

Many of the spokes contain shots of doors and windows, cracks in ceilings and one of water dripping into buckets on a wooden floor. Most of the photographs are out of focus, probably because Don has shot them from the shadows, far out of range. The light in the darker spokes suggests that the images have been taken early in the morning, making them cool in tone. Near the middle of the spiral, they begin to include people or animals within the frame. There is one shot of a postman, one of the drug addicts from earlier, then the unmistakable view of Maggie's back as she stands at her cooker, smoke rising from her mop of dishevelled hair. Two more images are of a cat, then a seagull whose eye stares back at the camera. Hughie puts his hand on a gap in the centre, right above a shot of the retreating drug addicts. As he feels a pinhole at his fingertip, Don moves behind him.

Perhaps that particular one wasn't for public consumption – nudie o the wee boy, or worse?

'Lost your finishin piece?' Hughie says tapping the space in the photos.

'Told you what they're after,' Don tells himself, 'waste of time – Grail's ours.'

'Mr Cameron, I'm not here on anyone else's orders.'

'Aye, right-you-are,' Don says, nodding his head up and down.

'What is it *they* are after. What's the Grail?'

Maybe the child porn.

Ignoring the question, Don starts tapping his foot on the floor, its force increasing as he hums an obscure tune that may have been 'Ruby Tuesday', pressure growing within the strange, hypnotic beat.

'Who do you think sent me?' Hughie asks. The foot tapping gets faster.

Its gonnae blow!

Looking at the wall where the picture is missing, then back to the old man, Hughie says, 'What's this Holy Grail, Mr Cameron?'

No reaction, foot gets louder.

'Mr Cameron?'

Still nothing, louder.

'Is it the photo Tommy has?'

'No!' Foot tapping rising again.

'Have you got it here? Can I see it?' The pitch in

Hughie's voice creeps up a couple of notches without his consent. **Push.** 'Just a few more ques—' Hughie starts to say.

'Right!' Don screams, almost lifting off the floor with anger. 'Out!'

Watch your back in case he's got a chib, maybe an axe.

Holding out a pair of pacifying hands, Hughie moves past the agitated old boy and makes for the door. He takes a breath as if about to speak.

'OUT!' Don shouts again, a shaking finger pointing the way.

Halfway out the living-room door, Hughie pauses.

Last chance before he slips out the axe. 'Mr Cameron,' Hughie says, a single open palm held up. 'Tommy has a mark on his neck, have you noticed it, did it happen when the boy was with you?'

Don's eyes widen in incredulity, fists drawn up to his face, his body contorting like a bag of rats fighting to get away from a fire. Snatching a set of keys from the table, he stands, neck pulsing, keys high above his head, ready to smite the unworthy transient who's strayed into his mystic's cave.

'Me! Tell him ... no, don't.' Don is arguing with himself until he remembers the heretic from the authorities who's lit the fire. 'Aaaaaghhhhhh!'

Keys clatter against the door, Hughie ducks out of it and rushes off along the hall as fast as he can. As he picks up his briefcase he hears loud ranting behind that begins to echo around the big sparse house, the man almost hysterical now, berating himself for letting another creature inside the inner sanctum. The Knight grits his teeth as Hughie feels a flush of shame.

WALKING ALONG THE LANE, Hughie feels the sweat cool and knows he is being watched from all quarters. The music at No 1 goes up, and although he can't see anyone behind the dark window, he knows they are there, he feels it. Pushing his shoulders back, he tries his best not to show fear, but his knees are at it again, a tremble going up through his hip into rolling guts. I took it too far there ... you pushed me too fucking far. *C'mon Hugh, don't be a fuckin weaklin.* Don't be a bully. The Knight begins to cackle at that one. *It's no your fault – that was one tightly wound mental case in there – who needed pushin; so maybe we've no evidence he's a paedo, yet, but he's definitely hidin some fuckin thing, something dark.* Just listen to you ... or me – fascist. God, I hope you're not the beginnings of my first schizophrenic episode. *That's the spirit, let the weakness in, let them win and us lose – attack yer-fuckin-self.*

'Tell them,' that's what Don said. Tell them what? Don't think he's a paedophile, but he does know the boy's runnin stuff.

And he spewed. Why? Because we put the word on the old cunt. Felt great, gettin stuck in, getting evidence. The Knight is growing inside him. *Almost dome stovin time!* Cackling, the Knight staggers back against the walls of Hughie's mind, eyes rolling in ecstasy, his black quivering tongue dripping bile. Passing

Davy Drug's house, the Knight pleads for him to – **raid the wolf's lair, punch Davy Drug to the floor, stamp his heid till his eyes pop out. Crush Thine Enemy!** Don't become what you hate ... we need a rest and to give all this muck time to settle, think it through, cut out all the static.

Davy and Scatter-cash are willin to let a wee strugglin wean do their drug runnin; one of the cunts burned him for bein late. I don't see the old nutter, Don, writin messages with stones and putting shite on yer door handle, even if he is fond o kiddies in their pants. Stop, please, I can't think. We need to relax, rally the troops. I could phone— **We don't need the help o your bent cop pal.** He's not— **We put the dealer cunts out o the boy's life, then go back for Paedo Van Gogh.** Shut it – shut the fuck up! **You weren't sayin that after the Manchester disaster, you ungrateful wee shite. You let that wee prozzy down, so don't repeat the crime.**

'Stop!' Hughie's face contorts at the mention of Manchester and he sees the stairs to his empty flat, more messages on the step, something waiting there. 'Need a drink.' He leaves the lane in a hurry, walking off into town.

Behind, on the lane, deep shadows hang on the window lintels and the panes look like impenetrable cataracts as their dirt catches the silver-grey sky. All the doors along the Terrace stay shut as the music inside No 1 turns off. No 2 is empty and No 3's ranting voice gives up as a murmuring breeze comes to the rushes of the waste ground.

NINE

THE GREAT REFUGE (DRINK)

'Morgan's and a pint of Stella, Rab.'

That stench of spilt lager on floorboards leaves a glorious sweet thrill in the back of his nostrils. West coast pubs on rainy days, especially after a stag night, are often the best vintage, so Hughie breathes deep and absorbs a lungful of his cultural inheritance. Skinny Rab, the Auld Hoose's skeletal super-sub glass-collector, has been promoted to the first team as two of the barmaids have gone AWOL, one thought to be in Magaluf, the other pregnant. Rab is the right mix of a big liver, addictive genetic predisposition and poor attachment to childhood parental figures – still looking for family in all the wrong places – always turns up. The pub is quiet, and the day shift is sparse, perhaps five punters plus Rab; it is the wrong end of benefits' fortnight.

Perhaps the Taliban are in town and nae cunt has bothered tellin us.

After downing most of his pint, Hughie walks up to the jukebox, brings out a shoal of twenty pence pieces and moves them around on his palm with a finger. Let's see, I fancy something funky. We'll have to go seventies sunshine rock to counter the dark mood, or eighties new wave if we want to go with it. Ah yeah, Steely Dan's 'My Old School'.

Alex Harvey, next? Manic and theatrical for our alcoholic brethren here – right up our street.

He goes back to his stool, empties the last of his pint and holds it up.

'You in a hurry?' Skinny Rab asks from the lager tap.

'Tough week, just glad it's Friday.'

Rab comes towards him with the dripping pint. 'All that kidnappin weans,' he says with a fly grin, 'must be tirin.'

Hughie's face stays blank. 'Another rum, slave.'

It is crossover time and what is left of the early shift hide in the dark booths along the back wall, drinking in silence. One of the booth lurkers is about Hughie's age, wearing clothes from the charity shop and sporting a skullet; he is nursing the dregs of a half-pint and holds a certain desperate look about him. No doubts he is hoping some old pal or partial acquaintance might stray in on the way home from work, slip him a few quid or at least top him up. Two seconds into the lead break of 'My Old School', Desperado begins tapping along in approval at the song choice. He grins at Hughie, his new musical appreciation twin, hoping to ponce a few pints while they discuss the finer points of seventies classic rock. Hughie looks away. At this time of day in an Argyll pub, it's easy to share a pint with a stranger that leads to six more, then you're laughing and talking about whatever you might or might not have in common, divulging things you wouldn't dare tell the wife if you still had one.

Through the window, Hughie watches people head home, his face going from tired to sad. When did I become so anti-social? Strangely, it's being a *social* worker that does it; you see inside society every day then wish you could forget what people can do; then you see them in the supermarket the day after you found out they're abusing their own child, butter wouldn't melt. When you finish up for the day, you can't hack talking to humans.

Desperado is staring into his half-pint now in a dull depressive stupor, having given up on hooking anyone. The guy starts rocking back and forth to the music – a wee toy robot caught in a snag in the carpet of life. Hughie sees this then closes his eyes.

Give the creep fuck all!

Hughie gestures furtively to Rab who leans in.

'Same again ... and give that guy a pint on me, don't say where it came from.'

Rab shakes his head as he sweeps up the tenner. He sorts Hughie first, then leaves it a minute before starting to pour a pint of lager. 'Sandy!' he shouts. 'Ah forgot, wee Katie left you a pint in the barrel, said you gave her a hand with a delivery.'

Desperado looks confused for a millisecond as he tries to remember something that didn't happen, gives in to good fortune and comes forward like a man of occupation and substance.

Aww, so you've helped the wee alky die a bit quicker, yer some guy, Hughie, some fuckin guy.

Moving to the window seat, avoiding further involvement, Hughie continues drinking at a steady rate. The light outside wanes, a flush of late sunlight catching the very top of the sandstone chimneys above the shops, somehow reminding him of Manchester before the crazy stuff began. His eyes glaze over, and he can see soft skin, its feel against the hand is exquisite as it rolls under the brush of his knuckles, sweet and soft. For a prostitute, she had a naïve look about her beautiful elfin face. It wasn't right, and he knew that, but her tears were so fucking real, her situation so impossible to extract herself from that he couldn't help himself. His head shakes. I wonder—

Enough!

This transports Hughie from his spinning thoughts, to where he stands in the Auld Hoose, glass in his white grip. He necks the rum, feeling a tingle in his throat as the layers of drink soak in and the evening comes seeking him out – he is glad it can still be bothered.

'Rab.'

The barman and Desperado ignore him as a dog race at Walthamstow passes the halfway point, their shouts growing into a hoarse crescendo, until the right dog, Rab's dog, wins, and the bouncing Desperado is dispatched to collect the winnings from the bookie's – back in the game son, back in the fucking game.

It is soon half-eight and the dayshift has gone up the road for a bowl of soup and a boozy kip as the young come piling in for the start of Friday night love stakes. The volume goes up. A group of girls from the bank come in together, bringing the smell of fresh air and perfume to the bar. He flashes a glance at one in a red skirt. He has ten years on her.

Forget it, at best you'll end up one of those grey-haired dads who stand outside the school waitin for a child while tryin not to look like a fuckin paedophile.

You're right, let's just drink, feed the jukebox and try not to look too lonely.

Another drink down the road, he pauses, pint glass on

lips, as he feels weight on the boards behind him. Before he can turn, a hand cups his arse and squeezes it.

What the F—

Hughie spins, drink in hand, thinking it is one of those lassies taking the piss, winding up the sado at the bar.

'Fuck!'

'No thanks,' big Lex says, that mad grin of his running ear to ear.

'You creepy big bastard!'

'Aye Shug, thought your luck was in there, eh?' Lex says as he pushes in at the bar, pointing Rab to the lager tap. He looks back into Hughie's face. 'Howz the child snatchin goin this week, Shug?'

'Got two in the boot of my car as we speak – take them out crisps later, let them breathe a bit.'

Looking down Hughie's suit to his pointy brogues, the cop begins to smirk, says, 'Still dressin like a poof, ah see.'

'Jesus, I missed you tank-topped sheep-shaggers.'

Lex is six-foot-three, a sergeant at the local cop shop, with thin white hair and skin the colour of a pint of semi-skimmed. To look more Scottish, he'd need to have a kilt on and a coil of Englishmen's balls around his neck. As he waits for the barman, he necks the last third of Hughie's pint and burps. 'Sorry, was gaspin.'

'You must be a good arse licker to make sergeant round here,' Hughie says.

'As long as it pays well, I'm in there.' Lex starts flicking his tongue out to a point and waggling it around.

'You've not changed.'

'And you're still a dreamer,' Lex says, punching his pal's arm, hard.

They clink pints, Hughie happy to see the big lump of rough testosterone from his past just waltz in as if he owns the place. Within minutes it feels as if they've never been apart, the shared bonds of a crazy youth flooding in to dissolve time. Hughie smiles. I feel human again, a tribe member.

Ah don't know if I'd trust the big fascist boot-boy – remember he's a hand strangler these days. Who would you trust?

'You never give it a rest, do you?' Hughie says as he catches his old pal scanning the pub's dark corners.

'Poof.'

When they laugh at one another, a few punters glance towards them, clock Lex, then look away. Hughie feels right at home beside a fellow guardian, another of the tribe of the excommunicated.

Fuckin key janglers, the pair o you.

'I need advice,' Hughie says, 'from a uniformed hand strangler.'

The big cop smiles at the Masonic dig, then burps in Hughie's face. 'No work stuff – bevy time.' He pauses and stares at skinny Rab who's come close enough to earwig; the barman moves back along the bar, wiping up the beer-spill. 'You thought about what I said last time, Shug?'

'What's that, that you thought you were transsexual?'

'No, about me nominatin you for the Lodge.'

'Eh, no, ehhh ...' Hughie can't look at Lex.

Embarrassin!

'Just, your dad was ... well respected at the Lodge.'

'I know,' Hughie says, still not looking up.

A silence wants to creep in.

'Well, you know it's an option,' Lex says, giving a nonchalant shrug.

They both gulp their pints.

'We still okay?' Hughie asks, now able to hold eye contact.

'Course, you tosser; we've got history, me and you.'

'You know it's all that standin naked in a bath with a dead goat wrapped around the waist that puts me off joinin, don't you?'

'That's the best bit,' Lex tells him, grinning.

Both burst into laughter, Hughie coughing his lager through his teeth.

The Knight is peering at Lex, rubbing yellow saliva from his beard. ***Might be alright ... he's certainly got balls, and baton and one o those nip yer eyes sprayers.***

Lex pours Hughie's rum into his and necks it to even the score, and they sit watching the growing group of swaggering young lads and pretty girls in tight clothes who parade around the pool table. The girls' vibrancy is intoxicating, gnawing through their middle-aged eyes, reminding them that their peak is long buried under the slurry of cheating wives, divorces and workplace cynicism. Both blame the job and consider one another brothers in arms, soldiers in the field who are accepted by the masses in the heat of battle but not so welcome out here in Civvy Street when it's all over.

'I don't want that,' Hughie says nodding towards the young girls, drink frozen in mid-air.

'Just as well, coz you've got no chance.' Lex breaks the spell by clinking his empty glass against Hughie's.

'I want a relationship with ... someone ... my age ... and nice.'

'Beggars cannae be too choosy, Shug.'

As they turn away from the distractions, Hughie leans in on his pal, whispers, 'D'you know Karen MacLean?'

'There's two,' Lex says, pushing him off. 'One's about sixty-five, plays bingo, has a bad hip and goes to St John's every Sunday; the other is, say … forty-four? Crackin body, works at the hospital; had a taste for the Yanks back in the eighties.' He gives Hughie a stern look. 'I'm hopin it's the latter you fancy?'

Hughie blinks slowly, and he nods.

'A bit mental, is she not?'

'No,' Hughie says, offended.

Listen to yer pal, he knows a nutjob when he sees one.

Lex throws a peanut up in the air, catches it in his mouth. 'You sniffing around her house yet?'

Hughie's drunk smile solidifies, his eyes dropping to his pint, trying to find a reply. Fuck he's heard about me looking in the window, got a call about me and the peepin Tom thing.

That's why he's here, send an old pal in, and take him down gently and quiet, nae fuss – Masonic style. There is a short silence as Lex chews on another mouthful of peanuts and gives Hughie an odd look.

'I … met her for a minute, the other day,' Hughie stutters, 'thought she looked …'

He knows.

Lex clocks the flush on Hughie's neck and begins to talk with the nuts spitting out, 'Calm it down, cowboy.' He pushes Hughie's shoulder a couple of times. 'Boy, you are out of practice at the datin game. That why you phoned? Perv advice?'

'Yeah, out of practice,' Hughie says, relieved.

'I just passed her, funnily enough.'

'Where?' Hughie says, looking confused again.

'Goin into the Cowal House hotel, with all her pals from the hospital.' When Lex tells him this, he lifts a brow and nods in appreciation of Hughie's choice of prey.

'You sure?' Hughie asks.

'Yeah, bout an hour ago.'

Hughie catches up again, body relaxing. Fuck, I'm getting paranoid. Lex is an old pal; he'd have looked in that window the other night. ***Well maybe we'll no go that far – maybe he's semi-fuckin-normal.*** The Knight is laughing hysterically now.

'Fancy goin down to the Cowal?' Hughie asks.

'Calm the jets, sniffer.' Lex looks into his empty glass and frowns.

Hughie takes the hint. 'Rab! Same.'

When nine o'clock hits, the arse-swaying, hair-flicking, heart-melting girls by the pool table go onto pints of cider and want attention. Their laughter gets louder, its pitch higher and, at times, hysterical. Lex and Hughie being apes just like any other, succumb to the oldest ploys in the evolutionary handbook by turning on their bar stools towards the ancient mating calls.

'I'm a fuckin baboon,' Hughie says.

They both laugh easy now. For Lex, this is because he usually only laughs with other cops; he knew far too much about this little community to ever be truly part of it. But if you want the heads up on the boyfriend of your wayward niece, how long the woman at the bar's husband has left in jail or the deal she has with the taxi driver who takes her son to school, Lex is your man. On the case, all the time, never resting and never off-duty – like termites and rust – fucking relentless.

Ask him about the dealers. Not yet. ***Now!*** No!

Lex catches him drifting off, gives his face a light slap.

'Ho! Rab. Keep an eye,' Lex shouts to the laconic barman, gesturing for him to watch the pints.

Hughie doesn't ask where they are going as Lex pushes him past the cackling girls, through the cloud of blue smoke and a mob of smokers by the back door, then up the steps and through the beer garden to where a newish Land Rover Discovery sits in the car park. Lex pulls a duffle bag forward from the boot and takes a thin blue jumper out of it, pulling it over his police shirt. Next out of the magic bag comes a lighter and a joint.

'We're stayin out for a few,' Lex tells him.

'Beats goin home.'

'Jezis, Shug, you are a negative fucker – no wonder you're not gettin any.'

Lex gives the back end of the pub a quick scan as he lights the joint then takes three deep blasts, handing it over. Hughie looks up at the darkening sky as he draws sweet leaf deep into his lungs. The sky holds that strange aching blue again. He coughs between words. 'Amazin ... the sky.'

Taking back the joint, Lex shakes his head, says, 'You gonnae tell me what the score is with your hands at any point?'

'Dropped a car bonnet on them ... down south,' Hughie says.

Lex looks at him as if disappointed, seeing through the paper-thin façade; he looks away for a second, then comes back and gives an accepting nod of his giant skull. 'Well, you always were a dozy cunt, MacDonald.'

'And we all knew you'd end up in a uniform, you blunt, bossy cunt.'

They snigger, Lex in full agreement as the joint jiggles

around in his fingers. After another two toots on the joint, Lex looks up into the night, his eyelids flapping easy over two big deep-set eyes. 'What were you on about again?'

'The colour of the sky, that blue ... the way it is right now,' Hughie says. 'Reminds me of when we were young, hopeful.'

Doubtful, Lex looks at him as the joint stub is pinged into the bushes. 'You don't need hash, you've already got a slate out o place.'

After checking his wallet for readies, Lex locks the back of his Land Rover while Hughie continues to stare at the sky, transfixed. It isn't that Lex doesn't see something in the fading daylight, it is that he would never give it up that easy. Watching your dad beat your mum's face to a pulp as a wean keeps you canny, always guarded.

'Just a layer of gas between us and icy space,' Hughie says.

Lex ignores this, marches off across the chewing-gum-strewn cobbles towards the Auld Hoose as if on an urgent mission. Hughie eventually lets go of the sky.

It's aw black and white to Lex, which will come in handy. Societal engineers need a bit o thick muscle now and then. No one knows he looks after his mum with dementia, and no one ever will – Lex just does it. People know in their bones that it's better if he's on *your* side than against you.

Running behind, Hughie jumps on his pal's back and gets piggybacked past the stink of the outcast smokers into the glowing pub.

Inside, the lights have grown warm and the noise level can be felt in the marrow. All the punters seem to have got pished or coked-up during Hughie's short absence and you have to shout to be heard above the laughter, dirty jokes and high-pitched female sob stories that spit from loose drunk mouths. Across this, clattering pool balls and the jukebox's booming bass weave a fuzzy magic – a dropped pint glass, with associated cheering, fires the starter gun for another weekend of paganism and debauchery; it is, without doubt, a profitable Friday night for the owners of the Auld Hoose. Skinny Rab, known for drinking away profits like a leaky pipe, is too busy working to partake, his face now miserable and dour.

'Our pints,' they both shout in unison, then laugh.

'Aye, aye, comin,' Rab says as he spins a pint glass under the tap, takes money from another punter and holds a phone between ear and shoulder, asking the boss to send in the reserves.

'C'mon!' Lex shouts, drumming his palms on the wet bar.

'So, you busy at the cop shop?' Hughie says in his pal's ear.

Lex gives an uninterested look. 'Don't worry, Hugh, there's enough skulduggery around this wee shithole to keep us both busy till retirement.' Lex bangs on the bar again, forcing Rab to scurry towards them, spilling their old drinks.

Hughie gestures for Lex to come near, backing into a corner to the right of the main door. 'Serious stuff now,' he says, 'I need you to deal with somethin – someone.'

'Is it this Karen?' Lex says and gives a letchy drunk grin.

'Nooo, it's more serious—'

'No chance!' the big cop interrupts, 'I'm no interested if it's work ... this is laughy time.' He is scowling now, irked.

'This guy is feedin off folk.'

'Sounds like half the taxi drivers in this town,' Lex says, waving Hughie away with a shovel hand.

'It's wee Davy Drug's mob; the clown's usin weans to do his runnin.'

Lex is listening while staring through his pint glass. He takes a big slug, pauses in thought, then wipes his mouth. 'Not interested,' he finally says.

'C'mon Lex, I'm gettin set on here.'

'What are you on about, now?'

'I don't think he's too happy with me goin about his wee fiefdom; some arse has been messin around at my flat, messages, shit on the handle, tryin to get inside my head.' Hughie gives the room a quick scan, before adding, 'His pal, Scatter-cash, well, he tried to give me a kickin the other day.'

Lex starts grinning at this last bit, asks, 'What'd you do?'

Hughie gives an uncomfortable shrug. 'He thought I was a nosey suit – took it too far.'

Grin widening, Lex pushes, 'You sort him out?' willing his pal on with a nodding head.

'I gave him a slap.'

'Good man – good man.' Lex is patting his pal's back now, making his pint spill.

'But I'm not proud of gettin involved.'

Like a delighted drunk dad, whose son has fought the school bully, Lex puts his arm around his friend's neck and drags him about in celebration, more drink spilling. 'For a lefty, you're a tough wee bastard,' he whispers in Hughie's ear.

'I almost lost the plot.' Hughie sounds worried as he lifts the giant arm off.

'So what, it was self-defence.'

What did ah tell you?

Big Lex is more likely to listen now that Hughie has shown the fire they both shared in the bad old days when they took on the Yanks outside pubs at two in the morning.

'What evidence have you got, apart from you batterin innocent members of the public?' Lex asks.

'Well, mostly hearsay, to be honest, but a lot of it.'

'Who's sayin what?'

'Well, there's Don Cameron at number three and Jim in the wee shop—'

The booze is beginning to get to Lex, he interrupts Hughie by putting a hand over his pal's mouth. His expressions are more exaggerated and angular. Screwing up one eye he gives a robotic shake of the head, says, 'What? So, you've got a madman and some equally fucked-up old Korea veteran? Great! Crazy bastards united.'

'What do you mean fucked-up? Jim's sound.'

'Hughie,' Lex says as if disappointed.

'Jim's fine.'

'Came back from Korea in a straightjacket ...'

'Says who?'

'... after shooting a wee lassie in the head. Probably sits up all night playin Russian roulette since his missus died.' Lex gives him an intense doubting look.

'That's all crap; you know it.'

Lex looks right into his protesting face, says, 'Neither is exactly a reliable witness in front of a sheriff, now are they.'

Hughie gives a conceding shake of the head. 'Is that stuff about Korea actually true?'

Lex holds his hands out to each side. 'Christ knows, that's what the Town says.'

'And *that's* reliable evidence?'

'C'mon, Hughie man, just drop it, we're havin a laugh here. If you want, I'll lift the wee arse that tried to slap you, but that's it.'

'I'm serious Lex!'

'Seriously fuckin pissed.'

Their conversation has an edge to it now and both slow it down, take deep glugs from their pints – the noise in the pub surges and pulses over them. They look around at the drunken punters until Hughie breaks first. 'We're old pals, are we not?'

'Don't make this personal,' Lex says, staring at him.

'But they have been fuckin with my head.'

'Ignore it, that type gets bored.'

'I can't,' Hughie's voice rises, 'I convinced myself someone was on the roof the other night, things moved in the flat, then the shit on the door handle.'

Lex looks at him as if concerned for once, protective perhaps, but it is hard to say because of the drink. 'If you let it get to you, it'll make you ill. Let it go. If it gets worse, I'll look into it,' Lex tells him, giving a conciliatory nod.

'I'm not worried about me.'

'Well, that's alright then.' Lex is pretending to be distracted by girls that have come in on a hen night.

'I worry about the young boy.'

'Youngsters are tough.' Lex eyes the bride-to-be, sipping his pint.

'He's a child for fuck's sake!' Hughie says sharply.

Although still pretending to perv, the side of the big man's pitted face has lost some of its harshness. He swallows, beneath the iron plates something shifts.

'Lex—'

A hand is held up to silence Hughie again. 'You're sure the lad's involved in the runnin?' Lex asks, still staring at the tight satin arses.

'Vulnerable wee lad, possible learnin difficulty, carryin hash around your turf. Then some arsehole tryin to strangle me and scare me off.'

Lex turns, catches him with a short withering stare that frightens. 'This better not come back to bite me,' Lex says.

'You'll help?'

Putting the giant hand back on Hughie's shoulder, Lex speaks very deliberately into his pal's ear, trying not to slur too much in the process, 'If you find out where the drugs are stashed, and you can put Davy Drug or the other fanny in the same place, you call me, and I'll hang them out to dry and take the credit. Everyone happy?'

'You'll do that?'

Letting Hughie go, Lex says, 'You know me. And it's *we'll* do it.'

'Fill em up,' Hughie shouts up the bar at the panicking Rab.

'Anyway,' Lex says, 'that wee shite Davy was always a toerag. His mother kicked him out, got sent to a children's unit over the river ... like a shite into the sewer.'

'I just want him gone.'

'If he needs ma attention, he needs to be acting like a right twat. Is this Davy a right twat, Hugh?' Lex says, grinning, getting louder for some reason.

'A total and utter twat!' Hughie insists. 'I mean who calls themselves Davy Drug, but a wet twat?'

Standing erect and laughing, Lex gestures over Hughie's shoulder. 'Pity the *twat*'s standin right behind you.'

'Yeah right,' Hughie says, 'the wee twat's right behind me. Very good, you're funny Lex – not.' He staggers back and forward a bit, punching Lex's arm, before adding, 'Hope the tosser's had an overdose of his own gear.'

'That'd be justice, eh?' Lex shouts.

Both are laughing hard now.

'Yeah, hope he chokes to death,' Hughie adds.

'That's no very fuckin nice,' a voice tells Hughie from behind.

Spinning, he finds Davy Drug staring at him. 'Jimi Hendrix died on his own spew, you know that?' Davy tells him.

'Did you just make that up?' Hughie slurs.

This brings an explosion of laughter from Lex who is now slapping the bar in delight, while Davy's face flushes red. The dealer is forced to react and pushes at Hughie's shoulder with a stiff finger as the chatter in the place drops. The barman tries to cool things down by reaching over and catching Davy's arm, asking him what he wants to drink. Too late – Davy is fired-up, focused on Hughie and Lex who have humiliated him by laughing at him as all the pub listened in. With a palm this time, he shoves Hughie again, harder, back against his pal, making Lex spill some lager and stopping his laughter. A scuffle starts, in which Hughie tries to keep the two others apart, Lex pinging Davy's nose with a flick of the finger.

What are ye doin? Nut the cunt and let Lex stove his dome in.

Despite Hughie's efforts, the big cop gets Davy by the scruff, tightening his grip until the dealer's neck wears a deep ditch of pressure that cuts off the air.

'Float back to your sewer,' Lex tells the dealer before pushing him away.

Hugging his pal, Hughie attempts to make the whole thing a big joke. 'Jesus, cool it, Lex; the clown's humiliated enough ... leave it.'

This comment makes Davy Drug's red, pockmarked face go into purple mode, and those detached eyes widen as he comes back for more, catching Hughie between the drunk sheriff and the too-thick-to-back-down outlaw.

'Fuck!' Hughie shouts.

Lex gives the guy a hard two-fingered poke to the fore-head, just above one eye. With the pub watching, Davy's unable to back down even though he looks like he's about to greet.

'Is that it?' Lex says, laughing, delirious now.

This taunt provokes Davy into picking up the nearest weapon – Hughie's pint glass – and going for it. Lex sweeps Hughie aside and comes forward, fists ready. There is some hesitation from Davy, the glass in his hand visibly shaking.

This allows Rab and Davy's girl to take the pint off the drug dealer and put it on the bar, then pull him wriggling back through the crowd towards the pool table. Davy makes an effort to show he is still keen to take on the big cop but goes fairly easy in the end.

'You're dead, the pair o you!' Davy shouts.

'Good job your girlfriend saved you, drug-boy,' Lex shouts back, then leans easily against the bar.

Chairs clatter to the deck and drinks smash as Davy storms out the back of the pub, trailed by his girl.

Rab, who is drenched in sweat, fires up the jukebox volume to lift the mood as he shouts, 'Who's next.' Behind the bar again, he downs a vodka someone has left unat-tended. People soon go on with the night without much thought. Girls laugh and men boast and tell tall tales of the week's events on the building sites. At that point, Rab gives a round of free shots to the lads who have been waiting at the bar and then necks another himself to steady the old nerves.

'Fuck, that was hilarious,' Lex says, looking genuinely elated.

'You're worse than he is.'

'If he'd got any closer with a weapon, I'd have been

justified in layin him out there and then.'

'You were settin him up?' Hughie says, lifting his shaking pint to his mouth.

Lex grins down at him. 'You wanted him gone.'

After several more nerve calming gulps, Hughie gasps, says, 'Rather you didn't do it in public.'

'Ahhh, still the thinker I see. Have to admit, I got a bit carried away there.' Lex grows serious for an instant, staring down a few guys who are still looking over. 'That wee prick's in the book now.'

As his heartbeat slows, Hughie downs his remaining lager in one long gulp, which helps. Lex just stands over him staring at the moving crowd of insects like some relentless, sentinel-brute.

'Jesus, you're as mental as ever,' Hughie says.

Old fashioned jack-booter, brought in on the job just in time.

Hughie begins to feel his gut turn and the old dark worries creep in round the back as the music turns up further. Girls are now dancing on any open piece of floor. Rab, who has now lost the plot, is drinking like a fish; he puts two free drinks in front of them.

'Looks like doubles,' Hughie says, holding one up against the light.

'Down the hatch,' Lex shouts.

The place sparks, girls cackle, and a roar comes up from over at the pool table as another pint glass smashes.

'We'll go and find your bird after ah have a pish,' Lex slurs, before staggering off towards the bog, scattering dancing insects here and there.

The crowd moves back into place and Hughie feels something move inside his guts again. He shakes his head to clear it. I better do a piss too, maybe it's that.

Off his seat, his legs feel weird, like rubber at the knees. This sends him veering off against the wall by the main doors. Looking down at his legs, he tries to see what is happening to him – nothing makes sense. Hughie starts to blink, trying to get his mind back on solid ground, but when he looks along the bar, Rab's eyes are different, inhuman and black-crow remote. A shiver makes the hair on his neck stand up as he touches his face which feels like ... rubber. The laughter in the room seems to be aimed at Hughie now as it pulses along with a techno beat from the jukebox, the rapper grunts in and out of the jagged melody with animal malice as the witches writhe along with it.

What the Fuck!

The Knight is sinking into the floor of Hughie's brain, choking greyness oozing through the gaps in his armour, drowning him. Hughie holds his throat as if something is in it. I'm not well, think I'm going to be sick ... this isn't the drink. He turns away from the unbearable stare of the ogre barman towards the orgy of young drunks again, bodies flowing back and forth to confuse him and stop him going after Lex. He feels stranded, eyes, lots of them, staring.

'What's ... goin on?' he asks himself.

A face, fleeting at first, appears amongst gyrating tight leggings and short skirts; it is staring at him, but he can't focus before the mass of bodies crash together again as if commanded. Closing his eyes makes the swooning paranoia worse as the demonic pub sways, his stomach turning and aching like it is bleeding inside.

Shite! What the fuck wis that thing starin over frae the pool table?

The curtain of sweaty bodies opens again, and a girl in a short white top and glossy leggings comes out of the mass, towards him. As she approaches, he tenses. It is her glazed pool-ball eyes, they are crazy weird and surrounded by thick make-up that draws him deeper. Somehow, she can see right through his defences and into his panic-stricken soul. Her hair hangs down like a cloak as she leans to the side and comes in close. Hughie draws back against the wall, where he clings on like a spider about to be washed down a plug-hole. Do I recognise her? I'm scared – where's Lex? She touches his shoulder, making him jump, now leaning into his space until he can smell caustic perfume burning his nostrils – her whispering scratchy voice chants in his ear.

'What?' he says through the downward crush of the music.

'... told me ... tell you ... watch ... beasts ... you're for it,' she whispers, her East European accent fading in and out like an ancient broken mantra, each whisper otherworldly, drifting like an infection into his ear, then round and round his whirling head, infecting the blood in his skull. She ambles back through the crowd as if in slow motion, her hips rolling and those sheer leggings appearing to be the scaled skin of some reptilian cross-breed.

What's the bitch on about, and who's that she's with?

Sweat runs down his forehead as he stares after her. Can't see past all these young idiots dancing around like fucking witches. ***There, look!*** In amongst the writhing throng, something sits detached from everything else.

It's him.

The sight of the drug dealer is enough to send Hughie towards the toilets again, but instead, he staggers sideways against the bar, is helped back to where he started by laughing strangers. His heart is thumping, his guts convulsing and threatening to unload; he knows Davy Drug is watching his every stumbling move, sniggering. Around him, others are part of it, sneering as the beat punches at his head.

'Time you were away home,' Rab tells him as he lifts their glasses from the other side of the bar.

The Knight's face appears in his mind, eyes popping, a giant zigzagged snake crushing his wind pipe as he spits orders between choking. ***Got … to get out o this hole … get home Hughie … runnnn …***

As he staggers, the door to the street seems to recede out of reach, his guts swimming in circles with his thoughts as Rab and Desperado let loose loud mocking laughter. Those bastards are in on it; they all hate me, hate social work … oh, fuck … help me. Lex?

You cannae help him now – get out! GET OUT!

The Auld Hoose spits him onto the hard pavement like vomit. His right cheek cooled by the damp asphalt as he breathes in fresh air and relief. He's escaped.

It doesn't last, he notices that there is very little feeling in his legs and the nerves in his fingers feel like live electric wires dancing and jolting on the damp ground, the charge making his frame spasm. ***Been poisoned.*** This fear isn't going; it's getting worse. In his head, an image forms – hordes of people coming after him and kicking his skull until it pops out grey juice onto the kerb. After a few attempts, he manages to get to his feet and stumble along the shopfronts, holding onto the walls and windows in a stooped run before collapsing a hundred yards further on. He looks behind, but no one is following, yet. The High

Street is quiet, and all he can hear is the noise of the pub, vibrating with evil.

I need help. ***C'mon Hugh, move!***

Falling again, outside what used to be Woolworth's, he cries out, his palms slapping the stone slabs. Strange, no pain. The street lights have gone weird, green to blue, and something crawls up inside his throat. ***Get up ...*** He takes a few breaths then throws up. ***Chemical weapons, we've been poisoned. Keep goin soldier.*** On his feet again, he goes on, the night an endless tunnel stretching off into a foreign land. Two hundred yards on, he leans against a parked car that looks familiar, but nothing else is really familiar any more, it is all dark – like the Town has been swapped for a village from Purgatory. 'Everything's ... melting.' And something alive and slimy is crawling up my throat again. He holds his neck as it claws at the inside. 'Help ... wooaaaaghhh!' It liquefies as it spills out his mouth and across the tarmac.

A sound comes. He looks up above his head, perhaps recognising the local Lodge building. It seems taller than he remembers, dark, with strobing lights inside and a hurdy-gurdy band belting out incomprehensible jumbled accordion sounds that eat at his thoughts like a set of teeth – chew, chew, chew. Faces appear and disappear at the high window, seem to see his terror, enjoying it. He looks away. It's then that he susses out the car; it is wee Chas's Jag.

Shout for help!

He doesn't put his hand out to save himself as he falls, his head bouncing on the kerb and his body jamming between car tyre and pavement. He doesn't dare move until soft rain begins trickling down his face. This is soothing until frightening thoughts come back like a rupturing nest of spiders, twisting and intertwining until he scratches his face to get them out.

Pull, man, pull yourself up.

As he is dragging himself up the side of the car, the window drops down under his weight and puts him back into the wet gutter.

'Look at the state of that guy,' a young man's voice shouts from across the road.

Shout for help. 'Please,' he whispers.

Laughter drifts off along the street and echoes around the corner of Moir Street – gone.

Twice he tries to rise but can't.

His mum's voice comes to him. It goes away then comes again, edging into the pandemonium in his head, telling the child Hughie, 'Bloody determined you are, thrawn.' His drunk father comes to him too, the smell of whisky breath, Dad holding him in a tight headlock, demanding submission during one of those overzealous kid-on fights that went on when he'd come back from Mill's Bar, steamin. Mum starts shouting 'Let the child go, you're hurting him, William.' A small, red child's face, his own, looks back at Hughie, refusing to submit to the drunken bully, refusing.

Rain bouncing on the road brings him back to his adult nightmare, and he stretches out his hand again, fingers touching their way up Chas's car door until he gets a grip on the open window. Gritting his teeth, he pulls himself up onto his feet. Once up, he wobbles for a moment, then stands still. I'm going to piss myself, it's coming out.

That wee shite is up there at the Lodge, sucking up to his mates while you're here on the fuckin front line, spiked by a drug dealer. The Knight's voice is cut off then comes back in fits. ***They're***

*comin ... **Amygdalanians** ... **lupines, wolves** ... **they're**—*

His guts move south. In desperation, he unzips his fly, staggering first back then forward onto the car where he sprays pee into the open window of Chas's Jag before stumbling off up the road, cock in hand – sure something is now stalking him behind. One girl, with frizzy, badly permed hair and heavy make-up, looks up as Hughie slides along the steamed-up glass of the Chinese takeaway like some sexual drunk slug. She shakes her head then turns away to the TV on the wall as if this is a regular sight on Friday nights. ***Get inside, Hughie, they're about us.*** The Knight falls into blackness, coiled in tentacles of snakeskin, black fur and flashing teeth. ***Ru*—**

The street lights flicker, something is coming up behind, he knows it as he staggers on.

The lock on the close gate is old and prone to rattle in high winds – it springs inward and he stumbles into the lightless close, hands out in front like a blind man escaping a storm. The black walls feel like they are coated in grease as he bounces off them. His body is cold now, the light from the street cutting through his useless legs, turning his shadow into a menacing claw on the damp stone floor. He stops dead when the streetlight runs out, only driven on again when he feels sweat or piss running down from his crotch, his belly full of writhing worms. Stamping his right foot in front to prevent tripping over a thing he's yet to imagine, he makes it to the stairs. The light switch he holds between his dirty fingers, clicks back and forth – nothing. Blackness and near blackness writhe on the edge of his ability to see. After spitting out phlegm to clear his airway, he goes on, then instantly stops. Sure he's heard movement, he points his useless eyes to the right of the stairs, where his memory places the basement door. A shape, sculpted by his imagination and hyper-vigilant ears, seems to be creeping towards him.

Lupine ...

He is trembling again, breath catching, his face screws up as he tries to see. Nothing, it has stopped. No! It's on the move again. A low growl comes from the swirling dark as it comes one soft step closer.

'Hughieeeeeee,' it whispers.

He recoils, fists up in front, heart thumping in his chest wall, but his legs are stuck, and he can't make them move. Off in the distance, he swears he can hear the echoes of witches, screaming and cackling, cutting off any retreat. Must get into the flat. He senses it moving to block him – the air moves – his head shudders as a solid mass hits him above his right eye, sending him backwards away from the stairs and safety. Terrified, he staggers and changes course towards the dull light of the High Street, his legs still so fucking useless. Scraping footsteps follow behind, bestial claws dragging. Another hard blow strikes his head at the back, even harder than before – his face slaps the stone floor. Digging his nails into the cracks, he tries to crawl away from the thing. He looks up at it. God, help me.

Hughie's skull judders again, rattling his brain against the inside – the creature doesn't want him to see it. The universe fluxes, rotating round his meat-slab body – the black void opening wide as he willingly dives headlong in to get away from the lupine-snake-beast of the shadows. Fear – snarling – blackness – Manchester's screaming – the Eyes – wet concrete again – sharp, dripping teeth – footsteps – witches cackling – shrieking – blackness and then, thankfully, nothing ...

He jerks into consciousness and sits up, blind, holding a protective hand out in front. Can't see. Where am I? Dead? Feeling his aching head with a trembling hand, he explores something wet tied to it. His jittering fingers identify a cloth that covers his forehead and eyes; searching beneath, the right eye is tender and caked in dirt or, more likely, dried blood. When he removes the damp rag and throws it away, his head throbs and the right eye feels like it is about to expand until it pops inside his skull. Aya, aya, aya! Where am I, and who just spoke? Did I imagine the voice? Returning both hands to his sides to support himself he explores the material that lies beneath him. Feels familiar – a duvet? What is going on here? Tilting his head back, he catches a whiff of perfume which forces his eyes open, breaking the scaly blood that binds his eyelashes and allows blinks of sharp light that bounce through his fluttering lids to burn like hot metal on his retinas. Too sore. He closes them again. Someone is breathing near me. Don't freak out—

'You are a dark horse,' a woman says. 'Need to watch your intake though.'

This provokes a spasmodic involuntary move backwards away from the voice. He turns his head, blind, towards the source of the voice but doesn't speak. Need to know what this is. He forces his crispy eyelids open again for a half second before they shut instinctively to stop the pain. The voice is very familiar, but his mind is still reeling and nothing feels even close to normal or real – everything is a threat. He keeps blinking, forcing the fog away, until one eye manages to hold the light, the other screwed tight shut

and more swollen. A silhouette, a thin one, appears. **Witch!**
As his vision adapts he begins to see or imagine Karen, just
sat there at the bottom of his bed, worried face, smoking a
fag, one of his medieval history books held out in front of
her under the light, the rest of the room in deep shadows.
The shadows still crawl with things, unknown things that
frighten him, but her concerned white face draws him back
like a beacon. A lump comes to his throat and he gulps it
away. It's a wet dream or she's about to grow fangs. Nah, it
really is her, all ... dolled up, as if out for the night. Strange
dark angel, come to take my soul. He tries to get up as the
lamplight spins and he falls back onto the pillow. She
throws the book on the floor, the fag into a cup and rushes
towards him; bending over, she looks into his eyes. Her
shiny long hair hangs down, brushing his cheeks for an
instant as she pulls him up and sorts a pillow at his back.
She hands him a glass of water that has been sat by his bed.

'Drink,' her soft voice insists.

**Don't fuckin trust her, could be more poison
– Witch!**

Cigarette smoke and perfume, mixed with the cold
outside air, come oozing off her to lift the hair on the back of
his neck. She holds the glass to his mouth and he takes sips
of the water past dry, quivering lips, in blind obedience. Her
fingertips touch his lip for an electrifying instant as she
removes the glass, her calming eyes study his beleaguered
face as he squints back at her, lost. He blinks in a minute
tremble as she steps back. What is going on here? Is this
real? Is this death?

Touch it, make sure it's real. I'm not sure – think
it's an angel ... yeah, a fucking angel.

'We found you lyin on the street, face all bloody,' Karen

says. 'Louise said you'd be okay, she's a nurse, a drunk nurse.'

His one working eye narrows, but he doesn't speak to her.

'You were goin on about eyes and wolves,' she went on, 'screamed at one point, kept rubbing your knuckles.' Karen sits on the chair he hangs his clothes on and lights another fag. After blowing out a plume of thin smoke, she holds the fag to the side of her face. 'You don't mind me smokin, not after me rescuing you?'

He blinks the one eye in response. I'm safe, in my room, in my home.

Thanks to this fuckin ... thing? Goddess. Wonder if I'm still tripping from being spiked? Wonder what Davy spiked me with, perhaps ... ketamine and LSD. The sheets, they feel ... almost normal now ... go towards the light.

The familiars of his everyday life, that mountain of washing, the broken alarm clock and the piles of discarded magazines – they all feel somehow reassuring, perhaps signs of a resumption, or the beginning of the resumption of normality. His mouth though is a different matter, it feels prickly like someone has left a cockroach in it. In half-shadow he takes on a creepy look, tongue running around inside his cheeks searching for dead bugs whilst his one functioning eye watches her every move.

Karen grows fidgety under the scrutiny as the last Bacardi and coke from hours ago wears off.

'Didn't nick anything, promise. Eh ... that was a joke,' she says and gives an anxious giggle.

Not speaking, he stares back, attempting to open his other eye, his contorted face twitching.

A witch, playin with yer head, say nothin.

'Oh, my pal Louise took a pint of milk from the fridge when she left,' Karen tells him at a rapid rate. 'Got kids who always need breakfast, I'm told. Kids must be a bummer ... if you're hung-over.'

He senses he is freaking her out and stops searching inside his cheek with his tongue, tries to smile instead, but feels that is even freakier with a face coated in dried blood. ***Oh, fuck!*** Angry pulsing comes on again from the back of his skull where he was hit, making him close his eyes when the wave of pain comes over. This brings back that creature from the darkness of the hall.

'Imagine, kids – nothin worse with a hangover,' she says.

'You said that,' he says sharply.

'Sorry, I'm nervous. Is your head sore ... where you fell over?'

Putting his hands up, he tries to stop her incessant questions. As he does this, he lets go of the cover that is around him, then notices he is naked. 'What the fuck, I'm naked. How?'

Pulling the blankets around, he hides his bits.

'Surprised you're so bashful after me and the girls found you lying on the pavement steamin, with your ... thing hangin out your trousers.'

'Oh, no.' He shakes his head then stops because it hurts.

'Too many vodkas?'

'No, honest, I was spiked,' he insists.

'That what they call gettin drunk now, is it?' She laughs a bit.

'I wasn't ... someone put somethin in my drink, followed me ...'

'Good job we came along before the police then,' she says, wriggling her nose.

'Thanks,' he says, head down.

'Weird thing was that I'd asked the girls about you earlier.'

'Me?' he says, glancing up.

'Louise, the girl with the blue dress, she knew you at school.'

'Blue dress?' he says, looking puzzled.

'Said you were handsome if a bit quiet, moody; then we find you pished in the street with your ... cock hangin out.'

'I was attacked!' he insists.

'Thought you were spiked.'

'I went for a drink, I got spiked, then I got attacked.' He catches his voice getting loud, gives her an apologetic weak smile.

'God, I'm pretty borin compared to you and your drinkin, drug-takin and fightin.'

They both stop talking for a wee while as the drink and drugs seep away and the first shoots of self-consciousness fill the gap, the room edgy with silence.

'Who attacked you?' Karen blurts out, unable to stand it.

'I ...'

Say fuck all.

'... don't know!' His tone shows unintentional irritation.

Standing, she throws her coat over her arm, makes the zipping motion across her lips, steps over his clothes and walks towards the bedroom door.

'No, it's not you ... my heads banging,' he tells her.

'I'll drop the snib on my way out.'

'You look ... pretty,' he says, nodding to himself.

Where the fuck did that come from?

She pauses at the bedroom door, looks around his messy bedroom, then back over his bloodstained face as he pinches his nose again and makes loud sniffing sounds, trying to hold the blood back.

'You know how to make a girl feel special, Hughie.'

'Sorry ... I'm ...'

Her hands go up as she shrugs and turns to go. This brings him to his feet where he instantly trips on the duvet and staggers backwards onto the bed, an arm clattering on the bedside stand. She rushes back and lifts his feet off the floor onto the bed, her eyes flashing real concern as she hangs over him. With a soft hand, she turns his head to the side, narrowing her eyes as she looks at his swollen face.

'Maybe we should take you to hospital?' she says.

'No!'

She lets go of him. 'You'll have a big bruise, from where you fell.'

'I didn't fall, someone hit me in the hall.' He stops as if thinking of something. 'Did you see anything, anyone?' he asks.

'We just saw you ... with your thing out,' she tells him. 'When we all carried you in, the old woman next door came down, told us where you lived; your keys were in your pocket.' Looking at his ponderous face, she adds, 'Don't worry, we'd covered you up by then.'

He stares past her. 'It must have run out the basement door.'

'It? We never saw a soul, but the roof fire escape was wide open; her from next door closed it.'

As if more aware suddenly, he looks right at her, feels her skin without touching it, picks up on her breathing and her sweet rum breath, then smiles a wide thank you. Their eyes connect and hold.

'Why did you never return my call,' she asks.

He becomes perturbed, lost in the confusing universe again. 'What call?'

'I left a message; with your boss.'

All he can do is shake his head; this prompts her to go on. 'I felt so bloody embarrassed about the other night, you seeing me ... through the window with that idiot ... I ...' Her words drift off into more awkwardness.

'Chas said nothin,' Hughie insists. 'If I'd known ...'

She holds his gaze firmly now. 'I was drunk, you know that, don't you? When you saw me with that guy.'

He took her hand in his. 'I'm the one who should be embarrassed, must look like a right sad bastard. If I'd known ...' He blew out a deep sigh. 'Chas didn't tell me—'

One of her acrylic fingernails silences him, pushing on his upper lip.

'Maybe, I'll call you Monday,' she tells him, 'maybe dead on five and maybe you'll answer, and we could maybe get something to eat.'

He starts nodding like a puppet.

'Your number?' she asks.

'What?' He feels scattered again.

'Your phone number?'

'Eh ... 77 ... 4356.'

'You better pick up, Hughie. Last chance,' she says.

She gets up and walks into the hall without even a backwards glance, her heels neatly stepping over the debris of his life, the swish, swish sound of her tights whispering into his hypersensitive ears.

So feline.

Another spell!

He comes to his senses late, holds the covers around him and hops after her just as she pauses to undo the latch on the front door. His grunting makes her look back at him in his cheap stripy duvet, with his bloodied face. Bouncing a bit nearer, he stops when he is sure she is about to speak. She doesn't and goes out without a word, the door closing behind her.

Left standing like some orphan pupa, the spell of normality she'd spun soon evaporates and the shadows grow within the holes in the plaster, the old building creaking with faint songs of menace. Hopping to the door, he turns the locks and slides the bolt over, before shuffling back down the hall, as if being chased, into the bedroom.

On the bed, his hand touches the warm surface where she'd sat, his body coiling into a foetal ball around the spot.

We've been doped with chemical weapons and you're gonnae trust that pheromone-coated sorceress. Jezis Christ, man! Swiping his sword back and forth wildly, the Knight fights off another horde of hallucinations that seep from beneath the gaps in the skirting boards and crawl about the cold empty flat.

Outside, a dog might have barked, but it is an intangible sound, so faint and far away. The weight of tiredness pulls him down, the bed a giant magnet, his head soon burrowing deep under the covers.

Fuck that witch, let's concentrate on that weasel Davy. The gutless fucker spiked us with chemicals, attacked like a coward when we're out of it – would've bashed our brains in too, if he wisnae disturbed. That evil wee bastard's no playin by the rules, Hugh. Nah, fuck all this love shit – this is a war, a fight fer survival – we need to get the cunt and get him good. Are you listenin to me? Hughie ya dozy cunt! Hughie … Hughie … Hughie … Hughie!

TEN

SOUL SELLING

Instead of pushing her away, he lets her burrow her head in, lets her thin arms hug him so tight it is hard to believe something so small can be so strong. She sobs above the buzz of Manchester traffic and he feels wet tears run over the hand that cups her cheek, feels her fragile body tremble and cling harder still. When she looks up, he pulls back in fright. No, this is wrong. Her memory melts in his cupped hands, that sweet face thinning as he watches it morphing to a small, pallid, smackhead's face, her wide eyes terrified. 'You ran ...'

Hughie!

He jolts awake, still wrapped in his bloodstained duvet. Refusing to uncoil, he hides his head from the day beneath the covers. The Knight hasn't seen it this bad; the nightmares, the sweats and the sleepwalking are usual, but the poison has amplified it all. The Knight is sat by a dull fire in Hughie's mind, on the lookout after three long nights of creeping paranoia, the hangover from the spiking seeming endless. The Knight looks at his host with disdain and revulsion. Using a rough iron file, he sharpens a rusting sword in slow, deliberate strokes, metal on metal, back and forth, back and forth. When the squealing stops, he lifts the blade in front of his emaciated face, locks gaze with Hughie, then runs his tongue along its razor-sharp edge – black blood dribbling from parched white lips, down his bearded chin. Spitting into the fire summons flames that flash and light up the Knight's solemn stare as he starts to whisper.

Although they were being slain, they slew, And till the world's end, they will be honoured. Y Gododdin.

Hughie flaps the covers over his head to escape the shards of light from the curtains. But the Knight is always there in the dark recesses, silent, his probing stare able to unnerve, make Hughie feel self-conscious, useless, even bullied without a word being said. There is nowhere to hide, no way out since Manchester. Hughie yawns, having had no real sleep for days, then feels a shiver run through his body as the chilly morning gets inside the bedclothes, spider fingers of cold creeping up his back to the neck. The Knight's beady eyes are still watching. With a shake of the head, the old warrior pushes off the stiffness of a long night watch, then jumps to his feet and into Hughie's bedroom, slashing at the air with his bloodstained blade, making Hughie flinch into full consciousness – eyes open.

Howz it goin, Father?

Hughie just stares at the hallucination with numb, blank resignation.

The Knight points the rusty sword, an inch from Hughie's face now.

Someone said they didn't need the Order of Light. Move back to sunny Argyll and live the

easy life amongst the bonnie hills and purple fuckin heather. The Knight leans in on him. *That's what you told me, is it no?*

Hughie rolls away, refusing to answer.

Well, it hasn't fuckin worked out that way, huz it, Daddy?

'What else can I do? That cunt nearly killed me the other night.'

We need to transcend the rules, muzzle the mutt.

His mobile rings, and the Knight is gone.

Jumping up, he reaches for his discarded clothes and wrestles with his trouser pocket to free his mobile, then hesitates a moment before answering. 'Hello.'

'Where the fuck did you go on Friday?'

'Lex,' he says, relieved. 'Were you alright after the pub?'

There is a grunt somewhere down the line, then Lex replies, 'Just getting in the van. Where did you go to? I came out the bog and you were offski. That wee weasel Rab said you had staggered out.'

'I was attacked ... spiked!'

'Sure it wasn't just the booze? I was blootered too, hardly remember a thing.'

'Some bastard almost cracked my skull open,' Hughie shouts down the line.

'What ...' Lex's voice breaks up and there is another crackle of voices in the background. 'Need to go, buddy, got a shout – catch up soon.'

'Do we still have a deal, about Davy?'

'What?' Lex says, sounding distracted.

'Davy Drug, remember?'

'What?' More noises as Lex answers the radio, then, 'Need to go Hugh—'

'Lex ... fuck off!' Hughie stares at the silent phone, then lobs it onto the bed.

Now up, he walks naked through the flat to the front-room window and peers around the worn curtain. It's Monday already, and across the way, the student girl is up and dressed for James Watt College. She sits messing with her fringe, combing it one way then another.

Hughie rubs his head where it still hurts and opens the window to let some fresh air into the smelly room, careful not to flash anyone. The sky is dull, fog coming off the Clyde, seeping up onto the High Street in the eerie silence. Shivering, he kicks a pair of dirty socks across the floor and heads for the kitchen to make a cuppa.

You've hidden in here fer days, nae discipline, nae guile. There are wolves all over yer turf – hunt the bastards down, skewer their eyes.

As the Knight nags, he pours the boiling kettle into the encrusted sugar bowl to loosen off the last of the sugar snotters. Spinning the hot water until it makes an opaque liquid, he then throws in a teabag. After fishing out the teabag and throwing it into a sink full of dishes, he opens the fridge, catching a whiff of decay that contorts his face.

Jeziz, Daddy, this place is lookin worse than Maggie's hovel.

It is then he remembers that he'd used the half-pint and Louise, Karen's pal, who he's never even met, nicked the new bottle for her kids the other night when her and the others carried him up the stairs while inspecting his cock.

'Bollocks!' He throws the sugar bowl of black tea into the sink, causing a crash and the demise of at least two dinner plates.

Clever stuff, really clever fuckin stuff.

Putting his mouth under the tap he gulps at the water as if his life depends on it, lets the water run over his face. Back in the living room, without tea, he opens a cardboard box to start unpacking it and scans his books: Medieval Scotland, Prehistoric Europe, the Enlightenment. He shakes his head and closes the lid. I could have been teaching history right now, arguing about the influence of the Moors on southern Europe with my mates or having a go at the dozy art teachers for holding back on the tea room kitty money; instead, I'm dealing with a gang of psychotic social misfits who no one else gives a toss about. He knows the Knight is waiting for a break in his thinking to start on about the other night's humiliating disaster. Rubbing his aching ribs, he wishes he'd had the sense to wear armour before going to the pub. Inside, his nerves leap as he hears an screetching file being drawn over rusted steel. Eeeeeeeeecccchhhhh!

'Okay, but any crap and I'll retire you once and for all,' he tells the empty room.

Where would I retire? I don't exist, cept for in yer heid, ya fuckwit.

Hughie grins to himself. I'll dream up a Cretan old folks' home where burned out crusaders get dumped and left to rot. 'I'm trying to help the boy, I'm trying,' he says. The room sits quietly around him, only disturbed by the odd car on the street now. Breathing in and out in long, slow breaths, he accepts the day and waits for the inevitable.

Listen, I can see yer makin an effort after

all the hurly-burly you've been through, ah really can. The Knight's voice goes low as if someone might overhear. *But ye need to clarify some objectives, identify targets*—the voice then goes from that gentle scratchy whisper to a yell without warning *—Polish these fuckers off before they kill some cunt!*

He can't see the Knight yet but feels his breath near his shoulder. 'I heard you.'

Aye, and ignored me, done a runner, left that wee lassie to fend for herself. You cannae even say her name these days, can you?

'That's not fair,' Hughie says, the lines on his face deepening.

Fair, Fair? Jezis, tell that to the wee thing down south. The Knight waves Hughie's naivety away with an iron gauntlet. *She's probably dead anyways.* You don't know that! You don't. *See what ah mean? Yer livin in a fantasy, pal.*

Pulling the throw from the back of the chair, he wraps it around himself, huddles in the armchair and cringes at the blurred memories of Karen and the bad trip. Hughie flinches as a wet whisper finds its way to his ear.

Point one: you've had a few days of feelin aw sorry for yerself; poor wee Hughieeee, aw didums. The Knight coughs, his chest rattling like a dying man.

Hughie shakes his head. That LSD and ketamine, or whatever the fuck it was, seems to have worn off – we're fine, are we?

Point two: focus on the drug dealin cunt who

tried to do you over, regain a grip on the board. Need to follow through this time – get the cunt.

No firm evidence that it was Davy who spiked us ... assumptions.

You're meant to get less naïve as ye age, Hughie, no more.

The wind billows the curtain with salty air and Hughie turns towards it, feeling the morning breeze on his unshaved face, his remote gaze taking him out of the window towards the clearing morning sky. Memories of him and his childhood pals playing in rowing boats rise to the surface – tight lines with mackerel on the end and the hush of the boat hitting the pebbled shore.

Aww, the wee boys playin at boats – that's all gone and you're a dead man if you don't wake up to what's goin down here.

Running a finger over his furry teeth, he loosens the debris, then washes it away with his tongue. Jesus, I feel rough.

What d'ye expect? This is no some romantic battle, this is warfare, twenty-first century style. Tell ye, you were almost murdered the other night, assaulted by chemicals beforehand. Chemical weapons! Fuck me, that's the sort o stuff that old Saddam lost his life for just threatenin to use, and he didnae actually have the fuckin stuff. Nah, we need to retaliate – hard.

The Knight steps out of Hughie's peripheral vison and into the room, clanking helmet in one hand and heavy dragging sword in the other, leaving footprints of bile on the floor as he walks. The Knight's eyes bulge in a skeletal face as he dons the helmet and points a rusted gauntlet finger at

Hughie. *D'ye think our heroes were messin about in the battle for Jerusalem in 1099? It might look alright on the written page, but it would huv been dirty – guts unravellin on the floor, grown men crying for their mummies – psycho stuff.* The Knight stops at this point, catching Hughie cold with a stare. *See this wee cunt Davy? He gets it; he's no fuckin about with daft rules, that boy.* The Knight is grinning at his sword now. *The good thing is*—he says slowly, looking back at his creator—*you kicked his blubbery sidekick Scatter-cash's skull in easy, put the dog down.* Raising his arms in victory, the Knight starts a wee circular dance, his armour clanging as bile starts spraying from the metal like black tears. When the dance stops, their eyes meet.

Now there will be nae runnin away this time when it gets rough – nae ditherin with yer morals like Manchester – agreed?

'I … I was hospitalised for fuck's sake, almost happened again the other night,' Hughie says in a pleading voice.

So, that's it? We're gonnae just run out on those we're sworn to protect – again. The Knight growls deep inside, walks away and kicks a whisky bottle across the room. *Yer like some weaslin fuckin deserter, Father, honest.*

Hughie hugs his knees tighter, looking guilty. 'Okay, I'm insane, but I won't give up.' He rests his chin on his knees and settles down to wait for his psychotic attaché's response. The Knight leans in, breath smelling of fish guts and whisky. *What did we get wrong down south, Father?*

Hughie keeps quiet.

We tried to take down the enemy all alone.

Giving a grudging nod, Hughie listens, still unable to look at him.

Let's use this Lex cunt and Jim, find the dealer's weakness and exploit it – bring the shitty wee cunt down, today.

Hughie looks surprised at the timescale, but the Knight ignores him, his sinewy spine bending ninety degrees until he resembles a contorted gargoyle. He comes close in again, his toothy grin sitting inches from Hughie's face. ***I know there were some unfortunate circumstances with the Eyes, but in the end, we failed the prozzy badly – poor wee cow. But we can turn the tables this time, eh?***

Hughie closes both eyes, tight shut, nodding.

It's time for fightin, not romancin. Who knows what yon Karen's motives are? Her timing was either very fortuitous the other night, or very, very fuckin suspicious.

She saved us.

And the line-up o Yanks, they say she's been through, it isn't exactly a good sellin point fer a wife, is it? Anyways, let's no fall out over a dirty wee … nice young lady when we have business to attend to. Right. Up!

On his feet, Hughie walks to the phone, still naked, dials the absence line and gets put through to an answering machine.

'Hughie Mac, social worker here, going to be off for a few days, it's my piles, they're bleedin pretty bad.' He smiles to himself. No one ever questions the old Duke of

Argyll's excuse, far too embarrassing for most line managers to handle.

The Knight is whispering rhymes again.

And our brave Champion onward goes, to meet in Town the Norseman's foes. Bjorn Cripplehand 1098.

ELEVEN
BETWEEN THE LINES

The poor, the police, the DWP, and social workers are caught up in an endless adaptive war of attrition within the petri dish. Those looking down on this don't have the functioning empathy system needed to recognise the things they see, especially societal bacteria like Davy Drug. Davy was damaged during development, by a system he doesn't know exists. But he learned to act defensively, instinctively, and will use wee Tommy, his younger self, as a human shield to prevent his own demise. Not once would he consider looking through the lens and up the barrel of the microscope; as blind as those who peer down it.

MAY HAS BROUGHT bursts of real sunshine at last, and Hughie sits sweating in the car on Bute Street, wishing he'd parked further down the street in the shade of that sycamore tree. He's here because he is going to end this. He also knows that Davy, like the rest of us, follows a set of rotating habits and behaviours he's not really aware of.

Homo sapiens (wise man) is perhaps an ironic label, because it suggests choice on the treadmill of sourcing stuff, eating stuff, crapping out stuff, venturing out into the environment to get stuff, trading stuff or doing stuff for others that will result in us getting a bit of their stuff; all to breed our own small copies. This biology we share with goats and ducks and spiders makes even the slyest of drug dealers easy to hunt down. Jim, the shopkeeper, has aided the mission thanks to his sponge-like memory, absorbing the gossip and routines, replying with nothing more than a sharp joke or edgy grin as he files the intelligence away. He's also seen as dodgy, all that stuff about shooting wee girls in the head has made people presume he is unlikely to assist authority. It has cost Hughie four pounds and fifty pence for a roll and a can of orangeade that he didn't want, to extract a starting point.

But after an hour and fifteen minutes of waiting and watching the lane entrance, Hughie is getting pissed off. Beginning to doubt his field skills, he closes his eyes tight and takes some long, easy breaths, daydreaming about Karen in a pencil skirt while the Knight hides in the back seat looking annoyed. His mobile rings again; it's the office.

You're no answering that – you're sick.

As Hughie silences the phone, Davy Drug comes down the lane and catches him unaware. Shite! **Don't move, that'll attract his attention.** Pushing back in the seat, he slides his legs down into the footwell and tucks his head down. There is nothing to do but lie low in silence now, hope the drug dealer doesn't knock on the window and grin in. Davy seems half asleep, despite it being so close to midday, ambling off unaware. A bit down the road, he comes alive, scanning ahead, his vigilance switching to high, a familiar sly smirk coming to his face.

After giving his heart a minute or two to slow down, Hughie gets out of the car and follows the dealer down towards town.

Davy stops at the first corner. After lighting a fag, he's off again, his Neanderthal swagger unable to hide the flashing eyes and hunched shoulders of low self-esteem. Hughie gives him time to move ahead. Jesus, Davy, don't think you've got what it takes to pull in a big deal and retire to Mallorca with the real psychos.

Reckon the chances o that happenin to this dope are about the same as the local authority terraformin fuckin Mars.

He follows his target over the crest of Victoria Road, jouking along, gate to gate, letting Davy pull ahead as they head towards the West Bay.

The breeze coming from the Bay is a relief to Hughie's sweaty armpits; the cool air taking the edge off a muggy afternoon of patchy sunshine.

The dealer stops dead without warning, lights up another fag.

A pale old woman with pink tinged hair and crazy red lips, who is pruning her hedge, stares as the gawky social worker steps in by the gateway of her big old-money Victorian house.

'Can I help you?' the old woman asks. Her loud tone telling him she is used to prompting answers from the hoi polloi; he freezes, gives a disrespectful grin as her powdered face takes on the look of an angry meringue. A look ahead sees Davy Drug still fighting to get his fag to light in the breeze. ***Can't leave yet!***

'Well, what are you after?' she demands.

'Eh ...' How can I explain myself? – Too hard. Another look up the road and the dealer is off again. Waving weakly at the meringue, for what reason he isn't sure, Hughie moves on up the road before she thinks to phone the police.

The Bay takes over on his left side, its long curving lines of pebbles and seaweed run away in bands towards the Victorian pier in the distance. This view seems at odds with Hughie's dark mission as it sits serene and beautiful under the sun and rolling cloud, only disturbed by the imperceptible movement of two tiny matchstick silhouettes – a solitary walker and a four-legged control beast that pulls the owner down to the hushing tide.

Watch, this prick's antenna is workin overtime.

The Knight continues to give this kind of expert advice as they creep out of town and along the Bay on Bullwood Road, keeping Davy just inside the crosshairs while observing from behind a line of trees. Off to the south, the sunshine breaks through cloud at the mouth of the Clyde, shafts of light dancing on the distant Irish Sea, lighting up the orphan speck that is rocky Ailsa Craig. Above the hunt, the ever-present gulls wheel around in lazy arcs, their strained warning cries distracting Hughie who looks ahead just in time to throw himself onto a bench and look casual as Davy stops, yet again.

Troubled by something, Davy stands by the railings, looking out onto the Clyde, oblivious to the beauty in the play of light or rolling waves, perhaps moving something troubling over and over in his head.

Perhaps the clown owes the big boys a few

score for unsold weed. Maybe his Polish girlfriend has wised up or saved enough dosh to bail on him. *That bitch, nah she likes the drug money too much.* We know nothing about her. *Drug dealer's hoor, what's to know?*

Davy came out of his trance, frowning up at the noisy gulls that mock him as he takes a long last draw on his fag, his face that of someone about to face something better avoided.

Hughie looks away, knowing people somehow sense when they are being watched for any length of time. When he dares to glance up, Davy is swaggering across the shore road and straight through the gates of a run-down hotel called the Tor-an-lee. Gone.

Go, go, go!

When Hughie reaches the stone gateposts of the hotel, his heart is pounding. He flashes his head around the post and catches sight of the dealer's back only ten paces away. Davy looks as if he is counting money. Hughie pulls back. This is fucking nuts. *Get a grip soft-lad, he's a weaklin druggie, we can do him over if needs be.*

Standing there, he feels both afraid and foolish as he hides from a small-time hash dealer on a bright weekday afternoon. This is crazy, go home, watch the telly, go for a pint. *This cunt drugged and beat yer heid in, burned Tommy's neck – he's for the off.*

Across the road, the tide is crashing up the stony beach, the deep groan of moving rocks under the retreating surf suffocating any noise Davy might make coming back towards him. A small car goes past, heading towards Dunel-lan, the drone of its engine cutting through the sound of the shore as the driver slows to have a look at the strange suit stranded by the wall.

Hugh, wake up – we need to go for it.

Pushing himself, he steals a look around the post again, catching Davy disappearing up a steep drive, the heavily wooded grounds wrapping around him and hiding what he's up to. Breathing calmer, Hughie thinks about the hotel and what Davy could want here. Back in the mid-eighties, the Tor-an-lee was a Yankee hang-out, good for live music and drunk women. It has been shut for years, maybe twenty – maybe a good place to hide a stash. For some reason, he remembers some of Uncle Malky's stories about the place hitting the skids when the Yanks left and the owner, a thin English guy called Marty Wilkinson, took to the bottle. It happened so quick, one minute his hotel was packed with desperate-to-spend-money Yankee sailors, and he was gold-plated, a big BMW in the driveway. Next minute, the Soviet Union collapses, the Yanks dump the Town on its back like an old hoor and go home – he's left with a big, damp empty house that's sucking the life out of his bank account. There was no way Marty boy could've seen glas-nost, Gorbachev, the whole totalitarian implosion, coming, no way.

Ho! Cunt features, yer avoidin what's goin down here – move!

I'm not sure ...

Another car and pensioner driver with a wiggly finger wave forces him to push himself away from the wall and through the wide gateway into the rambling grounds of the hotel. Towering beech trees, heavy with lime-green new leaves, hide the hotel from view as he creeps up the rutted drive trying to avoid any noise that might give him away. The steep brae has muddy car tracks on it that look new. He jumps to the firmer earth between these ruts, where long silencing grass hides the sound of his approach. Looking back from near the top of the hill, he sees the Clyde stretching both ways, most of the drive he's walked up is now lost in the trees. Tall and decrepit, the Victorian hotel, with its reflective windows, shows itself on the last twist of the brae, slowing his steps. Its boarded-up front door is a gag in the mouth of a dying giant. There is no sign of Davy, but a small quiver rises and falls in his legs.

Reach deep into yourself, do one thing right, before he hurts any more weans.

Hughie tiptoes right up to the building, all the way fighting the notion to run back down the hill and off towards town.

Chemical warfare, battered skulls and wee boys with fag burns on their necks.

Drawn to the big, dirty, dining-room window, he wipes the glass and peers in on a modern-day *Mary Celeste*, with mouldy tabletops, beer mats still in place; torn, yellow, upholstered seats lead to a dusty powder-white wooden bar with bottled gantry behind it. He notices that all the bottles are empty. Nice one, Marty boy, leave the debt collectors fuck all. Jezis, this is eerie; wonder who owns the place now?

What's that?

He spins on his heels, making the gravel crunch. ***Shhh-hhhhh.*** The sound of a door closing comes from the right-hand side of the big hotel. Hughie freezes for a moment, then moves to the left, along the front of the hotel to the other gable and hides around the corner. Adrenaline drives him into a pile of twenty-year-old beer barrels conspiring to give away his position; he catches one as it falls, but as he puts it down, it hits another and gives a dull clang. **_Shhhh, fer fuck's sake!_** Chest thumping inside his shirt, he fights his way onto a crumbling, wooden-decked beer garden that was built during the eighties' boom years. The gable of the towering hotel, with its curtainless, sky-kissed windows, glower down in its sadness as he creeps over the sagging boards. Ghosts of the past point to a sign, framed in rusting American chrome bumpers, that stands above the padlocked side door.

Come in, shoot Pool, eat a slice of Pizza and drink our chilled beers.

He is too anxious to cringe at the way people used to suck up to the Yankee dollar. **_Another distractin phantom; move on soldier._** Two steps on, his foot goes right through a rotten board, his leg disappearing and his knee smashing onto the firmer underlying joist. 'Aaaoww!' His arms flail and he clenches his teeth to stop himself screaming again as more of the deck gives way, the loud crash bouncing over the watching stone walls, giving warning that a clumsy fool is abroad in the world. Lying still, he listens for footfall and his imminent capture by Davy Drug. After a long scan, his ears pick up nothing but the dull hiss of the Clyde flowing past below. What am I doing? Where's all this going?

Get up ya twat; let's do the cunt.

He gets up slow, while expecting a drug dealer's voice from behind asking him, 'What the fuck are you doin here?' Thankfully, it never comes, allowing him to crawl off the fragile, mossy deck like a faltering child.

He creeps to the edge of the back end, knee bleeding inside his trousers, his fists trembling and cold sweat running inside his shirt. Peeping around the rear of the hotel, he scans an empty gravel car park that is overshadowed by mature beech trees and the back of the lurching hotel. Opposite, a series of stone coal bunkers lean against the steep bank that climbs up the hillside into birch wood. Stone steps run up behind the bunkers to the second-floor cottage that was once damp staff accommodation. The past comes to him again, stilling his shaky legs as it reminds him of a greasy haired barmaid he once kissed out here.

You need to cut out all this dissociative rosy memory crap.

But I'm shitting myself. Maybe I should go.

Voices!

It is hard to tell where the voices are coming from; he guesses it's Davy on the phone to someone, maybe his girl.

Get closer.

With slow deliberate steps, he leaves the cover of the gable and moves across the car park, the gravel quickly grassing him up. Halfway across, he spots a large, shiny, red Mercedes parked with its boot open, cardboard boxes inside. He looks up at the netted cottage window, unable to know if he is being watched. Sound comes from the steps at the side of the cottage. Abandoning stealth, he runs and hides by an open coal bunker. I'm trapped.

Some cunt …

A loud, muffled city voice shouts orders from the stairs. Stepping into the coal bunker and pulling the door over until its rusting hinges begin to groan, Hughie is caught between a potential trap and running into a scarier situation outside. He lets go of the door and stands still. This is all wrong; what do I—***Sshhhhhhhh.***

Multiple sets of footsteps come down the steps.

'Just do what he says; he'll soon fuck off,' Davy Drug whispers to someone outside the bunker door.

Two pairs of feet rush away. Hughie coils, ready to run for it, then stops dead as he hears movement right above his head – perhaps at the cottage window. Someone else is here, someone very heavy? I am trapped. **Shhhh.**

Dust falls on his head from the boards above, making him hold his breath. Davy and his accomplice return, shuffling in awkward unison across the weeds and gravel then back up to the top of the steps. He hears footsteps shuffle on boards as his trembling hand touches the damp walls. He tries to breathe the musty air again without making any sound. A small tremble starts in his leg and he feels the blood in his feet go cold.

Don't you dare go into one of yer turns, d'ye hear me, Hughie?

Something is placed on the boards above, displacing more fine dust that nips Hughie's eyes.

'Nice arse,' a loud Glaswegian shouts, up above. There is a slap and then a girl yelps.

Three pairs of feet now rattle across above and come down the stone staircase until they are at the bottom, just outside the coal bunker. He senses unwillingness in the dragging of some of the footsteps.

'Naebody seen you comin here, did they?' the big-mouthed Glaswegian asks.

'It's cool, Degzy man, honest,' Davy says, his voice higher than usual, almost whining.

'Right, let's get the rest o the gear,' Degzy orders.

They go off across the gravel.

Run …

Hughie can't move, shaking now. By the time he unfreezes, the Mercedes boot has thumped shut and the scuffing feet are coming back – he is trapped in the darkness. The dealers are struggling to work in unison as they carry something heavy; a casual, scuffing, supervising pair of feet follows behind. Hughie pictures the boss dealer, Degzy, goat-eyed. But who's the other one? Davy's bird?

The weight they carry drops on the steps.

'Careful!' Degzy shouts, his voice coming through the thin rotting door to touch Hughie's face.

'Sorry,' Davy answers.

'Right, there's eight Blu-ray DVD players up there, an three hunner pouches of backy. In this yin, there's fifteen laptops, ten blocks o resin that'll have tae be divided up intae ounces. Give these two ounces of H tae Scatter-cash and tell the idiot no tae cut it, coz it's aw ready been roon the block a few times.' Degzy speaks to Davy like a supermarket manager would to a new store-boy. 'She can help you, can't ye doll,' he adds.

'I will help, but not with heroin,' a foreign female voice answers, her words trailing off.

'Is she fuckin at it?' Degzy shouts.

'Okay, she'll do it; just havin you on,' Davy explains. 'Won't you babe?'

It's Davy's bird, that Polish witch frae the other night.

'I ... help,' she tells them, her voice still reluctant.

'Any whizz?' Davy asks, trying to move it on.

'You better no cause me any bother, doll.' There is an edge to Degzy's voice, a deep menace.

'She's solid, Degz,' Davy says, his voice getting jokey to de-escalate. 'You've got us workin like slaves, eh, ya lazy bugger.'

A hard slap rings out, Davy pleading, 'Don't hurt us, big man!'

Davy's girlfriend shouting, 'Please, please!'

Another slap rings into the bunker and the girl now yelps – seems to fall to the floor – more movement then puffing.

'This is no a fuckin joke,' Degzy screams. 'If ye fuck up, I'm the wan whose outta pocket or worse. Are you two fuckin idiots gettin this?'

The older man is raging at his staff, his familiar, intimidating aura seeping under the door and transforming Hughie into a small trembling thing in that instant. Hughie starts breathing shallow to avoid detection.

Don't freak on me, man, the Knight whispers.

'Course we are, Degzy,' Davy says. 'Dead sorry, big man.'

The girl is sobbing; Davy asks her if she is okay, perhaps helps her up.

'Right, hide this stuff up the stairs,' Degzy orders as if nothing has gone on; his voice quieter now, blunt, like a dull mash hammer.

'I'll put it in there, save us humphin it up the stairs, eh?' Davy suggests, trying to sound enthusiastic.

'Where?'

'The ... bunker ...' Davy says, hesitant.

Panic sets in as Hughie steps back from the door. The damp, filthy bunker absorbing him. A half-empty oil can by his feet threatens to scream out if he moves any further. The Knight, who is shaking too, puts a finger to his lips as his master's heart pounds off the scale, sweat bleeding down from his hairline onto his cheeks. Oh God, this is like before – damp, dark, I'm fucked, I'm fucked, I'm fucked. I smell it, that stink of petrol on the rag.

Oh for fuck's sake, not now, the Knight begs in a scratchy, low whine. ***Please, Father.***

Hughie feels his way along the slimy stone wall, stepping over the oil can in slow motion, backing himself into the dark.

Make yourself insignificant, ready to rush the cunts. It's back, isn't it? **Naw, don't be daft ... but you'll have to fight.** I can't ... I just can't. **Don't do this to me again ...**

Water seeps through the material of his trousers as his knees meet the bunker floor – jammed low in a corner, he begins to shake uncontrollably, imagining footsteps coming towards the door, the Eyes staring into his shaking psyche, mocking his patheticness, his cowardice.

It's pulling me back!

Jesus, Hugh ... No!

Can't stop it.

He trembles as the black bunker spins him out of reality into his past. Silence, blurred lights, distant cars on the M6 heading into Manchester, then more flashes and that low growling.

MOUTH'S STUFFED with a petrol-soaked rag, his punch-swollen face full of panic. Blurring, then he's sat staring at the thing in front of him, duct tape around the forearms and shins holding him to the rusted metal chair. Its dog snarls and barks – Hughie flinches – the crazy pimp with the eyes feeding on his reaction. Try to think; can't. Look at those eyes, they must have been raped, brutalized throughout child to have that goat-eyed ability to show no feeling, yet stare right inside you, into your organs.

There's a stink, perhaps stagnant water, perhaps his

guts or perhaps the Doberman had taken another shit. Panic. Hold it in, hold it in, don't scream.

The Eyes comes closer, Hughie's freaking, the cloth rag that silenced him is uncoiling down his throat, blocking off most of the oxygen, the petrol on it sending spasms through his throat that start to make his body convulse, pulling the rag in deeper until vomit cuts off the last sniff of air and hope. The metal chair is rattling now; the fight for life has begun – the dog's going ballistic – nearly feeding time. Too busy dying to feel the thud when his head hits wet concrete. A hand, almost gentle, sweeping the hair from his face. The Eyes wants to see his terror, to see that last desperate moment of panic before death. No, please ... it's over. Why? Because the ego led me here. Please, please, I don't want to go ...

The vomit's escaping, then choking coughs, then the precious air rushes in just before the dark can take him. The dog's teeth stop flashing, the Eyes controlling the thing, for now, dragging it away on the chain. Sounds, sounds of normal human activity and droning cars creep in from the motorway and hold the far distance, but they might as well have been a million miles away, in another universe, another dimension. He's not finished with me. The mutt starts again; a boot hits Hughie's head and his eyes roll into his skull.

'Shut up!' the Eyes tells the dog and the dog calms to a deep, frightened, whimpering growl.

Hughie is away from it all, in blackness at last.

He wakes. Rain? No, not warm rain ... urine. Hughie spits and coughs it back out as it douses him. In one movement, the pimp lifts his limp bound body by the hair and puts the chair upright again. Still tied, still terrified.

'Hello, you.' The Eyes is right there, an inch away, the words almost jovial, breath stinking.

'Please ...' is all Hughie gets out.

Knuckles folding like putty as three hard measured blows hit his right hand, the bones making a cracking sound. As the club hammer withdraws, the dam breaks.

'Aaaaaaaagggghhhhhhhhhhaaaaaaaaaaaaaaaaaaaaaaaa!'

His face contorts, and he pleads with his mind. Pass out – go to sleep until it ends – can't – MUST – CAN'T.

Hughie's head is hanging, his chest doused in vomit, his body shaking involuntarily within his bonds, guttural groans coming in waves with the pain.

'Now, don't you say a fuckin word unless I say so,' the Eyes whispers in his ear.

Head is tugged backwards, the cold hammer placed delicately on his sweating forehead. Hughie waits for it, the crying coming without control. He's going to stove my dome in, feed me to the dog then bury me out here in the scrub ... but I don't want to die, not here.

'Why did you fuck her?' the Eyes says as they put weight on the hammer.

Hughie can only puff and wince.

'Why?' the Eyes shouts.

'I ... I ... didn't.'

This sends the freaky-eyed pimp into an instant rage. Hughie opens his eyes, the hammer passing his head to hit his other hand, flattening skin and bone into the chair's hand rest. It, the Eyes, casually moving away, anger vented, leaving Hughie straining the bonds in wide mouthed, silent agony.

'She told me!' it shouts from somewhere behind.

Spitting out more acid, Hughie tries to speak, starts sobbing.

'Speak!' it screams.

'I didn't, I didn't.'

Woozy, head flopping about, Hughie goes down the tunnel to unconsciousness, anything to get away – like impala when the lion's got it by the throat – switch off your mind – go to sleep before you see your own organs.

The Eyes is back, slapping his face about. 'Talk,' it says, lifting a foot and resting it on one of his hands. 'Talk,' it says again as it twists the foot.

More gaping mouth agony, single begging screams. Black then light. Hughie's eyes rolling in and out of it all.

'What did you do?'

'She ...' Hughie chokes. Spits out something. 'She ... was ... was scared ... I held her—'

'You fucked her!'

'I held her, right? I kissed her head cos she was crying; she was scared to death ... th ... that was it. Please ...' He tries to hold it back, but the sobbing starts again.

The Eyes lifts the hammer off his forehead, crack him sideways on the cheekbone with the cold iron.

'Aaaagghhhh ... okay ... I started to ... care about her ... kissed her lips ... once.' Hughie can't look at the monster, tries to pull away from the hammer as it's placed on his skull again. 'That's the truth,' he whispers between sobs.

The hammer goes away, and the Eyes shakes its head in an exaggerated back and forth motion. 'What? All this, for a fucking kiss?' The bastard's laughing, almost hysterically now. 'You middle-class arseholes get involved with other folk's business; fuck with things you know nuthin about ... then can't handle the consequences.' It's back, leaning in as Hughie turns his head away from words spraying saliva in his face. 'Still, bet you're regretting it now, you Scottish arsehole.'

Rubbing its bald head, the Eyes seems to be coming to a decision as it paces through the shafts of light from the small slit window of the abandoned substation. 'You need to learn about reality,' it says holding the hammer up.

The big bastard has gone behind Hughie who tries to turn his head. Can't see it. It will smash my skull in, let my brain come out as I stare at the ceiling. Trying to stop the sobs, Hughie listens. What is that? A scraping sound beginning, becoming a whisper. Is it the Eyes talking, perhaps to its dog? The words unintelligible. Silence. Hughie braces himself for it. Jolting back. Savage barking and snapping ringing around the wet concrete walls from behind. A dull thud brings it to an end. Just a high-pitched whining now. Another thud and it's done.

The Eyes is still behind him and the whole world is filtering through Hughie's ears, preparing him for that moment when his skull disintegrates.

'Look what I can do,' it suddenly whispers in his right ear, making him pull away, 'to the things I love.'

The big bald-headed bastard comes into view, floating in the macabre nightmare, dripping hands still grasping the wet hammer, those eyes holding no pain or sorrow or regret. 'You fall in love with a fucking whore, fill her head full of ideas about recovery and jobs and houses and a life with babies. Surprise, surprise, the whore runs away, and I'm down two fucking grand a week.' It grasps Hughie's mouth and cheeks in a crushing grip, contorting his face as it moves right in close, eyeball to eyeball. 'I'm gonna let you live.' Looking for a response from Hughie, but he's barely conscious, can only groan.

'You're going to say nuthin – got it? If you fuck with me again, she gets what the dog got.'

Hughie nods best he can, eyes rolling to white for a moment.

'Understand, Jocko?'

Hughie blinks in agreement, as a sneer runs across its face, the sweat on that red bald head, dripping now. 'She gave you up right away, do you know that,' it tells him. 'Even told me where to find you.' A short snorting laugh.

Hughie's face crumples at this, his eyes shut, tears running.

Without another word, the thing lets go of his face, straightens up. Hughie's too far gone to react when it takes a knife from its pocket, cuts the tape around one forearm and gives the chair a light shove. Hughie's head cracks on the concrete, his eyes roll open and he looks past his own feet at a pile of fur, teeth and blood. The thing called the Eyes is shouting, 'Be seeing you, Jocko.' Blurry bits, stink, then it's ambling across the wet floor and off out into fuzzy bright daylight. A dead set of snarling teeth. Dog blood, man blood, mixing. He'll kill her, he will.

Something black, quivering and crawling inside now.

HUGHIE, **wake up, man.**

'Where—'

Shhhhh … don't speak. The Knight is whispering close in, sounding scared. **You're back in Argyll, been out for almost a minute – took a complete nervy.** Am I okay? **No, they're here too, out there**. The Knight is pointing a shaking gauntlet at the bunker door.

Outside, another scuffle breaks out between Degzy and Davy – shouting, Davy Drug crying out.

'Please don't hurt him,' the girl screams.

'He's a fuckin idiot!' Degzy shouts back.

Fingers scrabbling about in the dirt, Hughie grasps a rusted iron pipe and begins lifting himself on unsteady legs until he is upright and ready to fight yet again. His vision is blurry, eyes blinking in silence. ***That's it, soldier – let's kill the bastards!*** Hughie almost breaks his teeth as he grits them, ready to swing the pipe. I'll do it. ***Go for the skull – big cunt first***. As he grips the iron, his scarred knuckles begin glowing white.

'It's fuckin soakin in there, ya prick,' Degzy tells Davy on the other side of the thin door.

'Sorry, big man; I didn't think.'

'Jesus, are you two fuckin havin me on, the day?' Degzy asks. 'Get the gear up the stairs. Now!'

Stumbling double footfall goes up the steps to the cottage, followed by two heavier feet.

Move soldier!

Hughie creeps to the door as weight goes on the boards above his head; pipe in hand, he pushes the door open with his foot, making it creak. No one visible. The pipe clatters to the floor and he takes off along the wall, close in to avoid being seen from the window. Past the outbuildings, he thinks of going back the way he came in, then decides he'll be spotted, so launches himself over the drystone dyke that used to keep the sheep out. Landing in long grass, he crawls in between pale birch trees on his elbows. Panic reigns in his head as he gets up on one knee then throws himself back onto his belly as the dealers come back down the steps and stand just over the wall. They'll see me. ***Stay down.***

'I don't give a fuck whit the punters put in their veins, but you want them tae come back for more,' Degzy tells Davy in a tone of despair.

'I'm always listenin, big man.' Davy's voice is hesitant, fearful of a word out of place, none of his usual arrogance and lip.

This show of meekness seems to cool the boss-man's temper and corrects any misconceptions about the pecking order. 'You dae as your telt, and you'll dae alright.' Degzy's tone is almost paternal now.

'I'm listenin, big man ...'

'You still gettin the wee Mongol boy tae do the drops?'

'Oh aye, no chance of me gettin caught with the wee stuff.'

'What if he blabs?'

'Who'd believe him?' Davy starts laughing at his own cunning but stops when Degzy doesn't join in.

'If anyone was tae grass me up, you know what happens?'

'I'd never boss ... honest, big man ...'

'Just windin ye up, son,' Degzy says and laughs, Davy joining in immediately.

Lighter footsteps come down the steps, slowing near the bottom. Hughie sneaks a quick keek from behind a birch trunk, sees Davy's girl, looking petrified, not the cool chick from the pub, now unkempt, without make-up and far too thin. She stands tight up to Davy who is looking at the deck. Degzy turns out to be a big, tanned, leather-faced man, with a large belly held in a jogging suit; his hair is dyed blonde with grey tufts at his ears that give away an age around the late fifties. One of his wide, bare forearms has a snake tattoo on it and there are latex gloves on each hand. As he turns his gaze from Davy to the girl, she flinches, to his obvious delight. His eyes exude an easy malice, sitting just above a contemptuous, cruel grin. Hughie hides his head, imagining Degzy turning and catching him with that crippling gaze. Closing his eyes, he holds his breath and listens, but is forced to look again when his imagination interprets a short silence as the gang creeping towards him, about to pounce over the wall.

The couple stand, waiting for the big guy to let them leave or give another order. Her legs are visibly shaking.

'Lovely wee arse this one's got,' Degzy tells them as he eyes the girl, then winks at Davy. He sounds almost cheerful now the business is done, time for a wee play with the workers' heads. 'Give us a wee spin, Katriana,' he says to the girl, gesturing with a circling finger.

Katriana, shuffles round, her cheeks blushing, her shoulders and eyes down, while Degzy makes a small grunting sound; Davy doesn't say a thing, gulping and looking away, the humiliation complete.

'You should come up n stay the night at the Club when the wife's away, Katriana,' he tells the girl while grinning at Davy. 'Nae need tae bring this loser,' he adds, 'I'll show you the sights.'

She gives Davy a flashing glance as she says, 'Sounds good, Derick.' Her words don't match her expression of controlled terror.

The boss dealer comes in close now as if about to say his last, Davy's face taking on a shaming flush as the big bastard slaps the girl's backside again; Katriana pretends to giggle. 'Right,' Degzy says, looking at Davy for the slightest sign of resistance. 'If there're any more problems, you call in; only on the phone ah gave ye – got it?'

Davy just nods.

'Davy,' the boss says.

'No probs, big man,' Davy says, head still down. 'I'm listenin.'

Degzy has a look at his watch then snaps his gloves off, one at a time. The other two stand there, no rank, no choice, no way out, in front of the real and only law they know. Hughie hides as the big dealer's narrowed eyes break off from his crew and scan the hillside. Fuck, these high-end predators have good radar, and it's always on.

Wondered if it wis this Degzy cunt in the close the other night?

A single set of footsteps march away and Hughie breathes out with relief and lifts his head

'Get on with it you two,' Degzy says without looking back.

'Sorry, big man, sorry,' Davy says as the crunching feet continue off into the distance. The Merc door opens and clunks shut.

When the gangster drives off, Hughie sees Katriana slap Davy hard on the arm and start crying. 'He treats me like slut and you do nuzzing,' she says and goes to slap him again.

Davy catches her wrist, then grabs her hair until she relents. 'Give it a pack.' He pushes her away towards the cottage and follows, watching her carefully. Perhaps she has already run off from other men who couldn't keep her safe.

Stooping, ape-like, Hughie moves up the hillside for another hundred yards, then stands fully upright before moving higher. Only when well into the woods, does he dare look back. He looks at his phone for signal bars. **No police,** the Knight whispers. Below, he can still see the sagging pitch of the hotel roof with its broken grey slates that match the colour of the endless river. A speck, a single sailing boat, makes way down the wide rolling waters of the Clyde, her dull back resisting the sun. She sighs at his troubles, the brown peat bogs groan, and the crooked hills behind him bow in agreement at the utter wickedness of men. As the adrenaline slows in his system, the sweat begins to feel cold on his back. He drops to the ground. Putting his hand on his crotch and then to his nose, he sniffs piss. Giving up, his arms and legs flop out to the sides until he is star-shaped on the sphagnum-moss carpet. His suit stinks of damp cellar and is stained with coal at the knees and there is muck at the elbows; to finish the look off, piss cuts a shiny patch around the crotch and down one leg. Staring blankly up through the branches, black fingernails clawing at the green, he allows his absorption into Brigid's earth, with its leaves, twigs and the grasping mosses; away from the pain of this nasty little life, away from its monsters and his shame. Breathing in swells him up and makes the twigs crack beneath his shoulders, the silent birch swaying over him. *I could lie here until I die, and nobody would care or notice. By October, I'd be one with the rotting leaves, free of it.*

Hughie, nothing actually happened down there. I don't care, it's over, I'm finished with this. ***It's just the past bitin at yer arse. Anyhow, you know I'll never let you jack it in, become a weasel.***

Hughie doesn't respond, still watching the sky, eyes empty.

Right, right, we did well the day – that what you need? And I'm guessin that pishin yourself on the floor of a coal bunker feels a wee bit, well, degradin right now; but ye did no too bad, considerin you took a complete nervy. The Knight appears over him to block the cloudy sky, leaning in close, his yellow and black teeth dripping and his voice all scratchy. *At least we know more about these druggie bastards and have leverage.*

Hughie moves his head away from that thought, to the side so he can stare at the sky.

Ah know it's no easy on you – behind the lines is the toughest. The Knight moves to block the light again, one beady eye open wide, its pupil glazed and white with cataracts, the blind stare on Hughie. *This is light against darkness, Hugh. Those dozy, maladjusted, half-wit mongrels, versus us, the Knights o Light, only guardians of that wee boy.*

The lines on Hughie's face grow deep at the mention of the boy.

You held out well in there. None o that girlie style screamin you did in Manchester. But the boy, he's too weak.

Hughie looks up as the blueness breaks free of the clouds again. I'm done with it.

Fuckin coward! If we do nothin, you know the boy's done for.

'Fuck off!' Hughie shouts, the sound bouncing off where it is hushed by the trees. A keen-eyed gull, hears the shout and looks down through the birch branches – catching sight of a strange black-suited star creature – alone – gazing right back with watering eyes.

Getting to his feet, he looks for the Knight, no sign. Taking his mobile out of his jacket, he checks he has enough signal to call Lex. The Eyes comes to him; its shaking head enough to push the phone back in his pocket and Hughie off up the incline to where the trees thicken, and the air grows close, sweet and oppressive. I'll find the forestry track, drop down behind town and sneak home.

At the last hurdle, he stops. Water gurgles out of a pipe in the steep bank, spilling into a pool that catches the flickering sunlight. He looks around the woods, making sure he is alone. A warm breeze touches his face and murmurs in the swaying treetop branches, hushing his frantic mind, taking him from hysteria to mildly traumatised as time stands still around him. He notices the piss-patch again and, without a thought, strides into the cold water, only pausing and wincing when it touches his ball sack. Fuck, this is the worst day since the last worst day of my life. Nightmare. I'm a loser, a piece of rotting shite. I'll be hit by fucking lightning next or get raped up here by sheep farmers. He winces again, cold water filling his belly button.

Divine waters drive away the wolf fear; turn our dark thoughts to the universe's Light once more.

Ignoring this, he scrubs at the dirt on his hands. Clean myself up, tell anyone I meet I got caught in a freak rain shower or something. Main thing is not to get spotted in this state; if I do, they'll know I've cracked. Rubbing his knees now under the water his arms are immersed up to the shoulder, the rubbing becomes frantic and angry, this effort sends ripples outward to form a series of sparkling rings around him.

Holy Light of the Universe, banish the drawing darkness, stove in the teeth of the mongrels who serve it, gouge their eyes and melt their lupine tongues.

The scavenging gull cocks its head, then flies away, disturbed at the sight of a clothed ape thrashing in the forest pool. As numbness rises from his feet, he calms, the ripples abating. It is then he notices something weird, a morphing shape that waxes and wanes on the surface of the bright water – someone is behind him.

'It's no deep enough,' a voice says.

Spinning around fast, he sees someone looking down on him, the sunlight at the figure's back obscuring who it is. Hughie takes a step to the side, shields his eyes. It is a relief and simultaneously an embarrassment to see Jim, the shop-keeper, standing above, on the road, holding the handles of a heavy wheelbarrow of scrap.

'What?' was all Hughie could say.

'It's no deep enough to top yourself.'

'I was trying to ...'

He strides out of the pond in long awkward steps, the water trying to pull his trousers down. On the side, water gushes out of his clothes, making him pause until it slows to a trickle. Tugging his pants up, he hurries up the bank, red-faced.

'Some sort of nature freak, is it then?' Jim suggests. 'Or have you no got a bath at home?'

Putting the barrow down, he helps Hughie up the last steps onto the gravel track while looking over the dripping social worker. Nothing much else is said as they waddle off along the forest track between heavily scented, plantation spruce; Jim leaves behind a thin tyre imprint, Hughie a trail of evaporating puddles as he feels a chill seep into his bones.

After a bit, Jim cuts off without warning onto a narrow deer track that goes downhill and zigzags between wide tree trunks, his squeaking front wheel showing the way with its radar-like eek, eek, eek.

'A cuppa tea will sort you out,' Jim says over his shoulder.

Hughie follows, unsure of where they might get a cup of tea out here. The sweet smell of pine and bracken is gradually replaced by the stink of burning plastic as a small clearing opens out. Wisps of blue caustic smoke rise from three rusted oil drums with charred lids; below them, fires glow as the breeze comes and goes. A second wheelbarrow, full of burned copper wire shows what Jim got up to on the shop's half-day close. A kettle hangs over a smaller fire, surrounded by blue-schist boulders that prevent spread. Jim catches Hughie glancing back through the trees before sliding down a rough-skinned oak onto another clump of moss, his head falling forward in exhaustion. The soft moss beneath his backside seems unreal, prickling as if moving. Hughie stares at the fire and doesn't dare look away.

'Make yourself at home,' Jim says as he starts poking one of the oil drums with a branch. 'I was just about to get another load goin, but I'll make us a brew first, eh?'

Hughie knows he is acting odd and feels judgemental eyes on him. He is relieved when Jim goes off with the empty kettle towards the sound of running water. When the old boy returns, he sits opposite, placing the manky kettle onto the hissing fire, poking a few dry pine branches into the hot ash under it and skilfully blowing until the fire comes to life. Hughie hasn't moved, either peering into the woods or at the fire as Jim watches him. Birdsong comes in from the distance to mix with the crackle of the sparking wood; a sweet blue stink climbs and hangs lazily between branches and shafts of sunlight. Despite the sun and songs, Hughie sees black cracks between the trees, and reality where dark things linger. Both men's eyes meet, both feeling awkward for the silence between them. Hughie is shivering now, the older man with his fire stick, at home in his primitive world.

'Take them off, they'll dry quicker,' Jim says.

'What?' Hughie asks.

'Your trousers.'

'I'm fine.'

Pointing with the stick, Jim says, 'I'm no an arse bandit if that's what you're worried about. Not that I've got anythin against them boys, mind.'

This gets no smile out of Hughie, though he does shuffle forward until he can feel the heat of the fire on his wet shins.

'You in trouble?' Jim asks, rubbing his short beard and squinting over.

'I wasn't tryin to kill myself.'

Jim shrugs with indifference. 'Maybe no, but things are obviously gettin to you.'

'I'm fine.'

Jim nods into the woods. 'Did somethin happen back there?'

Hughie doesn't respond.

'No worth it, Hugh,' Jim says, the lines when he grins telling of a soul that has been around the block a few times.

About to talk, Hughie catches himself. How can I explain today's crazy fucking events without giving away the past? *Say fuck all.*

'Amazin how a wee walk in the woods can clear the head,' Jim says with thick sarcasm. It works.

'Arse-end of the world,' Hughie replies.

Jim starts cleaning out a mug with the sleeve end of his cardigan, looking up the hill. 'Maybe you're right – rock, sheep and scrub.' He gives a quick shrug before adding, 'At least you can more or less do as you please up here – fight the demons in peace.'

The fire licks idly at the black kettle until steam wafts

261

out the whistling steel spout in undulating peeps.

Hughie starts blinking. 'Doesn't the indifference get to you?'

Jim looks pleased, gives his head a thoughtful tilt. 'It's a wee town, with wee town attitudes.'

'Things grow here ... unseen.'

'Right, you're talkin in fuckin riddles now.'

Hughie goes quiet again, the simmer in his eyes going.

'Went away to the forces myself ... I was ... twenty-three,' Jim confesses.

Ears pricking, Hughie begins to move a bit in his body, warming up.

'Why'd you come back?' he asks.

'Ran into somethin worse than small-town shite.'

Hughie picks up twigs by his feet, angrily snapping them and throwing them into the fire, watching them catch light.

'You're regrettin comin back here,' Jim suggests.

'After today, yeah.'

'You going to say or is this another fuckin riddle?'

When there is no reply, Jim pulls his sleeve down to cover his hand and lifts the boiling kettle off the flames, sharing the boiling water between two steel cups. The teabags float up and spin with spruce needles as he stirs. 'Lot of people run away from bad stuff; end of the train line, over on the boat to Argyll, a wee house in the heather-covered hills – still no happy.'

Hughie takes the cup of tea, a wee tremor in his hand.

The fire gives a loud crack and sparks dance and fall.

'That why you thought ... I was going to top myself?'

'That and the fact that you were in a cold pool in the middle of the woods with a fuckin suit on.' Jim gives his wicked grin.

They sit for a bit without talking, sipping the strong tea and watching the smoke haze that now hangs in the woods. When Jim throws what is left of his tea over his shoulder, he says, 'Yank done himself here once. I found him hanging in that tree just through there.' He is pointing his empty cup to a stand of thin twisted oaks that lean lazily over the burn.

'Did you report it?'

'Course,' Jim says, 'after I emptied his wallet.'

Hughie tries smiling for a moment, but the breeze picks up and spins blue smoke into his face, the haunted look coming back. Opening his piece bag, Jim takes out two bread rolls and throws one at his vagrant pal, an offering. The fire hushes and Jim starts eating.

'I followed him,' Hughie says.

'What?' Jim's mouth is full.

'He was stashin drugs, at the back of a hotel.'

'Hotel?'

'The Tor-an-lee.'

'Drug-boy?'

Hughie nods in reply. He bites into his bread then struggles to chew it, eventually swallowing a big lump. 'Davy was loadin up knocked-off laptops, DVD players and hash ... smack too.'

'Smack?'

'Heroin.'

'Anyone else there?'

'Yeah,' Hughie says, eyes blank, 'that psychopath you saw with the Merc. Treated Davy's girl ... like she was cattle.'

Jim sits silent for once, his roll frozen in mid-munch, waiting for more of the story.

'I freaked out,' Hughie tells him. 'It went wrong ... I don't know, I just totally freaked.'

'You could've got done over, Hughie.'

Hughie goes to speak and stops. ***Do not mention Manchester or your spasms.***

'They follow you?' Jim asks.

'Don't think they saw me.'

Not happy with the vagueness, Jim stands up, looks off towards the trail they came down; his slit eyes scanning the surrounding woods with care until they find their way back to Hughie, who is just sat there, head in hands, hanging over his knees and wet trousers. 'Jesus,' Jim says, 'you're like a secret fuckin agent or somethin.'

'They tend not to piss themselves,' Hughie replies, head still down.

Jim starts to sit on his stump, then stands bolt upright again as the breeze comes rustling through the leaves, scanning for creeping gangsters. Here and there, amongst the birch trunks and bracken, fleeting shadows take on the shape of something hiding, waiting to come at him. 'What you goin to do now?' Jim asks as he eventually sits down.

'Do?'

'About the drugs, down there?'

'Don't ... I don't know.' Hughie throws his roll into the fire, watches the flames take it.

'Tommy will end up runnin smack.'

Hughie gives an exhausted nod. 'Would you ... help me put it on a plate for the police?' He is staring back at the old boy now, the tables turning.

'Depends.' Jim takes another bite of his roll, begins chewing in thoughtful rhythmic circles, pausing every now and then as if he is imagining a certain situation in vivid detail. He doesn't commit, then throws his roll in the fire too.

'Guess it's all down to me to help your dame Maggie,' Hughie says.

'Don't even try the guilt trip, I served my country.'

'Yeah, I heard.'

Jim gives that a funny look, gets up and goes about his wee camp from one task to another in meditative autopilot, poking the oil drums, stacking wood and stopping now and again to sip at his tea and roll thoughts over again and again in his mind like he rolls the embers back into the centre of the fire. Hughie just sits there, limp.

What's a man o his age doin creepin about in the woods? El fuckin Loco, nae doubts. Watch, he's creepin back.

Jim, kneels near Hughie and pushes a branch into the fire. 'You got a plan?'

'Tried to call a pal in the cops ... no signal.'

'They're useless.' Jim shakes his head.

'Maybe you could ... help me,' Hughie says. 'We could put the thing on a plate for the cops, show that someone round here gives a fuck.'

Jim shakes his head again. 'I'm far too old for this stuff now.'

'Never! You look fit as hell.'

A wide smile cuts across Jim's doubting face, but he doesn't bite. He takes his stick from the fire and waves it about, releasing sparks, as if from a wand.

'C'mon, Jungle Jim,' Hughie says, 'you're cunning, smart, you can help me sort this.'

'Jungle?' Jim says, suddenly puzzled, his smile and wand freezing.

'What?'

'You called me Jungle Jim?'

'Did I?' Hughie says, acting daft.

'Right there, a wee moment ago, I heard you.'

Hughie looks uneasy, his friend's gaze pushing him to say, 'Eh, well, I heard you, er, served in ... Korea.'

'Korea?' Jim says, looking slightly hurt, confused even.

Trapped in the woods with a murderer.

'Someone said ... you went a bit ... mental ... in Korea.' Hughie cringes at his own words, quickly adding, 'That's what they say ...'

The twinkle leaves the old shopkeeper's eyes, he throws his magic wand and he mulls over his new friend's words.

The old cunt might slit yer throat for that.

'What else do *they* say?' Jim asks, his voice breaking.

'Some say you went ... berserk—'

'Berserk?' Jim's hands shoot up and Hughie flinches.

'You, sorta shot ... a ... a young girl ... in the head. By accident,' Hughie adds as if this might soften it all.

'I was in Aden for fuck's sake!' Jim shouts over the fire. His eyes go wide as if trying to focus on something that makes sense in the world, a tide of disbelief washing over his face. This changes to anger quickly, and he turns it on Hughie. 'I shot *myself* you idiot; to get out of that fuckin nightmare in Aden.'

Holding out a pacifying hand, Hughie says, 'Sorry, Jim, it's just what people say.'

The shopkeeper's inner-program scrambles, his sense of himself has just been liquidised. After what feels like an age, he speaks, still staring with wide eyes. 'All these years, every cunt that comes into the shop has been thinkin that I'm a fuckin child killer.' He shakes his head, his gaze coming to rest on his big-mouthed pal.

'I ... I, guess so,' Hughie says. 'I didn't believe the one about you scalping the kid though—'

'Fuck!' Jim shouts.

Panicked and desperate, Hughie has to speak. 'Didn't think you'd care what people say.'

'Kinda different when they say you shot a wee lassie in the fuckin head.'

The Ferry ramp hitting the jetty echoes up from the East Bay to break the tension for an instant. The old man's face is so troubled.

'Sorry ...' Hughie says softly.

'Can't believe folk thought I was a child killer.' Jim gives a long shake of the head, trying to dispel it.

'Probably put people off robbing your shop over the years, ah guess.'

'Lucky ol me.'

'Saved on insurance claims.'

Something dawns on Jim, his brows wrinkling up. 'Wait a minute ... what age d'you think I am?'

'Eighty-ish ... someone said.'

'Cheeky swines, I'm sixty-nine.'

They both go quiet until Hughie starts to chuckle. Jim stares at first then cracks and joins in, unsure why. In that instant, Hughie is drawn further out of his trauma and Jim becomes aware of why people often avoid him or are overly polite. They have another quick cuppa and Jim hands out stale doughnuts which Hughie eats without complaint. Brigit embraces them as their healing laughter filters out into the trees to ward off evil.

Hughie gives a sincere nod, says, 'Listen, thanks ... for being here.'

'Ah, stop it,' Jim says as he looks at his watch. 'Nearly five, time to head back and have a perv at the lassie on *Countdown*. Some chassis that yin, eh?'

Hughie sits bolt upright. ***Aw aye, yer lady nutter-Karen was gonnae ring you about five.***

'You alright? It's okay, you're safe,' Jim says as Hughie flaps his arms about, trying to get to his feet.

Without warning, Hughie runs off, managing to shout, 'It's not that,' before disappearing into the trees.

Jim lifts a hand to wave, but his pal is long gone; all that can be heard is the occasional breaking branch with associated curses that fade into the distance. As Jim begins to walk away he is caught by a sudden overwhelming thought, stopping dead in his tracks, he turns and runs a few paces back after his pal.

'Tell the bastards, I didn't kill any wee lassie!' he shouts into the woods, knowing his friend won't hear.

With a roll of the shoulders and a big puff of air into his chest he walks back to the fire alone as the low sun falls behind the tall pine-tops that run like saw teeth above the campsite, leaving only thin rays of golden light to reach out and grasp the rusty oil drums, making them ache with an orange only seen in these woods when the short summer takes hold. He tidies up the tools and pours the kettle into the complaining drums to put them out. At least twice, he looks up to where his friend has gone through the trees, perhaps hoping he'll have changed his mind and might appear waving from above at any moment – no one comes.

As the sun drops further into the hills that guard the Town, its last spindly claw creeps along the forest floor, across the mangled tree roots until it kisses Jim's worn leather boot. The campfire hisses at him as he pisses on it and produces pungent smoke that attacks its maker's throat.

'Bastards,' is all he says before he zips his fly and wanders off towards town, leaving the shadows to swallow up the woods and his creaking oil drums.

TWELVE

REVERIES OF A SOLITARY WANKER

Back at the flat, he rushes across to the phone by the window, picks it up, and dials 1471.

Call received, today, at – seventeen hundred hours – Caller withheld their number.

'Fuck.' He goes to the armchair, sits down, then stands right back up and paces about on the rug. You idiot, the first chance of a relationship, and you blow it. What a tosser.

Nae good attackin yourself, there's enough infidel arseholes out there linin up to do that already. I need to live, distract myself. **There's always time for hoors and shaggin after you've proved yer no that coward.** I'm not a coward, I've carried the weight since it happened. **Still a bit of a coward.**

Hughie shakes his head. Distraction, the shrink said; the booze isn't working, so it's sex or love – something primal enough to push the terror away for a wee while.

Where'd this love come from?

Kicking off his shoes, he walks out of the living room

and into the bathroom, hangs his jacket on the door and drops all his other clothes on the floor. He stands starkers by the basin, looking at his black face in the mirror. Unable to bear his own stare, he turns away and puts the transistor radio on to drown out the thoughts. When he scrubs at his neck and face in the shower, the tray fills with dirty water that runs between his wiggling toes, the drain making a sucking noise. He sings along with the radio, 'Blitzkrieg Bop'. Primal Scream's 'Rocks' comes on next; thoughts of Karen in a pencil skirt induce more slushing endorphins that run like the shower to wash away the day's battle scars. The Knight's umbilical link to Hughie means that electro chemical signals go both ways; they share the spikes in happy stuff that oozes around the brain as well as the anger and the black depression juice. The Knight is pogo-ing around, outside the shower, like a pensioner on speed, his visor clacking up and down as his gauntlets flash jerky shapes through the steam.

Out of the shower and hopping around, Hughie puts on fresh underpants, socks, a clean shirt and a new pair of trousers. He sings bits of songs during a futile look for his striped blazer, then remembers it is at the cleaners. This leads to the sniffing of his suit jacket where it hangs on the bathroom door; unsure, he sprays it with a cloud of deodorant followed by aftershave to mask the smell of scrap metal bonfires, then pulls it on. He stands staring at the shelf in the bathroom cabinet where he'd left his razor yesterday.

That's weird.

Did I take it into the bedroom, looking for batteries?

As his paranoia wells up, he sits on the toilet, holding a knee that has started to tremble. I'm fooling myself, you can't be as stressed as I've been of late and not forget things. It's fine ... I'm fine. 'Don't think, just do,' he tells himself.

Something's no right here, Hugh, honest.

Stop it! Karen, focus on Karen. Those eyes ... that deep green ...

I'm beginin to wonder if you're some kinda perverted psycho muff addict, preferrin oxytocin to good old adrenaline that would let you see that there's something happenin in here. The Knight is peering out the bathroom door and up the empty hall, eyes wary, flicking side to side, sure that the castle has been breached.

The thought of Karen's face dissolves the paranoia, making Hughie smile to himself. He unzips and stands over the bowl, the sound of his pee gurgling and drowning out the Knight.

Okay, muff-man, ignore me; go ahead, fuck the wench doggie style. He slaps Hughie's back, seeping into his maker. ***But nae lovey-dovey stuff, okay; war's afoot.***

Hughie wipes the steam off the mirror, faces himself again – the month's crazy events, the dealers, the panic attacks, shit on door handles, all of it coming at him like a storm. His smile leaves and his jaw clenches. No, never give in, never give in, never give in. Lifting the toothbrush, he frantically scrubs away the taste of fear and spits it down the plughole, then stares hard at the Knight. 'Don't get in my fuckin way today.'

The Knight vanishes. 'Live in the moment,' Hughie mutters as the paranoia abates then comes back like the tide, relentless, all consuming.

As he hurries out the front door, stones scatter off in

different directions in the pitch-black. Another message from my psycho-stalker? Looking up, he notes the bulb is missing, again.

Hope that Glasgow psycho's not hidin, ready to pounce – he looked like a right eye jabber.

He stands, heart pounding, then whispers, 'Karen,' like it's a holy word. His footfall echoes as he runs down the stairs.

ON THE HIGH STREET, he whistles, and a set of taxi brake lights go on. Hope it was her that called; if not, I'll look a right twat.

'Supermarket, then Ardenvale, fast as you can,' he tells the driver as he gets in the back seat.

The smell of aftershave and smoke is enough to prick anyone's curiosity, and the balding driver starts asking questions immediately. Hughie evades any specifics and looks out the window. I need to forget my stalker – my fucking sanity is dependent on it. Her green eyes start flashing, a stocking top, a warm inviting smile.

Aye, wee Tommy will be fine, he's survived fer years, man – runnin about after drug dealers, keepin his old maw sober long enough to feed him, no to mention bein looked after by a paranoid schizophrenic who every fucker thinks is a paedophile. What's the worry, Hughie, what's the fuckin worry, man?

Stop! Opportunities like this are rare these days, and masturbation leaves me feeling like my life's over, a forgotten wanker waiting for death. The taxi takes a corner and Hughie and the Knight slide along the seat together.

———

HER CLOSED blinds move as he walks up the path, and she shouts, 'Come in!' when he nears the front door. Gripping the handle, he breathes in, twists it and goes inside. Right away, he catches a cocktail of perfume and cooking in the empty hall. After a quick glance in the hall mirror, he looks down at pairs of her scuffed shoes that sit by the front door. Should I take mine off? Nah, that would be pushy, presumptuous, she'll know I'm a chancer, kind of guy who takes women for granted.

Jezis Christ, are we overthinkin this or what?

He catches the panic, puts on that cool-axe work face until he can get his bearings; it immediately collapses. What's the worst that can happen?

She screams rape, you get arrested, lose yer job. Fuck off.

In the nook, under the stairs, he clocks her laptop with the Facebook screen up. She's no doubt consulted her pals on my late arrival. This all seems a bit … desperate, but at least we're both still searching … for something.

Don't linger like a brigand rapist in the hall, move along.

Poking his head into the living room, he sees her on *the* chair, ear to a phone, wearing a black satin blouse and knee length skirt and black tights.

Bingo!

As he enters the room, she looks down at his shoes, covers the handset and whispers, 'Take them off.'

273

Slipping them off, he stands awkward for a moment with the shoes at his side, like a schoolboy, then walks back to the front door to put them beside her shoes. When he creeps back into the living room, with a sheepish smile on his face, she still has the phone at her ear, her eyes focused on him all the time, listening to what sounds like a man shouting down the phone line.

'Sorry if I'm confusing you, Paul,' she says to her caller. 'What did you say? Goodbye.' The phone is abruptly hung up, and she fumes for a moment.

With the bottle of wine held out in front like an offering, he shows off his rusty dating skills to full effect. Uncrossing her legs, she stands up, face still cold. He gulps.

'Both sobered up since we last met,' he jokes.

She doesn't smile. Offering a kiss to her cheek feels awkward. What have I done? I missed the call = **lack of interest.**

Avoiding the kiss, she takes the wine and looks at it then back into his nervous face, her eyes asking questions without words, seeing more than he wants to show this early in the game. She is smarter than he'd thought, far more complex. The red lips are perfect though, glossy, like a TV advert in close up, and her neck, stark white against her black blouse, runs up in a fine line to a delicate chin and high cheekbones – the chemicals are flowing around his brain already, gushing and overwhelming all senses.

'Just had to cancel your replacement,' she says, her voice matter of fact.

'Sorry, I'm late ... caught up at work. By the time I—'

'It doesn't matter,' she interrupts, her voice turning soft and husky in an instant, throwing him again. 'You're here.'

A smile relaxes her hard face, eyes catching him again

and again in a series of bewitching lash-flashes. God, my knees are shaking.

In the fading early-summer light, she looks like a forties' film star with her tight clothes, tied back hair and manicured eyebrows. Way out of our league here, Hughie, way out. *Housin estate slapper, nuthin more – bang and go*. Please, just shut it.

'Do you smoke?' she says, twitching her nose in disdain.

Hughie turns his head to the side and catches a whiff of campfire smoke from his jacket. 'I just visited a client ... a real smoker.'

'Was his house on fire?' She laughs straight at him.

'Eh, no ...'

As he shrinks inside his smelly jacket, she gives him a wicked relieving smile, her face turning as if posing for the camera. 'I'll hang it up,' she says and begins pulling his jacket off as he lifts his arms like a kid. After sniffing and screwing up her small nose, she throws it on a chair.

'Fraid I went in a bit of a huff,' she says. 'When you didn't answer, called my ex. When I saw the taxi, I had to phone him back. God, I sound like a right .... Just gag me if I talk too much – not kinky gagging.' She finally shuts herself up, still smiling.

She keeps changin who she is this yin; sad, happy, mental as fuck, it's throwin me right off balance.

'Come,' she says and pulls his arm.

In the kitchen, he is seated at the table again while she pours the wine and fusses around the noisy, bubbling pots on the cooker, sipping at her glass, wooden spoon in the other hand. The wine glass looks a more comfortable fit, the spoon held like something new to her. He smiles, then finishes the glass in two long gulps.

'Need a drink when you do your sort of work, eh?' she says.

'Tough week, really tough,' he says, blinking.

'You want to try wiping shitty arses ...' She catches her words, looks into a pot, embarrassed, and stirs.

'You're fair makin me hungry with all that dirty talk,' he says.

His shit joke works; her shoulders relax, she puts the lid on the pot, comes and sits opposite him. They drink more wine between more of his nervous jokes as her husky laughter fills the room.

'One of my friends said you worked in her dad's pub when you were young; The Tavern. She said you lived with your uncle back then.'

He frowns, attempts a firm look. 'Is Sad-net good for relationship tips then?'

'Better than looking in windows,' she says in quick reply, her face showing instant regret.

He blushes.

'Sorry, I didn't mean that,' she says, 'I'm too sharp. It's living on your own that does it.' Her eyes reassure him.

'Is that enough?' he asks politely as he tops up her glass to the brim.

'Why did you live with your uncle? Sorry, nosey again ...'

Her shining hair catches the window light, and he remembers the prize, stepping back into the ring. 'My mum lived up country, and I wanted to live in the Town; Uncle Malky lived in town.'

'Your dad?' she asks, resting her elbow on the table and her head in her hand.

'I'm guessin you already know about my dad.'

She fake-frowns at this. 'Heard he was a bit of a drinker, turned to God then died kind of young ... sorry.'

Hughie, Hughie, Hughie, she's investigatin you now – total mental case.

Hughie claps his hands together gently. 'Well done. Jesus, how I bloody hate this wee town. Still saves on lots of small talk and chit-chat.'

They toast for no reason. As she puts the glass back to her lips, their eyes lock and don't move.

'Everyone says I went with three black Yanks at the same time.'

'It was just the two then?' he says right back.

After a pause that makes him think he's missed with the joke, she says, 'Yeah, one black, one white. I'm an equal opportunity kind of gal.'

Now sat close together, drinking vodka in the living room, the stink of burned stew hanging above them, he feels it. Her delicious, dangerous and unworthy stream, seeping into his muddy river; dark oils mixing in the spinning eddy, pulling them in. She isn't fearful of his odd-ball madness and he loves her biological clock desperation.

'I'm a lucky man, sittin here with you.'

Green eyes flash into his soul.

'That was sweet. More,' she demands

Touching her arm, he runs his hand up, stroking her sharp elbow with soft fingers. 'You're stunning, exquisite' he says in her ear.

She offers her neck to his lips and slides under him, her movement fluid, like a predatory cat sidling up to prey. Without warning, he pulls her into a kiss, cupping her face with his hands, touching her tongue gently with his; tentative at first, then passionate as they explore for resistance or lack of it. Breathing deepens, they pull at each other's clothes, the kisses becoming wild, almost rough, until he senses he is going far too fast and begins to kiss his way up her neck, feeling the tension rise from her waist where he holds her.

Bang, Bang, Bang!

Thrown out of the chemical trance by the banging on the front door, they look into each other for answers. The door hammers again.

Getting up, she straightens her blouse, pulls her hair back and goes towards the front door, leaving Hughie looking bewildered. Holding his breath, he hears the front door open, then her low voice begging someone to calm down. A man's voice can be heard now.

'You've got to be fuckin joking!' the red-faced bricklayer shouts when Hughie appears in the hallway.

Karen hangs her head and groans, the guy's giant caveman hand holding the frame above her head like a root, inveigling its way in through her doorway.

'You're a dirty fuckin slut!' the Caveman shouts in her face.

'Don't talk to her like that!' Hughie tells him.

When Hughie looks over her shoulder with his collar undone, the big lump flushes and swings a wild looping punch that catches Hughie square on the mouth, knocking him back against the wall where his head rattles on plaster.

'Bastard!' Hughie screams and comes back quick, fists up.

Karen never flinches, stepping in front of Hughie, she starts slamming the door hard on the Caveman's trailing arm – three times, each slam producing a scream from the Caveman on the other side.

'Out!' she shouts as the arm withdraws, and the door closes shut with a thud.

When she reopens the door after a few seconds, the Caveman is at the gate in fading light, he is holding his wrist, his face shocked, contorted with pain. 'My fucking arm ... you've broken it, you bitch!' he shouts the last bit at the top of his voice and slumps off up the road with a look of real hurt on his face.

Karen stands defiantly on her step and sticks a V-sign at the twitching curtains next door. Pushing Hughie inside, she slams the door and begins to shake, her arms holding herself.

'God, you're a tough wee thing,' he says as he touches her trembling shoulders.

He can't see any lust in her eyes now, only anger and embarrassment as she pulls away, holding her face, the emotion catching her as she perhaps starts to think of her gossiping neighbours bad-mouthing her again in the supermarket, the looks at work when the news gets through.

'Hey, hey, you're okay, you're okay,' he says, holding her hand.

A single tear runs down her cheek. 'I'm fine,' she insists.

Hughie feels his jaw ache and touches his lip, going pale when he sees the red blood on his fingertip. 'Wow, my knees.' He hits the deck like a bag of spuds, the world spinning away from him.

Karen's face hardens again, and her head shakes down at him. 'Fucking great!'

THE METALLIC TASTE of blood in his mouth is soothed by a big gulp of the hot sweet tea she's just handed him. Sat on one end of the sofa, he feels inside his mouth while looking up at her sour face. No teeth missing – it could have gone worse, somehow.

'More of a lover than a fighter, me,' he says, cradling his jaw.

'You're as bad as him.'

'Sorry,' he says and gives a hopeful smile.

She doesn't smile back.

Oh, oh, psycho-bunny time, again.

'This is what my life is like,' she says as she wipes his bloody mouth with a J-cloth, then spits on it and rubs too hard under his eye where he'd hit the floor. 'You're goin to have a black eye by tomorrow,' she adds, her face now looking its age; all the worry fissures opening up with stress, the make-up unable to cope with the job at hand.

'I'm okay.'

'Bloody neighbours loved it.' She sounds angry now.

'It's no big deal. Come here, gorgeous,' he says, trying to embrace her.

She pulls away and gives him the cloth to dab his own lip, goes off towards the kitchen. 'Think you're in shock, I'll make more tea.'

Holding his thick lip, he looks around the sparse room, notices a big tear in the wallpaper along the skirting, cigarette burns on the carpet near the artificial fire. Obviously, she ran out of money before she got to this room.

What a fuckin mess yer in, again. The Knight is scowling, shaking his head furiously at his maker. *Get out of here, quick, fore it all fucks up.*

Karen comes back, hot teacups in hand, and they sit on opposite ends of the sofa now, just looking at one another Her mascara has run on her red cheeks and she seems even darker since coming back from the kitchen. His white, bloodied face feels swollen, and he can't find the words to soothe her troubles.

'That was an unfortunate wee interlude,' he jokes, trying to shuffle along towards her.

Karen puts her cup onto the carpet, spilling it, starts crying uncontrollably, head hanging, hands on her face to stem the flood. That hair that shone when he came into her home a couple of hours ago, now dangles like rat-tails, her shaking painted nails coming through it in claws; fear and glamour all rolled together in a dull room on a housing scheme. She starts rocking back and forth, the sobs untethered.

Run fer yer life, Hugh – totally Loopy Lou, this one.

He goes to hold her; she shoves him away.

'I'm a disaster,' she warns him, her voice breaking, but sure.

They just sit there for a while. Outside, kids run past the window, shouting and laughing with excitement, their footfall and joyous voices telling the listening adults that the illusion of an endless childhood is still alive as it fades off into the dusk in fits and starts until it is all gone. This makes the gap between them feel like a chasm. Clear of the intoxicating smoke of lust, he sees behind her streaming make-up to where the hard knocks have left dents. Although she doesn't see it, his eyes are absorbing her pain. Still, she's so beautiful, a fallen angel, I'm sure. He hesitates before moving over from his side, and off the sofa, kneeling beside her. He goes to put a hand on hers, but she pulls away again.

'I know what it's like,' he whispers.

She sears him with black mascara eyes.

'What is it, Karen?' he asks. 'C'mon, let it out ... tell me.'

His insistence cuts a holding cord within her, her head falls, and she begins to shout at the floor, 'Tell you what worthless bit? My mum puttin me in care, the guys who said they'd marry me and didn't, the three engagements, the miscarriage, the shit job, the kids I haven't had, the neighbours talking about men fighting over the slag.' She looks at him at that, goes on, voice manic, 'You're as bad as him, and I've only known you five minutes. So, what bit do you want to talk about, eh, what bit?' After screaming the last few words, she starts crying again.

'I understand ...'

'Christ!' she says between her gritted teeth. 'Another bullshitter!'

'Listen—'

'No! I'm sick of listening to men; just ... fuck off!'

Fer Christ's sake, don't go near this nutjob; talkin like we're pieces of shit.

He puts a tentative hand forward, touches her shoulder.

'Just get out,' she says shrugging him off. 'Bullshitters – all of you!'

Standing up, he steadies himself, drops the cloth he'd held to his lip on the coffee table, then picks up his jacket and begins walking towards the door.

Obviously, she's a fuckin loon-tune – let's get the fuck out before she pulls out the whip and cuffs, starts knockin you about. This is not right, I've made things worse. ***Aw, ah see, it's damsel in distress time; gettin you hard, is it? That bastard punches you for nothin and now she's callin you all sorts. Wakey, wakey, Hugh.***

He wavers by the living-room door, then goes back towards her. 'I'm sorry, if I've done something ...'

'You still here?' she mumbles under her breath.

'I—'

'Are you a bloody retard or something?'

'Karen—'

'Go!' she screams in exasperation, fingers clawing her face, the venom hard to hold back.

Hughie son, grow a spine fer fuck's sake, man – walk away.

Cheeks flushing, Hughie stands, caught between things as usual. 'Okay, my turn,' he says.

No, no, don't humiliate yerself any further.

'Bye,' she says from inside a ball of matted hair.

He ignores the images the Knight sends him from the amygdala of police, handcuffs and rape charges; starts to ramble, 'When my dad died, I was fourteen. My best pal ... my best pal was run over when I was nineteen. My first love, she ran off with her college tutor, yeah that's right, a weedy fucking drama teacher.'

She stops sobbing and he goes on, 'Then my mum and my Uncle Malky, who had straightened me out a hundred times, both died when I was finally getting it together down south.' He looks for a further reaction. Nothing, so he starts again. 'I did alright for five minutes at uni, got a degree and started to climb the social-work ladder.'

She interrupts. 'Is this goin to take long?'

He ignores her completely. 'Course, I knew it would turn bad again, you know it in yourself – once you've tasted the black thing, you know it's never far away; it's just a matter of fuckin time really, till it catches up with you ... and it always does. So, I decided to marry a woman that I

283

never loved.' He opens his eyes wide at that. 'Christ, I've never said that out loud before. Of course, we couldn't have kids, which she said was my fault, told me I was a Jaffa. Guess what's next; the cow left me.'

He runs his hands through his hair, scalp tingling, his eyes still wide, not even looking at her any more, looking inside himself as he stands there on her carpet like a thin six-foot gaping wound, his soul determined to cleanse its pain, get it all out once and for all.

Don't tell her the worst bits, please man … have some dignity.

'Then,' he says, grinning, 'just to prove I'm clueless, I decided to try to save a prostitute from a people trafficking gang. I kissed her once, still not sure why, perhaps I was more lost than her. Anyway, I got tortured by her pimp for the pleasure – took a bit of a loony-tune turn, fell out of my job just as the bitch wife, I never loved, got pregnant to her work colleague, another teacher.'

Karen is immobile now but still hiding her face in a ball of hair, so he walks around to the front of her, staring down. 'Oh, and I'm now being stalked by some absolute arse who wants to do me in or drive me mad. That's not you, by the way, just some random drug dealers I attracted.'

Bending down until his head is close to hers, he gives another deranged grin, adding, 'So, don't talk to me about being fuckin worthless.'

What in the name o fuck have you done – the shame – it's all out in the open now.

She looks at him and he looks back, both seeing things they hadn't seen earlier when they were under the beguiling spell of infatuation. Her eyes are blotched with mascara that runs down one side of her face. His stinking jacket feels cold now on his sweaty back, whiffs of smoke catching the air as he nods, gets up and turns towards the front door. She stops him by putting a hand out; it shakes as she holds it there, her face looking so fucking sad now.

'What?' he snaps.

'You—'

'I should stay,' he says, interrupting. 'We could make up, or perhaps we could join my fucked-up life to your fucked-up life and make fucked-up babies; that it?'

'No.'

'Then what?'

Lowering her head, she says, 'I just thought ... he might still be out there ... maybe you should go out the back door.'

He changes course without another word, heads down the hall into the kitchen, makes for the back door with her following slowly on behind.

So what, the Caveman wins the prize of a female nutjob – who cares?

'No,' Hughie shouts at the Knight and goes out the door leaving it wide open.

Karen's face wakes from her own worries as she stands on the step watching him walk into the dark muttering to himself. She squints when Hughie pauses by the wheelie bin, the faint orange light from her kitchen only catching his static feet. Both are aware that if he takes one more step it will be the end to the whole twisted mess, over.

Up the scheme, a woman bawls on her children to come in, her voice carrying in the dark still air. He is frozen there, in the shadows, his shape silent and menacing.

'Hughie?' she says.

'What?'

'Bye ...' she answers, her words unable to say what she means.

The Knight waves her off with a dismissive gauntlet. *Can't you see, Hughie, we don't deserve carnal stuff; we've failed so far, need to crack a few skulls, then come back like a hero and pump the life out o the dirty bitch.* You know nothing about this stuff; nothing! *Let's get real here for a minute, son; yer hidin in the dark next to some fuckin smelly bin; even loose knickers over there, who likes men lookin in her windows, doesn't want you. This is humiliatin, son, totally humiliatin. HUMILIATION!*

She rubs her arms and steps back inside, about to shut the door.

'Fuck off, you old bastard!'

Karen looks out and around the dark garden, then peers towards him, trying to make out his shape and what or who he's talking to.

'I think you might be concussed,' she says as she steps onto the cool stone in her tights and tiptoes towards him. 'Come back in, you're hurt worse that I thought.'

As she gets close, she raises a hand, intending to move his head to the side to see if it is swollen, but she pauses her arm in mid-air, wary, knowing how unpredictable this one is. He gives a weird chuckle, and she senses his dark face staring back. She withdraws her arm and takes a small step back into the glow from the kitchen, where she feels safe. 'You okay ... Hughie?'

She can feel his eyes on her skin, her heart picks up a beat.

Yer humiliated!

'I deserve the goddess,' he might have said as he lunges at her out of the shadow, wrapping her in a wild embrace, spinning her away from the warm light and pushing her back until he has her pinned against the wheelie bin. She resists for a moment, her hands holding his face, nails paused to dig deep. 'Hughie,' is all she gets out before the strange attraction catches light and resistance swaps polarity, her hands running over his face and grabbing his hair tight, pulling his mouth on to hers. This is what she expects of men, force, will and want – she feeds on it, and it makes her feel desired, not buried here in the past with her dreams, instead she feels wild and alive. In the clinch, she bites his ear and he rips her blouse down over her shoulders and snaps her bra strap, sucking at her nipple before running his tongue up her neck like a dog might. A thought shoots through his head, a fleeting bird's-eye image of him taking what he wants on a bin, out the back of a council house in the poorest part of town.

Poor man's opera – monkey time.

Feverish animal grunts come out as he explores with his hands, touching and stroking wherever he wants. Arms around his neck, she puts her weight on to his shoulders, flings her legs around his hips, his hands running up her thigh, lifting her by her bum and yanking her skirt up to the waist. Throwing her arse up onto the wheelie bin, he tears her tights down, then her pants come off, thrown into the dark. Air rushes through her clenched teeth as his tongue goes up her thigh until it finds her soul's end. From a few gardens away, it sounds like a brutal fight as she bucks and claws his neck, and he resists any attempt to slow his bobbing head. Her thin frame tenses and tenses until she comes under a starry sky. A shrill sigh is the last thing to come out of her open mouth and sail through the hedges and along the neighbours' gardens as they sit, oblivious, in front of their tellies. Now limp on him, she lifts a weak hand

and rubs her hair about where her head has hit the wall hard. Sliding off the bin, she lifts his jacket off and undoes his zip as they stagger into the dark, kissing. On cold, damp grass, he fucks her on her hands and knees. At one point, he hangs back like a drunk space-cowboy, his head spinning as stars score his eyes, a dog now barking at her high-pitched breaths. A feeble motorbike drone ploughs in from the darkness, its sound dissipating up into the hills above town as Hughie comes with a breathless grunt. When he falls from her, onto the cold prickly grass, Karen crawls beast-like onto him, smearing his chest with gritty, earth-covered hands. She holds him. Breathing in unison now, they look up as pinpricks of light fade in and out of the thin cloud, the cooling night biting at any bare flesh. When the stars eventually break free and shine out, they look brighter than either can ever remember.

ANOTHER NIGHTMARE WAKES him in the night, so he watches her sleep for a while, sees her thin, bare calf slide out from the red bedcovers, caught by light from the street, her toes stretching in a little fan before withdrawing back under the warm bedding. The Knight is salivating, watching her through Hughie's eyes. Hughie rolls over to put an end to the leering and the crazed dribbling.

Don't act all high an mighty; we both know why you're here – monkey spurt.

Slipping out of her bed, trying not to disturb her, he sits on the side of the bed massaging his cramping calves with his hands. The bedroom is empty bar the bed and a dresser; she told him she is decorating it. He sniffs. It's those paint fumes that have dried my bloody throat out.

Standing up naked, he creeps to the window, pulls back the curtain. After glancing back at her to see if she's awake, he opens the window a couple of inches. Moving his face closer, he breathes the fresh air, feels a shiver run over his naked skin. The alarm clock on the floor says ten past three, while outside, the streets are silent. Stray streetlight illuminates her white face, but she never stirs – her long, blonde curls, dark roots and red cheeks are angelic, despite what they have both just done to one another. The soft pit-pat of rain begins to hit the window and a breeze catches the net curtain which flaps in his face, hiding Karen in a soft dreamy blur for an instant. The Knight looks down with him on her beauty, Led Zeppelin's 'Kashmir' belts out in his head, and he imagines for a moment they are on a boat on a lake under ice-topped mountains, the morning call to prayer filtering in from the water's edge and the stink of hashish mixing with fresh orchids. This is close to a life; wonder how I'll blow this one.

The Knight is sat by a furnace, whittling arrow heads with a rusty blade, his skin's deep pockmarks caught by the glow from the fire, his jaw clenched with a deep resentment. *Nice to see you're alright, gettin plenty. Bit of a pity about the wee lad Tommy, don't suppose he's doin so well tonight, mmm?* Hughie's thoughts are pulled into shade, he sees Tommy's face, contorted under his own thin duvet as people party in his house, music blasting his ears. He can hear Maggie laughing at ghosts of the past, drunk, as every sort of weirdo and creep wanders through her house – Tommy's big plate eyes run with tears of fear, awaiting the return of the cigarette man. Jesus, please stop! It's my condition, the trauma. ***Don't worry, you're nae different from the rest o yer motley species; selfish, always lost in yer own sordid wee deprivations – excretin and yearnin for more.*** The Knight spits in the fire and it flashes in his possessed eyes. ***Do us a favour, Hughie, leave now, before you hurt her too.*** When the Knight says this, he flicks the end of his blade towards the sleeping Karen. This is my condition talking, I'm not bad for her. The Knight tuts and shakes his head at this, looks back to his fire.

Tiptoeing across the room, Hughie slips back into the warm bed behind Karen where his thoughts calm. Beneath his touch, she feels so soft and warm. Heavy rain hitting the open window stirs her.

'Sshhh,' he says in her ear as he strokes her hair away from her face. He tastes the salty skin of her cheek as he kisses it three times – one, two, three.

'We could phone in sick tomorrow, both of us?' she whispers, half delirious.

'Spend the day together,' he whispers back.

It is hard to know if she heard as her soft rasping breaths tell him she has drifted off again. Holding her as you hold something delicate and precious, he watches the curtain flap and imagines they are on the Silk Road again, camping in rusty-red sandstone caves by the fire with his princess in his arms, camel trains drifting off into the Taklamakan Desert touched by moonlight. 'Achilles Last Stand' jangles around his mind as he falls into a blissful sleep. The Knight sits awake, planning.

THE FIRST THING he sees in the morning is the open bronze faceplate of the Knight who is squeezed on top of the wardrobe under the low ceiling in a space barely fit for a small suitcase. The Knight's legs hang down and bile drips off his toes; his head is at an angle to his shoulders that no living thing could accommodate. The Knight's beady eyes fall on him, searing and blaming as usual. *How can you start this?* he says, nodding at the wench then looking back at Hughie. *You know you cannae be consistent, know you just don't have love inside you.* I need something solid. *This isn't solid, this is more complication.* The Knight begins to whisper. *You told me you wanted to prove you had it inside you, show that someone cared about the poor boy up the lane. But you soon gave up when a half-decent piece o fanny turned up.* The Knight's face grows sour, like he's bit a lemon. *Turns out I wis right all along – no one cares, its every man for himself and it always has been – a Darwinian dogfight to the bitter finish, clawin at one another, fightin for pussy as we sink back into the bile*. Oh, shut up for God's sake. He's using my hangover against me now. Letting my past trauma seep through. Hughie clenches his fists under the covers.

Poor wee fuckin Tommy. As the Knight speaks, he leers at Karen's fine bare shoulder which pokes out of the covers like an angular fin. Hughie covers her up, then throws his legs out of the bed. The bed shakes, but she doesn't move.

Finish this Hughie. She wants a hero, no

another nutjob who takes panic attacks and pisses himself in coal bunkers; get out before you fuck her up even more than she obviously is. We're just no ready for all this. Please, I need someone. *Naw, you listen to me, you've been drugged, attacked and yer mates are no exactly jumpin up and down to help you; the druggy bastards are out there struttin about, ready to do you or someone yer connected to over.* The Knight looks at Karen's shape in the covers, shakes his head, face grave with sudden worry for her. *Don't get her caught up in this madness; she's an innocent. You know how it went before, with that poor wee prozzy.* But Karen's ... so ... *Vulnerable. We're not strong enough to carry her, not yet.* Okay, okay. *Let's just slip out, save her from their attention.* I said I'd spend the ... *Out, quick before she turns round, fore you put a target on her back.*

Her hair lies in rat-tails on the pillow, and he smiles to himself as he looks down on her and rolls the ends in his fingers. She doesn't need me in this state. His stomach moves the wrong way. I'll sort my life out, come back like a shiny paladin hero, sweep her off her feet, and find our own Silk Road. *C'mon, up an away before those curtain twitchers wake.* What if you are my fear of intimacy? *What if that Degzy cunt with the mad eyes drags her up here alone?* She needs someone to stick by her.

These bastards aren't fuckin about, they'd kill her or worse. Anyway, wee Tommy could do with some o yer stick-ability, could he no? The

Knight scratches his neck with the point of his blade, in the same place where Tommy's burn scar is.

Driven to his feet, Hughie slips his trousers on first as he is unable to find his underpants. Every movement makes a noise, even tucking his shirt in seems to rustle like a brown paper parcel being shoved into a letterbox. Dressed, he goes over to kiss her beautiful head that peeps out of the covers.

Don't. It'll wake her up and we'll have to explain stuff.

Hughie nods. We can go out Friday, go to the Auld Hoose together, have a meal and I'll find out who she is.

Hurry, son.

At the top of the stairs, he thinks about going back.

Quick now!

The stairs creak as he goes down them, and he thinks he hears movement from the room. Turning his head back up the stairs, he listens. I can't do this to her.

It's for the best, you know it.

He changes his mind, about to turn and go back.

'Look at you,' Karen says from the doorway of her bedroom at the top of the stairs.

She is standing, a sheet wrapped around her, hand on the door, her eyes empty.

'Karen ...'

'I lay there thinkin, he's going to say something,' she says, almost whispering.

'I ... I thought you were asleep, didn't—'

'Is that what you did to the prostitute – crept out, not a word?'

'I was goin to leave a note on your computer,' he says, but it sounds weak – like a lie does.

293

'Go, please ... just go,' she says.

'Let me explain—'

She slams the bedroom door to cut off his whining voice.

Unsure, Hughie goes down the stairs, stopping several times as if to go back up.

Did ye see her face there? She's not right, don't make it even worse by creepin back; we need to go.

At the bottom of the stairs, he picks up his shoes and goes out the door without stopping to put them on or look back.

Outside, the concrete slabs are wet, soon feeling cold through his socks. As he leans against her wall and puts his shoes on, one at a time, he hears crying filtering from the window he'd opened last night. Looking up, he sees the curtains flap, and the window shut and lock, the curtains pulled over. A hot flush of remorse stabs him, runs up his brain stem and flushes guilt all along every synapse in his head. Go back, man, and explain yourself.

What if those gangsters who've been puttin shit on yer door and almost killed you; what if the same cunts find Bunny Boiler up there. She's half simple, be easy meat for that lot, have her on the game in no time. Lead them away from her; do the right thing for once.

Walking down the hill, away from the scene of the crime, rain hits his face. It doesn't feel cold, doesn't feel of anything as his mind starts racing. I should feel like the apostles after the big man came back; instead, I'm creeping and sneaking off, embarrassed after a night of casual shagging, scared I'll ruin her life by bringing her close to dealers and gangsters, and me. Bet she's thinking I'm a gawky stooge, another *CREEPY* FUCKING chancer. Oh, Karen, I'm so sorry.

Awww, fer fuck's sake, you must be jokin, Hughie? This girl's clearly a fuckin tart, lives in a damp council house, her caveman lover HUMILIATED you by thumpin you about in front of the neighbours last night before slack-drawers let you shag her on a bin. Then, then, the nutjob HUMILIATES you further by chuckin you out in the rain after she'd sat on yer face.

'Please stop!' Hughie says as he wanders down the street.

The rain comes again, heavier, mixed with the sweat on his forehead, the windows all around staring like ravenous cameras, Karen's reputation to be liquidised into shite by lunchtime at the Co-op. He tries to straighten his walk, the Knight rolling another burning tyre of ruminations at him.

Strange that your drunkard cop pal cannae remember our deal to rescue the boy; like ah said, cops are useless, often bent and lazy as fuck. Even your geriatric, kid-killer, Jim, isnae keen to put his hands near the mutt's jaws. You know the score here, Hughie; don't act naïve son, connect the spine, connect the fuckin spine.

Hughie waves frantic arms at a passing taxi that slushes to a halt in the puddles. He throws himself in the back. It is the wee nosey driver from the night before.

'Had a good night,' the driver asks with an annoying grin on his face.

Hughie doesn't answer as water runs off him over the seats.

'You late for work?' the driver asks this time.

'Aye.'

'Social work offices, is it?'

'No, hold on.' Hughie looks past the confused driver, through the rain-soaked windscreen and blurring wipers into the distance. Something happens to the rage that eats him, a narrow blowtorch flame forming, then vertebrae fusing until Hughie sits upright in the seat, his face stoic and serious.

'Where we goin then, pal?'

'Just drive,' Hughie snaps.

THIRTEEN

DRAGONS BELLY

Vomit, when it passes the junction between the tubes to the stomach and lungs, can fill you with a small terror, a small glimpse of your last moment. He opens his mouth and lets it pour onto the road, despite being diluted by the rain it becomes even lumpier as the coarse tarmac of the road rises through it. He wipes his mouth with his sleeve and slams the car door. This is mental.

Robert Bruce or Charlemagne would say – he who dares wins, he who hesitates is a big fuckin fanny.

Pushing the door with his back, he bursts into the grocer's shop holding a package under his open coat. In the dull light of the shop, he looks haunted, raindrops bending his eyelashes and dripping onto the black package, which loosens in his grip and falls to the muddy shop floor with a thump. Jim is standing behind the counter, cornflake bowl in one hand, a spoon of flakes paused by his mouth in the other. The shopkeeper gives the fallen package a disdainful look, before shovelling the flakes into his mouth and crunching away, his gaze eventually rising to settle on Hughie.

'What's that?' Jim asks between chews.

Hughie picks the package up and rushes past Jim into the back-shop without asking for permission. Looking along the brown cracking paint on the ceiling, down past the porn mags and onto the manky, wet, muddy green carpet tiles, Jim shakes his head and whispers to the heavens, 'Sorry, love,' before following his creepy pal through the clicking beaded curtain.

'You alright?' Jim asks, turning off the racing. 'You're shakin.'

Hughie doesn't answer as Jim looks him over.

'Reckon you need to pack the drinkin in for a while.' Jim tips his bowl up and glugs the milk that is left at the bottom.

When the package slithers onto the food preparation table, it produces a small thud and sends a cloud of bread-crumbs onto the sticky lino floor. Standing together, they stare down at it where it sits across the checked tablecloth next to the brown sauce bottle, bread knife and salt and pepper cellars. After a silent moment, Jim points his spoon towards it, says, 'Been shoppin?'

Hughie peels open the cheap plastic bin bag to reveal twenty half-kilo slabs of vacuum-packed black stuff, all taped together into a tight block.

Jim looks troubled. 'What is it?'

'Like the stuff we smoked last week.'

Jim looks unsure, gives a doubtful shake of the head.

'Afghan black – cannabis.'

'Fuck!' Jim says as if suddenly realising what is in his shop. 'What the hell did you bring it here for?' He looks in panic towards the front of the shop.

'Listen, I've just stolen Argyll's next three months' dope

supply from a drug gang, transported it to your run-down grocer's shop rather than the police station ... I'm crappin myself; give me a fucking break.'

'That's my name above the door, remember. Last to touch the ball and all that.'

Putting his bowl down, Jim uses the spoon to burst a hole in the cellophane of one block and bends down for a sniff of the contents, raising his eyebrows in response to the strong odour from inside.

'Shop!' a voice shouts from through the bead curtains.

Jim looks at him. 'You not lock the door?'

'You kiddin?' Hughie whispers, shaking his head.

After a brain freeze moment, Jim rattles the sink with his multifunction spoon and goes through the bead curtain like a wary sloth. 'Alright, howz it goin?' he says to someone.

Left with the evidence, Hughie springs into life and covers the hash with an old raincoat from the hook above the lager stack. Tiptoeing to the back door, he turns the key to unlock it, just in case a runner is the next move, then stands listening for signs of trouble.

Aw, aye, great move. If Degzy or the drug squad burst in, there is nae way they'll find ten blocks o hash under a fuckin raincoat. Fuck's sake.

Voices from the shop are talking about the price of four or eight cans of beer.

'You'll need to come back when you get paid,' Jim says.

'Oh, come on, sir, just this once.'

It is the tinker from last week. The tone of Jim's voice shows that he's fazed, and the tinker is on it.

'Just enough for a wee drink; got familee visitin,' the tinker insists. There is a pause, then he adds, 'Magic, James sir, I'll be back the day after next ... to pay; won't forget this, sir.'

Listening, Hughie feels a single bead of sweat running down inside his shirt to chill his back and remind him how risky the game has got. There is the sound of the shop door shutting and a bolt going across into the frame, then Jim comes back through the curtain. He gives the raincoat on the table a nonchalant look. 'Definitely spy material, you are,' he says, face deadpan.

'He gone?'

'Aye, but this nonsense is costin me money.'

They sit and drink a cup of tea before Jim wipes his hands on his cardie, removes the coat and moves the plastic package to his side of the table. His fingers linger on the frightening alien thing, the surface smooth to the touch. 'What's the plan, Sid?' he asks, peering at the black cannabis resin through the hole.

It takes a minute before Hughie can answer, even then he sounds distracted. 'We sort this,' he says, looking towards the Terrace.

'This is fucking nuts, Hugh, and you know it.'

'You said Davy's out fishin most nights now.'

Jim is still transfixed by the package. 'Would we go to prison if we get caught with this much?' He looks from the hole in the package to the social worker, but Hughie isn't really there, eyes holding a dark focus, a brutal determination to do ... something.

'What time does Davy go out?' Hughie asks.

'The mackerel are runnin.'

'And?!'

'Alright, Crazy Horse. He goes to the pier at eleven or twelve,' Jim says, annoyed now.

'Does he have nights off?'

'Now and then.' Jim frowns, looking at his hands and then the cellophane coating on the package. He stretches, pulls a dish cloth off the sink and runs it over the package as if to get rid of his fingerprints.

'His front door?' Hughie asks.

'Door?'

Hughie glares at him for not keeping up, the sunken rage closer to the inside of the pupils now. 'We need to get through his door.'

'He doesn't lock it—'

'I could've brought smack, that keep you awake?'

Jim shakes his head at Hughie, then sits back in his chair, his thoughts spiralling as events start to bed in. 'Wee bastard's obviously movin up the food chain, eh?'

Battle's comin...soon.

Hughie nods, then gets up suddenly, as if unable to cope with what he has going on inside. He holds his guts and looks out the back window again.

'This is pure nuts, Hugh.'

'No cowardly shit this time; we're doin this.'

Jim waves his hands about and brings Hughie out of his trance. 'Where'd this, 'we', come from,' he says.

'We need to do somethin,' Hughie says in a whinging voice that is meant to imitate Jim. 'Well, we're doin something.'

Jim doesn't reply, sits watching his pal over his specs as he paces about like a mental case with lips moving like he's talking to himself.

'I need to go,' Hughie announces out of nowhere.

'You've got to be fuckin kiddin, right?' Jim throws his hands up in protest, staring in disbelief.

Hughie goes to the bead curtain, then turns back to Jim

as if half breaking from a spell. 'I won't be too long ... promise.'

'Meanwhile, I'm sittin on this lot. Nah! Fuck. That!'

Jim is about to let loose again when he notices his pal's eyes are red as if he's been crying; they are wide and glazed, holding a ghost of someone stalking off into the hills, cutting their wrists before slumping down beneath a peat hag. In the short silence that follows, Hughie is drawn to what haunts him most, staring past Jim and out the dirty window towards the Terrace. 'We don't need to do this,' Jim says almost tenderly, holding out reasoning hands.

'I have to go,' Hughie says and leaves.

'If you're late back, this lot's goin in the Clyde,' Jim shouts as the beads rattle.

It is dark enough, at last, around twelve thirty, but Davy Drug is still inside his house.

'Should we give up?' Jim whispers.

'Some soldier you must've been,' Hughie replies from somewhere in the shadows.

Jim had noted the same coldness about his pal when he came back into the shop an hour ago; he certainly hadn't had a shower, but may have been to the pub, his eyes redder with dark bags underneath them.

'I want to get the shite as much as you do,' Jim insists, 'but we've been here for too long.'

Hughie can sense Jim shaking his head.

'A bit longer,' Hughie offers.

Still don't trust this old cunt, weak spine; he's finished. The Knight stands looking into the mind's eye like it is a dressing mirror. He tightens a small knot on a bloody neckless of punctured fingers which he's hung around his black armoured chest plate. He then shows his sharp yellow teeth. ***It's an eradication tonight. Snare this mutt-bastard before he breeds. Crush it!*** The Knight starts to eat what looks like a kidney, blood dripping from his beard as his eyes meet Hughie's.

'C'mon, prick, out you come,' Hughie says loudly.

'Shhhhh,' Jim says. 'He's a drug dealer for fuck's sake, they're no exactly known for being reliable.'

'He's goin down!'

'What the hell has got into you? Let's go back inside, Hughie, talk it over,' Jim whispers.

No answer.

The bale of cannabis protects Hughie's knees from the damp of an earlier rain shower, Jim who is quite content to stand half bent over like a patient old military scout, is somewhere just behind Hughie's shoulder. A warm salt breeze floats up from the Clyde and unsettles the night which sits tight around them as they hide amongst the brambles and the long grass of the waste ground. Both are watching St Andrews Terrace for any sign of movement, like snipers, lost, far behind enemy lines. It is quiet save for Davy's dampened music and the odd shout from an open window at wee Tommy's house when the boy gets on the wrong side of Maggie and she lets loose that whiplash tongue. Don, in No 3, is home but seems to like sitting in the dark in his living room, perhaps feeling invisible to the predators who creep about this place.

'Did you hear a dog bark?' Hughie asks.

'What? ... No, nothin ... Let's go back.' Jim's voice is the opposite of his pal's – anxious, trapped by concern, and unsure of what is happening. After a moment, he says, 'Here, have this,' and pushes something into Hughie's hand.

It is impossible to see what he's been given, though it

feels small and narrow; Hughie stares blindly at his palm. 'What is it?' he asks.

'It's a joint, I rolled a few, to calm your nerves.'

'Christ sakes!' Hughie shouts.

'Shhhh, you'll get us caught,' Jim whispers. 'We could go back to mine and smoke it, think of a different move.'

Hughie puts the joint in his pocket. 'No wonder you got sent home from Aden, nutter.'

'Fuck you! This is kids' stuff compared to what I've seen.'

'Aye, that why you want to give up and run away, let this prick off the hook.'

'Not got a clue, have you?'

'We're fuckin doin this,' Hughie tells him.

He feels Jim push him, so he pushes back hard and they both stand up, facing each other blind and angry, start palming each other away, both tensing up as they can't see the next push coming. When they pause, Hughie can feel the older man's heavy breath, despite not being able to see his face.

Wolf!

They both drop down instinctively as a dim light goes on and a door bolt clacks – Davy Drug's front door opens. The dealer comes out, puts a bag down and turns on a torch. Hughie pats Jim's back in a gentle apologetic way. 'Sorry,' he whispers.

'Shhhh,' Jim says and shrugs his hand off as they peer up through the black tangle of brambles to where Davy stands at the front of his house, the silhouetted thorns looking like barbed wire.

'Who's there?' Davy shouts and takes a step forward, looking out over the waste ground.

Both men fall further to their knees as the dealer holds

his torch high, by his head – casting a light out over the grass – the reflected light making Davy's face look demonic. The torch beam moves slowly from side to side across the waste ground, Hughie balling his fists by his side. He's seen us. **Hold tight; easy, boy.** He's staring right at us. **Hold**.

They sit motionless, breath held, Jim gripping Hughie's arm, as the dealer moves a few steps towards them on the lane just fifty yards away. Davy Drug's head turns as if hearing every small movement and rustle of their clothes.

'It's time we sorted this thing out, once and for all,' Davy tells the darkness.

He bends down and takes something out of the bag, but they can't see what it is in the poor light. He holds a hand up with the thing in it, torch in the other. It looks like ... a fucking gun!

'Right, ya cunt,' Davy shouts, 'let's do this.'

Jim lifts onto the balls of his feet, ready to run, crushing Hughie's arm in an ever-tightening grip.

Davy, alone, bar the two frightened spies in the bushes, starts to dance about in the dim glow, waving the gun in the air.

What the fuck?

He spins fast, points it back at his house, says, 'Fuck you, Degzy man!' They hear the low puck that tells them that he's fired an air pistol at his own door; both drop down on their knees again.

Davy puts the gun into his jacket pocket with great ceremony and swaggers over to his front step where he stands as if looking down on his gunshot victim, legs apart, gangster arms folded, shining the torch on a small spot of rutted tarmac. 'No so fuckin hard now, eh, cunt!'

From the distance, a car horn filters through the layers of the night, distracting and pulling Davy's gaze off down the lane towards it. Without looking back in their direction, he moves to his bag, bends over it and puts the pistol away. The dull door light casts him as some hunched ghoul as he walks off towards Bute Street. His swinging torch beam strays onto walls and bushes making ghostly shapes come alive for an instant until he finally disappears. The light by his door cuts out, allowing darkness to cover the Terrace again.

'That was mental,' Jim says, letting go and standing up.

'That guy he was imagining shootin, that's the dealer he's got himself in with.'

'No keen on his new boss, I guess.'

'Didn't see fishin gear, did you?' Hughie asks.

'Where do you go with an air pistol at night?'

Stop fannyin around.

Hughie takes off his gloves then takes two mobile phones from his pocket, turns them on and gives one of them to Jim. As it comes alive in Jim's hand, it illuminates his scowling face.

'Right, if he comes back, or anything happens, you phone me,' Hughie tells him.

'How do I do that?

Hughie gives a sigh. 'Have you used a mobile before?'

'Nah, don't see the point.'

'Great,' Hughie says.

'You should have shown me how back at the shop.'

'How did you think you'd warn me?'

'I'd whistle.'

'Whistle? Are you fuckin senile?'

'Alright, don't have a go. I'm old, no daft,' Jim says as the tension rises between them again.

'Right, right, if you need to contact me, just push this button—'

'What button?' Jim asks.

'You got it?' Hughie asks after guiding Jim's finger to it.

'Oh, yeah; got it.'

'We'll meet back here, go to your shop and watch for Davy comin home. When he does, we phone the next number down and our pal Lex will nail the little bastard with the gear. Got it?'

'Course,' Jim says, indignant.

Hughie looks off towards the shadow of Davy's house, the night folding around it like a tunnel. Putting his glove back on, he lifts the cannabis bale, scrambling for a better grip of the slippery surface. His fingers come across the hole in the cellophane; it feels bigger than he remembered. 'Did you take more out of this?'

'You sure you want to do this?' Jim says, ignoring Hughie.

'You fly old bastard.'

'It's not too late; we can jack it in ... you're not thinkin straight.'

Without answering, Hughie stumbles forward into barbed wire brambles and darkness.

AFTER MAKING it to the edge of the lane, he glances back, but Jim is invisible to him. Nearer the house, the outside light comes on again and lights up his cowering silhouette.

Light's on a sensor, ya tart. D'you think the Black Douglas held back when he took on the Moors at Teba? Nah! Remember this Davy

cunt's a child abuser, almost burst your skull open, and you know he'll go after yer green-eyed witch soon enough. These wolves are growin stronger, spreadin in your territory – let's get the mutts snared and muzzled.

Taking a big calming breath, he walks through the light to the door, looking in all directions, ears searching for the next unseen threat. Turning the handle slowly, then pushing it, he feels a mixture of relief and terror when the door moves inward without complaint. His heart pounds in his chest as he takes a last glance back at the safety of the dark waste ground – imagining Jim sniggering to himself, joint between lips, waiting for Hughie to go inside so he can light up.

Move on soldier.

Inside the hall, the smell of joss sticks is pungent, no doubt there to fight the stinking damp. Underfoot, the floor feels sticky and it is made of hard floorboards rather than the carpet he'd imagined. He closes the door behind himself, lifts a hand and takes a single step forward into the black unknown. I'm putting myself in a trap. *Puttin shite on your door handle.* I'm a social worker. *Skull pop!*

He feels the shape of a meter box as his left hand explores the wall. He opens it. Flicking the power off, he ensures that any early return by Davy or his bird will be slowed by at least a few minutes as they fumble to figure out why there is no electric. The air catches his throat as he stands back up, perhaps a whiff of Dettol bound to the incense sticks and damp. Stepping forward, he immediately bumps into the wall, throwing his free hand out in panic. Christ, this is crazy. *Drugged in public.*

Moving slower now, he feels his way along the cold

walls, his caveman senses feeling the wall too close with echoing breaths. After a short way, the plaster wall changes to a wood frame and he pushes at what he hopes is the kitchen door, where he'll do the deed. His foot catches on something in the threshold, the bale thumping on the floor. Shite! Motionless, he listens for any activity, holding his breath and turning his head around like a radar dish. The air holds menace within it, his heart thumping as the hiss in his brain tells of all the ways he is going to get caught. **Child-neck-burn.** This is madness. **Children carryin smack**. Pushing at the door again, he taps the deck with his foot like a fireman, looking for holes or traps. He feels something soft beneath his shoe.

What the hell? Feels like ... a body!

He fumbles with a resistant pocket until he manages to free his phone, then sets it to the torch app. It lights his panicked face until he spins the beam down and shows a long, striped snake draft excluder made of blue and yellow wool with black buttons for eyes. He kicks it aside and goes in through the door into more darkness. After flashing the light here and there, it is clear that this is the living room, eclectically furnished with two odd worn sofas, a big telly, shelves full of comics and an old Pioneer hi-fi with big eighties floor-standing speakers, behind this the ever-present damp oozing walls deny any form of normality. He tries moving forward without the light from the phone, soon cracks his knee and bites his lip to hold back a scream. Phone back on, he looks down onto a low coffee table with a giant brass bong on it. The light then strays onto a portable gas fire against one wall with two large, out of place, gas bottles standing behind – the type used in big commercial properties.

Thief as well as a druggie.

Hughie shakes his head as the kitchen sink catches his scanning torch beam, shining through an open door at the far end of the long room.

Bingo.

He memorises the path to the kitchen, turns the torch off, so no one outside will spot it, and moves on, trying to avoid the piles of black plastic bags that lie near the end of the sofa. Half a dozen careful steps and he is into the kitchen where he thumps the bale of hash onto the sink. The Knight looks ecstatic and grins, his black teeth dripping saliva like wolf fangs do. ***We've snared him, he's goin down – Drug-boy's goin down.*** He starts laughing hysterically.

Hughie's heart spikes as he knocks a bottle off the drainer into the steel bowl of the sink – his senses flying out like long tentacles, searching for any sign of danger in what feels like a living, shifting creature rather than a house. Some faint light from the window allows him to perceive a dismembered motorbike, resting on its stand, no wheel on the front fork. It blocks an escape through the back door, three petrol cans completing the blockade. The window behind the sink is half open, to disperse the fumes which he had earlier mistook for Dettol. Night air drifts in, fresh for a moment until it loses out to the sweet stink of fuel. What a hole.

Do it.

From the window, he sees light specks through the trees, the respectable houses that hide the Terrace are giving off glimmers of warm, sophisticated light that seem very close, yet so far out of reach. He lets out a deep breath. I'm standing in someone else's home – a vigilante-house-breaker. ***C'mon, c'mon, do it now.***

He begins groping around the kitchen units for a stash, the tacky worktops, coated in something that sticks to his gloves. While planting the package under the sink, he knocks over half-empty aerosol cans that clang and ping. Fuck, fuck! He pulls his head up and listens for a moment, before pushing the bale to the back of the shelf. He finds more plastic petrol cans, which he arranges around the bale to make it look like a proper attempt at a stash. Closing both cupboard doors gently together, he gives a small sigh.

Snare set.

Back in the living room, he is forced to put the phone torch back on after tripping over a laundry bag. Its light catches on the glass of a line of photo frames on the wall, drawing his eyes to them. He moves closer, sees an out-of-focus Davy Drug, perhaps six or seven years of age, peering back with a mum-shaped woman stood by him, her arm hugging his neck on a bright summer day in the back gardens of the Terrace. They look so happy. Davy's smile reminds him of wee Tommy's when he got his new specs and a bag of sweets. Hughie puts the light closer. Kids are kids, I guess. The next photo is from the mid-eighties judging by the state of Davy's bleached jeans and the Iron Maiden T-shirt and not in town. Recognising one of the others, he screws up his face in the eerie glow. It is a group photo of six teenagers and a stout adult with a bald head and big tash. He knows the tash right away; it is the manager of Bishop-Hill Children's Unit who was known to be a right fascist back then, treated the kids like criminal inmates, rather than victims hiding from the storm.

'Well, well, Davy son, guess life's been kinda shit for you mate,'

A pink satin ribbon draws him to the last photo in the line, probably Davy's mum holding a bundle in her arms, her face full of hope, proud; what was her dream for her baby son then? Perhaps she thought he could get an apprenticeship, become a plumber or a joiner, maybe do well, go self-employed one day and take her on a foreign holiday to Spain or maybe even the Canaries. Hanging from the baby photo is a pink satin ribbon, with something written on it in small print:

Annie Stanz. RIP 1982.

Hughie blinks twice. Lex was wrong, she didn't kick her boy out ... she died. Somehow Davy ends up in with the psychos in Bishop-Hill.

Scum grows on rotten wood.

Standing back, Hughie turns off the light, suddenly seeing wee Tommy next door, with Davy, both standing at the foot of a crushing pyramid of bodies, in the swill, their faces contorted with the weight coming down on them. ***Turn it off.*** Tommy is crying, Davy in a hysterical panic, both trying and failing to keep their snouts out of the gutter as the swill rises up around them. The gutter infects them, stinks until no one wants to sit beside them at school, they don't have the right boots to play in the team or don't go to the gym, because the others will see the marks, the bruises. The GP thinks you're at it all the time and scolds your mum with his middle-class tongue in front of you, and she just takes it. Then that girl you fancied at school, smirks and totally blanks you as you try to pay the overdue rent. As a teenager, the police start slowing down every time they pass you, even on sunny days when you are in a good mood, on the way to the swimming pool. Three more years, and everyone is writing you off as soon as they hear your name, your address, their belief confirmed when the local newspaper nails it all to the wall in the Friday court report the month after you get caught with an ounce you bought for a posh mate in Dunellan. Each slight of the ego fractures that childish smile, replaces it with a blank stare that keeps them away. The iron raindrops from the pyramid keep falling.

Don't go limp on me; that cunt tried to bash yer skull in.

Rubbing his face with his hands, something strange tingles inside; his eyes and throat irritated, a distant high-pitched whine coming in from nowhere.

Fer fuck's sake, we're here to crush this mutt. Crush? Mutt? Crush the poor? That's not why I'm in here, is it? All my electrons, quarks and atoms aren't assembled in this form to do over the poor for … for … revenge.

Don't start this Hughie, not here, not now.

Davy was a child, brought up in poverty like me and wee Tommy. Davy's face is being pushed hard against the bars, tears running on his thin face as a tattooed psycho fucks his bleeding arse, thud, thud, thud.

You spineless cunt!

Hughie slumps down on one knee. 'This guy should have been protected by the likes of me when he was a kid, not set-up, framed, now we've failed. I'm infected.'

The burn on the boy's neck, yer skull gettin bashed, you get drugged; the Eyes from the south, they're winnin again, laughin at you cos they know you'll cave, be weak, nae balls—

Degzy fits the bill better for the first two and that wee barman won't look me in the eye since that night. As for the Eyes, Davy has no connection to that thing. Hughie's face freezes in a realisation. 'You've set me up,' he shouts at the

Knight. 'You're made of the same stuff – the Eyes, you ... it's all hate. You're the Amygdalanian, the rot in the wood. I could have broken free of that Scatter-cash, but you booted into his ribs, loved it, enjoyed it.' Hughie touches the cool floorboards. Jesus. I'm still traumatised. I've just dumped a beautiful girl, used an old war veteran, broken into a house ... for ... revenge?

Evenin up the score. Why not?

You've turned me into a deranged fucking fool, a vigilante burglar, stumbling around in my own wee fantasy world, trying to avenge the past. Hughie's head is moving back and forth. I'm not what the deranged voices in my head say I am; I'm the thing that notices its lies, its anger. That it's wrong. The Knight comes forward, mean slit eyes, his accusing finger lifted high, ready to manipulate and threaten. *Coward, remember Cathy, that wee prozzy down south? Probably dead coz YOU bottled out, cunt.*

Hughie's eyes meet the Knight's. 'No,' he says calmly.

That surety in Hughie's voice hasn't existed for years, but it comes in and lands on the Knight like an anvil from the sky.

You need me; don't you dare. The Knight's face shrinks to that of a little boy, frightened, hiding in shadows and his own imagination as his mum and dad fight, the father's voice making him cringe with every alcoholic bark. *You can't trust any of them, the police are useless, they're all useless, and that's why you can't tell them what happened to you. If you do this, you'll be alone, a nobody, a fantasist, a liar, a useless fucking liar.*

A blinding flare of insight cuts the Knight in two, smoke

and flames coming from his eye-sockets and mouth. His torso fights to the last, cursing his maker until it is ash on the floor of the frontal lobe.

'Oh, no, no, no.' Standing upright, he looks around the poor person's living room, starts to shake his head, plagued by ghosts of his mum and Uncle Malky, both looking worried and wondering what has become of their wee dreamer boy.

'Agghhhhhhhhhhhhhh!' He kicks the coffee table, knocking the brass bong to the boards. The damp walls that have heard it all before, soak it up easy. He moves towards the kitchen, feet shuffling fast and close to the floor to avoid tripping over anything until he gets to the sink.

A dog barks outside in response to a faint high-pitched screech as he ducks below the moonlit window and goes into the cupboard under the sink. Hash package in arms he makes for the front door, nodding to himself. Lob it in the Clyde, that's the best I can do.

'Are you kiddin me, ya clown,' a distant voice says.

It is muffled, but it definitely comes from the front of the house. Angry shouting starts when whoever it is can't get the light to come on. Then there is footfall coming down the hall, two voices arguing.

Hughie drops the hash at his feet and stalks backwards into the kitchen, pulling the door part over as the living-room door bursts open.

Davy comes in first, torch flashing here and there, while Degzy is still berating him from behind. 'If the cops took it, they wouldn't huv left the smack and the DVD players, would they?'

Hughie pulls himself further into the dark, his ears his only defence now as he stands welded to the floor.

'Where's that Polish tart o yours?' Degzy's voice is angry, paranoid.

Davy can be heard anxiously flicking the light switch with no luck – in his panic he argues back.

'I sent her to her sister's, she's freakin ... her brother OD'd on H and she thinks somethin's stalking us ... a spirit—'

Hughie cringes as a dull thud silences Davy and knocks him to the floor.

'Sorry, big man ... sorry.'

'D'you lot think I'm daft?' Degzy screams.

There's a rattling sound as Davy crawls over the floor, manages to light up his gas fishing lantern by the hearth. 'I'll sort the light; fuse must've blown.'

There is a scuffle as Davy is dragged about yelping, then he's thrown back into the hall. 'Sort it,' Degzy shouts. Another sound like the kicking of an arse and clomping feet receding to the front door.

Silence now, a dull ghoulish blue glow from the lantern. Hughie can feel the big dealer standing motionless in the living room, just ten feet away; his malignant aura seeping and crawling towards Hughie between the table legs and along the sticky floorboards. Almost freaking, he imagines Degzy's teeth dripping with anticipation, ready to slice him through the windpipe and let the useless social worker gurgle away his last seconds in terror. Hughie moves inside himself to break the spell. Evil, real hardened evil is close. I'm a rabbit, frozen stiff. He'll sense me soon enough, predators can smell the weak. Hughie glances at the open window above the sink, susses out whether he can get through the narrow opening without stopping before the lights come on and they grab him. I can't make it out – too late now – I'm a stupid fucking narcissistic idiot who thought he understood Nietzsche, kids on he's Übermensch. Wrong, sonny boy! Holding his breath, he reaches up and takes a long kitchen knife from a magnetic strip, careful not to dislodge the other knives and give himself away, points its shaking tip at the door, jumping as the big dealer shouts out in the next room.

'You leave that door open aw the time?'

In the distance, Davy says something that is hard to make out.

'Stupid cunt,' Degzy says to himself, then kicks something across the room, perhaps moving towards the hall.

Like prey before the death it knows is coming, Hughie is caught in the frozen place between fight and flight, unable to move any further. C'mon, c'mon, time to go, through that window and don't look back. But the weight of his past starts crushing him, that uselessness in the limbs that being a torture victim instils deep inside you, that overwhelming knowledge that you are already done for. I need to faint, switch off, so I don't feel it this time. I remember before, the Eyes, a stronger beast, holding me there like an empty coat, no barrier to what it was willing to do. Oh, fuck, its returned, in a different form – still my master.

A bead of sweat on his brow warns of another panic attack that will guarantee death, or worse, another slow torture.

'Yaooaaw!'

Davy's shriek comes through the house as a fuse blows, and the lights stay off. Degzy moves in response, perhaps going into the hall, but Hughie isn't sure and wants to look out the door. No! Must get out. The opportunity pushes him to take that one big step to the sink; peering into the dark living room as he lifts his backside onto the sink, knife still pointing at the gap in the door. All he can make out in the living room are backlit shadows and a strange silence. Don't think the bastard's gone to help Davy. So, where is he? He freezes again as Davy starts cursing at the antiquated fuse box at the other end of the house. Moving his bum further onto the sink, Hughie analyses all the shadows for signs of the big dealer; the scrambling dots on his blind retina making no sense. Despite the weight in his gut, he moves again, slow, until his backside is at the windowsill and he can feel the cool touch of freedom on his neck. He holds his breath as one shadow in the other room begins to stand out. There, close to the door frame. What is it? Sort of rounded. His guts tighten again as he thinks it moves when he leans his head to the side. Is that? An orb of grey dusted specks, just inside the ability of the human eye to observe hanging like an apparition in the dark of the gap in the kitchen door. A gulp sticks in his throat, and he doesn't dare blink. The thing seems to fade until silver light fills the room, the moon finally escaping the clouds. The orb is there again, clearer, with all the small grey specks he'd perceived before starting to glow and join up, the ball thing coming more into being until its shiny black eyes blink open.

'And what the fuck are you?' Degzy asks.

There is a silent moment, then the kitchen door bursts in and the gangster is on him. The knife falls from Hughie's hand as he tries to scrabble out the window on his back. Degzy grabs him near the knee and starts punching at his stomach. There's a burst of desperate flashing hands and feet as Hughie is hauled off the sink, his escape gone, his mind in chaos. Gut-punched, he falls to the floor. This thing isn't even human – my limbs are useless.

'Davy, get in here!' the big dealer screams as he puts the boot into Hughie hard.

Holding his hands in front of his face, Hughie tries to ward off the kicks until one gets through, jarring his cheek bone and collapsing his defence.

Only after he slumps against the kitchen unit and goes

limp does the kicking finally stop. It's happening all over again. Help me, help me, help!

Fight man, fight!

An electric memory in the amygdala fires Hughie back up onto his feet – his rising skull catching Degzy under the chin – the big guy staggers back from the force of the blow, while Hughie throws himself at the window, crawling over the sink, his hands catching each side of the window frame outside. As he makes the final pull towards the specks of safe orange light, his ankle is seized.

'You're fuckin dead, ya bastard!' Degzy shouts, more punches landing, some hitting the spine, some missing and clattering the thin steel sink. – the creature's frantic now, not human. Hughie sees its frenzied crow glass eyes as the thing spins him to get to his soft front. Hysteria is on Hughie, his hands grasping for a grip on anything to avoid the inevitable. As it pulls him back again, he feels something cold beneath his left hand and swings it without any hesitation, the bottle he'd knocked into the sink earlier bounces off the thing's head – its mouth open – that grip going loose for an instant.

'Got it,' Davy shouts as the lights come on all over the house.

The soft net curtains brush Hughie's face as he pushes on the sink and falls backwards into darkness, away from it, his body dropping through the open window frame like a rag doll before crashing onto a plastic wheelie bin. From there, he's thrown onto hard, cold concrete slabs, his palms slapping down before his head. Adrenaline prevents much pain and he's up on his feet and staggering like a wounded cat before running ten yards to thrash his way through a thin privet hedge. He instinctively drops to the ground once in darkness, spins and listens for pursuit. From dark cover, he watches Degzy's blank face at the window, staring out into the night, punching the sink in anger. Even though he's behind a swathe of hedge and tall grass, Hughie's sure the thing can see or at least sense him – the monster's mind radiating out, looking for his scent, able to pick up on his sweat and weakness at any distance. Hughie feels frozen again as it holds him like its cousin, the Eyes, once did. He can smell me, they all can.

'Davy!' Degzy screams, slamming the sash window shut and throwing the microwave off the wall. There are more crashes before its frightening silhouette stomps away from the window.

Hughie stays put for a while. Being that close to evil again is overpowering and he finds it almost impossible to convince himself that he is safe; the notion that that thing is tricking him and will pounce at any moment from nowhere clings to the inside of his head. He feels his crotch, but he hasn't pissed himself. After hearing what sounds like a distant scream, he imagines Davy being punched to a pulp then suffocated by rubber-gloved hands. Silent like a ghost, Hughie runs off across someone's dark drying green and vanishes over a fence.

JIM'S SHOP has no lights on. Hughie turns the door handle and goes inside, then locks it behind himself. As he gets to the counter he can see the old shopkeeper through the beaded curtain in the unlit, back room, propped at the window with binoculars to his eyes, watching the Terrace. Hughie clatters through the noisy bead curtains.

'Shit, you gave me a fright there,' Jim says as he spins round.

Hughie just stands there, his dark shape stalled.

'You got out okay?' Jim says.

'You didn't fuckin phone.'

'I ... I whistled ...didn't you hear?'

'That ... that was you?'

Hughie slumps down in a chair, but Jim can't make him out or see the swollen face and quivering hands, so returns to his binoculars.

'You were supposed to phone, we agreed,' Hughie says, voice on edge.

'The phone went mental, so I gave you a ... a whistle.'

There is a pause where the younger man clenches his eyes shut, while Jim moves his binoculars around the lane.

'It went all wrong in there,' Hughie announces. 'It's a mistake, I'm not phoning Lex.'

'What—'

'I mean it. I've seen photos of Davy ... his mum ... it's not right.' Hughie shakes his head in the dark. 'Anyway, he's probably gettin a beatin as we speak.'

Jim takes the binoculars away from his eyes for a moment, looks at the shadow that is his friend. 'It's too late, Hugh.'

'What are you on about?'

'It's too late,' Jim repeats.

'We're not phoning, anybody.'

Takin the phone from his pocket Jim holds it up, its face glowing green, says, 'They're on the way,' then throws the phone at Hughie, who catches it and looks at the last call.

'Why?' Hughie asks, his voice desperate.

'I see druggie boy comin back with the psycho you described. Tried to phone you,' Jim explains, getting agitated, binoculars held up in protest. 'I whistled, but you didn't appear ... I get in a panic, push all sorts of buttons ...

eventually, it starts ringing someone. Lex answers, so I tell him you're about to get done over. Then I ... ran off.' Jim looks away, out the half-closed curtain.

'Oh no, no, no, no,' Hughie says and starts beating his forehead with his palm.'

Jim lingers, his shadow in the window, unsure what to do next.

'I'm stoppin this,' Hughie announces, starts pushing at buttons on the phone, swears and starts again.

'Too late,' Jim says lifting the binoculars to his eyes once more.

Blue lights light up the Terrace, strobing along the brickwork and out onto the waste ground like surreal spectres. Tommy and his mum come to the window of No 2, to see what all the fuss is about, faces press to the glass, one on top of the other. Hughie manages to get a shot at the binoculars, but it is impossible to focus with his hands shaking so much, so they both creep out into the backyard of the shop to get a better view of the raid. They get drawn closer and closer, like guilty moths to the blue pulse of the police lights, which exposes two cops going around the back and the others grouping by the front door of No 1, bringing on the outside light. The dealers must be aware but are trapped like rabid dogs in a cage, no way out now.

There is a crash as Davy's door bursts in, and cops pile into the house, jostling one another in an adrenaline rush. Lex, as expected, leading the charge.

Jim and Hughie are now back to where they were sat at the beginning of their vigilante mission, through the fence and on the waste ground by the bramble bushes. Angry shouts come from the house, and Hughie begins to rise, wanting to intervene, but Jim pulls him back, 'Too late now, son.'

Strobing blue visions show Degzy inside the window, arms aloft, beckoning the cops to, 'Come ahead, ya cunts!' More banging and shouting, followed by Davy screaming and flashing torch beams in both the hall and the living room. The blue strobe flashes round and round, Degzy in time lapse, swinging the gas lantern like a mad skull, another flash as a torch hits his head. This brings a sudden orange flare, then more shouting and someone screaming in pain. Rocking back and forth, Hughie watches helplessly as the living room of No 1 erupts in flame. Hughie now running through the tall grass towards the lane.

Davy is first to be dragged out of the open front door, legs kicking as he is bundled towards the van, hair pulled back, arm pressed up his back, face streaming with blood that is perhaps the result of Degzy's treatment rather than the two cops who have him now. Davy tries to break away as a cop radioes for a fire engine, butting the other cop in the cheek, starting to run. In his moment of freedom, he sees Hughie standing on the lane, ten yards away, bathed in a dull red light, a blue flash coming and going on his face. He stops dead. 'It was you,' is all he gets out before a baton takes his legs away from behind. Cuffs on, Davy gets a free punch in the kidneys for being a cunt. Life is going the usual way for Davy as he stares up from rutted tarmac towards the devil in that suit.

Most of the noise now comes from the hallway where Degzy is putting up a good fight, the flames that have engulfed the entire living room pushing the battle into the hall. Lex's shouting grows louder and angrier by the second. An officer yelps, there are grunts and more popping from the blaze.

'Scum!' Degzy screams, then goes silent.

The front window blows out in a loud orange flash,

sparkling splinters of glass falling like snow as Degzy is hauled out the house through thick smoke. Lex has the dealer in a tight headlock as flames escape from the window and begin to lick up the front of the house like snakes. Having lost his hat, Lex's face catches the light, he looks possessed.

'Fuck me gently, you've done it now,' Jim says from the bushes, his mouth falling open as another explosion goes off sending the big cop and his prisoner onto the deck.

'Call the engines,' Lex shouts, then punches Degzy hard in the face, now owned by the madness of the Terrace and proximity to his own death. Degzy goes limp.

The Terrace gives a dull groan and flames spit out of its eaves and along the broken cladding. With all the shouting over, the police gather themselves together and stand Degzy up. Like Davy, the big dealer suddenly becomes aware of Hughie, standing silent, further up the lane. He turns his bloodied face to the cops, eyes narrow, and asks, 'What is that?'

After giving Hughie a glance, Lex says, 'My pal.'

Both men are dubbed up in the van with Davy staring through the grill. Hughie looks away as the van rolls silently down the hill, away from the burning building, radio squawking, its blue lights strobing the waste ground where it exposes Jim, stood like a statue, sparks drifting past him into the darkness.

As the rest of the cops troop off, Lex is left uphill of the fire.

He demands an update on the fire engine as he walks towards his pal. Seeing smoke wafting from under the slates all along the terrace tells Hughie that there are no dividers in the lofts to hold the fire back; this sends him running to Maggie's door, banging on it and pulling at the handle.

'Who's in there?' Lex asks as he catches up.

'The wee lad and his mum.'

'Move!' Lex demands as he kicks in his second door of the night. Maggie comes out, pushing Tommy in front of her, both choking and spluttering. 'What in the name o hell have you lot been doin?' Maggie asks.

Hughie shrugs at her and Lex stares at the side of his face.

'Are you okay?' Lex asks Tommy.

The boy nods his head, the flames at No 1 reflecting in his glasses.

'Who done that?' Tommy asks Hughie who looks towards the fire, unable to find the words.

They all stand stunned on the grass, the sheer pace of the gas and petrol fuelled blaze frightening to watch.

'Is Don okay?' Maggie asks Hughie above the roar.

The two men look at one another then sprint to No 3. After a load of arguing, they manage to get old Don to come out, but this is only after threatening him with arrest.

Jim, Don, Lex, Hughie, Maggie and wee Tommy, who holds his mum's hand, stand there beneath an enormous cloud of smoke that bounces the firelight back onto the surviving bay windows. The Terrace brickwork is glowing orange now, like a forge in the depths of hell. As if catching them watching, the smoke drops, choking them and chasing them across the waste ground towards Jim's shop. Only Don and Hughie hang back to hear the roar within No 1 that tells them the second floor has collapsed into what was Davy Drug's living room. Hughie's face is tortured. Davy's photos, the ones of him with his smiling mum, they will be ... gone. He just stands with Don as the flaming creature sucks and breathes through any gap, nail-hole, or cracking window that might feed it with air –

ravenous, it surges and grows again. At the other end of town, sirens cut into the night and half-asleep husbands are sent to look out of windows by their curious, tranquilised wives.

Don turns, watching the social worker's face in flickering orange.

'Wait till wee Chas hears about this,' Hughie says to him as he puts a supportive hand on the old boy's shoulder.

'The Grail,' Don says, pulling away and running off towards his house then disappearing into its open door.

By the time Hughie gets into the hall, it is full of black, choking smoke, so he drops down to escape the worst of it, pulling a T-shirt off a radiator to cover his nose and mouth. He crawls along the damp carpet, stopping every few feet to cough or rub his burning eyes.

'Don! Don!'

In doing this, he drops the rag and takes in a lungful of smoke that burns his chest and chases him back towards the front door, but he is disorientated and runs head first into the wall, stunning himself to the deck. I've done it now; going to die trying to save a possible paedophile.

Something gets hold of him in the dark, pulling him up by the collar and running him out towards the door. Smoke and bodies burst out over the front steps and onto the hard tarmac of the lane. Things are all weird, spinning until he finds himself lying beside Don who is spitting out phlegm, a manic grin showing off his bad teeth that shine like a vampire's in the glow of the blaze.

'Why did you go back?' Hughie shouts.

'The Grail. It'll protect me and the boy.' He pats his chest and crawls away from the smoke onto the grass.

Hughie follows, neither getting up.

Firemen and more police appear, running towards

them, trailing long hoses from the engine that can't squeeze up the lane's narrow width.

'Are you two okay?' a fireman shouts over.

Don grins at him, like someone who's just swum the English Channel, while Hughie can't speak for choking.

'Anyone in there?' the fireman asks.

Holding out a hand for a second, Hughie manages to say, 'All empty.'

'You sure?'

'Hundred percent,' Hughie says and falls back in the grass.

As if hearing this, the Terrace groans and something within Maggie's house falls inward with a loud crash. The fire beast is finding its strength again and roars through the broken windows as they lie there looking up.

'You smell that?' the fireman asks holding his head into the blast.

Shaking his head innocently, Hughie ignores the stench of cannabis that is engulfing the waste ground before it lifts high above and drifts off into town within clouds of black smoke.

'Get back!' another fireman shouts, waving them away.

Going through the hole in the fence to Jim's backyard, they walk slowly, looking over their shoulders every couple of steps when another crash draws their attention back. They both know the beast is going to eat up all Don's art, his scrolled second from Glasgow School of Art, all of Tommy's cosy familiar nooks and the only picture of his dad on the planet, Davy's inherited trinkets and images that reminded him that someone once cared about his rotten soul – the beast devours them along with the poverty, the dodgy electrics and the damp stinking squalor.

They hesitate at Jim's back door. Maggie can be heard

coughing inside, her son asking for sweets in an excited and oblivious tone.

'Don't mention our detour ... and thanks ...' Hughie says.

A look is exchanged, and Don smiles.

In the back room of the shop, cups of tea and beans-on-toast are already on the go as Jim puts in a good shift. Lex is stood away from the others, head at an angle, listening for a return on his chest radio. The rumble of another collapsing floor echoes through the open door, the fire hissing back at the inadequate hoses until Maggie starts crying, and Lex gives the door a kick shut.

Jim nudges Hughie to one side, saying,' You ought to tell your pal where to find the rest of the stuff.'

Shaking his head and warning Jim with his eyes, Hughie goes towards the sink to get water for his burning throat. He gulps at a glass of water, wishing it was whisky, then stops to gasp.

'I'll head back to the office, organise transport to take you to A&E,' Lex tells the motley crew. Something is sitting on his thoughts by the look of it, lots of unanswered questions and loose ends perhaps, the kind of stuff that bugs nosey cops or gets them in the shit. 'You okay, wee man?' he asks Tommy, who gives his jiggly dance and smiles, sweet rotating in his mouth, more in each hand. Benefiting from the slackening of rules during the crisis, Tommy is in with both feet.

'You're something else,' Lex tells him and ruffles the boy's hair.

Jim gives Hughie a nudge as they follow Lex towards the door.

'What will happen to the pair you nicked?' Hughie asks quietly, out of the other's earshot.

Lex stares, his face showing the beginning of a black eye. 'The dope, we couldn't get near it.' After thinking he adds, 'The big guy might have previous, and it was him who started the fire. But Davy will walk after a few weeks in the clink for resisting, maybe.' Lex pulls a face and shakes his head.

When he opens the door, the noise of the fire engine's pumps comes in. He turns to them just before going. 'I'll say it was anonymous,' he says, 'but where'd you get your info?' He looks at both their faces in turn, then fixes on Hughie.

Interrupting before Jim can speak, Hughie says, 'I seen the pair carry it in … while I was visiting the boy … earlier.'

Lex gives a doubtful nod. 'If those two pricks have anything else stashed, we might get their prints on it.' He stares at Hughie again, and his pal shrugs.

'Okay, I'll get a statement from you, at some point.' Lex gives them both a last look, goes out and closes the back door behind himself, leaving the refugees to their supper.

Jim isn't happy, staring at Hughie who puts a finger to his lips. Hughie comes in close, whispering, 'I know, I'll sort it.'

Unimpressed, Jim goes back to his customers as if it were an average afternoon in the shop. Maggie sits beside the euphoric Tommy, her satin dressing gown tight at the waist, her legs akimbo, sobbing into a cup of tea, between puffs on a fag. Don avoids eye contact when he is handed a plate of food, sniffing the offering for poison, then going off to a corner where he sits cross-legged watching the muted TV that bathes the room with silver light. Jim locks the back door as if to keep something from getting in.

'Make yourself useful,' he tells Hughie, waking him from a remorseful trance.

'Do what?' Hughie asks.

'Hang Don's jacket up and get me some sweets for boy-wonder out of the store.'

Hughie turns on the light in the toilet that Jim calls the storeroom, looking for somewhere to hang the jacket. Some of Jim's work shirts hang on hangers, and boxes of sweets and booze sit on everything else, including the loo seat. His throat feels scorched as he looks at his face in a broken mirror on the wall. It looks like a husk, soot in every crevice and pore. Exhausted, he reaches up to hang Don's jacket on a spare hanger, feels something square sat in the breast pocket, a white edge peeping out. He remembers Don patting it when he escaped the fire. He undoes the button fastener, then pauses. I get to see the Holy Grail at last – bet it's a picture of Don's mum; total shocker if it's a naked kid. Lifting it out and turning the photo to the light, he catches his breath, a strong sense of dread making him sit down on a stack of lager cans. 'This is not holy,' he whispers, eyes fixed on it. How could ... how could I have got it all so wrong?

'You havin a shit in here?' Jim says, popping his head around the door.

Hiding the photo in his pocket, Hughie nods his head, tries a fake smile as he picks up a box of Freddo bars, his face looking so pale, worried.

'That wasn't your fault out there ... it was inevitable,' Jim reassures him.

Hughie doesn't move.

'Hurry it up,' Jim orders with a fatherly grin and goes back out the door.

Christ, listen to the old prick, givin us orders; he shat himself out there, left us for fuckin dead.

Hughie searches after the Knight's voice, through the bile black corners of the frontal and parietal lobes of his brain until he finds him hiding in the amygdala. He is naked, backed into a corner with sword in hand, swiping at his maker with panic and terror. Jim does things because he cares ... he might fuck up, but he cares. You, you pushed me to go against my own nature, the rules of the Order. Why? Because you want never-ending revenge for what happened in Manchester; you don't care who the victims of that revenge are or might be, it doesn't matter to you. Turns out us two arseholes got a lot of it wrong. The Knight's head becomes encased in gagging lead and he falls through a floor of snapping teeth into a liquid limbic dungeon, arms flapping, silent. You are dead to me. The words echo around his mind, to every fissure, fold and crevice. No reply. Hughie touches the photo in his pocket and leaves the storeroom with the box of Freddo bars.

JOYCE SENSES something is wrong down the phone.

'I can't explain it all,' Hughie tells her, 'but we need rooms for a mum and son and a single for Mr Donald Cameron.'

As he says this, Don grins up from a comfy chair, orange bean stain on his shirt.

'Hughie,' Joyce says and leaves a gap, 'you know you're a crazy bastard, don't you?'

'Phone 775850, when you get the rooms confirmed,' he tells her. 'Jim will put them in a taxi.'

After hanging up without warning, Hughie bends down to give Tommy a hug, but the boy pulls back.

'Is he still an arsehole?' Tommy asks his mum.

Maggie stares at Hughie for a long while, her lined face

like an old sore. 'Looks like we'll be getting a new house at last,' she says. 'Give him a cuddle.'

The boy's arms go around Hughie and that pulsar smile fires about the room to break the others from their dark thoughts. But it doesn't last, and the blackened faces begin to look exhausted, the events now taking a toll. It goes quiet inside Jim's kitchen, apart from the television which has gone into late night mode – a busty woman spins a roulette wheel and the camera zooms into blurred stripes of white, black and red.

As Hughie tries to sneak out with a coat hanger and a pair of marigolds he's stolen, Jim catches him at the shop front door.

'Where you goin now?' he asks, looking at the gloves.

'Sorting it,' is all he says, shutting Jim in.

Like a bedraggled automaton, he zigzags the streets until he finds it two down. He puts the gloves on and fiddles with the back passenger-side window, which eventually relents and drops, then leans in, opens the door and pulls the seat forward to access the boot. The alarm doesn't raise his heartbeat a single skip. From the boot, he pulls forward the DVD players, then pats around with his yellow rubber palms until he touches the pack. He has no idea what it's worth as he looks at the heroin. Rubbing the DVD players and the smack with his sleeve takes over a minute, but he doesn't fluster, too exhausted. After putting it all back together he walks away as the yellow indicators flash in time with the whine of the alarm. The phone box under the gargoyle of the Burgh Hall is working for a change, so he dials the number, and interrupts a woman who answers. 'There's a car on Hill Street, alarm goin; tell your sergeant it's there. Tell him!'

ON THE DARK landing outside his flat, he turns and looks up at the fire exit. The exit door is hitting the frame as if pushed back and forth by an unseen hand.

'Fuck me gently,' he says and forces himself to climb the last ten steps where he steps out onto the roof. A breeze has begun to lift and push the cloud, above him, the stars are visible again, the whole place dark save for the dull glow of street lights from the other side of the building. On the air, there is the faint smell of burning wood and maybe cannabis if you can recognise it. About to go back down, something catches his attention off to the left. Did it move? Further along the cast-iron fire escape, which runs along the back of the next four buildings, something flickers as if his line of sight has been crossed. He listens. Nothing, just the warm air rolling off the Clyde towards the hills and the faint noise of drunk laughter from way down the High Street at a lock-in at the Auld Hoose. Rubbing his grimy face and eyes, he notices a faint glow through a window of the Lodge building. I guess the Masonic lads are up late, fucking goats, playing naked boy-scouts games or whatever secret societies do at this time of night. He begins blinking, sure there is movement on the long walkway. Can't be Davy Drug, that's for sure, he's tucked up in the nick with the gangster. There it is again. His pulse lifts but soon drops as a car engine fires up somewhere off in the distance, breaking the spell. Too weary to consider any more heroics, he plods off the roof, pulling the door hard shut, then shoves a rusty bolt into place. **Never block the fire exit**, the sign says. Not unless there are other things to fear, worse things, things that creep about on roofs in the middle of the night. He rattles the door to make sure it is tight shut. I'm totally fucking paranoid now.

After flicking on the light just inside his door, he sniffs his hand and draws his head back. 'Fuck me!' Moving inside, he bolts the door with his clean hand, turns the mortise lock and flicks the Yale snib on. At this point, he clocks the shit he's smeared on the wall when he flicked the light on. What is going on? Before doing anything else, he goes around the rooms of the flat, using his clean hand to turn on the lights and lamps until every room is lit, and he checks for creatures, monsters and night-stalkers. While scrubbing his hands in the bathroom, he stops to sniff them now and then, never convinced that they are clean. He feels too tired to wash his coal-man face and just lets his trousers drop onto the bathroom floor. After taking the Grail from his jacket pocket, he lets the jacket fall with the rest and walks away in his shirt and socks.

Whisky, a big glass of it, accompanies him to the bed where he lies back on stacked pillows, the drink sat on his chest, the photo in his other hand. He looks from the Grail to the flaking ceiling that hangs beneath the rooftop.

'Surely not,' he whispers, his eyes dropping again to the photo which he tilts into the faint light from the window. 'Is this the same creature?'

Outside on the street, a lonely car passes, its engine hoarse, cutting the early-summer night and the thin window glass – fading in echoing fits and starts until it can only be heard in the imagination. Perhaps it was a solitary house-wife making her way back home after meeting her fancy man, racking her brain for a believable excuse for being away so long. He looks up as the ceiling creaks with the wind. Maybe my stalker drove off ... maybe the bastard's still here. This pushes the glass up, the whisky tipping down his throat, small drips escaping to stain his shirt. As the glass empties, his eyes grow heavy again and he imagines the roof fire exit door open once more, creaking to and fro in the soft breeze.

'How did I get it all so wrong?' Hughie asks his dead mum and Uncle Malky who shuffle into his mind as reinforcements. They both stand mute, no reply.

As the town's inhabitants finally give up, his hand goes loose, the empty glass making a dull thud as it hits and rolls along the carpet. Snoring soon echoes against the screwed-shut windows as he lies sprawled out on the bed covers like a fallen bird, the Grail clasped to his damp chest.

FOURTEEN

THE VISITATION

Red eyes staring, tears and a high-pitched sobbing, smoke. Please!

'Who?' he says as he sits bolt upright, his hand scrambling for the lamp, knocking it off the bedside cabinet onto the floor where he hears the bulb smash.

The faint light of the digital clock shines a red glow on his head as he cocks it to one side, still listening for things. Nothing, just another nightmare. Lying back, he puts his hand to his chest, then panics, sends one hand under the covers until it finds the Grail lying beneath him. Need to get more sleep but can't sleep, so I'll just lie here like a prick pretending. Rolling on his side doesn't help as his senses are now hyper, tuned to every crumple of the pillow, creak of a cooling radiator, or bump when Mrs Murchison through the wall gets up for a piss; all of it instantly analysed in detail for its origin, level of threat, and then matched against an opposing de-catastrophizing, anti-panic programme the shrink taught him in PTSD school. Paranoia always beats the rational mind; some monster is always waiting, pressed tight against the other side of the crumbling plaster, its mass ready to burst through at any second. The condition is so tiring because the body just isn't designed to stay on high alert for years on end. He rolls over, again. I need to get up, insomniacs like me never sleep like normals. Even harder when you've got whisky inside you to boost the system like a hundred watt per channel amplifier wired to a cheap transistor radio. Stubborn and fried, he lies in bed another ten minutes, listening to the place breathing before rumination forces him to throw his feet out of the duvet.

Early morning glow and birdsong ooze from the top of the heavy curtains to justify his activity, the rough carpet feels cold beneath wiggling toes. Leaning forward, he picks up the lamp and the bits of broken bulb and puts them on the side, so he won't step on them later when caught in his worries. A stink of whisky wafts up off the duvet to add to the taste of barbecued wood that clings to the back of his throat. He shivers through the hall, flicks the thermostat for the boiler, then goes into the kitchen to fill a kettle, chased by the eerie early light that only shift workers know. The tap shudders and sends a signal up the pipework to the other inmates of the building, telling them that he is still alive, and it is his turn to wander about inside his locked flat, alone.

'Still here,' he tells himself.

There is a slight tremor in his hand as he carries his over-filled tea cup into the living room and puts it down beside the armchair, where he coils up in his dressing gown and lifts his feet up. Leaning down, he turns out one of the lamps he left on in the night, stale air from the floor catching him with a mixed scent of sweaty socks, smoke and spilled whisky. He checks the Grail is safely tucked deep in his gown pocket. The clock keeps him company as the tea goes cold and the day washes in. Eventually, nine o'clock arrives, and he sits up in the chair.

'Who is my worst enemy?' Is it my inner vigilante or the creature of the Grail? At least my intention was good, totally misguided and driven by trauma and paranoia, but I care, I do ... I care. *It* is different, *it* is a monster, a real sociopath; that's clear now, and I must've been so mind numbingly blind to not pick up on something so fucking obvious.

The phone rings, breaking his train of thought. He ignores it and it stops. Sitting in silence, his fingers soon find their way back to the Grail in his robe pocket and he takes it out, holding it up so he can stare at it again. She looks humiliated, her face contorted with tears, mascara bleeding down her wrinkled cheeks like black blood. Behind her, he's in a rage, eyes narrow with effort, teeth clenched and beads of glistening sweat running in the contorted lines of a swollen face. Hughie gulps his dry throat. Is that all sex is in the end? – An angry ape turf war where wombs are the prize, vaginas just gates to be kicked down in the battle for genetic domination. It is hard to be sure it is rape, but she looks so upset. What can ... what should I do now? What risks if I expose the truth? He starts to hug himself, then stops as he remembers old Don the schizo's habit of doing that. The photo is held close, so he can see the blurry detail, his head starting to shake gently at it. These sociopath-types can lie ... lie more convincingly than I can tell the truth; in the end, it's all useless if you don't have a witness; life's all anecdotal, that's Scottish law, why cops ponce about in twos, why rapists walk free. If the victims are keeping quiet, what chance have I got? Listen to me, the peeping Tom, the last of the reliable witnesses, talking myself out of my responsibilities within this filthy wee saga. Holding the photograph between his palms, he prays to his mother's and Uncle Malky's memories for wisdom. This little thing could blow the arse out of the whole fucking ship if I want it to – sink the rescue boats. Next door's toilet flushes yet again and he hears it rush and gurgle in the cast-iron soil stack within the wall on its way towards the sewer below, under High Street. Miss Murchison must have had the runs. Why is she so isolated? Why doesn't she talk?

Hughie throws open his robe and stands up in one motion, then puts the photo in the printer-scanner and presses auto scan. While he waits, he pours the dregs of a bottle of Drambuie from last night into an empty tea cup, sips it and grimaces. 'I'm just as bad, am I not?' he asks himself. One-night stands, fires, getting assaulted and drugged, fist fights with poor people; even breaking into houses and planting dope. Jesus, I don't fuck around these days. I'm a nutjob alright, but perhaps the only guard on the wall. In his peripheral vision, he catches sight of an iron foot – the Knight – looking to step in to help him out. A knock at the front door makes him look towards the hall. The Knight vanishes. Standing dead still, he listens, but the sound of the scanner cutting in grasses him up right away, its sound echoing out of the gloomy room and down the hall.

Who in the name of fuck?

Shit! It can't be Davy Drug or Degzy, not unless they're out on bail or have escaped. Moving into the hall on bare tiptoe, he creeps down it, a weight of dread on his chest – this doubles as he stands on a loose board, giving away another sign that he is in. Lifting a cricket bat, which he bought when the stones in the close had started to change to shit on the door handle, from beside the front door, he raises it high and to one side. As his fists clench tight around the rubber handle, it makes the scars stand out around his knuckles, white symbols of the work of monsters, proof of the real world. I'll brain it, crush it! Stepping closer, he tilts his head.

'Hugh?' it says.

He doesn't dare speak, but his fists loosen.

'Hugh, it's me.'

Right up at the door, he holds his breath and turns an ear to it. 'Is that you?' he asks, his throat catching.

'Who else says it's me and sounds like me? Open up, I need to talk, idiot.'

Lowering the bat, he turns the mortise key slowly until the latch withdraws into the lock. The door is still tight. He hesitates as he holds the heavy slide-bolt, then drags it across and un-snibs the Yale at the same time – the door is now loose in its frame. He turns the handle, keeping the door firm within his grasp in case he has to force it shut again. With the gap at a few inches, he peers into the light-less hall.

'You're a hard one to get a hold of,' Karen says, then pushes in the door.

There is little resistance now as he stands in his pants and dressing gown, holding a cricket bat dangling by his side. Karen sweeps past, heels striking the boards as he catches the scent of fresh air and perfume. Like a boy, he follows on.

In the front room, she turns around, looking him up and down with a screwed-up face. 'You look ... rough,' she says.

His head hangs, unsure what to say as Karen puts a poly-bag and a pint of milk down on the coffee table, goes to the window and throws the curtains aside, letting blinding light flood the room; Hughie holds up the bat to block the glare – for a moment looking like an escaped lunatic in a searchlight. Her small nose twitches, and she waves a mocking hand to waft away the stink of booze, socks and man-sweat. With a hard pull, she lifts the window up several inches, letting in briny air.

'Oh aye, your neighbour over there is a bit of a prick-tease, is she not?' she says, staring across the street.

He doesn't answer, gives a loose shrug.

'What's with the bat?' she asks.

'The bat?'

Looking back at him and narrowing her eyes, she says, 'Have you got Asperger's or something?'

'Sorry ... I'm not well.'

'Joyce is worried, wants you to call her today.'

He thinks for a moment, blinking at the light. 'You know Joyce?'

'She told me you took three weeks leave without notice, were acting all weird since the fire thing.'

'You know Joyce?' he repeats.

Karen ignores him, looking at the bat again with a worried look on her face. He throws it over by the telly, where it clatters against the stand, its handle scattering some DVDs.

'You know about the fire?' he says.

'It was a big fire, Hughie; everyone knows.'

Backlit by sunlight, she looks like an angel, her gaze drifting to where he's slung the bat then around the chaotic room, an awkwardness coming between them.

'Present, from Joyce, not me,' she says, picking up the poly-bag and holding it out towards him, the shape of a file seen through the polythene.

'Thanks.' He takes the bag, opens it and stands staring into it.

'Is it what I said the other mornin?' she asks, her cheeks reddening.

He says nothing, stands frozen, peering into the bag.

'Felt a bit ashamed,' Karen admits. 'You creepin out the door, me knowing I'd have to pass you all embarrassed in the street within a week ...'

'I wasn't creeping out!'

His outburst immediately sounds too harsh, a new weight in the room. He hides his pants and white thighs by wrapping his gown around him, tying the belt tight, still looking like a secure unit escapee. He goes to say something but catches himself. When the war's over, perhaps then I can tell her about all this madness; not now, no way. Don't get her involved, keep her safe 'My head's full of work stuff ... I can't explain,' he tells her, hands held out, avoiding her gaze.

'Joyce did phone me,' she insists, 'I'm not just trying to worm my way back in, wanting a shag.' Pausing, she looks from his hairy shins to his soup-stained robe then onto his hung-over, badly shaven face, before adding, 'Thankfully,' to save what pride she has left.

'I've got stuff goin on, Karen.' He feels like an abuser at this point, walls building and his mouth drying out as they stand there. He wants to take another drink of whisky but doesn't want her to catch on.

Her face goes the other way, grows soft as she tries to make him look at her. 'Why don't you open up?' she asks.

'Karen ...'

'After what we did, and how it happened, I really needed you to come back the next day, with flowers maybe ... we'd make up.'

He doesn't react to this, takes a pair of trackie bottoms off the back of the sofa, pulls them up under his robe, hopping about on one foot for an embarrassing moment where he thinks he might fall over. He pulls socks from the radiator, leaning on the wall this time as he puts them on. She is still looking at him; it is unbearable.

'It's me, right,' he says. 'Main thing is, it's not you, it's me. There's other things goin on in this town apart from—'

'Be honest with me, Hugh, please.' Her sad green eyes flash, haunting him, making him look.

He moves about the room to lessen the spell. Must resist her pull; she's not safe around me, like the other girl, an innocent in the war. But I love her! He is stopped by his own thoughts and resembles a stroke victim as he stares at nothing.

'Sit,' she says, looking worried by the expression on his face.

He sits, hands gripping the edge of the sofa as she looks down.

'Oh, Hughie, what are you up to?'

Unable to cope with her gaze, he looks out the window at the sky. 'I forgot it was summer,' he says, red eyes blinking.

'What's wrong, Hugh?'

'Don't get caught up in this,' he warns her.

'But I want to.'

'Why?' he says, his unshaven face contorting in disbelief.

'You know why,' she says gently.

Getting up again, he moves away from her, picking up the bag she brought. 'What's this?' he snaps.

'Joyce asked me to drop it off.'

Karen's face loses all its light at that moment, her arms wrapping around herself as she stands, clearly wondering why she makes such a fool of herself so often. She would never have known it, but he notices that she's dyed her hair a reddish-auburn and straightened it; notices how the light cuts through it to warm her perfect, worried face; notices and can hardly resist those caring eyes that he knows lead to a warm ocean. He takes the file out of the bag. She's a goddess. No – stop it! A portcullis of nobility slams into the floor of his mind. Do the right thing for once – let her go.

'Hugh,' she says, waking him.

He stares at her coldly before asking, 'How do you and Joyce know each other anyway?'

'We've been bevy twins since school,' Karen tells him.

'More people knowing my stuff.'

'It's called friendship—'

'Fucking incestuous!'

She looks hurt when he cuts her off, but he doesn't rectify it.

'What is it, Hughie?' she pleads.

He ignores her, studying the first page of the file, his jaw tightening when he clocks the names. As the file thuds back on the table, he gives her a look, empty, even heartless. 'You'll be headin off then.'

Something finally gives inside her, a shadow falling around dulling eyes as she tidies herself to go. She flashes the greens and leaves a long silence where he might save the day, but he refuses.

'I'll see you out.'

'Don't bother,' she whispers.

Her steps are self-conscious but calm as she leaves him and marches out the door and into the hall. He doesn't follow, her steps quickening as she races down it. He hears the door snib being pulled at in a panic – the door slamming so hard behind her it bounces back open, then her heels clacking on the landing and away down the stone stairs while he stands bolt upright in the living room, rocking back and forth. Don't pull her into this mess, Hughie. Don't—

Running along the hall and out onto the landing, he hangs over the iron banister rail. Perhaps hearing him, her heels stop below in the close, waiting for him to call her. He clenches his jaw to hold her name back, gripping the banister so tight that the scars shine out in the grey light. He takes two steps down the stairs in his socks before stopping and holding his eyes hard shut. The cold stone beneath his feet seeps up with despair as her heels click-clack off out of the close onto the High Street.

Cupping his skull with both hands, he tenses then lets it all go. 'Aaaagghhh!'

Despite it being quarter past nine on a sunny June morning, the walls are still damp, and he can feel them breathe as they close in around him, sneering at this weak, foolish child.

The scars shine on his knuckles like some reminder of the plague as he pushes on the locks, entombing himself in the flat again. The beep of the scanner draws him along the hall towards the living room, the machine beginning to print out copies in a series of clacking jolts. As they fall by his feet, he stands there absorbing what they tell, alone.

The scanner flashes: SEND TO COMPUTER?

Pushing 'okay', he bends and picks up the photos, turning one of them around several times, as if trying to make sense of what he is seeing. His gaunt stubble-covered face looks at it cold now, as you would a piece of evidence that has the potential to damage your reality.

'Smart enough to leave little behind,' he says. 'But you underestimated the peasants, you bastard.'

He rubs his top lip as the face of the creature looks back at him. It is blind drunk, all red and puffy. Maggie's face worse, upset, with mascara tears running down her cheeks, hair pulled back, her clothes ripped down around her waist.

Her outstretched arms and hands are struggling to hold its weight. Hughie's attention is drawn to something worse, something that truly makes this a dragon-killing Grail of a picture. In the top right-hand corner, you can make out a child's trainer with a patch of pink – wee Tommy's ankle. This points to further emotional and psychological abuse.

Lowering himself onto the sofa, a wolf begins howling in Hughie's head, sharp teeth dripping with saliva. He sits there, face frozen, just staring.

'Everyone knows, but no one is willing to stand up,' he says as if trying to convince some part of him that still wants an easy life that it is time. Was it him who clobbered me? Must have been hiding in the hall for ages, waiting or tipped-off by some bastard in the pub. If Karen and her mates had never come along ... He knew I was broken, then got a fright when I kept digging.

'Turned me and Davy Drug on one another without even tryin, like we were stupid slavering dogs.' He begins to drift. 'I wanted it, somehow.'

Just as desolation is about to move in again, he catches a whiff of her perfume, faint at first, perhaps real or perhaps imaginary or a wish. It is so sweet, growing like a rushing breeze that clears the fog, rattling the rotten stems and loosening things that fall from the distant memory, drawing them down on him. When he closes his sore eyes, he sees his mum. Look at her face, it's that day. She's so strong for us, despite just burying her husband. Oh, there's Uncle Malky ... he's smiling despite being jumped in the close in John Street where he got a hard kicking – but he came back home without a moan, made a joke of it for me and my brother's sake, then made us mince and tatties. There's John, my wee brother; I caught him under the covers with a torch, thought he was looking at porn, but it was his homework. I can still see his blinking eyes, all red and tired, yet relentless to learn; he got his Highers the next year, and a degree, four years before me – not bad for scum like me and him. Trish, my sister, waving as she left. Big round tears hung on Hughie's lashes as he sees himself from above, sat on the chair with his mum to his left, John and Trish to the right and then Uncle Malky right in front; they stand like sentinels, kind looks on all their glowing faces. He finds himself shaking, the tears running over a faltering smile; the beast that hides behind the peeling walls falling back, crawling off up the plaster, in full retreat.

'I've let everyone down,' he tells them.

'Never submit to live in the bonds of slavery entwined, my son,' Uncle Malky recites.

It is from *The Triumph Tree*, mystical words from saints, bards and warriors that he'd found amongst his Uncle's books, the same books that got him into history in the first place.

'But I kissed a prostitute's head. I slept with Karen,' Hughie tells his guardians.

'Hardly crimes,' his mum whispers. 'The Manchester girl was a lost soul.' She sweeps in. 'You tried so hard.'

'I abandoned her at her lowest ebb,' he insists, his hands held out in front of his face.

'You thought he'd kill her, and like any other good man, you did what you could,' she says, her lilting island voice soothing, leading him.

'Face it, I'm a mental case,' he says.

'But you've always been mental, don't start worryin about it now,' his brother jokes, making Hughie grin and wipe tears from both cheeks. The brothers laugh at one another for a moment and it feels so good.

'Remember, it's all just a glorious blink,' Uncle Malky

tells him as he folds his arms, still wearing that burgundy jacket that Hughie said was purple to wind him up. 'On deck, sailor.'

The smile on Hughie's lips is so rare it feels uncomfortable at first, so he lets go of it. 'God, I'm talkin to the dead now; mental,' he says.

'Hoah!' his brother shouts. 'These two idiots might be buried corpses up the High Road, but I'm in Australia and she's in Yankee land.'

Trish cuts in, 'You never phone or respond to e-mail, you twat!'

'Well, Australia's like being dead really,' Hughie replies.'

'Says the peeping Tom,' Trish responds and winks at him.

Hughie looks straight at his siblings. 'I miss you two,' he says.

'Dig below the pain,' his mum whispers in his ear, 'find your soul's roots, who you are.'

'I'll try,' he says and closes his eyes.

When he opens his eyes the Guardians are gone, not there. He feels his mood go to dip, then thinks about his mum's words again. 'Okay,' he says and tentatively puts one foot on the floor. Breathing deep, he hunts after Karen's scent.

E-mail finger poised on the mouse, he stares at the screen.

TO ALLEN FERGUSON, Director of Services. See enclosed picture of Charles Wright, Area Team Leader and senior social worker for the Authority, having sex with a vulnerable client while her son Tommy Anderson is in the room.

If he is not removed from his position, I will go to the press by this week's end.

YOURS sincerely
Hugh MacDonald, social worker, BA Hons.
Cc Faye Knowles,
Andy McBain, Head of HR.

THIS WILL CAUSE CHAOS, open ten cans of worms and set even bigger fires; why not let it lie? The last molecules of Karen's perfume fire him up – the proof that a Holy Spirit exists. He clicks the mouse – *SEND*.

Looking off out the window into the patchy sky, he searches for reassurance as the traffic starts up on the High Street, the curtains flapping in the breeze are soon sucked into the gap in the window – his smile falls as the room darkens and the fragile summer recedes away from him as if following the lost dream of Karen away up the road. He puts his tired head in his hands, knowing what is ahead, knowing his allies are mostly dead ones.

FIFTEEN

WHERE THE CROWS DINE

The beep from the car door lock breaks the quiet of the car park. On the way around the side of the building, he thinks it strange not to meet anyone else. This adds to the feeling that he walks towards the gallows and that urge to run away again, get on the ferry, then the train, never ever return. He doesn't even notice the seagull swoop down and lift a scrap from the main road ten yards away as he goes in the main door alone. From the first stair, he can hear the keyboards clacking out a message in undulating waves: stay away.

When the office door creaks open, the typing fingers stop, and every single face turns towards him – most people quickly looking away, but the keyboards staying silent. Paranoia manifests en route to his desk, taking the form of a weight in his lower stomach and legs; the feeling that he might trip on nothing and land face down on the floor, haunting every step. When he gets there, he makes an odd grunting noise and looks around at them all, challenging any one of them to eyeball him, but no one does. The keyboards begin rattling again.

Hughie gives up looking for a fight, notices fresh, wet,

coffee mug rings on his desk's surface. Looks like some bastard's been rooting through my stuff this morning, looking for things, marking their territory while wanting me to know it. Hughie follows the mystery rooter into his desk drawers in search of an envelope to put the evidence in.

Across the room, Joyce offers a quick smile that soon falls away, but he notes she doesn't come near. The wires have been rattling all week with rumours and leaks, while he's been sat at home ruminating. Now he has returned, the crows are gathered en masse for the feast, not one leaving for the client home visits which should have started. He smiles to himself.

This is it. I'll treat it all as a workplace Old Firm game – right nasty, but winnable. The admin guy from Criminal Justice gives Hughie a brief nod, then looks away. Can't blame them really, always good to watch from the sidelines. Anyway, these affairs often throw up promotion opportunities or at least a new desk near the window.

He puts a square of sticky tape over Maggie's face, then puts the photo in the envelope and writes The GRAIL on its front. The worker drones look up in unison as he stands and walks past them all to the photocopier. Wiping his hands down his trouser pockets, he takes the evidence from the envelope and places it on the scanner screen, pressing the lid down hard, its surface hot against his sweaty hands. He feels them watching as he searches the finger pad menu, someone's chair creaks as the weight comes off it. Joyce appears next to him, her usual mischievous smile absent.

'Why didn't you answer,' she asks under her breath. 'Have you heard about the Pink Bird?'

He looks at her, puzzled. 'What about her?'

'She's dead.'

The brave façade he has held over the last ten minutes evaporates and he begins to blink uncontrollably.

'He's trying to say it was your fault; that you were behind with your assessments. The woman's sister in Corby is going ballistic, want's ... someone's job.'

'Poor wee Pink.' He looks at Joyce, trying to get his bearings again.

'He's behind this.'

'Who?' he says, still reeling.

'Petite Merde,' she says as if this would be obvious.

It finally dawns on Hughie, who shakes his head. 'She was fine.'

'Poor old cow got an infection in the care unit, first week, drifted off the next day.'

'I didn't know ...'

Joyce looks up at him, her face becomes pitying. 'He's tellin everyone who'll listen, that you're a ... useless drunk.'

He takes this blow incredibly well, though his hand still goes up to rub his neck, a clear tell for the watching flock.

Everything freezes as the main door crashes open and Chas stomps in, suited up, new blue tie on, face like thunder. Joyce veers off, disappearing amongst the desks. Inside the Team Leader's office, Faye, and Allen Ferguson, the Director of Services, both stand up and look through. Chas ignores their hand flapping invitation and walks around the office in a hurried arc towards Hughie, scaring anyone who dares lift their eyes with a staunch glance.

'You, fuckin insect,' Chas shouts from ten paces.

Hughie doesn't parry but fumbles at the buttons on the photocopier, which begins to nosily churn out copies of the evidence. Letting go of the machine, Hughie stands firm, feeling his gut wobble, but managing to keep his face still, calm somehow.

'I have worked for fuckin years tae raise this place up, covered arses and fought for fundin, for jobs,' he says, stopping an arm's length away from Hughie. 'You're a lying, spineless weasel, MacDonald,' he says, jabbing the air with an angry wee finger.

As the room spins, Hughie feels a concrete car park of expectation from the onlookers dropping on him; it catches his breath, tempting him to release the Knight from retirement. Silence reigns for a moment, save for the onslaught of the tireless copier, both staring at each other.

'You're finished,' Chas says leaning in.

'You abused a young child. You also abused his mother who came to you for help; time to pay the piper.' Hughie's words are spoken with such clarity and purpose that they become a cold rapier, sharp, and brutally effective as they stab his opponent's psyche and twist deep.

Some of the staff sit up at this point, perhaps seeing Hughie for the first time, perhaps seeing a man who'd climbed the management ladder down south, but most of all because their fear is diminishing. Although they can't see the holy armour his mum put on him in the car, they can now see a strong man in a very difficult place who is playing a blinder.

'I've done more for this town than you could believe,' Chas shouts, catching his fist in the air and putting it down.

Hughie puts his head down and shakes it. 'No, you're a sociopath, Charles, who's been caught in the act.'

A clear chink in the sociopath defence has been found, followed by another penetrating wound. It leaves Chas blinking, a cavernous hole exposed behind his bluster.

Hughie gives a soft smile. 'Still smoking the cigars?' he asks, then watches as a deep red runs up Chas's cheeks and neck. Here it comes, c'mon punch me in the face, then I'll fall back in front of witnesses – the psycho's mask removed.

Chas, however, is made of well-seasoned badness. He steps back from the brink to leave Hughie feeling disappointed.

'Made a mistake here, son,' Chas says quietly as he cools. 'A big one.'

Everyone in the office has abandoned sleekit glances and are all sat up and gawking at the pair without shame or fear of reprisal, though Hughie notices that no one has tried to intervene.

Beeeeeeeeeeeeeeeeeeeeeeeeeeeee

The photocopier beep makes Chas look down at it and something begins to dawn in his eyes. Hughie stands to the side, blocking his view of it. That body check would have been enough to get him one of Chas's spit-ball bollockings only a day or two ago, but things have just changed. The boss steps back again, warily looking across the pool of staff as the arena shrinks to the size of a phone box.

'Right, you two; in here!'

It is Ferguson, the Director, shouting from the doorway of the small office. 'Perhaps our laundry's best done in private, what do you think, gentlemen?'

Hughie tries to bend and pick up his A4 copies as Chas marches off.

'You too, MacDonald,' the big boss demands.

In a panic, Hughie lifts the lid and puts the Grail into the envelope, abandoning the idea of a bigger copy as he hurries into the office. Once he is in, Ferguson stands at the door, trying and failing to stare down the flock of staff who are now cawing to one another, the place feeling almost unruly, work abandoned. The office door slams.

SIXTEEN
THE BIG MATCH

Chas's office is more of a five-a-side pitch compared to the arena-like main office they have just left. It is hot, claustrophobic and stinks of too much testosterone – ideal for a closed-door grudge match with unknown rules. The blinds between the offices are pulled down and all of Chas's certificates, his BA in social work, his management training certificate, along with twenty other paper testimonies to his glorious ability and past success, sit above them like dubious witnesses, presuming their champion will prevail. The brief words Ferguson and Chas shared as they met, the thing Joyce said about poor wee Pink Bird – fills Hughie's head with paranoia. The large table that has been squeezed into the room for the showdown leaves little room for the four chairs needed. Chas tries an early attempt at control of the game by sitting next to Ferguson. Hughie stands there, unsure, Faye's smile appreciated as she points at the chair on her side. Ferguson, the top man, has the look of a foul-tempered, top-rank referee, dragged to a lower league game on a wet night due to staff shortages. He is an overweight man, and probably fond of alcohol going by the colour of his broad, pockmarked Highland nose. His discomfort and resentment drip down over the folds of fat at the back of his neck with the sweat. Without him having to say a single word to them, they know he personally blames each and every one of them for this embarrassing shameful event.

Faye lays out papers, only giving copies to herself and the big boss; Chas and Hughie exchange more eyeballing, neither backing down. Outside, the main office has gone silent and you can imagine a cluster of ears on the other side of the blind. Clasping his hands together as if about to pray, the big boss rests them on the desk to focus his minions before the sermon. They wait for him to speak, but he says nothing. Instead, after looking both men over, he turns towards Faye, nodding at her.

'Good afternoon, gentlemen. Allen has asked me to start us off and chair the meeting,' Faye says. She is composed, despite being put on the spot and has an air of confidence well above her usual arrogance that oozes from every move-ment. Hughie looks over at Chas who returns a similar quizzical expression. Something was already moving in the universe.

'If these ... developments, are handled delicately,' Faye begins, 'I believe their impact can be minimised.'

'Minimised!' Hughie says, his head shaking furiously.

Ferguson hushes him with an irritated finger to the lip.

'Why is she running this, anyway?' Chas adds.

Ferguson slams the desk and sweat bounces from his neck. 'Be quiet and listen to what Faye has to offer; both of you.' He is already struggling to restrain his legendary temper, despite the match just kicking off.

Putting her spectacles on, Faye looks over some prepared notes. She is calmness personified – there's a new Queen in the Castle, boys.

'If we deal with these allegations and counter-allegations internally,' she says, 'the department will avoid unfair criticism.' After giving Hughie a look over her specs, she goes on, 'If we drag these anecdotal arguments out it does no good for the vulnerable of our community.' She turns to Chas. 'The media will crucify ... us if this gets out.'

Ferguson nods in agreement with his own, well-read, script.

'So, we bury his abuse?' Hughie says, staring at her.

'He's makin things up now,' Chas shouts over him, 'trying to cover up his own mistakes and that poor wee woman dying.'

'How did I not see what you are?' Hughie says, eyes narrowing as he turns on Chas.

'Idiot,' Chas replies.

Ferguson slams his hand down hard, then glances towards the main office and army of earwigs. 'Enough, both of you,' he says through his teeth as he holds a trembling finger to them both.

Hughie draws back first. Ferguson's well pissed off, not keen on dragging buried secrets into the light. If a stare could hurt you, his is ready to snap my fucking neck. Need to play calm. This isn't just about one sociopath, like Petite Merde here, it's about all the bastards who've covered his back over the years and gave the mutt too much chain. Ferguson's scared.

'There are ways we can solve any issue,' Faye says to bring them back in, 'if we are willing to compromise.'

Hughie groans but doesn't dare fuck with the big boss by talking this time. He stoops his head, shaking it and biting his lip. Can't give up, play man, play the game.

WOLVES 1 KNIGHTS 0

Hughie takes the envelope out of his pocket at this

point, makes a show of sliding it across the table towards Ferguson. Bury this, you cunts. On the envelope is written: The GRAIL. Ferguson wants to claim it, but Faye puts her hand on it before he can. She gives the big manager a wary look, and he withdraws and relaxes. Why have a dog ...

'Very dramatic; what is this?' she asks Hughie.

'A photograph of a sociopath having sex with one of our vulnerable clients,' Hughie says, looking hard at Chas.

'Infringement of my private life, that's what this is,' Chas says, nodding in agreement with himself.

'We already have a similar digital image,' Faye says, looking back at her notes. 'We have to move on.'

Hughie ignores her. 'In the photograph, you will see a young boy's foot and ankle. The foot of Tommy Anderson, the ten-year-old son of the woman having sex with Charles here.' He points a hitchhiker's thumb towards Chas who tenses like a dog poked with a stick.

'We need to m—'

Hughie interrupts her. 'I tried to investigate possible abuse this boy received.' He pauses. 'But Charles refused to back me, even denied ever bein involved in this case.' Turning and looking hard at Ferguson, he adds, 'He'd been the family's case manager before I got involved; we found a file that confirms it three days ago. He's also a child abuser and possibly a rapist.'

'He's a fantasist,' Chas says, his hand sweeping away the accusations.

'Enough!' Ferguson demands.

A hush falls as Faye takes the photograph from the envelope and studies it in detail. Ferguson then leans over the table and she turns it to him. He squints at it for the umpteenth time that week, and looks suitably disgusted, his slow judging gaze leaving the photo and landing on

Chas like a weight; this, finally, is the full heat of the inquisition.

Trying to act nonchalant, Chas reaches out towards the photograph, but Faye moves it away and returns it to the envelope, then leaves it on the table, where it sits like a sheathed sword.

'Is this the original?' she asks Hughie.

Hughie nods. 'Yes, it is.'

WOLVES 1 KNIGHTS 2

Chas doesn't explode as expected, his eyes become cold, the rage now entombed in a dull stony scowl. Hughie is watching. This isn't right, he should have exploded by now, made a cunt of himself; I win. Shite.

'Can I defend myself?' Chas asks with offence in his voice.

'Speak,' Ferguson says after raising a hand to shut Faye up.

Chas gives his bloated chin a nervy a rub, weighing things up. 'This boy's a liar, basically,' he says. 'I've done nothin.' He lets out a long sigh through tight lips. 'He's usin my … private life to muddy the water. Why? Because he's havin an affair with one of our foster carers, instead o dealin with vulnerable dementia victims.' Chas starts nodding at his own story, adding, 'He's also been seen lying drunk in the gutter in the rain, thrown out of a pub.' After a sideward headshake, he looks from Ferguson to Hughie. 'Getting a leg over and being constantly drunk seem to be his priority; the Social Work Council might even consider him a rogue worker.'

'You were going to explain this photograph,' Faye says, tapping the envelope with a finger, drawing them all back from the spell.

'Let him speak,' Ferguson tells her.

This really rattles her, but she does as she is told. Hughie is lost, face frozen. What the fuck is happening here!

'I told MacDonald,' Chas continues, 'that sleeping with this ... woman, was unwise. But, he ignored my advice, and my express order, and began to see her; he even had the gall to ask for a placement for her, so she could make a few quid on the side.' Chas gives them a regretful wise look, his head slightly bobbing as he implores them to see Hughie's widening flaws. 'That raised my suspicions,' he tells them, 'so I did some background research. Seems that this is not the first time MacDonald here has had inappropriate relationships within his work life.'

Even Faye looks at Hughie this time. Hughie just sits like a simmering kettle as a new woven reality begins to swallow him whole.

'There are some indications that MacDonald has connections with underworld figures in the Manchester area,' Chas says with some authority. 'His ex-wife told me he was tortured by a drug dealer and pimp, all this after havin an affair with a prostitute; his ex said that he refused to involve the police.'

'You contacted my ex-wife!' Hughie shouts, exploding out of his seat.

'I did ma job.'

'Psychopath!'

'Look at his hands,' Chas says.

As the others look, Hughie sits back down and withdraws his hands from the table, face shameful. Now on a roll, Petite Merde opens his hands and gives a twisting shake of the head to the others, as if he's proven some point. He has more. 'As I explained when I called Allen, we have a relative who is insistent on taking the death of her sister to the Welfare Commission.'

'What call?' Faye asks.

Chas continues, 'It seems that MacDonald here, neglected the case of an eighty-year-old dementia victim, while he was fightin in pubs and runnin around after pieces of skirt—'

'Charles!' Ferguson says, hand slamming down again. 'Is that it?'

'Only some feedback from the fire brigade; seems they attended a botched drug raid where a house was burned out. MacDonald here was on the scene, yet I couldn't find a note of him in the police log.'

Slowing his heart, Hughie holds his nerve and the urge to explode. This is not going well, he's like a druid, painting and repainting reality. *I'll get burned at the stake if this keeps going.* Hughie looks at Ferguson and Chas, senses skulduggery, more spells. *Maybe I'm already finished.*

WOLVES 4 KNIGHTS 2

'This is why we are not going to air this in public,' Faye intervenes, sounding like the wisest woman alive. 'We will look like a shower of imbeciles, worse.' Her tone is sharp, but her veneer of cool authority is back in place. This is confirmed as they all catch a weary Ferguson nodding. 'So, let's move this on, with facts,' she says. 'Find a workable solution.'

'So, if you throw enough mud, you get away with anything?'

'*Listen,* Hugh,' Faye says, almost putting a hand on his arm, her head tilting in reassurance. 'Charles has agreed to step down as Team Leader.' She looks at Chas for agreement, her face stern.

'Do we still want tae to go down this road?' Chas says, looking to change tactics.

Faye heads this off. 'Well, I too have done a bit of research,' she says so quietly that everyone turns and listens. 'Seems that many of these awards on these walls may not be legitimate—'

Ferguson halts her revelation with a rap of his knuckle on the table. 'Move on please, Faye,' he orders.

Hughie's eyes widen as he looks around the office with its rows of framed certificates. He is a fake, a one hundred percent sociopath. Little bastard!

Faye takes another slightly frustrated breath. 'I have also been made aware that the properties that make up St Andrews Terrace, belong to a company owned by Charles's wife. And that there were building enforcement issues ongoing with all the properties, before the unfortunate fire. Can you confirm this Charles?'

'It's my private life again, nothing to do with the Authority,' Chas insists.

Hughie looks at Chas, gobsmacked. Bastard's like an onion, layer upon layer of lies and dirty schemes. 'That's why Maggie wouldn't talk!' Hughie blurts out.

'Your wife's ... interests, also take in flats No 3 and No 4, 37 the High Street,' Faye says and flashes a look at Hughie, who looks inward, putting it all together.

'You were in my flat, you fuckin psycho!' Hughie shouts, heels stamping the floor under the table.

'See, he's unstable,' Chas tells Ferguson.

Hughie gulps. 'Old Miss Murchison seen you, didn't she? Did you threaten her tenancy too?'

'Confabulation,' Chas says, 'the man's paranoid.' Ferguson's face grows redder and they all get a grip.

'Did Charles ever make you aware that his wife owned

your flat or your neighbour's flat or St Andrews Terrace, where your clients' live, the place that burned down?' Faye asks Hughie in the silence of the short calm.

Hughie shakes his head.

'Did he make you aware that he let out substandard properties to vulnerable clients?' she asks, hammering it home.

'No,' is all Hughie can find as he stares over at Chas. He's wounded again, bad this time. Well. Fucking. Played. Snowball.

'Is your wife also named on the board of Merctan, the company that owns the Auld Hoose and part of Mill's bar,' Faye asks.

'Not relevant, move on,' Ferguson says. His technique is to give Faye the ammo, let her fire at a few weak kneecaps, wound the cocky rebels, then take the gun off her before he gets any blood on his own reputation. After a fly look at the wall clock, he gives the nod for Faye to start to sum up. The others, exhausted, listen and stare at each other.

'These are the facts,' she tells them. 'The photograph … looks real and Charles has not denied his connection to the substandard properties that are let to our clients. In fact, he has confirmed many of the accusations by sayin that we were involving his personal life in this discussion.' She pauses, ticks something on her notes, looks at Chas and adds, 'Although we do not have any *evidenc*e of criminal behaviour, Officers of the Authority are judged by their behaviour and expected to hold a high standard and show transparency in their affairs while in office; using weak excuses, will not do any more.' She turns to Ferguson. 'Allen.'

WOLFS 4 KNIGHTS 5

Faye sits back in her chair at this point and crosses her legs, looking like a classy assassin with the job done.

A noise comes from the big office that sounds like a desk being dragged about; this allows the big boss to gather his thoughts before he has to do what has to be done. When they return to the moment, Ferguson's blunt eyes are on Chas. Hughie swears something passes between the pair, a red flush taking Ferguson's neck, perhaps a nepotistic root coming to the surface. The others notice his hands have landed on the envelope with the Grail in it; no one speaks as he withdraws it. He clears his throat to assert that he is taking charge of this squalid little game. 'Right, no more discussion,' Ferguson commands. 'Faye has been made Area Manager as of two days ago; this will be verified at interview within the month. MacDonald, you will work directly for Faye, so she can keep an eye on you and guide your obvious talent for ... investigating things.'

'Wait a minute, this isn't about me,' Hughie says, voice almost desperate while Faye holds his arm tight to reassure.

The big guy shakes a finger. 'I would have disciplined you for bringing the department into disrepute MacDonald, but Faye here has fought your corner well.'

Hughie looks confused, like a player who's taken the ball full in the face, unsure of what side he is on or the current rules of the game.

'I ...' Ferguson pauses, his face conflicted for a moment. 'I have also had talks with Charles.'

Faye's cool evaporates at this point, her face falling as Chas grins at her from across the table.

'I thought—'

'Faye, if you will let me finish,' Ferguson says with a certain tone that silences her. 'Charles has decided to ... retire on ill health.' A silence falls on the room as he goes on. 'Dr Haze from Inverchualinn Surgery, Charles's GP, has convinced me that certain chronic health issues may have impaired Charles's judgement of late and ... we have agreed that he will retire as of today, on a full pension, of course.'

'So, we ignore him putting a cigar out on a child's neck,' Hughie says into the desk.

'MacDonald!' Ferguson shouts. 'I am not going to speculate on the activities of a child who assists drug dealers.' Ferguson glances at Chas, the probable source of his information, then comes back at Hughie, bearing in on him, red face close to eruption. 'Be quiet,' he says holding up that finger, 'not a fucking word!'

Chas is going like a gimp at a hanging, his head furiously nodding with glee; it then morphs in an instant, as only the true psychopaths can, becoming dignified and calm. Opposite, Hughie is stunned, hatchet to the psyche. The wee cunt's acting like a heroic retiring club captain; they'll say he was a bit unorthodox perhaps, dirty as fuck others might suggest, but needed during times of potential relegation.

'Thank you, Allen,' Chas says, half bowing to the big man. 'I have discussed this matter with several of the senior councillors, and I feel that my time in this job is over. I am grateful for all of Allen's advice and goodwill over the years and hope we have left the county better than we found it.' He stares right at Hughie. 'I hope I can soon serve the people of Argyll again, as a councillor.'

Ferguson, the referee, is struggling to look Faye in the eye – blackmailed before the match.

WOLFS 9 KNIGHTS 5

Now the game is over, Ferguson is quick to his feet, rising like an angry ox, ready for the off. He comes to

Hughie. 'The best thing that this department can do is move on,' Ferguson says in Hughie's ear.

Chas catches Ferguson as he turns to escape out the door, pushes his wriggling hand into his reluctant boss's, shaking it for an uncomfortable length of time. Even Ferguson, the Teflon don, looks like he is handling dog shit, which he may well be. He withdraws his hand from the regrettable Masonic grip as soon as he can, but Chas is between him and the door, reluctant to let him go, glorying in an unexpected win.

'You'll be supporting me in the council elections, I hope?' Chas asks with pressure of speech. 'I'm running in your ward. How's your Maureen, anyway?'

'Yes, eh, I'll have to go, Charles. Late for a service review.'

'You still got a good handicap, big man?' Chas asks, oblivious to the rejection, piggy face all intense.

Faye pulls Hughie to one side. She looks older now and speaks quietly to avoid any further conflict. 'Let it go, Hugh' she whispers.

'How can *you* let *this* go?'

'We'll be crucified in a court, just don't have enough.'

'Don't go with this,' Hughie pleads.

After glancing at Ferguson, she says, 'Maybe he knows too much.'

'Like you gettin banged in a shed at the bowling club?'

Faye catches this full on, her reaction telling Hughie that she has heard the whispers, her eyes losing what spark they had left. 'I knew it was him ...' she says, her voice almost crumbling as it tails off.

'Not nice, is it?' Hughie insists. 'And you're willing to let him move those lies into council chambers.'

They both look over their shoulders at the other two, the

big guy stuck there with Petite Merde. Leaning his head right into her ear, he says, 'You thought you had a deal with Ferguson, but the bastard has everyone by the balls, everyone.'

Perhaps balanced by the force of Hughie's manic face and bitterness, she finds her foothold and falls back on her game like a real contender, takes his raised fists in her hands and brings them down slow. 'Departmental survival, that's what's important here,' she says while fixing Hughie with her resilient eyes. 'Who'll house wee Tommy if we all get shafted and the press roll in – he's a narcissist, he'd love the tabloids wading in – you shagging a prostitute, in with drug dealers and me ... well, let's not go there.'

'But it's all lies, Faye; he's splitting us.

'Stop,' she tells him. 'It's done, Hughie.'

Ferguson puffs out and finally pulls away as Petite Merde is in mid-sentence, coming to her and shaking Faye's hand with relief and appreciation. 'Thank you, Faye. I'll call you next week, for lunch.'

All the wriggling corpses are back under various carpets, and the necessary crap has been swallowed. With a nod, the big boss holds out a hand that he hopes will bring it all to an end. 'I knew your father, Hugh; we were ... close back in the seventies,' Ferguson tells him, hand still outstretched.

Looking at the hand and knowing everyone is watching, Hughie says, 'Masonic grip to seal the deal, eh?'

'Or perhaps a new start?' Ferguson says.

As they shake, Ferguson pulls him close. 'You can help us fix what got broken here,' his voice seems to hold true regret, but it is impossible to say for sure.

Hughie gives a weak smile, tries to nod. That's it now, I've shaken on it, in with the bricks, the pricks and all the skulduggery – I even know where some of the secrets are hidden now. ***Welcome home, Hughie my son, welcome back to yer glorious ancestral birthplace on the Coast of the Gaels – ya spineless fuckin prick! Fuck off!***

Faye sees Hughie's rapid blinking eyes. 'Thanks, it's for the best,' she whispers.

By the time they all group at the office door, most of the claws and fangs are hidden behind polite smiles, except for Hughie who just looks empty, his soul drowned, hope a lie. The Queen has regained her cool and the etiquette flows easily from her narrow lips. She thanks each person in turn for attending, especially Ferguson for coming into the field and getting mud on his shiny loafers. Faye ignores Hughie, not wanting to point the others to his defeated face; she even gives a fake grin and professional nod to Chas, then opens the door.

Chas stops dead, preventing the others from leaving Faye's new office. They try to move forward, but Chas is frozen and almost holding them in and away from something. At once, their eyes are drawn upward, over Chas's head, along the ceiling and around most of the strip lights as their mouths fall open.

'Oh my God!' Faye says.

Forty or more copies of the Grail, with most of Maggie blanked out, hang above Chas in the big silent room. One has been enlarged with Social Worker of the Year Photoshopped along Chas's sweaty face.

'Fat fucking bitch!' Chas screams at Joyce who stands by the photocopier, determined.

After ripping half a dozen off the walls, Chas spots the copies taped to the air conditioning duct. He leaps up several times, hands flapping at thin air between attempts, like a desperate child, his face panicked and close to tears. The jury of crows watch, their cold scrutiny stripping him of any rank and gain he's dug up during the meeting. Pulling a chair across the room, he clambers onto it, whimpering noises beginning to escape his lips. The chair is shaking as he snatches the photocopies from the ceiling duct, one by one in desperate swipes that leave odd bits of photocopied body parts hanging in paper triangles here and there. Pity sets in and some are forced to look away from the humiliated creature that dances in front of them, yet no one moves or tries to help him. His sweaty red jowls glow as his panic grows. With stubby fingers, he grasps the last big A3 copy, which fights to hold on. He puts all his weight into it and this sends the chair wheels spinning and shooting off to the side.

It is Friday morning, not even lunchtime, when Charles Wright falls from grace and hits the office floor with a thump.

Hughie and Joyce stand still as the others capitulate to their humanity and rush to help the small slumped figure on the ground. He growls and shakes them off as his mask comes off. 'You fucking arsehole cunts!' he screams as he staggers to his feet. 'Fucking insects, hoors and cunts … all of you!' His eyes are running with tears, his stare rabid, the creature finally exposed in the glare of the fluorescent strip lights. Unable to carry all the pieces of paper, he starts stomping one piece into the floor, before storming towards the main doors. Joyce, who is standing silent and brave, visibly flinches as he screams, 'Ugly, fat slut,' in her face. He kicks the exit doors wide open, and half runs down the stairs.

Joyce looks hurt, the shame he often induces in her

floods in to make her bow her head. But something inside has changed, and she runs after Chas, out onto the landing and shouts, 'Bye Porn King!' down the stairwell – she will later call this his retirement eulogy.

Ferguson looks like a broken giant as pieces of paper float down from the ceiling where they lie like reminders of his inability to control the chaos. He slopes off to the toilet with his briefcase drawn up to his chest. Perhaps, he really has taken on too much or perhaps he knows he'll have to hang about in the office in case Chas is waiting by his car to start the poison speeches, the blackmail and the sickening pleas for an invite to dinner – a skin crawling situation to avoid by hiding in the bog and reading the *Herald* for a good half hour at least.

The staff return to their seats like exhausted punters leaving a nail-biting thriller with a last-minute penalty and the inevitable pitch invasion. They sit whispering, unable to concentrate on work. Faye is down on her knees, pushing a waste bin around, putting all the torn shreds of porn-paper into it. Joyce, awake to the new order, bends down and begins to help her new boss tidy the mess she's partly created. A look is exchanged between the pair that tells Joyce she hasn't followed the head coach's advice. 'I'll make you a coffee, eh Faye?'

Hughie is sat at Faye's old desk, his feet up on it, hands behind his head, the sight of the new ruler bent over in that skirt, tidying her hard-won dominion, is a decent and fitting finish to a bloodthirsty stramash. He catches Joyce as she heads past him on her way to pick up Ginger Nuts and Kit Kats for Ferguson's return from meditation.

'You're the hero here,' Hughie tells her.

'I'm still shaking,' she admits.

'You won this; we were useless.'

'That file I sent you, it was Faye who found it in Petite Merde's desk.' She squeezes his shoulder and walks off. 'The wall art, that was my idea.'

He feels more naïve than ever as he leans back in the chair, the other staff busily hitting Facebook hard to plan the weekend and pass on the word.

Faye comes over, pushes his feet off her old desk and sits on it. He notices she is allowing the atmosphere of anarchy to continue for some reason.

'Not very queenly, you cleanin up after a sociopath,' Hughie suggests.

'Go, before he comes out of the toilet. See me on Monday.'

'What will I be doing on Monday, *Boss*?'

'Whatever I tell you to.'

They can just about find a smile between them, both knackered now the fight-juice has seeped away.

'What about Joyce, she in your bad books?'

'You kiddin? Joyce is the hardest worker in here, she's going to be my PA.' She prompts him to get up with a wiggly finger. 'Just go, Don Quixote.'

Unable to resist, she drifts off towards her new office, and he nods respectfully to the new monarch. It is somehow calming to know she is in charge, and he watches her start to take down all of Chas's fake glass-framed trophies – a grin coming to his face as he hears the first one hit the metal bin with a loud smash of glass. Videos of a man jumping about in an office begin to go viral in the Town.

Final Score

WOLF-CUNTS 9 KNIGHTS **of the LIGHT 13**

. . .

POLICE WARN **that there is potential for violence after the match.**

Hughie relaxes when he notices the prick's Jag is gone from the car park, his mood lifting as he walks round the back, suddenly noticing the wee puffy clouds that sit along the ridge above town, the afternoon's bright sun kissing their silver edges as the smell of cut grass catches the nose for the first time this year. He smiles at the hills as he puts his briefcase on the car roof – feels the place give a grudging nod in reply. Only when he opens the boot to put the case in, does he see that someone is already in the front passenger seat. The car door handle feels hot in his hand as he gives a small accepting sigh, then slides in behind the steering wheel. He smiles to himself for some reason and gives a shrug of the shoulders.

'You lost?' Hughie asks.

Chas never flinches, sits still, looking out the window until, eventually, his head turns and fixes on Hughie, his pupils dead, red rings around the white edges of his eyes — psycho stuff – haunting – serious. Chas takes a cigar out of his breast pocket, looks at it then at Hughie, his hand showing a quiver of repressed rage as he lights it up and blows smoke out into the car. Hughie doesn't bite at the cigar child-burner reference.

'I will ruin you, son,' Chas tells him, looking out the windscreen again.

'I know, I know.' Hughie's voice is equally calm, paternal even.

'I'll run you and yer *new* prostitute out. You're finished.' Every line on Chas's face grows deeper as he speaks until he resembles a small, sullen demon, the sun silhouetting him from the side and blackening his face.

'Listen, I'm tired, why not write to me from retirement,' Hughie suggests, smiling at it kindly.

This calm, makes the creature called Chas upset, its right eye narrows, its lashes hold a slight quiver; all its power is gone, and it is unable to stop a rosy anger from climbing its neck.

'Messy flat you've got,' Chas replies. 'You drink a hell of a lot.'

'Don't bite,' Hughie's mum whispers in his ear, while the Knight is nodding for Hughie to headbutt Chas from the rear-view mirror. Hughie can't help but smile again. 'I don't give in easy, you've got to give me that, surely.'

'You ever lose any photographs of Mummy?' Chas asks.

'Kleptomania's curable, I hear.'

Chas comes again, angrier, words loose. 'You must know ma wife's employee, Skinny Rab; serves interestin drinks, I'm told.'

Hughie looks at him then gives a dismissive shake of the head. He must be hurting so bad, willing to try anything in order to hold a place in the universe. Least I know it wasn't Davy that drugged me now. 'No matter,' his Uncle Malky says, his voice philosophical, 'this one is see-through now, finished.'

'Bet you thought you'd sleep better,' Chas says, his tone rising, 'now Davy's banged up.'

'I know it was you in the close that night, hit me with a stick, smearing shit on doors, then creepin back across the roof to the Lodge. How do you transport shite, by the way? In a bag?'

'I won't stop,' Chas says, leaning in.

'Do you know why I won?' Hughie asks Chas.

'As your landlord, I'm giving you two hours' notice; to get out ma fuckin flat.'

'See, we're social apes, believe it or not.' Hughie holds his hands out, moving air about as if helping to explain. 'We're reliant on reciprocal altruism. That's helpin one another to you folk who didn't really go to university.'

Those jovially delivered words go in like a dart through a soap bubble.

'Weak fuckin dreamers, the lot of you,' Chas shouts as he crushes his cigar between his fingers, bouncing it off the windscreen.

'In societal evolutionary terms, you're a free-loader; sociopath.' Hughie's tone is obviously mocking now.

'I'll ruin your name, your nigger lovin hoor's name—'

'Turns out we can figure your kind out by memorising the tit for tat of everyday interactions.' Hughie nods his head in amazement at human knowledge.

'What the fuck are you on about? Cunt!' Chas shouts, his mind crashing off the road into a tree.

'Psycho apes give themselves away over time; the lies add up, stretch too far ... the liar exposed.' Hughie blows out slow, makes a sad whistle.

Chas explodes. 'Yer father was an alkie, and yer uncle was a drunk gay boy dreamer.' Desperation leads to a pointing finger and more bluster. 'You've already started down that road, drink in every room; in with a bunch of oddball alcoholics and a nigger lovin hoor!'

Hughie gives a nonchalant agreeing shrug of the face. 'But, I still care about people, and they actually, amazingly, care about me.' He sits back against his door, searching Chas's red face. 'While you've been exposed as a fraud; whoever you are underneath it all, no one cares any more, son.'

As if remembering something important, Chas drops his clawing finger and produces the brown envelope with the

Grail written on it, shakes it furiously in Hughie's face. 'Ferguson thought it was only right that he returns this tae me, known the guy for years.' His voice is fragile, quavering. 'I'm not alone son, no way.'

Hughie coolly leans over him and undoes the glove compartment, which clunks open and hits Chas's knees. Pulling a fat envelope out and over onto his lap, Hughie opens it up then pauses. 'Remember that trick you showed me, son?'

'What the fuck are you on about?' Chas asks, watching as his enemy takes white cards from the packet and fans them out like a cheap magician would.

'When I was lookin for help with wee Tommy,' Hughie says, offering up the cards. 'Pick one.'

Chas hesitates, his eyes shifting around their socket between Hughie's face and the cards. He goes to take one, then stops.

'Scaredy-cat,' Hughie says.

Chas is lost, wants to resist, but needs to know everything; if you don't know everything, how can you protect yourself from the darkness that twisted your soul all those years ago. Placing a thumb and forefinger on one card Chas snatches it away and flips it over. He sees Maggie's body, her face pixelated out, then his own fat nakedness behind her in pin-sharp clarity. After staring at the copy, Chas puts it in his pocket covering his action with the other hand.

The pack is offered up again by Hughie, taunting with a fanning action and a glimpse of the underside. 'Pick another,' Hughie says, 'pick any one you like.'

As Chas snatches at another, Hughie loosens his grip and the cards fly everywhere, each one exposing a copy of the original damning photograph, each one staring back at

Chas, accusing, mocking and humiliating like a hundred hysterical voters laughing in his face.

'You cunt, YOU FUCKIN CUNT!' Chas screams, his strangling hands going for Hughie's face.

The attempt is easily caught, and Chas's face lines with panic as his stubby fingers are bent backwards by a younger, stronger man. He is then pulled forward, Hughie's forehead butting Chas's brow with a small, firm thud. Hughie looks deep into him, his eyes are merciless and ready to give up everything for the pleasure of beating the monster into a pulp.

'Anyone brought up where I was, can do this stuff,' Hughie says, twisting the fingers until Chas cries out. Making a fist by his head, as if about to punch Chas in the face, brings Hughie's mum out from the back seat, she leans over them and whispers in her son's ear, 'Phone your brother when you get in, he misses you.' She looks at Chas's grotesque face with pity and adds, 'Even this was a child once, before the infection. Don't become that.' Hughie releases the monster and sits back in his seat, sweeps his hair back. 'Sorry, Mum.'

Chas falls back in pain, his face frightened, confused eyes darting around the car. 'Who're you talkin to?'

Ignoring him, Hughie sits up in himself and fixes his collar, looks out the window, his voice low as he gives out orders, 'If you go near Karen, or the boy, or anyone else I even half know, I will leaflet drop the whole of the Town with these photos.' He turns and looks at its fearful face. 'You'll be the next Jimmy Saville.'

The poor creature is lost, hands quivering, eyes scared as it stares back. Hughie feels a moment of remorse then catches it after his Uncle Malky speaks up from the back seat. 'No, the message must be hit home hard; sociopaths will always come back – they can't change – you need to make your mark on their psyche, that's what they understand.'

'Thanks, Uncle,' Hughie says, then makes a fake lunge at Chas who is now fighting for the door handle, his fingers numb from being bent back, his attempts becoming more and more desperate until the door springs open and he spills out backwards onto the tarmac floor of the car park. As he lands on the tarmac on his backside, he looks so small and frightened, as if he's seen a monster within the tall, gawky social worker who blew in from England less than a year ago.

Leaning towards him, Hughie throws all the remaining photos and Chas's cigar butt out of the door as if tidying the car of something meaningless. The photos hit the deck and the breeze catches them, tumbling them over and over in different directions. The car starts, and he slams it into reverse. Chas is forced to scramble further away on his arse as the car shoots backwards, the open door almost taking his head off. Braking hard makes the car door slam itself shut, leaving the middle-aged, small-town sociopath to crawl around picking up copies of the Grail. Hughie feels another rush of pity, finds it hard to remember what is so dangerous about the poor thing scuttling here and there as the photos fight to escape, each one a little reminder of the truth and how easily men fall – how the lies they hide can still come back to haunt them, even when they're buried deep, almost forgotten, in the schizophrenic mind of a better man.

As he revs the car, Hughie spots Faye, through his sunroof, standing at her office window, looking down regally as the old King crawls on all fours; there is little pity in her eyes, just high-born coolness. Joyce, smiling, looks more human by the Queen's side, slightly back from the spotlight

377

– the loyal Priestess who understands the dark art of street fighting.

As the car shoots off, it almost clips Chas and blows a couple of the photos into the hedge that separates the social work offices from the police station. Killing Joke belt out from the radio as the car spins in a long veering arc, out of the gate and onto the main road. Accelerating up into second, Hughie laughs out loud as he catches, Uncle Malky, the Knight and his mum, who sits between the two old fools on the back seat, all bopping to the music, sequenced hand movements going left to right. The Knight's visor falls down over his face and Mum and Malky high-five.

'Love is blood, love is blood,' the four sing at the tops of their voices as he shoots past the police station and up the High Street, away from his flat.

ABOVE THE SOCIAL work car park, Gull flies across the blue sky in a slow lazy sweep, his reflection undulating along windows of the social work offices, his keen eye clocking the old Ape King staggering to his feet below. Gull's screech hangs like a laugh in the warm breezy summer day, his white front catching the light as he morphs into a silver ghost that turns and flies off in search of something more interesting. Two lazy wing-flaps and he disappears over the top of the Jobcentre on his way to the chip shop bin on Church Street.

SEVENTEEN

THE LOST HOUSE OF THE HOLY
ORDER OF LIGHT

Gull sails in a lonesome arc, his yellow orb eyes taking in the whole cold white world, filling him with dread as the hunger comes again. He searches for a crumb left on the pavement or maybe a tiny scrap from an overflowing bin. Nothing. Fuck all. Moving so slow it is amazing to folk that he doesn't just fall out of the sky. But this gull is from an ancient lineage of survivors, his forefathers flapped this same cold air as they watched the wasteful apes, following the birch and oaks north when the ice age ended. The apes soon became useful as they fished, hunted, and planted stuff in the ground, always lazy and prone to waste and spillage. Gull's ancestors saw the head-tops of countless invading empires after that, all wasteful with food, though the Romans didn't quite make it, content to give up just south of Argyll, on the Clyde–Forth isthmus, where they threw together the Antonine Wall; there they sat on their cold toga'd arses, staring north at tattooed Celts and into the rain clouds, always dreaming of sunshine and wine; those longings soon chasing them off south again.

The Scotti from Antrim, then the Vikings, in turn,

sailed up the claw-like sea lochs like a ravenous disease, spilling blood, guts and tasty waste on the thin soil and rock. Gull's folk scavenged willingly from all as the landscape and local gene pool absorbed every invading race. Next, the Saxon–Norman–English; usually content to bribe local clans to cancel one another out, rather than get their feet wet by wading ashore where it was hard to grow corn. Luckily for the gulls, the Cold War got going and this sent the most wasteful tribe of all, in their nuclear submarines, up into the shadows of the haunted green hills. These apes were particularly crazy and were soon throwing food and radioactive waste into the deep Holy Loch on a regular basis. The local folks and gulls came to know these new multicoloured conquerors as the Yanks of the Great Dollar Empire, who'd made a deal with the distant English Parliament in London, to hide nuclear bombs as far away from the South-East as possible, amongst those who had lost their voice. Against the odds, the locals rallied again, found currencies that could be used to calm the invasion – cannabis for whisky, spilled Fourth of July hot dogs on dewy grass for the clean-up gull squad, bread thrown overboard to the same birds when the Captain was off-duty for air rifle target practice. Then there was a new lawnmower from the Commissary or cheap strong vodka for invites to parties, laughter and a possible date with your sister; parties were always good for people bonding, and for gulls when the bin bags burst the next day. Gull's mother remembered the sad day the *Yankee Empire* lifted anchor, after thirty-one mad, gluttonous years, leaving the Town on its back like a prostitute with a learning difficulty; Davy Drug, Wee Tommy and Katie, the Auld Hoose barmaid, amongst others, were the only tangible, beautiful gifts left by the shoreline. Sat beyond influence, the Roman walls and Highland boundary, caught between Central Belt derision and Gaelic disdain, Argyll did what it always does in hard times – the people and gulls shrug it off, get back to looking inward, eternally dodging the rain showers as they try to make a living out of haunting beauty, thin soil and hard stone.

The breeze off the snowy hilltops cuts into Gull, his plumage ruffles, every flap of the wing gruelling as he runs on empty. Looking down, he spies a local man standing by the white lane. A man who carries similar ancient blood to his own, who has, like Gull, been forced out into this bastard weather by that incessant need to find things.

'JESUS IT'S COLD,' Hughie says.

He catches sight of the grey ghost disappearing over the rooftops as he pulls his gloves out of his jacket pockets; his hands ache in this weather and the scars shine white on a purple background of poor circulation.

Gloves on, he sweeps the thick piled snow off the car roof and turns away to start the hunt. The cloud feels so low, like it is touching his head, so he pulls his collar up and walks off through a soundless bluster of snowflakes, skliffing his way up the lane – crow-black against bright-white.

His new shiny brogues compact the deep creaking snow, warning those he is stalking that someone else is mental enough to be out and about on this December Tuesday morning. The snow was early this year and came in the night, like an unwelcome and suffocating family member that most had forgotten about, or thought was dead. A north wind has escorted it in, making the nose and ears red and the eyes water, forcing the locals to put on hats and huddle around gas fires that cost a fortune to run as freezing drafts find ways through the patchy repairs of summer to stab them where their jumpers rise up at the back. All this on top of the continued austerity, growing xenophobia and brutal cutbacks, which shudder hardest on these shores so far away from power. Despite all this and the newspapers predicting further doom for the masses, Hughie has noted that the trails of slush still lead through the Town's streets to the warm pubs where people cackle out their drunken banter straight into the scowling face of global Armageddon. Argyll genetics, from Fergus Mhor, the father of the Gaels, to Hughie MacDonald, hunter of the downtrodden and feckless, have sewn hard stoicism and a perverse stubbornness into the very marrow of every bone in the county.

Stopping and holding his steamy breath, his ears search the foggy white world for signs of activity as battalions of snowflakes come at him then lie down with their fallen comrades to hide the oily broken tarmac in a thick cleansing blanket. Like Saint Andrew himself has agreed admission, the snow stops, leaving a few last dancing flakes to spin and touch his pink cheek. Ahead, there is a burst of joyful spectral laughter, voices seeping towards him, in between the layers of hushed silence. He smiles. Further up the lane, dark smoke rises from the ruins of the Terrace, through its low, crumbling, scorched, sandstone walls, which six months back were kissed by fire. The place seems somehow at peace with that memory and even the harsh black timbers that collapsed with the roof on that night are now hidden under a healing altar cloth of pure white. The characters within the ruined shell look almost medieval as they scurry to and fro, feeding iron drums that send more black puffs of smoke into the low sky to choke the gulls.

'It's the Order of St Andrew!' Hughie shouts.

The three scrap workers look around as he steps through two small piles of rubble that were once the front door of No 1.

'Watch out – screw on the landin!' Jim says.

They all smile at this dig at the man in the suit and go back to work. Hughie raises an eyebrow and shakes his head as Tommy, in wellies and a karate suit, helps old Don load another bundle of plastic coated wire into a smoking oil drum, while Jim, the idle foreman, rolls another fag. Glancing sideways at Hughie's disdainful face, Jim says, 'Your fault.'

'Mine?' Hughie says.

'Aye, yours. You got me back into the smokin.'

'It was more the child labourer breathin in caustic fumes that had me worried.'

'Tommy away frae there!' Jim shouts, then shrugs as the boy totally ignores him and prods the fire with a flaming stick. 'Does what he wants that one,' he adds.

'It's good this, you keepin people busy, after all that went on,' Hughie says, then gives a warm smile.

Jim shrugs. 'Industry cannae rest in these times of austerity.'

'Thanks, anyway.'

Jim licks his fag paper, finishes the roll, then pops it between his lips. After lighting it, he blows out, smirks and says, 'Are all your lot, in the social work, nutjobs?'

'You shot any more Korean kids lately?'

Jim's face doesn't show any emotion or reaction. 'Just the odd one now and then ... when I'm bored.'

Tommy and Don begin to play-fight using Bruce Lee moves all around the snowfield that was once Davy Drug's living room. Hughie wonders whether there might be an

383

ounce of hash left under the charred black remnants that poke out of the snow here and there like demonic reminders, whispering about the madness – Tommy's laughter banishing them as it echoes out into the lumpy white waste ground.

Jim draws deep on his roll-up, leaves it in his lips, the smoke eventually seeping out of his mouth and up his side-burns avoiding his stoic, spectacled eyes. 'You're different,' he says.

Hughie looks down his new coat to his feet.

'It's not the clothes.' Jim's eyes smile. 'You're not that guy I met up the Bishop's Glen, you're tranquil, like a priest – but not a dodgy one ... though you do hunt down kids.'

Hughie moves from foot to foot to stay warm, all the time smiling at Jim in his woolly bobble hat, black tackity boots and paper-thin zipper jacket. 'I remembered that all this is just clusters of atoms, a transient phase,' Hughie says.

'Jesus, what is it with you and riddle talk?' Jim asks after taking the fag out of his mouth.

'I took it too seriously, forgot about just lettin go of the sides now and then.'

The old shopkeeper tilts his head back, looks up into white fog util snowflakes dust his glasses. When he looks back at Hughie, he nods in agreement.

Over by the oil drums, Tommy is giggling hard and Don's eyes are watering with joy as a snowball bounces off him and the pair continue to dance like fools. Despite the cold and the grey, it isn't the fires that lift the place, it is Tommy's laughter, its infectiousness and joy attaching to anyone who gets close enough. The pulsar has grown from a victim to a ten-year-old entity that makes the world a better place, just by being there. Hughie is proud he spotted the star seed in its infancy and helped liberate it. Even deadpan

Jim starts tittering as Tommy shrieks and executes a Yoko-Geri slap kick to Don's right knee; Don feigns pain and staggers backwards to the lad's and onlookers' delight.

'This pair are amazin together,' Jim says as he points his fag towards wee Tommy and Don. 'Amazin, man.'

Hughie turns to him and Jim is suddenly unsure of what he's said wrong, what he's done to deserve such a wicked mocking grin from his pal. 'What?' Jim asks.

'Man? Is that like, Wow-man! There's no hash in that roll-up, is there?'

'Nah, had to give that lark up; kept gettin the munchies, almost ate half my fuckin stock.'

They chuckle, a snow flurry pushing them closer to the oil drums where Hughie takes his gloves off, and they hold their hands towards the hot metal, both watching the boy messing about.

'We haven't talked much about what went on in the summer,' Jim says.

'Nothing to say,' Hughie replies, eyes turning downward. 'Maybe I broke more than I fixed ...'

'Nah, it had become rotten, needed puttin an end to.' Jim pats Hughie's shoulder, gripping it hard.

Taking on the past seems easy now, and Hughie is soon looking around, overacting paranoia before leaning into Jim. 'A wee karate-suited bird tells me you've been'—he looks around again—'*helpin* Maggie with her new flat.'

'We're just pals,' Jim says, going all stiff and pink. 'We're just pals.'

'You dirty old man.'

There is something hopeful and beautiful about fresh pink emotion on the cheeks of an old clapped-out veteran. It thrills Hughie's soul as they stand together.

A fresh surge of heavy snow comes in with the wind

behind it, hitting the hot drum lids, melting in an instant with soft hisses. Hughie beckons Tommy. 'C'mon, I'll take you to karate,' he shouts.

This sparks a final frantic kung fu fight between Don 'Mad-Skull' Cameron and the tiny bespectacled 'White Ninja' as the wind calms and a slow veil of white blobs falls amongst them, entombing the ghosts from the dead homes – in that instant, the place is transformed, healed, like a beautiful snow globe with only the good bits trapped inside.

Tommy and Don bow in acceptance of a hard-fought draw and Don's hand pats the boy's shoulder; the boy shrugs it off – his reaction to adult affection almost normal again. Above the town, the once ragged treeline lies under layers of winter that weighs down branches and moulds bog and heather into a big white duvet. Argyll is hibernating, and the Town nestles in her winter folds, the streets empty of folk, any noise that would normally bounce and echo around her hills falls mute and hushed on her covers.

Only the distant deep foghorn sounding up the Clyde and the occasional burr of a muffled car engine spoils the tranquillity as postmen, home helps, and the meals-on-wheels ladies, fight, slide and shuffle their way to people's doors.

'Howz the Warden?' Don asks Hughie as he walks right up to him. Don's voice is clearer, his eyes less manic, perhaps dulled into an enforced calm by the right meds.

'I'm taking Tommy to karate at one, it's been great for his confidence, then back to his mum for three,' Hughie explains, as if to the boy's uncle. Hughie bends down. 'You not freezin?'

The boy shakes his head in a blur. 'Bet the kittens are fuckin freezing though.'

'What about the puppies?' Hughie asks.

Tommy looks at him like he is well down the autistic scale, pulls away and runs off over the rubble and down the lane kicking snow into clouds as he goes.

'Tommy!' Jim shouts, but the boy ignores him.

'Leave him, I've got him blocked in at the car.'

'It's not that sort of kitten he's on about,' Don says with a piss-taking voice and grin.

Looking puzzled, Hughie humours him with a patronising nod.

'Kittens are young rabbits,' Don tells him, 'Tommy used to watch them on the waste ground in the summer, knows they hide down burrows in winter.'

The penny drops, and Hughie looks after the boy.

'Not as fuckin clever as he thinks this one, eh?' Jim says to Don; both men laughing at the rare sign of ignorance in the smart-arse social worker.

Pulling his leather gloves on tight Hughie makes a V-sign at them, which ignites a frenzied two-fingered reply from Don and a pursed-lipped, 'Oooooooooh,' from Jim as he leaves them.

Out of the rubble, he walks with long, slow, relaxed strides, kicking the snow up in front in powdery white clouds like the boy. Bending, he lifts a handful of snow, listens as it groans under the pressure that sculpts it into a snowball, then throws it up in a high arc until it hits the back door of the Church Hall of Saint Andrew with a satisfying thud, his mum and Uncle Malky away off in the distance, laughing. Scooping up more snow he throws another, but misses this time, laughing now for no reason. A small light spot in the low grey cloud catches his eye, and he glimpses a momentary realm where mounted knights traverse down from the heavens in zigzags, the horses' tails flicking like lightning. The knights aren't holding swords, instead rusted lanterns whose light clears the frightened mind, shining below the rubble of people's lives, setting fickle fires of hope and clarity for those who think to look up. Snow smothers everything as the grey cloud drops lower. Pulling his collar up, Hughie breathes in and blows hot breath through his gloves, like a transcendental dragon, the snow-melt seeping through the thin material to chill the skin below. I am wise now for one reason – I know the self is an empty vessel – without others, it stays that way. Those who can see, try every day, wee bits here and there, all in an effort to stop the world from tipping over into shite. Fuck knows if we can ever stop being just some crash barrier against Armageddon and rise through the rotting hull to seize the wheel. I don't know, I don't. But, I do my bit, I keep going. Hughie dances around on his toes like a child, arms flailing, making a big circle in the snow, not caring if the onlookers from the glowering B&B can see or not.

'Like rust and termites, fucking relentless,' he says out loud.

Thirty snow plough strides on, he can see the car, his heart and the breeze speeding up in unison. Despite the big waltzing snowflakes, their eyes meet across the hundred yards between. He watches the mercurial Tommy being funnelled into the back seat of their Volvo and can't stop grinning as he gets closer. It was the Petite Merde, who cunningly brought us together for his own ends, but he made that classic psycho's mistake – certain everyone thought like him. The fatal flaws he perceived as desperation and naivety – were, in fact, hope and optimism. Sure, I'm fraternising with the sullen-eyed aboriginals, that's okay. I've gone native, and there's no going back.

You're in too deep Hughie boy.

Wee Tommy, keen to get to karate, bangs on the car

window for them to hurry up. But Karen doesn't break her gaze as her man comes down the lane, her eyes wise and still, perhaps wise enough to see tomorrow and not blink or give anything away.

'What the Petite Merdes of this world bring together; let no man, or retired knight, put asunder,' Hughie whispers to himself.

Her hand touches his cheek as they meet, and he kisses her palm.

'Forgot to say, some guy ... DI Taylor, phoned from Manchester this morning,' Karen tells him.

'He was checkin on someone for me.'

'Everything okay?'

He smiles. 'Couldn't be better.'

'You still okay ... with all this?' she asks as she wraps her arms around him and gives a groan, embracing him tighter until both sway from side to side.

Looking up into the snowfall and beyond into the seamless grey, he breathes deep, filling his lungs with icy air. 'This makes me and you kinda immortal, does it not?'

Taking off one glove, he slides a hand inside her coat, touching her warm body, his hand moving down until he feels a kick come from her swollen belly that widens his eyes and brings a smile to her rosy cheeks.

'Soon enough,' she says.

The foghorn on the Clyde sounds for the boats who sail into the blinding mist, and the snow begins to settle on their shoulders, both oblivious to anything but one another in that moment – a new trinity confirmed.

Deep in Hughie's amygdala, a faint voice stalls and fails to break into the frontal lobe, hushed and hoarse, the utterance holds a certain level of defiance for an instant, but soon sinks under the waves of endorphins and is drowned. When their car moves off, Tommy's hands are visible at the rear window, waving around to the music on the radio. Wispy puffs of exhaust fumes fight the cold air and there's a satisfying crumpling sound, as tyres cut snow tracks down Bute Street into town. Way off, towards the hills, a grey gull flaps home across the darkening horizon as more snow falls.

Patience ... and time.

Lightning Source UK Ltd.
Milton Keynes UK
UKHW010609010519
341862UK00002B/511/P